REVIEWERS' PRAISE FOR "ECLIPS

"Sure to please!" - *Midwest Book Review*

"Belongs in most libraries' adult & YA collections." - *Library Journal*

Eclipsed by Shadow is an adventure about the love of horses that young and old will love to read ... The book will pull you in to the darkness of history and not let you stop reading until you get to the end." - *Allison King, Rebbecca's Reads*

"The legend of the Great Horse tells of an angel who asked to serve mankind when Adam and Eve were cast from Eden. Readers find themselves caught up in both the instructive history and the fascinating historical episodes. The novel's sequels will be eagerly awaited."- *Reader Views*

"The author, John Royce, who really knows his horses and his history, has crafted an extremely erudite novel that pitches the reader into the thick of events you remember reading in History classes lo those many years ago ... The action never ends. (Charioteers, rampaging Mongolians!) The fear is palpable. (I won't give it away!) And always, there are the horses."
                    - *Lynn Scanlon, "The Wicked Witch of Publishing"*

"5 Hearts!" Heartland Reviews' GRREAT selection
                    (Gifted & Reluctant Readers Explore Amazing Titles)

———•◦•———

READERS' PRAISE FOR "ECLIPSED BY SHADOW"

"To me this is the equestrian's version of the Harry Potter series. I think I made record time in finishing the book... I couldn't pull myself away, once Meagan got to Rome I was stuck in the book. I can't wait for the next book to see what happens to our young equestrian dreamer." - *Sabrina R., California*

"Up front I want to say that I loved the book! I love the different times. The author did a wonderful job of doing research into the eras mentioned to include daily life and the culture. For anyone that loves horses and loves to read, this is an excellent, well-written story." - *Crystal W., Camp Ramadi*

"Eclipsed By Shadow is definitely one of the best horse books I have ever read. The research was impeccable, and told the truth, not just the romantic, nice parts about it ... Definitely a page turner, with a suspenseful ending that left me pining for the next one." - *Anika C., Georgia*

The Legend of the

of the

Great Horse

- Book I of III -

Eclipsed by Shadow

by John Royce

Micron Press

For information, please contact:
Micron Press
71 Prince Street | Boston, MA 02113.
inquiries@micronpress.com

Although the author and publisher have made every effort to ensure the accuracy and completeness of information contained in this book, we assume no responsibility for errors, inaccuracies, omissions, or any inconsistency herein.

First printing 2008

Royce, John.
    The legend of the great horse. Book I, Eclipsed by
    shadow / by John Royce.
        p. cm.
        "Book I of III."
        SUMMARY: Travel to a time when primitive man stalked
    horses as prey and witness the development of
    horsemanship in ancient and medieval cultures.
        LCCN 2008923312
        ISBN-13: 978-0-9724121-3-1
        ISBN-10: 0-9724121-3-1

        1. Horses—History—Juvenile fiction.
        2. Human-animal relationships—Juvenile fiction.
        [1. Historical fiction. 2. Horses—Fiction. 3. Horses—
    History—Fiction. 4. Animals and civilization—Fiction.]
        I. Title. II. Title: Eclipsed by shadow.

        PZ7.R81597Leg 2008   [Fic]
                        QBI08-600107

Edited by JENNIFER AHLBORN
Cover artwork by MARTI ADRIAN © 2008
Original book cover drawings by JOE MILSTEAD
The coin image is a reproduction of an ancient Greek coin featuring the flying horse Pegasus. (Corinth, 7th century B.C.)
PRINTED AND BOUND IN THE UNITED STATES OF AMERICA.

To My Mother & Sister,
who shared their love of horses

Please refer to the ⊰**Glossary**⊱ for unfamiliar terms.

Horses are for all ages, but depictions of historical
conflict in this book may not be enjoyed by
very young readers.

The travels in this story are fiction,
but the intention is to present historical accuracy. Where
license is taken, it is to portray the spirit of the times.

Disclaimer: According to observation
and science, horses cannot fly.

The Legend
of the
Great Horse

— Book 1 —

Eclipsed by Shadow

California, USA
2001

Home

MEAGAN AWOKE WITH a start and sat upright in bed. The dream had come again. The dream of the flying horse.

Early light was outlining the window blinds. Meagan threw back her sheets and dressed quietly, as it was summer vacation and her parents preferred to sleep through dawn. She tiptoed out of her room and down the hardwood stairs to the kitchen. Closing the back door gently, she slipped though the pasture fence and raced into the backyard.

Auburn-haired and with a streak of tomboy, Meagan Roberts was not an unusual girl of twelve—except for the lucky fact that her family kept horses. (Actually, they only kept *one* horse, an aged mare, but very soon it would be two.) Hay and pine shavings greeted her at the backyard stable's entrance, in her opinion the best smells in the world.

"Moose?" Meagan turned on the barn's dim lights. The cool morning air was silent. Of course, she did not *really* believe the foal had come in the night: the veterinarian said it was still too soon. As with all the other mornings, she expected to find Moose munching her hay contentedly, enormous and alone in her stall.

The pregnant mare's formal name was *Bright Lights*, but she was called Moose for her bay coat and rambling gait. Meagan had loved the huge mare since her second birthday, when she had been held up on Moose's wide back, terrified and grabbing fistfuls of mane, crying to be taken off immediately and put back on forever.

Peering over the stall door in the quiet pre-dawn, Meagan tensed. The evening hay lay untouched. She opened the door to see the floor dug into mounds. Her beloved Moose lay in the wrecked bedding, dark with sweat, her sides rising and falling in fast breaths. A violent kick sent a spray of bedding against the wall. Meagan bolted for the house, crying, "Mom, Dad! Hurry! Moose is sick!"

Her mother was down first, tying her robe as she came. "Stop shouting, Meagan. We can hear you."

"Moose is *sick*. She's lying down and she's kicking!"

Jennifer Roberts frowned and called upstairs. "Tom, I'm going to check on the mare." She addressed her daughter calmly. "Meagan, some broodmares lie down before they foal. It is only natural."

"I know, but Moose didn't eat her hay and she's *sweating*. Please, Mom, *please* hurry!"

"We'll go see, Meagan. Just don't let Moose know you're upset. She is probably resting."

But Jennifer paled at the sight of the dark mare groaning in the straw. Meagan hung back in the doorway, watching her mother enter the stall and kneel beside Moose. Meagan could see the whites of the mare's eyes, something only a frightened horse would show.

"Tell your father to call Dr. Parker," Jennifer said quietly, "and bring back some towels." She stroked the mare's head. "Good girl, Moose, easy now. Everything is going to be fine." One large ear flicked as the mare listened.

Meagan was not the only one who held Moose as a constant in her life. As a teenager, Jennifer had watched the birth of the bay filly that was to be her companion through school, boys, marriage and children. She had watched Moose grow from a gawky foal into sleek prime, and now into the matronly shape of a broodmare.

Jennifer forced herself to keep talking. This was Moose's first foal and complications could happen. "Rest now, that's a good girl." Moose must have been in labor for hours, an alarming sign—mares usually foal quickly, within thirty minutes of labor's onset. The horse's coat was covered in dried sweat and caked with bedding. "You'll be all right, girl, you have to be. No one else knows all my secrets." Jennifer smoothed a sudden wet spot on the mare's muzzle.

Her husband, Tom, came to stand outside the stall door. "They're paging Dr. Parker. Don't worry, Jen. She'll be okay." Meagan stood silently behind, holding the towels.

Moose groaned and lifted her head. The horse's normally full flanks were drawn and soaked in sweat. Heaving herself up, the mare began circling the stall.

"Meagan, would you bring the halter?" Jennifer made herself keep the words calm. "I don't understand. Last night everything was fine."

The distended mare stopped and lowered herself onto the spoiled bedding, diving into the throes of a contraction. Jennifer took a towel and the halter from her daughter and knelt beside the mare again. Gently holding the mare's head down to prevent her from rising, she stroked a towel over the sweat-soaked coat, murmuring, until a surge of pain drove the mare to paw violently and wrench herself from Jennifer's grip. After a few circuits around the stall the mare lowered herself again to begin futile straining.

"Where *is* he?" Jennifer asked, her voice tight. Moose half-rose and buckled back to the floor, thrashing in the bedding. Jennifer retreated to the doorway to watch helplessly. Mother and daughter listened to the sounds of car engines, closing their eyes when each passed. The eastern edges of the sky were showing blue when a vehicle finally slowed and turned into the driveway.

Dr. Parker was a short, grizzled man with a face too weathered and creased to reveal his age. With a glance at the mare, the veterinarian set his black bag down. "I need one of you to help," he said matter-of-factly, and was surprised as Jennifer stepped forward. He had expected the husband but no matter. With horses, experience mattered more than a strong arm.

Waiting for the right moment to avoid being kicked, the veterinarian quickly knelt and haltered the mare. He pushed her lips back to see the gums: they were a pale, deadly white. He pinched a bit of skin on her neck and it stood stiffly instead of springing back. Dehydration. Handing the lead rope to Jennifer, he moved to palpate the mare, reaching inside to feel the unborn foal. The canal was dry; the water had broken hours before. When finished, his face was grim. He went to his bag.

"You have to make a decision. The mare or the foal." He said it gruffly, plunging a hypodermic into a bottle and inverting it. "She won't deliver a live foal without a cesarean, but the operation will kill her. If I don't the foal will smother." In silence he finished preparing the injection, and then looked squarely at Jennifer. It was not a cold look, or even without concern. It was the look of a man who knew the pain of the answer but required it.

"She was fine." Jennifer turned frightened eyes to her daughter. "Can't..."

"I need a decision, or it will be too late for either."

Jennifer stared at the towel in her hand, hearing Moose's uneven breathing. "It's her first foal ... she doesn't know what's happening."

The vet began to dab alcohol into a sweat-soaked spot on the mare's throat. He spoke more softly, "Mrs. Roberts, there's a chance we can save the momma. A small chance, but we might. Send your daughter out and let me try to save your mare."

"Is the foal alive?" Jennifer asked in a small voice.

"Right now, yes."

"If we waited for another foal..."

The man hesitated. "I know you want this for your little girl, Mrs. Roberts, but your mare won't have another foal, even if she makes it. You should know that. She won't have another."

Jennifer looked up at Meagan, a tiny shadow behind her father. Huddled, a new generation waited. *No.* It was too soon for this horrific calculation. A long moment passed as the two mothers communed silently. If Moose's time was over, hers too was passing. It was too soon ... it would always be too soon.

"Save the foal," she whispered.

The vet almost protested but instead gritted his teeth and returned to his bag. He quickly pulled a narcotic into a new syringe. *A shame, a damn shame,* he thought. He handed Jennifer the slack lead as she stroked Moose's once sleek neck.

The mare barely flinched at the needle. Jennifer felt something inside herself drift away. "Please take Meagan outside, Tom." She watched them leave, trying not to think, not to feel. There would be time enough to grieve.

A cesarean on a horse is graphic, but Jennifer watched impassively. This was no longer her mare but something slack and lifeless. It took all of the veterinarian's experience to deliver the foal, and it was several minutes before the limp, crooked creature, bathed in blood, began to respond to the doctor's efforts. The vet covered Moose with a blanket and called for Meagan and her father.

Meagan came in apprehensively, eyes large at the spindly newborn. Tom started towards Jennifer, who was kneeling beside the blanket, staring. He hesitated.

The vet was talking quickly. "It's a filly, a big one and with good reflexes too. She's going to be fine." He spoke in relief. Delivering a dead foal was bleak business and the Roberts need never know how close it had been. He looked at Meagan standing by the door with shining eyes. "I need some help rubbing down the baby. Any volunteers?"

Meagan's eyes jumped to her mother.

"Go ahead," Jennifer nodded. "Let Dr. Parker show you."

The vet held the foal and demonstrated how to rub the wet coat to mimic a mare's tongue. Meagan touched the foal tentatively at first, but was soon rubbing as the doctor showed her, stimulating the newborn's circulation.

Meagan's eyes fixed on the still form under the blanket. "When will Moose…"

Dr. Parker stood up stiffly, futilely brushing his pants. "I'll fix up a bottle and leave a feeding schedule. The foal needs to be fed every two hours the first few days. It will be easier if you can get her to drink from a bucket, and safer—we don't want milk down her lungs. It's going to be a lot of work, I'm afraid."

"I'll do it!" Meagan said quickly.

"We can manage, Doctor." Jennifer looked at the lead rope she still held and dropped it. She watched the newborn struggle to keep her head above Meagan's aggressive toweling and suddenly realized a strangeness about the foal. She looked at the vet in shock.

He smiled wryly. "I was wondering when you'd notice."

Jennifer went to the corner and looked closely at the foal. "But, *how?* She has Moose's head and her nose ... maybe her ears." Stroking the filly's nose, Jennifer traced the swirl of white in the center of the golden forehead. "But a palomino? It can't be." She shook her head. The stud fee had been large and hard to raise—she and Tom had justified it by telling themselves a poorly bred horse cost the same to feed as a good one.

"What are you saying?" Tom asked. "Is there something wrong with the baby? What is a 'pal-meeno?'"

"It means the golden color." Jennifer ran a hand down the filly's blond coat. "It's not a defect, except you don't see many palomino thoroughbreds. It's pretty doubtful we got the sire we chose."

Tom was puzzled. "Are you saying Moose didn't agree with our choice?"

"Looks like Moose needed a chaperon." Dr. Parker said it kindly. "I can write something so you can get your stud fee back."

"No," Jennifer said immediately. "She's a thoroughbred and should be registered as one. We will talk to the stud farm."

The vet nodded. "I'll see what I can do, Mrs. Roberts."

"Please." Without spirit, drained, she went to Tom. He circled an arm around her waist and pulled her to him, ignoring the dirt. Together they watched the new arrival wriggle in Meagan's grasp. It is normal for a foal to stand, splayed and wobbly, within an hour of birth. The newcomer seemed determined to be timely.

Jennifer avoided her childhood companion lying under the blanket. She would not let herself wonder if it had been the right decision.

*The daughter who won't lift a finger in the house
is the same child that cycles off madly in the pouring rain
to spend all morning mucking out a stables.*

- Samantha Armstrong

"SEE, DAD, HOW she doesn't pull at all?" Meagan led the foal another step. "Are you watching, Dad?"

"I certainly am," Tom answered proudly. Two months had passed since the foal's arrival, and he had watched the little animal's progress with amazement. A newborn horse daily consumes a fourth its weight in milk—some twenty-five pounds a day. In Tom's opinion, his daughter had handled the round-the-clock bottle feedings heroically.

The foal explored her new world on stilts: a horse's legs arrive almost full-sized, attached to an absurdly small body. Equine newborns demand as much attention as a human infant, but only for a short time—horses are one of nature's most precocious animals. Though the foal's short coat still resembled the blonde fuzz on a peach, already she was showing an interest in greenery.

Absorbed in his daughter and the foal, Tom did not notice the slightly bent figure of an old woman approaching. The warm voice with a slight quaver was only a few feet behind him when she spoke. "Quite a sight, isn't it, a child with a pony?"

Tom turned to see an elderly, white-haired woman with a firm gaze. "Yes, ma'am. Yes, it is. I am Tom Roberts ... and you are?"

"It's lovely to meet you, Tom. Just lovely." The woman carried a cane she seemed to use more for resting than walking. She called to Meagan, "That is a beautiful pony you have, dear!"

"She isn't a pony, ma'am," Meagan answered, preoccupied. She was checking the foal for imperfections—a new grownup was nothing special. "Ponies stay little. Horses grow up tall."

"Oh, yes! I remember reading that. Quite correct, dear." The old woman tapped her polished cane against the ground; it was of expensive wood and capped with a jeweled handle. "I see your young *horse* has a very smart owner to take care of her."

Meagan blushed and said "thank you," and quickly refocused on priorities. It did not seem possible there could be yet *another* bot egg on the foal's leg. The egg was a tiny yellow dot stuck to the end of a hair: if the foal licked the spot, the common parasite could travel into the horse's digestive tract.

"Meagan," Tom prompted, "why don't you bring her over?"

She peered closely at the foal's inside leg. "Yes, sir..."

"Don't disturb the child," the woman protested. "Your daughter must attend to her duties. I came only to witness." She took a deep breath and said admiringly, "Here stands the noble partner of poets, warriors and kings. Beautiful color, too. Gold. It would be fitting."

"Yes, ma'am," Tom said politely. In his observation horses attracted eccentrics like flies.

Meagan plucked the offending hair and examined it. Satisfied, she straightened and began leading the foal to the fence. The animal followed willingly in playful spurts.

The woman's eyes were kind. "What is your name, dear?"

"Meagan Roberts, ma'am."

"Both of you are so lovely. Have you named your pony—excuse me, I mean your young horse?"

"No ma'am. I haven't been able to think of a name yet."

"Yes, well, don't worry. Animals often name themselves. The proper name will come along." The old lady pointed her cane to the foal's diamond-shaped head. "I see you are halter training early. It is sound practice from what I've read."

Meagan stroked the quietly standing foal. "It was easy. It's like she already knows everything ... well, she is a *little* skittish, but that's just her breed."

"Show me a circle, dear. I would love to see." The woman called out encouragement as Meagan started the obliging foal in a figure-eight. "Excellent dear, *very* nice!" She leaned toward Tom. "What is the age of the horse, young man?"

"Oh, I'd say about two months now. You would not believe how she's grown."

"They do grow alarmingly. Tell me, do you remember the precise date the horse was born ... the 21st of June perhaps?"

"That sounds about right. It was a weekend, I remember."

The elderly woman leaned on her cane. "Palomino, too..." she murmured, frowning.

Meagan finished the circles and brought the foal back to the fence. "See, ma'am, she doesn't even nip!"

"She is perfect, dear." The woman hesitated. "Though it will be some time before you can ride her ... you understand *that*, I am sure."

"Yes, ma'am. We have to wait until she is three. Her bones have to mature."

"Very correct, dear. You *must* not ride too soon. Well, I am grateful for the demonstration. It was charming to meet you all." The woman turned away.

"Ma'am," Tom called. "I'm sorry, I did not get your name..."

"Just an interested party. It was a delight meeting you. Wonderful family, such a pleasure." The woman continued a congenial murmur as she disappeared down the driveway.

———

Although there were gloomy days of mourning, Moose's death never surfaced in conversation. After a few well-meant failures to comfort his wife, Tom stopped bringing the subject up. Meagan's tears dried as the foal grew, so he was left with his own feelings.

Tom had become used to the old girl, watching Moose shadowbox on cold mornings, kicking and running from unseen enemies. He smiled to remember the mare's contortions to snip a blade of grass beneath the fence while ignoring a full rack of hay; or of Meagan presenting Moose with a paperclip or other harmless object, and watching the massive horse back away in alarm, only to return curiously with neck outstretched, sniffing, a picture of foolishness. It impressed him that the immense, powerful animal possessed such a gentle spirit.

Tom would not have considered himself a horse-lover. In fact, most family arguments were over the time and money spent on horses. Still, he had come to appreciate the solemn tranquility the presence of a horse creates. He remembered a quote from one of Meagan's horse books, a passage written more than two thousand years ago by an ancient Greek general: *"If such a majestic beast is subordinate to our will, then surely man is master of the world."* Tom thought the old man had it exactly right.

He remembered moving to this house. It had been chosen for good reasons, including better schools and more space, but mostly it was to have horses (which, if pressed, Tom would agree was a good reason). At first he understood little of the fascination the animal held for so many, but his only daughter was one of the great joys of his life and he gave her anything in his power to give. Also, his father-in-law raised horses, so Tom was plainly outnumbered.

When Meagan's interest turned to riding, Tom did his part to encourage her. Meagan started lessons on condition of good grades and she kept the bargain. She spent summers at her grandfather's ranch, feeding, brushing, shoveling—whatever one did with horses. He came to understand riding was only a fraction of the experience.

Eventually a pony was leased for competitions and of course there were always lessons, for horsemanship is both subtle and vast. Tom earned frosty looks when he suggested that if Meagan still needed lessons maybe riding was not her sport.

Tom and Jennifer had talked for years about moving to a bigger place—before he was involuntarily retired. Downsized or right-sized, it meant the same to him. He found a recruiter and a realtor on the same day. The realtor worked faster.

The lot was small, with a driveway running past a two-story house to its all-important asset: a stable converted from a garage. The prized edifice had two stalls, a tack room, a feed room, and a small paddock that took the place of the backyard. He liked it and Jennifer loved it. They decided that night.

The original plan was to care for Moose in her golden years: the mare was eighteen and an equine's lifespan is approximately twenty-six. Well-kept horses can live longer, however, and quiet rides had been anticipated, and meditative hours of horse keeping. Not the least, a good deal of money had been spent on a stud chosen specifically by Meagan's grandfather to enhance her bloodline—Meagan's young horse was to be his crowning achievement. The foal was to go to a pasture to mature, and Moose was to be the horse in their lives until then. Of course things had not gone according to plan.

As a distraction, the new foal filled the backyard pasture with the commotion of ten like her mother. Now when Tom brought his morning coffee onto the patio, instead of sharing Moose's silent camaraderie he was met by the foal's antics.

On most mornings, Jennifer joined him at the fence. In her opinion the foal was unusual. "She puts up with everything, Tom, almost like a puppy. It must be the bottle feeding."

Tom said nothing. To him it was just the old mare showing through.

"I thought of a name for the foal!" Meagan announced happily at dinner. "Just like the old lady said, sometimes animals name themselves."

Jennifer looked up. "Which old lady is this?"

"A neighbor, I think," Tom answered. "She was wandering backyards the other day."

"I want to name the foal ... *Promise*." Meagan poked her plate. "I thought of it while I was brushing her. Do you like it?"

"*Promise*." Her mother smiled. "I think it is very nice, Meagan. We can register her as 'Bright Promise' to keep Moose's name."

Meagan nodded vigorously. "May I be excused? I want to tell her goodnight."

"After you put your plate in the sink." Jennifer stood and followed her daughter into the kitchen. "Don't be too long, Meagan, you have homework to do. And don't forget to tell Promise goodnight for me."

Tom joined Jennifer in the kitchen. "Well good, it's about time the horse got a name. She is getting too big to be just 'the foal.'"

"We should be thinking about the move, Tom." Jennifer was determined to give Promise a natural foalhood, in a pasture with other horses. Arrangements had already been made.

Tom watched his wife start the dishes. Her auburn hair was pulled back, her features clear. Jennifer always dismissed the suggestion that she was beautiful, but Tom disagreed. Both mother and daughter were like the thoroughbreds they loved, possessed of long lines, graceful and athletic. Jennifer's most striking traits were the ones Tom had fallen in love with and his daughter had inherited: green eyes and auburn hair—and also a fiery temper and an intractable stubborn streak.

Words came into Tom's mind as he watched his wife, something her father had said the night Tom was married. His father-in-law generally spoke little, but on that night he put his arm around Tom's shoulders and gave him advice. "She can seem a bit tough at times, son, but Jennifer is a good girl. She's like all the Owens women. They came west by oxen and went right back for their horses, and no one got in their way." His father-in-law's eyes had been full of amusement, but his expression grew serious. "You never got to meet any of the old girls. Just as well, son. Be a shame if they'd scared you off."

———

The following afternoon, Tom came home to more than the usual commotion in the backyard. Through the kitchen window he saw his wife standing in her gardening shorts, arguing with a plump man in a finely tailored suit. Tom opened the back door and stepped onto the patio. "Hello," he called cheerfully, "may I help?"

"Please, Tom," Jennifer said crisply. "I can't seem to tell this gentleman 'no.'"

"I don't believe I've met the fellow." Tom walked forward and introduced himself with a handshake; the visitor's hand was soft and moist. "Tom Roberts, glad to meet you. I see you've met my wife, Jennifer."

The man nodded unhappily. "I am pleased to make your acquaintance, Mr. Roberts."

"His name is Fred Jeffrey," Jennifer said curtly.

"Jeffries, actually," the man corrected. "Fred Jeffries."

Jennifer did not apologize. "The man wants to buy our filly, Tom. It seems to be an offer he won't let me refuse."

"But *sir*," the man protested. "My offer is more than fair."

"Oh?" He caught Jennifer's look. "The horse isn't for sale, Mr. Jeffries."

"You don't understand, sir. I can pay you much more than the horse is worth." The man was sweating profusely. "Substantially more. I don't understand all the bother."

Jennifer frowned. "Do you see, Tom?"

"Mr. Jeffries." Tom smiled patiently. "You have to understand, the horse is not for sale. It is our daughter's horse, so thank you, but no."

The man looked at Jennifer and back at Tom. "Of course. I did not mean to cause you excellent people any trouble. Thank you for your time." He turned and walked quickly back up the driveway, mumbling as he went.

"Who was that, Jen?"

"I have no idea, Tom. He wouldn't say." She walked to the fence and held out a handful of grass. The golden filly moved closer and took the stalks delicately. "It is just as well we are moving her to pasture soon."

Tom saw a hand waving in the kitchen window. "Have you reminded our daughter about the move?"

"No, I will talk to her tonight at dinner."

"You can tell her now."

The backdoor opened and Meagan stepped out wearing school clothes and a ponytail, a well-groomed young lady who barely resembled the rough-and-tumble child soon to re-emerge in jeans and a T-shirt. She ran to the fence and deposited her schoolbooks on a patio chair. "Hello, Promise," she sang. "I missed you."

Jennifer cleared her throat delicately. "Meagan, dear. We have to talk."

"About what?" Meagan answered carefully. It was never good to be called "dear" by her mother.

"We need to discuss moving the foal out to Mary's pasture. I think it's time."

"Remember, honey, we talked about this," Tom added gently. "Your foal needs room to run."

"But she runs a lot now." Meagan reached down for fresh grass. The foal watched with interest, ears pricked.

"Meagan, please listen," Jennifer said seriously. "There will be horses at the pasture and Promise needs to socialize."

"I know, but that was before, when Moose was going to be here."

"It is not going to be forever, Meagan. You can see Promise on weekends, and before you know it—"

"Why do you keep saying that, like three years isn't forever? Why does she have to be so far away?"

"Because that is what we can afford, Meagan. There are certain realities. This will save money and it is better for Promise. Horses need room when they're growing. And it will only be two-and-a-half years, not three. We've gone over all of this."

Jennifer's tone was becoming reminiscent of the one she had used with Mr. Jeffries. Time to make a judicious exit, Tom thought.

"If Dad kept his old job we could afford to keep her closer."

Tom froze. There was silence enough to hear Promise's munching. "Is someone going to answer that," he asked evenly, "or should I?"

"I am sorry, Tom—Meagan, apologize or go to your room." Jennifer crossed her arms when her daughter did not move. "Young lady, I remind you who is paying the bills. Unless your attitude changes, and quickly, you may not be seeing Promise at all."

"I'm *sorry*." Meagan picked up her books defiantly and stormed into the house. She did not, however, slam the door.

Tom stood a moment, wondering if he should say it. He took a breath. "Look, Jennifer, maybe it would be best if we kept the foal here. We *did* tell Meagan she could have a horse. It's the whole reason we took this place."

"There's no point in arguing, Tom. It is already decided."

"I know. Like mother, like daughter."

"It's for the *animal's* sake, Tom! We agreed on this. Am I the only one who remembers?"

"But does the foal need to run around so much? I mean, we aren't even sure we have a real thoroughbred." The breeding farm had been unable to explain the foal's coloring.

"Is this about the stud fee again?"

"Of course not, Jen. Asking you to be reasonable seems to be an insult when it comes to horses."

"If you want the money back, Tom, go ask for it. That's reasonable, isn't it?" Jennifer brushed past him into the house.

"You're only proving my point!" Tom called after her. He added wistfully, "I win ... ?"

——

Closing the door to her room, Meagan dropped her books on her desk and lay on the bed. "It isn't fair," she told the stucco ceiling. She turned on her pillow and stared into space.

On her bookshelf was an old favorite, *The Sword in the Stone* by T.H. White. She had loved the book since reading the first page's fanciful description of a young knight's education. Meagan imagined the joy of having to stay after school because she couldn't properly sit the trot. She knew exactly how the young King Arthur felt when he lifted the sword and discovered his destiny: it was the way she felt on the back of a horse.

Meagan's unhappiness was not only about missing Promise, even so soon after losing her beloved Moose. *It will be too late,* she thought miserably. Her one goal, her abiding passion, was to ride internationally, to represent her nation in competition— a goal that required hours of training a day and decades of hard work. Few of her friends understood. Like all equestrian sports, jumping remained strangely unseen by the great eye of American television, so in a sense she loved an invisible sport.

In her experience, people often assumed horse jumping to be an ancient pastime, though it is actually one of the youngest sports. Jumping was first organized in the early years of the 20th century, and has since grown into an internationally competitive sport with millions of competitors and fans worldwide. Meagan wanted to make a living with horses: her mother was a respected horsewoman, as was her grandmother before her. Meagan believed she had the gift and worked hard to prove it true. Learning about horses seemed more like remembering; it was an old love buried deep.

It may be only small injustice that the child can be exposed to;
but the child is small, and its world is small,
and its rocking-horse stands as many hands high,
according to scale, as a big-boned Irish hunter.

- Charles Dickens (1812-70) Great Expectations

PROMISE DID NOT leave that weekend, however, or the weekend after. Jennifer put the move off until the horse's registration papers could arrive—it was a sensible precaution, she told everyone. Once registered, Promise could have an identification number tattooed on the underside of her lip, to be traced if stolen. The truth was that, like Tom, Jennifer was reluctant to send Promise away. The best-laid plans can fail, and though Jennifer promised Meagan she would ride again, it was hard to make a twelve-year-old wait. And harder to send her horse away when there was no money for lessons or leases.

Horses had been Meagan's life since she had first been lifted onto Moose's broad back. Her books were horse books; her toys, horse toys. Riding lessons and a pony were all Meagan wished for on birthdays and Christmases. Every conversation included horses.

To answer her daughter's passion, Jennifer had arranged for three instructors. The first had been Jennifer's own father, who spent summers teaching his eager granddaughter the nature of the animal and its care. Though Meagan enjoyed Western riding she longed to jump, so an Old School, cavalry-type drill sergeant was found, an instructor with a reputation for turning out tough, disciplined riders with classical basics. After watching one drill session, Tom was sure his daughter would give up riding altogether. Meagan did more than survive the cavalryman, however: she thrived. Difficult horses were given to her and she succeeded, and steadily moved up the competition levels. In time, Meagan attracted the attention of a prominent trainer. The man's credentials included international competition and the coaching of two former Olympians. He became Meagan's trainer that afternoon.

One week later her father lost his job.

Jennifer knew why Tom put his foot down. Money was scarce and horses could be only a small part of the new budget. But Tom never understood, not really. To him, once Meagan was out of pigtails and able to steer a horse, riding lessons had diminished value. It was Jennifer who understood what horsemanship demanded and the values it instilled.

Meagan was ambitious yet Moose had to stretch as the jump heights rose above three feet. Jennifer had realized it was time to find another mount for her daughter: at the age of seventeen the mare was ready for fences to start lowering, not rising. The idea to breed Moose had seemed the perfect solution. If they raised the animal themselves, the family's tight finances could support a prospective foal. It *was* the perfect solution … almost. A mother may not divulge all her hopes for her daughter, but Jennifer had done her best to put the impossible within reach.

Tom reached into the car for groceries as a parade of girls streamed down the driveway. Their assortment of bright clothes and neon sneakers mounted a garish assault on the senses. "It's the Ponytail Brigade!" he greeted them. "All hail the mighty Promise! Remember, no feeding fingers to the horse."

"We'll help you!" announced a little girl in a fluorescent jumpsuit staring up at him.

"No, we won't," snapped a girl Meagan's age, wearing lipstick. "We are going for yogurt, remember?"

Meagan stood before him and pleaded, "Dad, can I *please* have money for the store? Katie's mother is taking us."

"I think your Mom is making dinner, honey."

"I will just be a little while. I'll come right back."

"Ask your mother." He hoisted the groceries out and closed the car door with his foot.

"I'll open the front door for you!" called the girl in the jumpsuit.

"Thanks, honey. How old are you?"

"Six," she answered proudly.

"That's a good age. Stay there."

———

Halloween was memorable, as is any disaster. It began with Meagan's decision to use the good tablecloth to make Promise into a horse-ghost. She was explaining this to her mother when the foal bolted and shredded the linen. In the interests of family harmony, it was agreed Tom would take Meagan trick-or-treating this year.

The tablecloth was mended for its new career as a horse costume, and father, daughter and foal set out—though Meagan's authentic "Headless Horseman" pumpkin-head quickly succumbed to an inquisitive nudge from Promise. At the first house Tom nervously agreed to hold the foal and let Meagan trick-or-treat. While waiting, the foal glimpsed the top of Tom's wallet in his back pocket and mistook it for a treat. Tom's shouts attracted children from all over the neighborhood. By the time Meagan returned, Promise was disrobed and Tom's wallet was a sodden lump. He handed the lead rope to Meagan without a word.

Switching duties brought little improvement. Meagan grew upset when her father invited pennies and apples in place of candy and, more ominously, Promise discovered Halloween bags contained her favorite red fruit. A boy standing too close was ransacked for goods. The hysterical child streaming candy and costume down the street concluded the evening.

Thanksgiving Day arrived with the foal still in the backyard. It was a day of relatives, picture taking, and general feasting on the patio. Tom acknowledged the patched linen tablecloth with thanks that the day was not Halloween, while Promise helped the children closest to the pasture fence finish their salads.

"I needed a saddle pad," Meagan said in disappointment, sitting in the stable aisle surrounded by Christmas wrappings and bows. Promise looked on hungrily, a demented blonde reindeer wearing fake antlers and a white beard.

"Well, Meagan," Tom said evenly. "I guess Santa couldn't fit that in his sled with all your other gifts." He pointed to the toys, stuffed animals and horse tack propped along the wall.

"You won't need a pad for a long time yet," Jennifer soothed. "The old one is fine for training."

Tom was always surprised how much patience his wife had with this kind of nonsense. They had scraped to make Christmas a good one and a little appreciation was due. He knelt down. "Look honey, a new halter. Let's put it on her and see how it looks." Meagan pouted and shrugged. "Well then, let's put the wrapping paper in the garbage and see how *that* looks."

"Is it necessary to make everything a point, Tom?" Jennifer asked curtly.

"Fine, dear," Tom replied, mentally counting. He decided to take a short walk outside the stables. He did not understand this obsession with horses. Yes, they were beautiful animals—he stopped in surprise. A man in a black-and-white checkered suit was standing on the patio, someone vaguely familiar...

"Mr. Roberts! I'm so glad to see you again!" The visitor was beaming, arms spread in a grand gesture. "I am coming to lend some Christmas cheer! I have another offer for that little horse of yours."

Now Tom recognized the visitor.

"I can pay you twenty thousand dollars for the little beast. *Twenty* thousand dollars, sir! I ask you, is that not more than reasonable?"

Tom was dumbfounded. The offer was ridiculously high for a backyard foal, enough to cast doubt on the man's mental state. Tom saw a look of fear come into the man's eyes as Jennifer emerged from the stables.

"Mr. Jeffries!" At least Jennifer had no trouble recognizing the visitor. "How have you been? Do you know it is Christmas morning?" The man stuttered something about a counteroffer and being reasonable, but Jennifer surprised him. "Do you have a card, Mr. Jeffries? You never know, we might be interested." She said it smoothly, ignoring Tom's open mouth.

Fred Jeffries produced a card from the depths of his coat pocket and handed it grandly to Jennifer. She took it and nodded pleasantly. "Thank you, Mr. Jeffries. We'll be getting back to you." She watched the man swagger down the driveway. "Wouldn't want to lose this," she told Tom merrily, tucking the card into her blouse's front pocket.

Later that afternoon, Jennifer and Tom relaxed on the patio in a post-Christmas stupor, watching Meagan and two neighborhood friends put wrapping paper to work on the long-suffering foal. Everyone seemed in a safe mood.

"Okay, Jen, I'll ask. Why did you tell that man we would sell the foal?"

She took a careful sip of coffee. "The papers are taking too long. I haven't told Meagan yet, but I am having Dr. Parker freeze-mark the foal instead. Promise could go to the farm next weekend ... who's to tell Mr. Jeffries we didn't get a better offer?"

"I see. We move the foal to pasture and tell this Jeffries person we sold her. Only one problem, Jen. The man offered us twenty thousand dollars."

"Twenty thousand ... for *our* foal?"

"I don't think he'd believe we got a better offer."

"*Twenty thousand dollars?* I told you the man was strange. We are definitely moving the horse on Saturday. *I'll* call our Mr. Jeffries."

"Mom, dad, look!" Meagan called. The foal was barely recognizable, buried in layers of wrapping paper and ribbons from the neighborhood trash.

"Yes, honey," Tom answered. "A little Christmas nightmare."

"Take a picture!" Meagan held the lead rope as her friends supplied Promise with a steady stream of carrots.

"I would, Meagan, but we don't want evidence for the animal abuse people."

Meagan was up early the morning Promise was to go to pasture. The backyard was framed in morning mist, colors grayed. A horse trailer had been borrowed and parked in the backyard so Promise could become used to its strangeness.

"Good morning, Promise," Meagan called softly, coming to the stall door and unlatching the top half. "This is the big day, girl. You are going to meet lots of new friends."

Promise put her head over the door and nickered. "Move over, silly," Meagan said, pushing the horse back to enter the confined space. Running a hand down each leg, she made sure the filly had no bumps or swellings from the night. "Today you'll see what that big metal box is all about."

She slipped a halter on the filly; Promise fidgeted, but Meagan insisted on walking politely to the paddock. Once free, Promise tossed her head impudently and trotted stiffly away. The horse's palomino coat was a washed-out tan in the early light as she bounced toward the borrowed trailer, then swerved abruptly and ran the perimeter of the small pasture. Meagan watched, letting her filly "get the kinks out" from a night in the stall. After three circuits Promise came back to Meagan in high, floating steps, nostrils wide from exertion.

Meagan let the horse sniff her outstretched hand. "Not yet, you're getting breakfast in the trailer. You can eat hay until we get there. As much as you want. It will be fun."

Promise nudged Meagan's hand impatiently. It was unlike her favorite person to ignore her Sacred Duties, namely retrieving lovely buckets of grain from the feed room. The filly snorted disapproval and began another run around the pasture.

Meagan hated to admit it, but her mother was right. In the volumes of horse books she read, pictures showed how each hoof holds spongy tissue to pump blood into the body with the weight of a step—four little hearts, one in each hoof. The backyard might be big enough for an older horse like Moose, but a growing foal needs space to buck and gallop, to learn the skills of a creature of motion.

Promise came back to Meagan, nudging her hopefully. "Go on, play. It's not time yet." Meagan watched her young filly blow in annoyance, and said softly, "You're leaving. I might not like it, but you will. And I don't want any stories about you causing trouble." Meagan had decided not to show that she was upset. Tears would only make her parents feel worse. The foal needed to grow up and it was selfish to want Promise to stay.

She watched the filly walk to the fence, searching for blades of grass making the error of growing too close. This was an ending for Meagan. At twelve, two-and-a-half years seemed an unchartable lifetime to wait. She could not find words to explain, but already she missed the intimate solitude of riding and the quiet rhythms of a ride. A horse has musical gaits: a four-beat walk, two-beat trot, and rolling three-beat canter. Her world was going silent.

———

The ride to pasture was uneventful. The pasture's owner, a boisterous woman named Mary, hooted as Promise dived into her held bucket of grain. "Loads like a trooper! Usually do at this age, you know. It's at two you get problems—*just like kids!*" She shrieked with laughter at her observation.

Tom cringed. He wanted to like Mary, he truly did—the woman was their horse's new caretaker, after all. Still he winced at her loud clothes and hair, and jokes, not to mention her voice. Everything about the woman held volume.

"Thank you again, Mary," Jennifer said. "This is going to be perfect."

"Oh, sure! Got to have room for the little ones to stretch their legs!" Mary handed the lead rope to Meagan with a screech, "'Course they look pretty stretched already!"

Meagan surveyed the foal's new home as Promise nosed her happily. The property ran beside a ravine so blanketed with scrub vegetation it was impossible to see the other side. Barns and feed sheds huddled near the front of the pasture. No one lived on the property but a variety of dogs served as hospitality. A small herd of mares, foals, and elderly geldings grazed at the bottom of a long slope.

Preoccupied with nipping the lead rope, the foal hardly noticed being led through the gate and unclipped from her tether. "Go on, dummy," Meagan said, pushing her away. When Promise nudged harder for the lead, Meagan put it behind her back.

A noise attracted the filly's attention. Down at the bottom of the hill, one of the broodmares squealed and trotted disdainfully to a fresh patch of grass, away from a neighbor. Promise watched the herd intently, ears high.

Meagan swatted the filly's rump. Promise trotted a few steps and came to an abrupt halt, standing in concentration. Then the horse bolted, running toward the herd and veering off. The grazing mares ignored Promise's antics until she arrived properly and made formal introductions. Another youngster nuzzled Promise in an invitation to play.

"It's sort of like *Born Free*," Tom observed.

"She's going to be fine, young lady!" Mary exclaimed. "Just fine!"

"She really is," Jennifer assured her solemn daughter. "This is going to be good for her."

Meagan nodded and bit her lip, hard.

I am not expert in horses and do not speak with assurance.
I can always tell which is the front end of a horse,
but beyond that, my art is not above the ordinary.

- Mark Twain (1835-1910)

RANDY WELLS WAS a small-time horse trainer and he liked it that way. His was a reputation best maintained by avoiding those actually knowledgeable about horses. Randy had long ago discovered that some people rode most beautifully from the vantage of a cocktail party. These individuals, if wealthy, found in Mr. Wells a man most appreciative of their talents.

The man knew his market and he had the look. Tall, handsome and with most of his dirty blond hair, Randy once spent a summer in Britain and affected an accent to sound "born to the Hunt." He took care to look the part, going nowhere without at least a polo shirt and usually boots and breeches. If he was feeling puckish, Randy carried his riding crop.

At forty-nine, the man was past his prime and trying very hard to prove otherwise. His wife had had enough of his affairs and removed their children to Florida. Randy now divided his time between trying to win back his family and his general pursuit of women. He preferred those with nice cars, but would settle for a tan.

The phone was ringing. Randy put a hand to his head—it had been a riding crop night. "All right," he mumbled into the phone.

"You are not going to believe this, but the last horse is *gone.*"

Randy groaned when he recognized the speaker. He wanted a drink; even water would do. "Congratulations."

"You may keep your congratulations. We do *not* have the animal in our possession. The lady of the house says they sent the little beast to her father's stables somewhere near Las Vegas. To be *sold*, imagine the gall."

"Did you get the name?"

"Yes, it is one Larry Masterson. He was the breeder of the little animal's mother, so I was told. Am I to be impressed?"

"I meant the name of the place. The stables itself."

"It is Nevada we're talking about, sir. It is a desert. How many stables could there be?"

About two thousand, Randy guessed. "Talk to you soon, Freddie."

———————

"You have a letter, Meagan," Jennifer called upstairs. "It looks like a party invitation."

Meagan came onto the landing. "Open it please," she said with audible indifference.

Jennifer almost insisted that her daughter come down. The pouting about Promise had no end in sight. Sighing, she instead opened the envelope and pulled out a stiff card with lines of engraved script:

> *To My Young Friend, Ms. Meagan Roberts:*
>
> *Mrs. Eleanor Bridgestone wishes to extend a cordial lunch invitation to you and accompanying parent or guardian, and hopes to receive the honor of your company.*

"That's odd. There is a date but no phone number." Jennifer looked up. "Who is Eleanor Bridgestone?"

"I don't know," Meagan shrugged. "I've never heard of her."

Jennifer glanced at the envelope. 156 Haversham Avenue, in the Heights. Nice area. "Come, Meagan, think. Is she one of your teachers? Maybe the principal?"

"I don't know any Mrs. Bridgestones, honest." Meagan sighed dramatically and closed her bedroom door.

This is a funny way to ask for a parent-teacher conference, Jennifer thought. There was no postmark, so someone had delivered the card personally. She called into the living room, "Tom, do we know an Eleanor Bridgestone?"

"Not me," he called back.

"It might be someone with the school, but there's no RSVP number. Why wouldn't they do this on campus? Meagan says she doesn't know."

"Our daughter isn't really talking to us, Jen, if you haven't noticed. But it wouldn't hurt to meet one of Meagan's teachers. Want me to take her?"

"No," Jennifer said thoughtfully. "I will..."

———

Randy turned down his television set when he heard the phone. His dinner date was overdue. Picking up the receiver, he delivered a cultured greeting with a full dose of British. "Good *e v e n i n g.*"

"Good evening yourself," came the sullen reply.

Randy turned the television volume back up. "Freddie, if you're calling about the horse, have no worries. I drove by and the little beastie really is gone." He had surprised himself by actually following up on the request, but after all, business was business.

"As I presumed. I am here in Las Vegas. *What* a zoo."

"Oh? I've always liked it. Do yourself a favor and try the Blue Candy Lounge." Randy flipped through the channels. "How many stables have you been to?"

"Bother that! Would you believe there are *hundreds* of stables in this terrifying state? I will need some assistance."

"Oh really?"

"When I called back to ask some very simple information, Mrs. Roberts was extremely short with me. She even hung up, each of three times I called in a row. How rude."

Randy stopped at a channel giving sport scores.

"This is not going well at all," Freddie said huffily. "I *must* know the name of the father's stables."

"It shouldn't be too hard since you've got the vet records. I have a friend at the Jockey Club who can tell me where the dam was foaled. Chances are it's the same place."

"The damn?"

"You know, the momma. Daddy's the sire, momma's the dam."

He let it go. "So, this jockey's club will know where the horse's damn mother was born?"

"Foaled, you mean."

"All right, *foiled*. Whatever you people say. I suppose these expressions are ancient." Freddie hung up thinking horse people were imbeciles.

It had been a strange association from the start. Randy had met Fred Jeffries at the race track, drinking upstairs in the Club House. Randy saw only an oddball dressed in a green tweed jacket too small for him; it took time to realize Jeffries was costumed to look the part of a gentleman horseplayer—laughable then, doubly so now. Randy saw alcohol flowing and hoped an introduction might send some his way. He was right. After they watched a race together, Fred bought Randy a drink.

"Why, thank you kindly," Randy said affably, toasting. "To the next race!"

Fred took a swallow and fixed an unsteady eye on Randy. He had lately taken to drink. "You sound like someone who knows horses, Mr. Wells. It just so happens I need one of your breed..."

Randy did not know exactly what to make of the remark, so he nodded, downed his drink and returned his attention to the race telecast. Fred held up his glass and gave a mild toast. "To new friends. May we enjoy a very profitable association."

Randy turned back, friendly once again. "Good word, profitable. What kind of association were we speaking of?"

"Let us just say I have an employer with an eye on a particular horse, who wishes assistance in its procurement." Fred grandly gestured to the bartender for another round.

"Help with a purchase, you mean."

"A *procurement*, yes. Actually, we are talking about three *procurements*." Fred had been repeating the word, thinking it lent sophistication. He leaned closer, smelling heavily of beer and something Randy guessed must be cheap cologne—unless the tweed jacket had been stored too long in a damp basement. "You see," Fred confided, "my client has an idea to make a special collection of horses. Seven *procurements* in all. So far, I have only been able to get four of the beasts. There are three left to obtain. I told my employer I wouldn't let her—him—down." He pointed to a group at a large table watching the races. "One of the horses is owned by the people sitting over there. Mr. and Mrs. Fielding. You probably know them. They have an animal running today."

Randy squinted. "And you want to buy it?"

"No, no, the horse *we* want is just a babe, only six months old. Those people own it, unfortunately. I made them a generous offer of thirty thousand dollars for their little beastie. At first they said yes, until they inquired of my employer. *Then* the price went up."

"Because of how wealthy your client is?" Randy interrupted with interest.

"Exactly! Which is why I have need of a middleman." Fred brightened. "Do you have a pen?"

Randy turned to ask the bartender.

"No, no, never mind," Fred said impatiently. "Pretend you had a pen, and were holding it right now, and I asked you who invented it. If you could answer correctly, you would have named my employer."

"He invented *pens?*"

"Well, bought the patent, or something. I don't know. That's where the money came from, anyway." Fred wound down into a mumble, thinking he should have waited for a pen. It hurt the presentation. "There are a lot of pens in the world," he finished lamely.

"And lots of money," Randy added optimistically.

"I never realized how attached people can be to a *horse*." Fred Jeffries was exasperated by the project. He had studied at the finest schools in Europe and was Head Chef in the home of one of the wealthiest families in California—he considered it beneath his station to be outdoors. However, he *never* refused the wealthy and had smiled gratefully at the request.

"It very much depends on the approach, I have found," Randy said with sympathy shining in his eyes. "You say these Fieldings were going to sell for thirty thousand. What happened, my good man?"

"They raised the price to seventy-five," Fred said with a shudder.

Randy whistled. "Talk about charging what the market will bear."

"I am going to look incompetent, which is something my employer does not allow." Fred was clearly in distress. "I am now operating under cover. The whole experience has shaken my faith in humanity."

"Oh, we mustn't lose that ... what did you have in mind, exactly?"

"Well," Fred clasped his hands together and knitted his brow. "The way I figure it, all you horse types must know each other."

"It *is* a small world." Randy did actually recognize one of the group, a formerly wealthy widow with a passion for gambling. He had never seen the others in his life, but he kept a smile on his face. "My people," he said serenely.

"So, these Fieldings will know you aren't connected to my client. You should be able to pick up the horse for thirty grand and sell it to us. With a broker fee to you, of course."

"Oh? A fee of ... ?"

"I believe the figure of five thousand dollars has been mentioned."

"I *see*. But I have a question. If your client is so wealthy, why does he care about such a small amount of money? I mean, a lot of people could toss that out and not think twice."

Fred cleared his throat. "Do you *know* many rich people, Mr. Wells?"

Randy shrugged modestly.

"Because, if you did, then you would know rich people hate nothing more than giving money away."

"Even for a special *procurement*?" Randy rolled the word out in his richest accent, amused at Fred's furious eyes. "Just so I have it right, your client will pay thirty-five thousand for the horse. If I can come up with the animal, that's the price?" When Fred assured him, Randy smiled. "We can do business."

It was the easiest money Randy Wells had ever made, even with expenses.

At first, the Fieldings were genuinely reluctant to sell their young filly, as she was well bred and carried racing potential. But Randy made an offer too good to pass up, so a deal was made pending a routine veterinarian check, a standard procedure in horse sales. Everyone was shocked when the check turned up early evidence of arthritis, hairline bone fractures and a dreaded disease of the hoof's navicular bone. Of course, Randy's shock was from the high price of the faked diagnosis.

Randy pulled out of the deal with an injured air, leaving the Fieldings desperate to find a buyer for their newly worthless filly. Fred Jeffries' call the next day was providential and the thirty-thousand dollar offer was eagerly accepted. When Fred suggested his veterinarian could do the pre-sale check the following week, Mr. Fielding generously offered to accept twenty-five thousand for an immediate purchase, without a physical exam. Mr. Fielding understood how eager Mr. Jeffries was to have the horse ... could payment be made by certified check?

The young horse was delivered directly to Fred Jeffries' employer. After Randy saw the facilities—and once the checks had cleared—the men became chummy.

"There are only two horses left to procure," Fred confided to Randy. "That will *finally* complete my employer's little collection. I should never have told my employer I was a horseman. I wanted to impress, but *this...*"

"About the collection," Randy pressed. "What are the other horses like?"

"Well, they all are baby-girl horses ... I forget the word. In fact, all the horses were born on the same day in June, on the summer solstice. Don't ask me why. It is my employer's request."

"He is an eccentric," Randy volunteered. "I understand completely. It must be hard to attend to your important duties when you have to bother with this menial horsetrading."

"*Horse*trading," the man sniffed. "The word is perfect. It is all haggling and playing games. Why can't you simply order a horse, like a sausage or a pie?"

"That is why we have commissions," Randy said smoothly. "There is a human element involved."

"Maybe *that* is the problem." Fred sighed dramatically. "I have done a good job, I think. It was easy to buy the first few horses, I had only to pay a certain purchase price. Very civilized. But then came this Fieldings unpleasantness, which is hopefully over."

"It is all behind us," Randy reassured him. "What do you intend to do next?"

"I don't know. I feel two headaches coming. Both remaining owners have refused to sell. One is owned by a mother, I think. She is quite upsetting. And then there is the Colonel's horse."

"Let's discuss the Colonel..."

The horse in question belonged to one Colonel Winthrop. The colonel had ridden at Fort Riley before it was disbanded after World War II. His father, Old Cavalry himself, had pressured the young man into joining. Winthrop had lived the life of a horseman, mucking his way through military service. It was difficult and forced, and he never forgave the animal.

Those unpleasant days echoed still, as most of Colonel Winthrop's relatives were horse people. For the past fifty years the Colonel had politely endured horse talk and invitations to ride but kept himself clean of it. To his dismay, his daughter-in-law gave him a young Morgan filly named Guinevere for his seventy-third birthday. Convinced the salutary effects of horsemanship would carry her father-in-law hale and hearty into his later years, she assumed, as did everyone, that the good Colonel was suffering from the lack of a good horse.

Colonel Winthrop was the type of horse enthusiast in which Randy Wells specialized. Randy saw instantly why Fred Jeffries was having trouble. The Colonel was reluctant to sell because the filly was a gift, and in his social circle decorum was the utmost consideration. It was merely a service matter.

An corruptible horseshoer provided a means to the profitable end. After a routine trim, the Colonel was given the sad information that little Guinevere possessed a severe case of forging. The poor filly would forever clip herself when going faster than a slow walk, and was fit only for grazing and lead-line chores. Of course the young horse seemed fine *now*, but it was only a matter of time...

Colonel Winthrop admitted it would be criminal to subject the horse to the strenuous riding he enjoyed. By a stroke of fortune the helpful horseshoer happened to know of a petting zoo accepting young horses ... in fact, a representative named Randy Wells would be in the area the next afternoon with a trailer. And yes, the zoo would be happy to accept a modest sum as a charitable donation.

The transaction increased Randy's curiosity about Fred Jeffries' mysterious client. Acquiring race stock was understandable, as was the pursuit of a certain breed, or even a color or trait. But when Randy asked Jeffries to describe the foals he had successfully "procured," there seemed to be no connection except age and the fact all were fillies. Of the six young horses purchased so far, there were two of mixed ancestry, one Standardbred, one Arabian, one Quarter horse, and the stout Morgan, Guinevere.

Randy hoped the final horse would provide a clue. It did not. The last purchase was to be a backyard foal out of a Thoroughbred dam, with one glaring characteristic that made the collection even more mysterious: the foal was a golden palomino.

A young palomino Thoroughbred should not be expensive, to Randy's mind, for its coloring cast too many doubts on its ancestry. All Jeffries needed to do was make the family a generous offer. Or so it had seemed.

Meagan's grandfather, Larry Masterson, was a man with little time for foolishness. He watched impatiently, waiting for the man who had parked at the front gate to walk the quarter mile driveway to the main house. The visitor wore an expensive, fashionable suit and stopped every few yards, as if he could not make up his mind whether to keep on.

This must be the one, he thought. *Can't say Jennifer didn't warn me.*

For his part, Fred Jeffries was annoyed and not completely sure he was off the farm road. A mailbox was a perfectly reasonable place to park, he thought irritably. He was coming to detest the state of Nevada. Waving, Fred evaluated the old rancher leaning against his beaten red pickup, wearing a plaid shirt and jeans belted under an enormous buckle. Tall, slim, white hair still full, the man was probably in his late sixties and seemed the perfect hick.

"Hello, sir." Fred offered his hand. "My name is Fred Jeffries. I flew in to see about one of your horses." Fred pumped the rancher's callused hand, impressed by his own softness.

"You don't say, Mr. Jeffries." Larry gave a warm smile. "It's not often we get real city people here."

"No?" Fred glanced back down the long driveway.

"Don't believe I've ever had anyone park up at the gate, either."

"Well, the mailbox was there and where I come from we—" Fred paused, startled by the sight of a black bull watching from a paddock behind Masterson. "It's a bit more centralized." He swallowed and looked around. "God's country. You've got to love it."

"You say you've come about a horse?"

"Yes! Yes, sir, I have. I understand your daughter sent a certain young specimen here a few days ago from California. Seems I didn't offer quite the right sum and surely you don't mind negotiating..."

"A palomino filly? I seem to remember. Nice little horse, too."

"Oh, she's a beautiful animal. So, which way to her little house, or cubicle or whatever?"

"We sold her yesterday."

"Sold her?" Fred repeated, blinking. "Why?"

"Couldn't jump very well, so we sent her off." Jump training is delayed until a horse's fourth year, but Jennifer had insisted the man would never know. Larry's expression was straightforward. "Sorry about that."

"Do you know where she went?" Fred wished fervently that the little horse had jumped better.

"If you don't mind my asking, son, what are you wanting this particular horse for?"

Fred thought quickly. Jumping was out. "Oh, pulling wagons, you know. I was hoping to contact the new owners to see if they might be interested in selling."

"Pulling wagons? But that filly's a thoroughbred. Born to run, son, not to pull wagons."

"Well, she'll need to race some, too." Fred ran his fingers through his hair. The old man was worse than his daughter.

"Race *and* pull wagons, son?"

"Oh, yes, working the farm, betting on weekends. Family pet. Wife's idea, really." Fred felt himself begin to babble. "Can you say where I might find her?"

"No, can't really say. Maybe they said something about ... oh, Canada, I think it was."

"*Canada?*"

"Yep. Probably do her good. Horses love cold weather— thickens the blood. Pull better."

Fred nodded at the unbidden horse lore. Canada. In January. He was afraid to ask the next question. "I hate to trouble you, but do you know *where* in Canada?"

"Some auction, I think they said. Vancouver. No wait, maybe it was Toronto." He instantly regretted saying it when Fred took inspiration. "Sorry about the filly, son. You shouldn't bother trying to track her down. Just find another one. There's lots of them, you know."

Fred shook his head, looking at the bull and then back at his car.

"Need a ride?" Larry offered.

———

Sitting on open air metal bleachers in Toronto, Fred Jeffries decided once and for all he hated horses. Well, not so much horses as the people they hung around. Who else but horse people would put on a damn outdoor auction in the middle of a Canadian winter?

It was about five degrees below zero, and Fred was colder than he had imagined it was possible to be. His coffee had cooled in the short walk from the coffee stand. Across the tundra, he thought, shuddering. Six layers of clothes immobilized him, and Fred felt their main use was to keep him from sticking to the bleachers.

The auction began at dawn with the cattle. Fred had come an hour late, but the lady in the registration trailer assured him the horses had not yet started. On the bright side, when he asked about a palomino filly *everyone* thought they had seen her. This was the only January auction within a hundred miles of Toronto and Fred had taken a chance. He thought happily of his next bonus.

"Mr. Jeffries?" a voice asked respectfully. Fred craned his head around his stiff parka to see a red-faced man standing beneath the bleachers. "Are you looking for a palomino filly?"

Fred scrambled down from the bleachers. "Yes, I am! Do you have her?"

"I think I might. She is a beut." Happy to have found an eager prospect, the man tromped around the main ring and through a series of sheds. Fred followed close behind, stepping carefully. They rounded a shedrow and Fred saw it: his Holy Grail, in the shape of a little yellow horse.

"That's her!" Fred exclaimed happily. He would have hugged the animal were he not mortally afraid of horses. "How much?" he asked eagerly.

The red-faced man set back, hooking his thumbs in his waistband in a self-satisfied slouch. "Well, sir, I couldn't show my face at home if I didn't bring back at least eight hundred dollars for her." The man set his face into a kind of frown illustrating his unmovable position on price.

Fred stared at him. *Eight hundred dollars?* He looked at the little filly with new disdain. "Talk about coming down in the world."

"She's a nice horse, sir. You can see that."

"Maybe you should talk to her last owner." Fred wondered why his employer would want such an obviously poor specimen. The wretched animal couldn't even jump.

"But sir, I bred this horse myself. She hasn't had another owner."

Fred looked at the man in confusion. "Didn't this horse come from Nevada?"

"Nevada? Why, no sir! This horse was bred right here in Ontario." The red-faced man laughed heartily without noticing that Fred was not joining in.

"What in the—"

The trader stopped laughing and followed Fred's eyes. Across the short lot between sheds, another golden horse was being taken out of its stall.

"No concern, Mr. Jeffries. Just another entry. Palominos are up next." The man came closer and lowered his voice. "Tell you what. If my horse doesn't go through the bidding I save the fee. Let's split the difference and say seven-fifty."

Fred had a horrible thought. He walked to the nearest stall and looked inside. Sure enough, staring back was yet another golden horse. "What's this?"

"How do you mean? You wanted a palomino and I have one. Right here, for sale."

"I didn't know they were a damn *species*." Fred felt helpless. He very much missed his comfortable kitchen. Then he had a sudden thought: at eight hundred dollars each, he would buy them all! "Good sir," Fred said, pleasantly recomposed. "How many of these type horses are there?"

"Hey?" the trader asked, confused.

"You know, these pal-o-minos. How many are here?" Canadians were so dense.

"About forty, I guess. Sixty at the most."

Fred's face fell. "I see. And how much to trailer to my house?"

"I can do that for you," the trader grinned. "How far do you live?"

"California."

The man's smile dropped from his face. He crunched through the snow and began to untether his horse.

"That much," Fred mumbled. He felt like pounding his fist in frustration, but he couldn't feel his arm below the elbow. Forget the stupid horse. He was going home.

In the afternoons the programme was:
Mondays and Fridays, tilting and horsemanship...
- *T. H. White (1906-64)* The Sword in the Stone

"Hurry up, Meagan!" Jennifer called upstairs as she transferred her wallet and keys into her best purse. Meagan ran down the steps holding her shoes. She was dressed in her powder blue, knee-length dress—the one she most hated. The dress meant church and receptions and graduations, not being able to go outside or even to *think* of going near horses. Today it meant a boring lunch with some lady named Eleanor Bridgestone.

The doorbell rang. "I'll get it!" Meagan called, hurrying past her mother. She opened the door to a proper gentleman in a black formal livery and humorless expression. Meagan greeted him in a small voice, staring.

Jennifer walked up. "Hello, I am Mrs. Roberts. May we help you?"

"Good afternoon, *Madame*." The man's tone was deep and dignified, with a trace of French. "My name is Nelson, and I am here at the behest of Mrs. Bridgestone to offer transportation to the afternoon's lunch."

Jennifer looked past the man to an imposing limousine parked on the street. "Thank you, but I had planned on taking my car."

"As you wish, *Madame*. You may follow me if you like."

On the drive, the streets went from pleasant domesticity to the kind of neighborhoods people drive slowly to sightsee. Tree-lined roads wound around properties set back and fenced by walls, their opulent yards and mansions glimpsed through iron gates. The home at 156 Haversham was hidden behind a vine-covered brick wall that encircled the property.

Jennifer followed the limousine as it pulled into the drive and stopped at the wrought iron entrance. Remote-controlled gates slowly swept open. She was growing nervous: this home certainly did not come from teacher's pay. Columns lined the front of a majestic mansion, framing banks of chrysanthemums. Unbroken lawn spread from either side of the flagstone driveway. The landscaping was minimal and perfectly kept, simplicity made imposing by scale.

The limousine's driver asked Jennifer to park on the ample circular drive. He then led Jennifer and Meagan down a long walkway to the front door, where another gentleman waited stiffly to greet them. This man was formally attired and wearing gray gloves, which surprised Jennifer. *Gloves, in this day and age?* She did not consider that for a certain slice of humanity—its most thin and materially endowed slice—the days and ages change very little.

Jennifer grasped her daughter's hand and marched up the stone steps past the man and into the interior. Inside was the spaciousness of a cathedral. Paintings were mounted along paneled walls between bay windows, over floors of lustrous mahogany. A massive staircase dominated the entry with a sweeping arc to a balconied second floor. Their guide stopped before the entrance of a formal room.

"Welcome," a quavering voice greeted them, brave in the vast space.

Meagan gave a little exclamation and whispered, "Mom, I *do* know her."

"Come in, please. I am so happy you could join me." Thin, withered hands motioned to a facing couch. "Nelson, please show them in." Jennifer grasped Meagan's hand firmly as the butler led them into the room.

The elderly woman's smile mapped lines across her pale features. Her silver hair was pulled back to reveal a strand of white pearls looped over a simple charcoal dress. A bejeweled cane leaned against the arm of the couch. "I am Mrs. Bridgestone, and you must be Jennifer. It is so good of you to come." The woman smiled knowingly at Meagan. "I believe your daughter and I have already met."

"I am pleased to meet you, Mrs. Bridgestone," Jennifer said graciously. "My daughter did not tell me you two were acquainted."

"We met on a delightful occasion last summer. How is your beautiful young horse, dear child? I won't make the mistake of saying 'pony' again."

Meagan was about to say the horse was fine, thank you, when her mother interrupted. "We sold her two weeks ago," Jennifer said firmly. "We had an offer too good to pass up."

Meagan looked at her mother in surprise.

"Yes, so I understand. I was sorry to hear that." The old woman looked past her guests and motioned to the butler. He carried forward a silver tea service.

Jennifer kept her smile fixed. "Your home is so lovely, Mrs. Bridgestone. Though I must say, I am confused about the nature of this meeting."

"Of course you are, dear. Allow me time to explain." The elderly woman waited as the tea was poured, accepting her cup with a polite murmur. "I am afraid, Jennifer, that by the end of this meeting you will think me a crazy old lady." She held up her cup. "I do enjoy my tea and I hope you like it. It is an Indian orange pekoe blend I have made specially. I have to, they stopped making it years ago. With so many changes, this is my little stab at permanence." She chuckled. "Tea. How little you become satisfied with."

Jennifer restrained herself from eyeing the extravagance of this single room.

"I have gained some experience with horses since we last met, Meagan." Mrs. Bridgestone sipped her cup delicately. "What did you name your young horse?"

"I named her Promise, ma'am. It was how you said, that animals sometimes name themselves."

"They do indeed. At least, that has been my experience." The woman thought for a moment. "*Promise*. Why, that is a lovely name! It is quite apt too, if somewhat misleading..."

Meagan looked shyly at the floor.

The woman reached for her cane. "Before we have lunch, I think you two might enjoy meeting a few friends of mine.

Nelson, could you assist?" The man stepped forward to help Mrs. Bridgestone to her feet. "I've had a recent illness," she explained. "Nothing too serious, but it *has* slowed me down."

Jennifer and Meagan followed into a wide hallway that ended at a glass door. Beyond could be glimpsed lawn and white fences. A bay-colored flash floated by in the sliver visible through the window.

Meagan opened the glass door and ran out. Emerging into sunshine, she gasped to see a storybook stables nestled within a brilliant green landscape. White fences wrapped crisp lines around wood-shingled roofs and raked paths. Hanging chrysanthemums flanked yellow-and-white Dutch stall doors. The building looked more like a decorated cake than a working facility.

"Mom, look!" Meagan ran to the central paddock and leaned over the fence toward a husky bay horse. "It's a filly too!" she called. "She is Promise's age!"

"I own six horses altogether, Jennifer," Mrs. Bridgestone confided. "All fillies. The stables are new, and I've secured the services of a horseman to watch over them. A groom..." The old woman leaned on her cane and gazed at the stables. "What a lovely profession."

"Have you had horses long?" Jennifer asked.

"No, actually not long at all." Mrs. Bridgestone took Jennifer's arm as they walked on. "I admit to a mostly academic knowledge of horses, Jennifer. I loved horses as a young girl, yet I have come to actual ownership late in life." They came to the paddock fence and watched Meagan stroke the young filly's soft coat. Mrs. Bridgestone raised her voice, "That is Guinevere, dear. She is my newest addition. An entrancing disposition, as you can see."

Meagan held an open handful of grass to the stout filly. The animal comically snorted the leaves away.

Mrs. Bridgestone leaned to Jennifer. "Tell me something, dear. You have practical knowledge about horses. Are they really as intellectually ... *limited* as one hears? It has always upset me to think so."

"You mean, are horses stupid?"

"I have heard it said, and I am sorry. They are such splendid animals."

"Don't be sorry, Mrs. Bridgestone." Jennifer was amused. "They are so different than humans. Right now that horse is watching Meagan, you and me and almost everything around her. And she will never forget, because horses have a photographic memory. Horses hear and smell as well as a dog, they are so sensitive they can feel a fly's landing, and can even recognize people by the vibration of their walk."

"Yes, yes," the old woman said, "I have discovered the most engaging facts in my readings. Did you know that the horse's eye is one of the largest in the animal kingdom, even larger than an elephant's? I understand horses are timid because in nature they are prey. Have you found that to be true?"

Jennifer nodded. "It is hard to imagine how differently a horse sees the world. But the more you try, the better they respond."

"How charming. It is fascinating how closely horsemanship and culture coincide. When Europe fell into the Dark Ages, their horsemanship deteriorated into barbarism. It was not until the Renaissance that humane methods were rediscovered." Mrs. Bridgestone stepped to the fence and reached a frail hand to stroke the filly's neck. "In owning a horse, I feel I own a living piece of history." Guinevere reached to sniff Mrs. Bridgestone's hand. The woman smiled. "Magical beings, aren't they? There is history in their hoof beats—or is it hoof steps? I should tell you, my friends and staff have questioned my sanity since I started my horse project ... sometimes a touch of madness produces the sanest result." She sighed, watching Guinevere trot off with her tail high. "I was surprised to learn horses have never been domesticated. Equines are a much older species than humans and their instincts remain. Horses return easily to the wild, as with the American mustangs. I like that, somehow. In all the centuries they have never forgotten themselves."

"Yes," Jennifer said regretfully, "though we don't need horses anymore. Now they are only expensive playthings."

Mrs. Bridgestone looked at Jennifer sharply. "I wouldn't say that, dear. I wouldn't say that at all. People are no authority on what they need. Ignorance about our needs is one thing that separates us from animals. Oh, I *truly* wish we had had this meeting long ago, Jennifer. They say horses rush men to folly. Well, they do it to old women, too."

—————

Lunch was a lavish affair amongst yellow flowers, white linen and silver. Nelson served as guide to the steaming plates and cups of fresh fruit. A distant raised voice from the depths of the mansion caught Jennifer's attention: the sound had a strangely familiar wheedling quality.

"That is only my Mr. Jefferies, dear. Temperamental but very loyal. He is the only member of my staff who does not whisper about my horse obsession." Mrs. Bridgestone directed Meagan to a covered dish. "Try the quail, dear. It has raspberry dressing and watercress. You may find the contrast interesting."

Meagan tasted the portion presented to her by Nelson and wrinkled her nose.

"Meagan!" Jennifer admonished. "Remember your manners."

Mrs. Bridgestone chuckled. "I am reminded of my late husband, Ashton. He couldn't abide hot meals, rest his soul. Said they raised one's hopes too high but a sandwich never disappointed. My Ashton wasn't one for disappointments." Mrs. Bridgestone reached for the tea. "Meagan, you may prefer the lamb. The mint dressing is quite good."

"I'll try some," Meagan volunteered. Nelson scooped a generous spoonful onto a side dish and set it close. Positioning a speck onto a tine of her fork, Meagan tasted the dressing and smiled broadly.

Mrs. Bridgestone took a sip of tea and savored it. "I mentioned I was new to horse ownership, Jennifer, but I have always held the animal in respect. I do not think it is too much to say horses gave us civilization."

"I learned about ancient nomads who lived on horseback," Meagan said earnestly. "They conquered the largest empire *ever*, from China to Europe."

Mrs. Bridgestone smiled. "The Mongolians, dear. They invented the saddle's stirrup which allowed knights to use lances. Many nations have had their influence, for equestrian nations have led the world." The woman set her cup down delicately. "Like horsemanship, civilization is not an obvious process."

After lunch, Mrs. Bridgestone adjourned to a warm room whose coziness made Jennifer wonder if brandy and cigars would be forthcoming. A low fire burned in an ornate fireplace, below a polished marble mantle inscribed with flowing letters in a foreign language. Dark leather punctuated with brass fasteners covered couches and stools, and framed art of horses filled the walls.

Beside the door, a pedestal bore a brass sculpture of a bearded, trident-bearing man mounted on a flipper-tailed horse. Meagan stood before it and reached out a finger.

"Don't touch, Meagan," Jennifer warned.

"No, let her, Jennifer. The child won't hurt it." Mrs. Bridgestone walked slowly to a pair of facing couches in the center of the room. "That is a statue of a Hippocampus, dear. They were the mounts of Poseidon, god of the sea. The ancients believed the horse came from the deep ocean wearing the froth of the waves for its mane. Do you like it?"

"Yes, ma'am," Meagan answered quietly, and walked in wonder to an antique vase set upon a white pedestal. A team of horses charged over the curved surface.

"You may touch the vase, dear, it is only a copy. The original is sixth century B.C. Do you see the images of black horses over the red background? It was an early, crude form of vase painting called 'black figure.' Red figures were developed later, but I like the severe lines. Personal taste."

Meagan softly agreed.

"They were interesting people, our forebears the Greeks. That particular vase shows a four-horse chariot called a *Quadriga*. Chariot racing grew so popular under the Roman Empire that it was considered a form of madness. It was the first mass spectator sport."

Meagan walked on to an antique globe, hands clasped behind her. Dancing curlicues of fanciful horses adorned its colorful seas.

"I obtained that piece in Delhi, dear. I have a friend who believes the horse is the only animal to have reached Nirvana. He says Allah placed fear in the horse so that he would remain earthbound, to be an inspiration and guide to mankind. You will find religion and horsemanship very much intertwined."

Jennifer moved to sit across from the woman. "It's very nice to be here, Mrs. Bridgestone, but I am still not sure why. As lovely as this has been ... I thought this meeting might be school-related?"

"If you mean education-related, yes. Horses are said to be excellent teachers and only so much can be taught in a classroom." The woman cleared her throat delicately. "Do you believe in legends, dear?"

"Well, I suppose I believe, like most people, that legends began with a grain of truth or an explanation for something."

"Yes, I think that must be true." Mrs. Bridgestone looked toward the window and stared out for a time, as if she had forgotten her visitors. When she turned back, her eyes brimmed with tears. "I have a legend I would like to tell you. It is obscure yet quite lovely. It tells of Man's banishment from the Garden of Eden. I have it written down if you would allow me to read it. Nelson, the letter?"

The butler stepped forward to a shelf, retrieving a folded letter. He placed it on a silver tray and presented it formally to Mrs. Bridgestone. Putting on her eyeglasses with a shaking hand, she took the letter carefully and tilted her head to read:

> *In the Beginning, Man so angered the Lord he was cast from the Garden. In the midst of the Lord's wrath an Angel came onto Him. The Angel asked permission to lead Mankind back again to Paradise, and wished to be given a shape to best serve Man in his exile.*
>
> *This love stayed the Lord's wrath. The Four Winds swirled into a shape of beauty that moved to thunder ... the Angel took form and became the first Horse.*
>
> *Since that time, the Angel has lived an unbroken line of lives, inspiring and teaching, even as the Angel's children have carried Mankind to mastery of the earth. Upon each death the Angel takes another form and again a Great Horse is born.*

Meagan listened raptly. "I *like* that story, Mrs. Bridgestone!"

The woman refolded the letter and set it upon the tray. "I am happy to hear that, dear." She pointed to a portrait of a magnificent horse, head bowed, carrying a haughty rider in white. "That painting shows the stallion Bucephalus, one of the eminent Great Horses of history. When he was first presented to King Philip of Macedonia, no rider could mount him. The king's own son was a boy about your age, and he called out—"

"I'm almost thirteen," Meagan interrupted.

"*Really*, dear? Splendid." Mrs. Bridgestone smiled at Jennifer. "They grow so quickly, don't they? It seems my grandniece went from diapers to driving in the space of an afternoon. Well, to continue, when the King's son saw the wonderful stallion being led away to be banished, he cried out, '*What an excellent horse they have lost for lack of skill!*' Naturally the king was annoyed with his son's manners. To teach a lesson the King had the horse brought back for his son to try what the others had failed.

"The boy had noticed the young horse was shying from his riders' shadows, so he turned the stallion into the sun and mounted easily. He rode Bucephalus for thirty years, and conquered more armies than any man before or since. Do you know that boy?"

Meagan shook her head.

"He was Alexander the Great, dear. The stallion Bucephalus carried his master from Egypt to India, and no one else ever rode him. Not once."

Meagan moved respectfully to an onyx sculpture beside the painting. The work was of a horse sitting on his haunches with both forelegs stretched in front of him. "Who is *this?*"

"That was the Great Horse El Morzillo, dear, the mount the Spanish conquistador Cortés rode to conquer Mexico. Cortés was forced to leave his prized stallion behind with natives who knew nothing of horses. They fed him only meat and wine until the poor animal wasted away and died. Frightened of Cortez's wrath, the natives made an enormous statue of the horse to worship. When missionaries returned—I want to say Franciscans—they threw the statue into the lake surrounding his temple. It is said El Morzillo looks up from the bottom of that lake, still waiting for his master's return."

Meagan walked to another pedestal. It supported a horse's head, a fragment of an originally life-sized statue. The visage was warlike: the stone mouth was open as if in rage.

"That is a cast of a Greek original, dear, made in the time of the Roman Emperor Trajan." Mrs. Bridgestone pronounced the name *Tray-jin*. "He reigned at the turn of the first century, about nineteen hundred years ago when Rome was at its height. It is a darkly fascinating time, the moment before western civilization began to disintegrate. With the fall of Rome came Europe's Dark Ages. Remember, dear, that Western Civilization has died once before."

Behind the pedestal was a large painting of a chariot race, head-on, with the crowd and track rendered in rousing detail. Meagan stood beneath it, staring in awe.

"The actual work hangs in the Manchester Art Gallery, dear. As you can see, the ancient Romans were modern in many ways. One of my favorite old writers was Cornelius Tacitus, who wrote scandalous histories of Rome. Such an insightful mind, writing so bravely as his world sank into madness ... that is a horse's manger, dear."

Meagan was stopped before a crumbling box mounted on a low pedestal. The object was corroded and gray from age.

"It doesn't look it, I know, but that is *said* to be the remains of the manger of the Roman Emperor Caligula's favorite race horse, Incitatus. Caligula had a stable of marble and gold built for the stallion, complete with furnishings and servants. Though horses are strict vegetarians, Incitatus was fed mice dipped in butter and marinated squid." Mrs. Bridgestone added more quietly, "Of course, the man was considered dangerously insane."

Meagan walked on. "How about this painting, Mrs. Bridgestone ... who is the old man with a long beard?"

"That is El Cid on his Great Horse, Babieca. El Cid was a Spanish warrior who led armies on his famous white charger. There are stories which claim El Cid was mortally wounded at the siege of Valencia but Babieca was left alive. Before dying, El

Cid left clear instructions. The Spaniards marched from their city at midnight with Babieca cantering at the head of the Spanish troops as always, but with his dead master propped in the saddle and tied by his long beard. The attackers thought El Cid had risen from the dead and they fled, ending the siege, and so it is said that El Cid won his last battle after his own death. And no one ever mounted Babieca again."

"Those are interesting stories, Mrs. Bridgestone," Jennifer said, meaning it. "Everything here is so lovely ... but I'm still very curious. Why have you invited us?"

Meagan turned politely to listen.

"Yes, well." Mrs. Bridgestone fingered her necklace. "I suppose there is no better way to tell you, except to just say it. To put it simply, circumstances have ... oh me. It seems your foal is the *next* of the Great Horses."

Riding a horse is not a gentle hobby,
to be picked up and laid down like a game of solitaire.
It is a grand passion.

- Ralph Waldo Emerson (1803-1882)

"REALLY, MRS. BRIDGESTONE?" Meagan's eyes shone with excitement. "*My* horse, Promise?"

"I am almost certain of it, dear. My sources indicate a Great Horse was to be born on the summer solstice of the new millennium. A female, born at dawn. The birth happened last year."

Jennifer held her hand out to her daughter. "Come sit down, Meagan. I think we need to listen to Mrs. Bridgestone."

"I did mean to visit again to tell you personally," the woman said apologetically, "but I've been housebound and left it to others. To put it plainly, I am ashamed."

Jennifer smiled broadly. "Oh well, Mrs. Bridgestone, I'm just glad you told us now. Meagan, come sit down this instant."

"You see, Jennifer? I knew you would think me a crazy old woman."

"No, no, I don't think that at all. It's just that ... what are you saying, Mrs. Bridgestone? That our foal is descended from the first horse? I suppose that could be true..."

"No, dear. Not just any horse, but one of the blessed incarnations of the Angel that so loved Mankind he forsook Paradise." Mrs. Bridgestone smoothed her dress nervously. "I know how it must sound, but all religions have a story of the Creator giving the horse to mankind. Paganism, Christianity, Islam—think of Pegasus! Is not the winged, white horse the very image of an angel?"

"Well ... yes," Jennifer answered carefully. "I suppose. Is this a good thing?"

"Certainly a Great Horse is most often a blessing. Quiet service is a horse's way." The woman hesitated. "However, there is a certain prophecy concerning this incarnation. This Great Horse carries a somewhat ... *dark* description, if we believe the sources."

"Promise is a palomino," Meagan said, disappointed. "Does a Great Horse *have* to be dark?"

The woman smiled. "You are very attentive, Meagan, and that is an excellent quality. The equestrian influence, no doubt. To answer your questions, perhaps we should see more of the Great Horses in history. Nelson?" After taking assistance to rise from the couch, Mrs. Bridgestone proceeded alone. Jennifer followed the woman to a glass case at one end of the room, holding Meagan's hand tightly.

Mrs. Bridgestone reached a frail hand to an overhead light. A multitude of objects came to view beneath the glass top: papers and photographs, and what looked to be a scrap of parchment. She tapped her finger over a vintage photograph of a dilapidated horse beside an equally done old man. "That was my first horse, Pumpkin, and the man was Cappy Beardon. Cappy had been in the cavalry, if that tells you how long ago this was. He fought in the last battles against the Nez Perce Indians." The woman pointed at a framed map hanging on the wall behind the case. "A man named Joseph was Chief of the Nez Perce Indians, one of the last tribes hounded into life on a reservation. He led his people on what is known as the Trail of Tears, sixteen hundred miles of retreat in the face of a vastly superior army. The feat was so amazing, military leaders still study the tribe's tactics. The Nez Perce were cornered and forced to surrender only forty miles from the Canadian border. In surrender, Chief Joseph gave a famous speech."

"'From where the sun now stands I will fight no more forever,'" Jennifer said respectfully.

Mrs. Bridgestone smiled. "Very good, Jennifer. After the surrender, Cappy was given charge of Chief Joseph's mount. It was an Appaloosa, and one of the Great Horses."

"Appaloosas are spotted horses," Meagan volunteered. "They were bred by Indians."

"Exactly right, dear." Mrs. Bridgestone tapped the glass over the photograph. "Tremendous horsemen, the Indian people. You probably know horses originated in North America and migrated to Asia, and were likely hunted to extinction on this continent. Horses are in the native people's blood. You should have heard the stories Cappy told about that horse! Some men wanted the Chief's mount for themselves as a trophy, but the horse put them all in the infirmary. *No* one rides a Great Horse without the owner's permission." The woman made this last statement firmly, as if stating a conclusive fact. "Some in our cavalry had an idea to exterminate the Appaloosa breed, but Cappy helped disperse the surviving horses. He personally returned the mount to Chief Joseph. In his later years, Cappy came to work for my father." She tapped the glass again. "He gave me my first and only riding lessons on Pumpkin, an old cavalry horse Cappy kept in a neighbor's stall. The lessons were a secret because my father hated horses. He absolutely forbade me to ride."

"That is terrible, Mrs. Bridgestone!"

"I thought so too, dear. My father was afraid because of a famous old movie that showed the sensational tragedy of a little girl falling off a horse to her death. *Gone With the Wind*, indeed— gone with a puff of hubris, they mean." Mrs. Bridgestone sniffed irritably and leaned back over the case. "Oh, here is something amusing." The woman pointed to a section of yellow stone covered with chiseled markings. "This is an Egyptian tablet with hieroglyphics recording the gift of a Great Horse to Pharaoh. The horse was consulted on important matters of state and his decision was final."

Meagan giggled, and Mrs. Bridgestone smiled. "It *is* amusing, isn't it, dear? I imagine it was a peaceful reign." The old woman touched the glass above an engraved placard. "This is a famous ode in the style of the Greek poet Pindar. He was famous for his tributes to Olympic heroes, both men and horses. This verse is dedicated to a chariot horse that won a race in about 480 B.C."

Meagan squinted at it and wrinkled her nose. "It doesn't make sense. It is just weird scribbles."

"It is Greek, dear."

"Can you read it, Mrs. Bridgestone?"

"Oh, a bit, not much anymore. However, I know this poem quite well." The woman leaned over the placard and held her glasses close:

> *Hail the fleet hawk of the earth,*
> *thunder announces his approach.*
> *He gives one man victory,*
> *all men ecstasy.*
> *In this One the gods have taken form.*

"Of course, Pindar isn't so flowery," Mrs. Bridgestone explained. "It was not the Greek way."

"I took Latin all last year." Meagan said gravely, wanting to impress. "I made an A."

"That is wonderful, dear! Latin is a much undervalued element of education. We should read for ourselves the lessons of history."

Meagan looked around the room, making sure to see everything. "It's all so amazing, Mrs. Bridgestone. Is everything about Great Horses?"

"Yes, dear. I have another room devoted to Celtic and Asian horsemanship, which can be another visit altogether." The old woman studied the display case, engrossed in sharing her treasures. "Now, here is something."

Meagan and Jennifer moved to look. Next to the old photograph of Cappy and Pumpkin, a gold coin stamped with a winged horse was mounted on dark wood. Beneath it an inscription read, *The Legend of the Great Horse.*

"That coin was the first piece of my collection. Old Cappy left it to me. It is an ancient Greek coin honoring an immortal race of winged horses called the *Pegasii*, of whom the Great Horse Pegasus was the first. I had it mounted to remind me of the dear man who taught me to love horses."

Meagan looked more closely. The embossed horse was riderless, wings open and head high. "It is very nice, Mrs. Bridgestone."

"It is in mint condition, I am told, remarkably well preserved. I will let you guess the next object."

"Now, *really*, Mrs. Bridgestone." Jennifer said, leaning closer. "I can guess, but it *can't* be..."

"Yet it is." The woman lowered her glasses to study the graceful spiral of silver that shone upon black velvet. "A reputedly authentic unicorn's horn. The unicorn is one of the most famous of the Great Horses. The horn was kept by a brotherhood of knights who had safeguarded it as a relic. I had to purchase a fallen-down castle to acquire it, but my sources were correct. The spiral horn was under a stone tablet beside the moon garden's pool in the innermost courtyard."

"The 'moon' garden?" Meagan asked.

"Yes, dear. Such a garden's flowers open only in moonlight. It is said a unicorn's horn has great healing powers, and drinking from the horn is said to remedy poison." Mrs. Bridgestone chuckled to herself as she considered another photograph. "My late husband Ashton took this picture when we couldn't buy the original. It is of the prophet Mohammed riding the Great Horse Buraq into Heaven. The hoof print can still be seen in Jerusalem where he leapt away." She sighed, reflecting. "Legend says Mohammed starved a herd of horses for seven days, keeping them without food or water. When he released them to the river, he sounded his battle cry, and five of the mares came to him without drinking. Mohammed made those five mares the foundation of the Arabian breed."

Beside the photograph of Mohammed's Great Horse, a section of parchment was written over with flowing script. "This is one I quite like, dear. It is a Medieval passage from about 1190, providing guidance on how to know a Great Horse from witch-horses or horses possessed by demons." Mrs. Bridgestone looked over her glasses at Meagan. "Our friends in the Dark Ages were quite concerned about that sort of thing. I should point out that medieval writers speak of a breed of large horses developed to carry Knights into battle, which they call the Great Horse. My belief is that one of the Great Horses was confused with a general breed. Scholarship was not highly prized in the period."

Jennifer and Meagan crowded toward the case to see the passage. The words on the ancient paper were well preserved and legible. One section was covered by yellow glass for highlight:

The Mageste Beste is kneughne moste certis by tide of birth
At Prime whanne the sonne ronne fro the earth,
Ich wight not ryde, save conssente by hir maister wille.
It muste be few wight beknowen the treuthe
Ichone Maistere is tolde by a furst.

Jennifer and Meagan puzzled over the words as Mrs. Bridgestone moved slowly to a couch and settled onto it. "The language is a little strange. Old English, you see."

"What does it mean?" Meagan asked.

"Well, the first line reads, 'The Magic Beast is known most certainly by time of birth.'"

Jennifer was reading carefully. "What is 'Prime?'"

"The second service of the medieval church, just after sunrise. I interpret it to mean the Great Horse is born at dawn, 'when the sun runs from the earth.' That is a typical metaphor of the day."

"And the next part?" Jennifer said, reading slowly. "'Ich wight not ryde?'"

"*Wight* means man. So the phrase says, 'Each man shall not ride the Great Horse without the consent of its master.'" Mrs. Bridgestone closed her eyes and concentrated. "Few men know the truth, each new master is told by a first."

Meagan shook her head. "I don't understand it."

"Well, we must be sure you do," Mrs. Bridgestone said seriously. "First, a Great Horse is born at dawn. That is an unusual time for mares, as they usually foal near midnight. Secondly, no one can ride a Great Horse without the owner's permission."

"That's a good rule," Meagan said grinning, quite satisfied with the discussion.

"And third, only the owners of a Great Horse will believe the legend."

"Why? It makes sense to me." Meagan squinted at the last line. "What is this word, 'ichone?'"

"That is how they spelled 'each one.' So much of Old English is spelled strangely to us yet has the same sound. Each *one* of the masters, the owners, is told by a previous owner of the Great Horse. As I am telling you."

"You owned a Great Horse, Mrs. Bridgestone?"

The wrinkled face clouded. "No, actually not."

"So why—"

"It is a very nice story." Jennifer hushed her daughter with a glance. There was no need to disturb this nice woman's fantasies. "How did you find out about the legend, Mrs. Bridgestone?"

"Old Cappy told me. I was ten years old when the old man moved away. Father said Cappy had gone away to die. He was very callous about it." The woman took a short breath. "Cappy was simply gone one day. Father gave me the duty of cleaning up.

"It was so small, his room, smaller than our gardening shed. A mattress, a desk and a crate full of papers. A dirt floor. I cried when I saw it. I had never really seen poverty before, I mean the cruelty of it." The woman dabbed her eyes. "Cappy left me his old horse Pumpkin, his papers and the coin. I tried to keep Pumpkin a secret but Father found out. It was late on a Tuesday afternoon. I remember it exactly..."

Mrs. Bridgestone paused and shifted on the couch. "Excuse me, Jennifer and Meagan. I never expected to become a rambling old woman." She dried her eyes and pointed to a small lamp beside the couch. Under the lamp's dim light was a letter creased with folds, lying flat in an envelope of plastic. "That letter was in Cappy's trunk. I would like Meagan to read it. It concerns the next Great Horse."

Meagan went to the table. The document was written in a strong flowing script, the ink blurred but still legible. "It's written to Captain Daniel Beardon, on June 21, 1901. That's the exact same day Promise was born, a hundred years ago!" She read the letter aloud:

Captain Beardon,

To speak in person would be my wish, but I believe we will not meet again on this earth. I have a duty I cannot fulfill. It is another grief that weights my heart. In the mountains of a place far south of this land a horse works to feed a struggling family. To them I should go to tell of the gift they possess. But this land is my prison. The chain is broken.

I have new dreams. A path into light is fading. I have heard whispers foretelling a birth. I give you the poem of my dreams.

A hundred years hence on this westmost shore,
The Great Horse comes to men once more.

History lights the future's course,
With lessons learned from the Horse;

So born of loss and mother's grief,
The Great Horse takes a mighty leap.

Eclipsed by shadow, the golden spark
Shall wing her rider into the dark.

If this is a warning, Captain Beardon, the intent is clouded to me. But in my dreams every night the Great Horse is mounted and darkness falls.

Hear with your own ears for the Spirit speaks to your people in ways not heard by my own. You are to have this message. So I believe. At least this duty has been met.

Captain Beardon, sparing my horse and companion was an act of a people that can know righteousness. I am proud to call you friend.

Joseph
June the 21st*, 1901*

Jennifer took a deep breath. "That *is* interesting—isn't it interesting, Meagan? *My*."

The old woman spoke softly. "I had an investigator search the state's veterinarian records. Seven female foals were born in California at exactly dawn on June 21st, 2001. I have acquired all of the foals. All, that is, except yours."

"Of course, Mrs. Bridgestone," Jennifer said breezily, "you don't take this seriously?"

"Oh, but I do, dear. Most seriously."

"Mrs. Bridgestone?" Meagan asked, hesitating at her mother's expression. "Do you really think Promise could be the Great Horse?"

"Yes, dear, I do." The woman's tone was solemn. "My sources call her the Great Traveler, with power to bring darkness to the world. Of course, we wouldn't be sure unless the Great Horse was actually ridden, but that must never happen." Meagan's eyes were wide. "I admit it is strange. In all my readings, Great Horses have never done evil. Perhaps this event has something to do with the millennium change. I can't explain it."

"Maybe it's a *good* kind of darkness," Meagan suggested hopefully.

"Unfortunately, there is more. Chief Joseph was not certain of the meaning of his dreams, but I have found other references that are less reassuring."

Jennifer interrupted. "*Less* reassuring?"

"I think I can best show you, dear. Nelson, could you light the Charlemagne piece?"

The man strode to a darkened corner of the room and flipped a switch on the wall. A spotlight revealed a coarse, stained medieval woodcut showing the figure of a rider on a winged horse. The awkwardly drawn figures were descending into a black abyss.

"It is not good work," the woman said frankly. "There was not much quality in the Dark Ages. Look beneath, at the engraving." She winked. "Or don't you read old Saxony?"

Jennifer and Meagan leaned down to see the scratched lettering, frowning.

"The horse of light dawns with the second millennium," Mrs. Bridgestone quietly translated, *"and will show its rider the darkness.* I have to take that as a warning."

Jennifer glanced at Meagan.

"A variety of sources speak of chaos and ruin brought on by this Great Horse," Mrs. Bridgestone continued. "Wars, fires, desolation, things of that sort. I can only think it has something to do with the start of the new millennium. Which of course was 2001, not the year 2000 as widely celebrated."

Meagan returned to study Chief Joseph's letter again, reading each line carefully. "Maybe this is why Promise is so good. I never had to halter-break her, even. She just followed me around—she never even nipped."

"How was she about her hooves, dear? My little Guinevere is somewhat difficult."

"Perfect. She picks up her feet if you look at them too long."

"Well, my Guinevere gives the blacksmith a dickens of a time. Oh, I must remember they are not 'blacksmiths' anymore. They are called *farriers*. Honest profession, I think, like country doctors used to be." The woman closed her eyes. "I have lived a long time, dear. I am afraid some nostalgia is justified."

"Mrs. Bridgestone..." Meagan avoided her mother's forbidding glare. "How do you know a Great Horse, if they are all different?"

"Because there is one special thing all the Great Horses share. It is inscribed on the mantle ... a lovely piece, isn't it? Remarkably well preserved, from one of the Louis' periods. The marble was found in the ruins of an old stable at Versailles. The inscription is French and says, *'Great Horses Live in the Imagination.'*"

Meagan nodded slowly.

"Great Horses have thrilled mankind since before recorded history," the woman explained. "All the Great Horses live in the imagination: General Lee's horse Traveler, Secretariat, Man O'War..."

"Or Mr. Ed?" Meagan added helpfully.

Jennifer smiled. "So the legend can be taken another way? Maybe even as something good?"

"I'm afraid not, dear. From my research, the consequences of mounting this horse are uniformly unpleasant." The woman shook her head sadly. "It is a pity. The flight of Pegasus has always been described as a dream state, nothing so dark. Be that as it may, I've decided to act. I have gathered six of the possible Great Horses here to live in safety, and I hope to find your former horse, Promise, as well."

"Mrs. Bridgestone," Jennifer said diplomatically, "it seems a lot of trouble, building a stables and all this. If there was truly a danger, wouldn't more people know?"

"I recall you to rule three." Mrs. Bridgestone said it conclusively. "Only the owners of the Great Horse will believe the legend. I believe the legend, so you see, I am to own a Great Horse one day. My duty is clear."

"Perhaps," Jennifer said gently, "it is only a legend."

The old woman gave an embarrassed laugh. "I do know how it must sound. That is why I invited you to see my collection."

"A man came to buy our horse ... was he your groom?"

"Oh, no dear. You are speaking of my chef, and I am sorry, truly I am. Mr. Jeffries can get carried away, but he is quite harmless. He is an experienced horseman, so when I had a short illness he took over the purchases." She reached over to Jennifer and patted her arm. "Mr. Jeffries tells quite a story."

Jennifer smiled uncomfortably, wishing she could be truthful. Meagan's beseeching eyes aside, Jennifer decided she could not trust someone who actually believed legends about supernatural horses, even such a nice-seeming old lady.

"I am sorry the horse is gone," the woman sighed, "but perhaps it is for the best. It is in Fate's hands now, where doubtless it always was."

Jennifer glanced at Meagan. "I am very sorry, Mrs. Bridgestone."

"Don't be, dear. It is my error. I should have told you the truth sooner, and all this would be settled." The woman smiled warmly at Meagan. She nodded to the butler and readied herself to stand. Holding Nelson's arm for assistance, she escorted them to the door. "You simply must come again. I haven't shown you my collection of Epona the Horse Goddess. It is quite startling. And I still have to tell you about the Golden Bridle."

Meagan straightened. "What is the Golden Bri—"

"Thank you for having us," Jennifer said, taking Meagan's hand firmly. "It has been lovely."

"Of course." The woman held out her hand. "I do thank you for coming, and I hope to keep in touch. Will you be getting another horse?"

"Another horse? *Oh*—yes, of course we will. We will take some time off to concentrate on other things, but Meagan will be riding again."

"I am happy to hear that, dear. Horsemanship was a foundation of classical education for many centuries. The old texts are clear that riding trains not only the body and mind, but also the heart. We seem to have gotten away from the tradition and it is unfortunate." The woman's face grew grave. "If you discover the whereabouts of the Great Horse, please alert me. I would like to bring her here for safety. You may think me eccentric, but my concern is quite sincere."

"Mrs. Bridgestone," Meagan asked politely. "What kind of darkness do you think will happen if someone rides Promise? Is it for *sure* a bad thing?"

"It seems so, dear." The old woman leaned close, and the measure of centuries seemed to weigh in her words. "No one would want to see all that we have shown horses..."

"Now that's a horse of a different color"

- anonymous saying & line from **The Wizard of Oz** *(1932)*

JENNIFER SAW A light through the slightly open door of Meagan's room. "Honey, are you all right?" she asked, leaning in.

"I'm fine, Mom." Meagan lay sprawled on her bed among piles of books. Her misshapen school bag indicated more. "Our class went to the library today."

"It's getting late." Jennifer opened the door wider and stepped inside. "Are you working on a project?"

"Sort of. Dad bet me double allowance I couldn't find a hundred quotes about horses." She pointed to two stacked books, *The Quotable Horse Lover* and *Horse Quotations*. "And please tell him the saying is to give 'free *rein*,' not free *reign* with a 'g'. He won't believe me, so that's our new bet I'll win."

Jennifer looked at the assortment of books surrounding Meagan. One described cattle drives, another cavalry, another the racehorse Man O' War. A medieval knight charged in full armor across one cover, and another book's open page showed prehistoric horse figures adorning cave walls, drawn as if by a gifted child.

"I thought if Great Horses live in the imagination, people would remember them and put them in books. I'm finding lots of Great Horses. I didn't know there was so much *history*." Meagan pushed a magazine toward her mother. The cover article was entitled *Scythian Gold*. "This tells about Scythian nomads who didn't have cities at all. When their kings died, they made huge burial tombs and filled them with gold. They sacrificed servants and soldiers and even horses, and put *them* inside the tomb, too."

Jennifer took the magazine. The cover showed a striking work of raw gold in the shape of a crouching lion. She thumbed past photographs of gold jewelry: griffons, eagles, lions, and horses tumbled over the pages in gleaming decadence.

"*I* think there are better things to do with gold than bury it with some stupid *king*," Meagan sniffed as she focused on a page. "And so far the only Golden Bridle I've found was for the flying horse, Pegasus, which doesn't help at all. Oh Mom, look! Here is a book about dressage. My coach was always making us learn about it." Meagan sat up to read a passage. "*Dressage is a system of training based on humane principles. The ancient Greek cavalry general Xenophon makes reference to an earlier work, proving dressage is well over twenty-three centuries old.*" Meagan made a face. "When my coach said dressage was old, I thought he meant like when *he* was young."

Jennifer picked up a volume entitled, *The Devil's Horsemen: the Mongol Invasion of Europe*. An earth-toned tapestry covered the jacket, and closer inspection revealed a scene of battlefield chaos. She bit her lip. "It's good that you're reading, Meagan. But history isn't always a happy subject."

"It's interesting. I think my textbooks make it boring on purpose. Did you know that people didn't even know horses could jump until the 1800's? Why can't my schoolbooks talk about stuff like that, instead of stupid battles you can't remember anyway?"

"Battles are important, Meagan."

"Sure, Mom." Meagan shook her head as she read. "*So* many horses died in wars. Over eight million horses died in World War I, and in World War II the German invasion destroyed the Polish cavalry with tanks and *planes. Isn't that horrible?*"

"History is brutal, Meagan. Your grandfather always says the best thing about the good old days is that they're over."

"Not *all* of it was bad. Look at this picture of Versailles! Maybe people just didn't know as much and that's why they had so many wars." Meagan looked down at the colorful page and frowned. "No one thinks about history, how it really was. At least, I never do."

"Don't forget your other studies. Sorry, I have to be mom." Jennifer leaned to kiss her daughter on the forehead. "Read for a little while, but don't be too long ... what's this?" She leaned down to retrieve a clothbound notebook that lay open on the floor.

"Oh, nothing. It's a journal I keep under my bed."

"Well it's not under your bed." Jennifer placed the open journal on the bedcover.

"There's nothing in it yet. All I have so far is the poem from Chief Joseph." The lines were carefully penned from memory with a few scratch-outs: *A hundred years* ~~before from now~~ *ago on* ~~the~~ *this westmost shore...*

"Meagan, we've discussed this. We had a nice visit, but someone like Mrs. Bridgestone could make life very difficult."

"I just want to know more about the Great Horse. What if it really *is* Promise?"

Jennifer wished the answer could be different. "Meagan, there are no such things as Great Horses. I like that you are taking an interest in history, but you can't believe in fantasies."

"Mrs. Bridgestone *said* only true owners will believe the legend," Meagan replied stubbornly. "You are just proving it."

"I'm sorry, Meagan." Jennifer glanced down at picture of chariot race with teams of galloping horses. "Horses can make people act very strangely. Now, will you promise me? No talking with Mrs. Bridgestone."

Meagan shrugged. "Maybe we should bring Promise back home, just in case. Maybe she is too dangerous to leave out there."

"Meagan?"

"I said *okay*."

Jennifer went to the doorway. "There are some nice things in history, too. There is a lovely story about a trotting horse named Hambletonian."

"I know, I have pictures of him."

"Tell the books goodnight, Meagan. Rome wasn't read in a day." Jennifer closed the door behind her and returned downstairs. She sat beside her husband on the couch. "I'm worried about Meagan, Tom."

"Of course you are, Jen. It's how we know you're her mother."

"She is not making friends. She won't participate in school activities."

"Meagan makes friends. Are you forgetting the Ponytail Brigade?"

Jennifer shrugged. "She spends all her time reading history books. It's that silly legend. Meagan is absolutely convinced."

"Yes, she told me. It sounds like this Bridgestone woman is a bit ... should I say it?"

"There is nothing wrong with being a little eccentric, Tom."

"That wasn't the word I was going to use."

"She is a harmless old lady, Tom. She grew up hearing a romantic legend and wants it to be true, that's all."

"I noticed you didn't tell her about Meagan's horse."

"I just don't want any trouble." Jennifer frowned. "I wish you had *seen* everything, Tom. I'm worried about Meagan's reaction."

"Don't worry, Momma. You can't fight all her battles. She is growing up."

Jennifer bit her lip as she nodded wistfully.

———

The dreams of a flying horse stopped. Meagan did not think of it immediately; it was only upon reflection that she realized her nighttime visions of riding a winged mount had ceased. The dreams had begun so gradually, and now they were gone.

Promise grew quickly. The filly's cream mane grew long and thick, and her tail gradually lengthened past her hock. Meagan visited the pasture on weekends and spent too-short hours grooming and practicing groundwork.

For her part, the filly was living a horse's dream. She had boisterous playmates, acres to run and grass wherever she dipped her head. Meagan was not living her dream, however— for a time she simply endured. The Great Horse legend was a secret she could not tell without being scoffed at, and she learned to keep silent. Keeping secrets was not hard for her. Horsemanship itself was a beautiful secret to most of the 21st Century world, so she had practice, and she endured.

Mrs. Bridgestone called punctually on Promise's first birthday. Meagan answered the phone to hear the woman's cultured, warm wishes, but invitations to tea were reluctantly put off under the watchful eye of her mother. The woman called again faithfully when Promise turned two, but this time Jennifer answered the phone. The exchange was cordial but brief.

Two years of long car trips passed. Meagan turned fourteen and moved up in school, and commuters driving the rural road alongside Promise's pasture became familiar with the herd of horses in various shades of black, grays, browns—and one gold streak that galloped among them.

Fred Jeffries' old accomplice, Randy Wells, had a sudden stroke of luck. His latest adventure in dating was a woman who owned Arabian horses and was friends with a neighboring family: the Roberts. Randy's interest was sparked when the woman told him the story of a palomino foal born in her neighborhood. To say the least.

Hard times had hounded Randy since the windfall from Fred Jeffries' mysterious employer. The worst moment had been the call from Fred saying his employer had put a price on the palomino of two hundred thousand dollars. *Two hundred thousand dollars!* Such an amount would clear Randy's gambling debts and pay for a move to Florida, where he could be close to his estranged family and—worst case—many tan women.

Randy casually inquired of the location and, quite incidentally, the feeding schedule. He was at Promise's pasture with a trailer before dawn the next morning.

Heavy clouds curtained the morning's light. The previous day had been like early spring, but today was going to be gray, damp and cold. Pneumonia weather, Randy grumbled to himself, tramping across the pasture with a halter.

The ground near the pasture's stables was cut by horses' hooves. The stables door was fifteen feet tall and was meant to slide on a track now rusted and bent. Randy braced all his weight to force the door open. Once he was inside, the early gloom made it hard to see. It didn't matter: a golden palomino would be easy to spot.

Walking down the aisle, Randy peered into each stall. He was surprised not to see the filly's pale yellow coat in the semi-darkness. He walked back down the aisle slowly, looking again. Finally, Randy risked turning on the lights.

Fluorescents blazed overhead, and every horse in the stables stuck its head into the aisle in hopes of an early feeding. Randy swallowed in disappointment. The palomino horse was gone. Someone had taken the palomino away.

Long after the lights were off and Randy was gone, Promise remained watching with the other horses, hoping the man would come back bearing buckets.

Jennifer was on the phone with a friend in the neighborhood, a staunch horse-ally named Marge. "You wouldn't believe it, Marge! I'm just glad we had her freeze-branded. No one would believe it's the same horse."

"Jennifer, no! That little filly was as palomino as they come!"

"Not anymore. Have you even heard of a palomino changing to black?"

"*Never!* Lipizzaners are born black and turn *white*, but this is odd, Jennifer, you know it is." After six children and a long succession of ponies and horses, Marge was not easily surprised. "She is the right age for it, though. What happened?"

"We had Meagan's fifteenth birthday party out at the pasture, so we went early to groom. Promise is shedding her winter coat and when we started to curry, underneath the hair was just solid black." A sudden thought crossed her mind, *'eclipsed by shadow...'*

"Jennifer?"

"I'm sorry, Marge. It's nothing." Superstitious nonsense, Jennifer scolded herself.

"I was just saying I'd bet my last dollar it was the warm winter we had."

"Must have been. The horse looks so much like Moose now, it makes me want to ride again. I say it's our turn next."

"It is, honey. It's long overdue."

"We're bringing her home Saturday. You have to come see."

"You couldn't keep me away! I can't even *guess* how thrilled Meagan must be."

"No, probably not." Jennifer bit her lip as she hung up the phone.

Much had changed in the two years the filly had been at pasture. A teenager's heart can change so quickly and so utterly. Meagan began making friends Jennifer did not like, and her conversations had turned to boys and clothes. Grades dropped. Prohibitions met rebellion. Meagan was currently grounded for crimes Jennifer remembered doing all too well in her own youth.

Jennifer walked into the backyard, where Tom was painting the pasture fence in honor of the imminent horsecoming. "Got the neighborhood alerted?" he called, squatting to reach the bottom of a board.

"Alerted and ready with carrots. You know, Tom, it's strange that it happened but I'm glad Promise shed out to black. It makes me feel better about bringing her back home."

"Yep. No one would guess it was the same horse. Kind of makes you wonder about that old legend, doesn't it?"

"Oh hush, Tom. Is there an extra brush?"

"Sure, go ahead." Tom pointed to a paintbrush lying on a can of white paint. "I'm hoping to lure Meagan into helping. You know, get her into the spirit of things."

A call sounded across the pasture. The next-door neighbor came to their common fence and waved a sheaf of papers.

"*Cromwell*," Tom muttered, putting his paintbrush down: relations with these particular neighbors were strained. "Come with me, Jen. Don't make me do this alone."

In contrast to the Roberts' bare paddock, the Cromwells' backyard was a landscape of pedigreed flowerbeds and manicured lawn. Tom walked to the fence and put his hand over. "Afternoon, Mr. Cromwell."

The man ignored the gesture and shook his paper. "There are to be no changes to this property fence without my permission! Says so in black and white."

"I am only repainting it, Mr. Cromwell."

"And what gives you the right to paint *my* fence?" The man rattled his paper again. "That animal's coming back here—yes, Dottie heard about it—and you intend to raise this fence without my permission! I want to see plans!"

"I intend to raise the fence?" Tom asked in confusion.

Jennifer spoke up. "I'm sorry, Mr. Cromwell, I haven't discussed it with my husband yet." She avoided Tom's gaze. "It is just that Promise has grown so much in the past two years. The rest of the fence is tall enough but this side is too low. I am worried our horse might get ideas."

"Your other horse never got ideas!" the man growled.

"Moose was older and settled, Mr. Cromwell. She wouldn't have crossed a garden hose if she knew better."

"So you intend on bringing a wild animal to disrupt my home, is that it?"

"It is only for safety, Mr. Cromwell. We don't want Promise trying to jump out."

"You are not touching this fence! My attorney is writing my conditions. You'll be getting it next week." The man shook his paper a final time and stomped away.

Jennifer smiled weakly and walked back with Tom. She picked up the extra paintbrush. "Missed a spot," she said lightly.

"That is because I have to hurry. Never know the next assignment for handyman Tom."

"Oh *Tom*, one of Marge's sons can help you. Meagan could baby-sit in exchange."

A young woman's clear voice called from the patio gate. "Baby-sit for who?"

Jennifer often had trouble believing how much the past two years had changed her daughter. Meagan was flippant now and aloof, and her only focus was not having one.

"Hi, honey." Jennifer answered cheerfully. "I was telling your father that Marge could use some help. Some babysitting money might come in handy."

"Do I have to?" Meagan passed through the gate and flopped into a patio chair. "Those kids don't mind me at all."

"Children that don't obey, what is the world coming to?" Tom stretched. "Meagan, how about finding some paint clothes and helping me out? Your mom is too slow."

"I've got homework."

"Wow, your first homework this semester. The timing is amazing."

Meagan looked away, studiously bored.

Tom bent down to pick up the paintbrush. "Mary is bringing your horse over on Saturday morning. She should be here around noon if traffic's good. That is, unless Promise can whinny herself over by magic." He grinned. In Tom's outspoken opinion, it was a mark of distinction for their horse to be the subject of a wealthy eccentric's private legend.

"*Really*, Dad." Meagan gave her father an exasperated glare. "You don't have to keep making fun."

"Fun? Heck, the horse has me convinced. I'd like to see *you* change your hair color in an afternoon. Oops, no. Sorry, I wouldn't."

"Can we drop it, please?"

"Ok, honey, you pick the topic. Either TV or teachers you hate."

Meagan rose to her feet with a loud sigh. She walked into the house and shut the door loudly—but not quite slamming it—and trudged upstairs to her room. She kicked off her school shoes and sat heavily at her desk. The day had left her sour. Horses had once made the maddening routine of school bearable. More than escape—though it was—riding had given her perspective and motivation. When the foal had left, she had felt isolated, adrift in a horse-born, motor-bound culture that seemed to have forgotten the partnership. Now she was reticent about Promise's return, almost afraid to care too much.

She had discovered a way to stop her loneliness: shopping and socializing. Poor scholarship was an unfortunate requirement of membership to the necessary cliques. This requirement was not difficult to meet, however, since even Meagan's interest in history had been successfully doused by endless classroom drill for numbing, pointless testing.

Staring into the mirror, she pulled her auburn hair up and posed, then let it go in disgust. Everyone said she had pretty eyes, but she saw only boring brown hair. She pulled the offending locks into a ponytail and deftly secured them with a scrunchie. She opened a drawer to find a hairbrush ... and stopped at a photograph.

It was a picture of Promise, taken during Meagan's birthday party a few weeks before. She remembered how her friends had tiptoed in their "clean" shoes, worrying about manure. At first they had touched Promise on the shoulder and stepped away, frightened, but by the end of the day all were petting and feeding carrots to the willowy thoroughbred.

She studied the photograph more closely. Promise had grown up so beautifully. Standing a little over sixteen hands, the filly's waist was still tucked with youth, her long neck still narrow. Meagan remembered how Promise had shed from palomino; it had been exciting to strip the clumps of gold hair away to a sleek, black coat.

Looking at the photograph, Meagan remembered believing Promise was one of the Great Horses of history. She had thought it would be fun to travel to the "good old days," when people knew about horses and life was simple, without the problems of the modern world. Once she had read stacks of books about famous horses, and even daydreamed that Promise would gallop into her classroom and magically take her away. Of course now she was fifteen and knew better.

Meagan flipped the picture and read the words: *She looks so much like her mother! Moose always listened and never told. She was my best friend and I hope Promise is yours. Love, Mom.* An image of the filly's amber eyes came into Meagan's thoughts. The gaze always held a faraway look...

It is a myth that horse-crazy youth grow out of horses. They may grow into other things, but a certain word, name or picture will instantly bring the memories back. Though Meagan could not pursue every equine dream and had to accept limitations, horses could still be a life-affirming joy.

Meagan put the picture back in the drawer and closed it slowly with a new sense of excitement. She had planned on doing homework with Katie tonight, but she *should* help Dad paint—her mother really was too slow. The tack room needed cleaning and the old wraps might still be good. Meagan looked with fresh interest at her old horse magazines stacked in her closet. Old friends. She could hardly wait to thumb through them again. Life was returning to normal.

—————

Promise arrived home to great fanfare. Jennifer organized a party for horse friends, and neighbor Marge was there with an infant on her hip. Another friend, Pamela, was in attendance—a woman who had in effect traded her husband for a string of Arabian horses. Pamela was escorting another of the parade of male companions since her divorce.

A trailer rig backed slowly into the Roberts' driveway. The blanketed hind end of a horse could be seen above the half-partition. The pasture-owner, Mary, shouted as she jumped out of the cab: *"We made it!"*

Jennifer hugged the woman. "Thank you, Mary. You have been wonderful." She moved to unlatch the trailer door as the woman led the horse backwards.

Tentatively, lifting thin limbs high, the blanketed filly backed cautiously down the ramp. Meagan waited politely, carrots behind her back. Tom kept a wary distance.

Jennifer took the lead rope and let Promise sniff her outstretched hand. "Now don't you look good, my big girl! No treats, sorry. You have to talk to Meagan." She held the lead out to her daughter.

"Can we take the blanket off first, Mom? I want everyone to see." Meagan spoke softly as she unfastened the quilted covering, reassuring the filly. She folded the blanket across Promise's back and lifted it away.

The filly had grown into glossy youth and looked every inch a thoroughbred. Her slender neck swiveled as she eyed the crowd, velvet nostrils flared. The air around the delicate filly seemed to quiver.

Pamela gasped. "She looks just like her mother!"

"Meagan!" Marge concluded after a circle. "This animal is a testament to your grandfather! Tell him that for me. She is a nice prospect. *Very* nice."

"Oh, she *is!*" Pamela made little claps. "How much fun for you, Meagan! You two could do *anything!*"

"She'll be ready to ride any time. Her knees should be closed," Marge added, referring to the necessary hardening of soft cartilage in a young horse's limbs.

"Probably, but we are having Dr. Parker x-ray to make sure." As she folded the bulky blanket in quarters, Meagan could almost ignore a twinge of conscience from Mrs. Bridgestone's warning. "We are going to teach her to longe in the neighborhood arena. Before I ride her, I mean."

"Why, that is one of my specialties," a man's voice spoke suddenly. It bore a British accent.

Pamela turned to the man beside her. "That is a *wonderful* idea! Everyone, I want you to meet the *most* fantastic horseman—my stallion Lord Azahd and *his* sire, Gimlu Azahd Zambuk, both *love* him to death."

Jennifer stepped forward and offered her hand. "I am Jennifer Roberts, and this is my husband, Tom."

"Pleased to meet you." The man grasped her hand warmly and then shook with Tom. "I am Randy Wells."

"Meagan, you *have* to have a session with Randy," Pamela insisted. "Everyone says he is such an expert!"

Randy nodded appreciatively at Promise. "This really is a gorgeous animal. Too bad she didn't stay palomino ... Pamela told me all about it."

"What's wrong with the color?" Meagan asked, frowning. She stroked Promise's sleek neck. "Black is nice."

"It's only that I especially like palominos," Randy answered smoothly. "Does the animal travel well?"

"Like a *dream!*" the pasture-owner Mary loudly assured him. "She does anything you ask!"

Meagan saw the man's broad smile and wondered why she felt uneasy.

Promise was almost mature enough to call a mare. Ever since first hearing of the legend, Meagan had inspected Promise carefully for signs of being ... well, a Great Horse. Close (maybe obsessive) observation had found nothing unusual about

Promise, however. Surely nothing that would indicate a ferry-man to the netherworld's darkness.

How will it be to ride her? Meagan often wondered, usually with an involuntary gulp. Rational thoughts reassured her that everything would be fine: mounting Promise was to be only the usual unpredictable first ride. The improbable world of horses was challenging enough without superstition fogging the way.

"Trot her back!" Dr. Parker called. Meagan turned Promise in the paddock and urged her toward the barn. The veterinarian squatted to study the dark filly's gait, checking for straight movement. Good conformation and gaits are indicators of soundness and performance.

Equine practitioners, or horse vets, are an important ally of a horse owner. Dr. Parker had visited Promise's pasture several times for examinations, tests and inoculations. Today he was giving the young horse a more intensive physical and she was passing easily. "Looks good, Meagan. Straight as an arrow. Tell your grandfather I am impressed."

Meagan called to her mother watching from the fence. "Dr. Parker says he is impressed!"

Jennifer walked up to offer the filly a cut piece of watermelon, holding it as Promise seized the rind and nipped off a chunk. "Moose always loved watermelon," she said as the horse dribbled and let pulp fly. She patted the filly and stepped back, eyes bright.

Promise stood patiently in the stable crossties as Dr. Parker measured her topline. "Sixteen-one," he announced, speaking in terms of *hands*, or four inches, the ancient measurement for horses. He assembled his equipment and began a series of x-rays, holding plates and the emitter on opposite sides of the mare's knee. "She stands nice, very quiet," the veterinarian commented. "We'll have the results soon, but in my opinion the horse could begin saddle work any time."

The dark thoroughbred stood quietly, as if listening.

I think that if I become a horseman, I shall be a man on wings.
- Xenophon (c. 400 B.C.) Greek Cavalry General

PROMISE WAS TO be three years old on Monday, June 21st, though like all registered thoroughbreds her official birthday had been the first day of January. Meagan planned a celebration complete with specially-made carrot cake. On the day before the big event, the front doorbell rang. Jennifer opened the door with a smile. "Mr. Wells!"

Randy was wearing boots and breeches, and a hard hat for effect. "I'm so glad you let me come, Mrs. Roberts. I love seeing young horses and I've heard such nice things about yours." He glanced out the back window, hoping for a glimpse of his four-legged windfall.

Jennifer closed the door. "I'll join you shortly. Meagan's in the backyard getting ready."

"No, I'm not, mother." Meagan stood at the top of the stairs, still in her school clothes. "I'm finishing homework."

"Homework—oh, *good*—but you remember Mr. Wells. He was nice enough to come see Promise today..."

"I forgot, sorry. I'll get dressed and hurry down."

"No, don't hurry, please!" Randy insisted. "If someone would just show me the way I will wait in the stables. I just love being around horses and I miss them so much. Since I've sold all my estates, I mean."

"Of course," Jennifer said pleasantly. "I'll walk you back to the barn. My daughter will be down as soon as she's dressed."

Randy patted the cell phone clipped to his breeches and smiled. "No hurry. I just like spending time with the animals. Noble beasts."

Meagan returned to her room and dressed. While looking for her boots, she noticed her journal in a pile of horse magazines that lay on the floor beside her bed. That's odd, she thought. She had replaced the notebook under her bed and didn't remember taking it out. She stooped to pick it up. The page was open to Chief Joseph's poem she had copied: *eclipsed by shadow the golden spark, will ~~bring~~ take her rider into the dark...*

My parents are going through my things, Meagan thought irritably. She closed the notebook and returned the journal to its usual hiding place. The argument could come later. She hurried to put on her boots.

Downstairs, she found the pasture gate open. The stables were empty. Meagan's first thought was that Mr. Wells had taken Promise down the street, to the neighborhood arena. She glanced into the tack room and saw the longe line. What kind of trainer would forget that? She took down the line and walked anxiously up the driveway.

The street was quiet. Meagan walked fast, wondering what Mr. Wells could be doing. She crossed the ditch and rounded the line of trees that surrounded the arena, and stopped.

The arena was empty.

——+——

That night Meagan cried herself to sleep. Police had been called and neighbors alerted, but nothing had been heard. Jennifer tried the phone number Pamela knew for Mr. Wells—it had been disconnected.

When she did finally sleep, Meagan dreamt of riding. She soared with Promise across clear stretches of green. Fences rose up before them and she twitched in her sleep as she and Promise soared over ... and then up into the bright sky. Meagan opened her eyes to the gray of early pre-dawn and lay in bed, staring at the ceiling remembering her remorse.

So the dream of the flying horse had finally returned. It gave her no comfort now; the vivid image seemed to mock her loss. Meagan stood quietly and lifted the window blinds. The early sky was gray and turbulent. Birds chirped in the cool pre-morning. She folded her hands on the window sill, ready for tears. Promise was gone, stolen. Even if found, the poor young horse could easily be traumatized. *Please be safe, girl,* Meagan prayed, putting her head in her hands. She happened to glance down to see a dark shape.

Promise was standing on the patio.

In moments Meagan was down the stairs and out the back door. On the patio, still in her nightgown, she stopped in shock. The filly's bridle was pulled halfway off and both reins had snapped. Cuts covered her lower legs and a scrape along one shoulder was crusted with blood.

Promise's nostrils dilated as she raised her head in jerks, backing a step. "Easy, girl," Meagan soothed, approaching. "Let me clean you up and get you some food."

"I am afraid there won't be time."

Meagan turned to see an unknown man standing beside Mr. Wells. The trainer held the most incongruous of objects—a gleaming handgun.

"Your horse came to say goodbye," Mr. Wells said evenly. "She's caused a bit of trouble." As he stepped forward, Promise tensed and blew out strongly. The man stopped. "See, Freddie, I told you the horse would come back here."

"But how did she escape?" the unknown man asked anxiously. He seemed out of breath. "The animal is a Houdini! Across all the traffic, too!"

Mr. Wells waved his gun toward Meagan. "It looks like that headpiece is about finished. Why don't you find something else? Fast."

"I *do* wish this wasn't necessary," the second man told her apologetically. "Understand I would never be in this trouble if it weren't for these animals. I wish I'd never *seen* a betting booth."

Mr. Wells waved his gun again and Meagan ran out into the tack room, thinking in panicked flashes. Her parents were still upstairs asleep. If the men were going to hurt her or her family, they would have done so—they only wanted Promise and there was no time to do anything except cooperate. Meagan took the halter and walked back to the patio.

She spoke softly to her frightened filly. Promise let Meagan come close, but gave no signs of relaxing. Every fiber in the horse was prepared for flight, and her wide eyes never left the two men. Meagan reached to carefully remove the broken bridle.

"Leave it on!" Randy growled, stepping forward.

Promise flinched, tearing the bridle from Meagan's hands and racking her raw mouth as it twisted. The horse stepped into a patio chair, tangling herself and almost falling. Hooves clattered on brick as the filly bolted across the patio and through the gate to escape. She ran bucking wildly into the pasture, running to the farthest corner.

Meagan remained frozen as Randy stooped to pick up the halter she had dropped. He threw the harness to her. The halter fell on the bricks.

"You are scaring her," she protested.

"Go get the horse." Mr. Wells pointed his gun at Promise. "Now."

"Don't make us do something unpleasant," pleaded the second man. "Not after all the trouble—I went to *Canada* for the beast and had chilblains for a month! Be a good girl and we won't hurt her."

"Get the horse," Mr. Wells repeated.

Meagan retrieved the halter and walked numbly into the pasture. Promise moved off to avoid being cornered, running back and forth along the low side of the fence. Meagan stopped. "Easy, girl. Everything will be fine." She cried softly as she spoke to her treasured filly. Promise stood off trembling with confusion in her dark eyes.

Meagan remembered a game she sometimes used to catch Promise, one the filly always played. She plucked a handful of grass beside one of the fence posts and walked forward slowly. The filly's ears pricked when she saw the motion, remembering. With quaking lips, the horse took the crushed handful of grass gently, nostrils still wide, ears alert. Meagan slipped the halter on, careful not to scrape the cuts.

Randy Wells and the other man approached. Promise raised her head and showed the whites of her eyes.

"Don't come yet!" Meagan called. "She is still too scared."

"We will take care of the horse. You just bring her over."

"It'll be all right, girl." Meagan led Promise a step toward the men. The filly put her head low into Meagan's hair, trembling. "Come on, girl, you'll be fine." Promise took another tentative step, stopped and snorted, then went another. Meagan hesitated. *What am I doing? She trusts me.*

Glancing at the fence joining the Cromwell's yard, Meagan saw an escape. It was a risk on an untrained horse, but the fence was low. With a quick motion, Meagan jumped up and pulled herself onto Promise's back. The filly swung around, accepting the weight and understanding instantly.

Meagan heard shouting behind her as Promise reached for the safety of speed. The pasture was small but both horse and rider meant to go beyond. Fluid strides lengthened, swallowing the earth in quickening gulps as the pasture fence rushed towards them. Wind rose in Meagan's ears, and time stretched into a series of still photographs as the young thoroughbred gathered and stretched. The ground blurred and together they lifted into the air.

———————

Meagan folded against Promise's neck as they ballooned over the fence—but the landing never came. She opened her eyes to see the top of the Cromwells' roof ... the ground was dropping away. Promise's mane lightened and grew long in her hand. Shining wings rose around her, blocking the rooftop before they swept down. She was riding a winged white horse.

Promise rose like an upward gust. Meagan turned to look back at the dumbfounded men in the pasture until an expanse of green leaves blocked her view. The horse glided between strokes and was easy to ride, but Meagan never eased her hold. Wind whipped as if at a gallop as the city slid away beneath them.

They coursed across the sky into a bank of clouds. Cottony mist blew around them. Promise skimmed a cloudbank, frisking and reveling in motion. Together they scaled towering cumulus and glided down vapory canyons. Meagan clung to the horse's warm neck in the frigid air.

Rising above the veil of mist, the horse paused with wings outstretched, trotting the air in slow time. Low thunder rolled beneath them and lightning lit the cloudbanks in gold and red. Meagan felt her mount shake, trumpeting into the wind.

Folding great wings, the horse dropped into the blackness. Meagan screamed as they plummeted through flashing mists and tearing wind. They plunged into open air below the clouds, dropping toward the floor of the world. Arid plains and solid rock rushed to meet them.

North America
20,000 B.C.

Prey

MEAGAN OPENED HER eyes. Thin wisps of clouds brushed the bluest sky she had ever seen. Her first thought was that she had woken from a dream. Groggy, she watched the clouds drift.

That dream was the most realistic of all, she thought absently. She noticed shapes above her and focused. A line of shadowed children stared down, silent as pigeons on a ledge. She closed her eyes again. *Great, my riding friends. Every time I fall off I have an audience ... wait—where is Promise?*

Her head cleared with sudden memory. *What if the dream*—she sat up quickly and stared at her surroundings. She was still in her nightgown, perched on a rocky cliff over an expanse of prairie grassland. An empty landscape spread before her, basking in late afternoon sun. *This is strange,* Meagan thought, swallowing. Solid rock walls rose on either side of her, marbled with green moss and snaking black fissures. Nothing manmade was in sight.

"Have you seen my horse?" she shouted to the children watching from above. No one answered, but in the silence came a familiar rumbling. The ground was beginning to vibrate.

Meagan climbed to her feet and looked around in astonishment. She stood on a ledge overlooking wide, empty fields. A canyon corridor opened here, onto the ledge.

Where am I?

She started to call again to the children above, but the vibration suddenly broke free into rushing sound. Rounding the angle of the canyon wall, a galloping herd of horses swept towards her in panicked fright, thundering echoes off the canyon walls.

Meagan darted to the cracked rock wall and clawed up the side as the sound of horses exploded behind her. Whinnies echoed through the corridor. The first horses to see the cliff's edge skidded before being pushed into the abyss by the horses behind. Shrieks tore the air. In seconds, the train of sliding horses passed, leaving the last animals milling in confusion. New sounds started overhead: howls of the ragged children. Hanging against the canyon wall, Meagan stared disbelieving into the empty dust.

A squat gray pony and a splay-legged colt stood frozen near the cliff's edge. The gray swerved and joined the surviving horses as they bolted back up the canyon to safety, leaving the newborn alone and bewildered, facing shock.

Meagan dropped to the ground and walked carefully towards the foal. The animal watched with round black eyes and trembled. Wrapping her arms around its short neck, Meagan rubbed the withers, the high place where a horse's neck and back meet. "It's okay, little one," she said, softly pressing against the trembling muscles. "I don't know what happened either, but we will get you home and everything will be fine."

The children were coming up the corridor, swinging thick sticks in time with their strides. The foal struggled backwards out of Meagan's grip and she called to them, "Wait, you're scaring him!" Then she stopped in shock. Not only were these children not her riding friends ... they were not even children.

She fell back, letting the foal bolt away. The creatures took swipes as the animal passed, and then crouched, eyeing Meagan. They were a child-sized, frightening kind of adult— hairy, scarred and deformed. They wore rags that did not cover enough and were grumbling to each other in guttural hums, plainly working up to boldness.

Meagan backed to the canyon wall and moved quickly along it. She reached the edge and, keeping her eyes away from the poor horses' remains, lowered herself over and clung to the rocky wall. Looking backwards to gauge her fall, she dropped to an outcropping. She knelt upon landing and moved against the cliff wall for protection. Below her, a chattering, hooting stream of people poured around the base of the canyon.

Several of the strange creatures peered over the edge above, looking down at Meagan. She pulled up her knees and buried her face in her hands. *I should have listened to Mrs. Bridgestone,* she thought desperately. *I should have found out more, I should—*

A dark figure dropped onto the ledge with a soft thud and scrambled to face her, howling. The face was a man's, deformed with scars and twisted into a snarl. Meagan cringed against the rock as the man-creature came closer. His first swing was erratic and wild, and he looked to his companions overhead. While he posed, mouth open in a victorious cackle, Meagan rushed forward and struck the filthy creature squarely in the chest with her hands. The man fell backwards off the ledge with a startled expression.

She looked up. Dark heads were silhouetted against the blue sky. There was a squabble, and shoving, and then another body thudded down on the ledge. Without hesitation Meagan pushed the dazed creature over the side and looked up, waiting. One by one, the heads disappeared.

Meagan crawled to the edge and looked over. Both of her victims had fallen into a crevice and were slowly squirming out. Twenty or so of the strange people were tearing and hacking the horse carcasses. Women threw wood and chunks of meat onto a raging bonfire.

Broken rocks were the only path to the ground. Meagan would have to drop to the top of a boulder eight feet down, and then slide around the slabs of stone to the base of the cliff. *I can do it though,* she told herself, once the freak family is gone.

A sudden thought occurred to Meagan, so terrible she could not even say it in her mind. She desperately searched the rocks for the broken body of a black thoroughbred. Half-squinting, it was moments before she could breathe again. Promise was not there.

Feeling her heart begin to calm, Meagan noticed one of the people watching her. A girl close to Meagan's age was standing near the edge of the canyon rocks, staring up. The girl's chest

was bare and stained with drying blood; her lower covering
was a ragged animal skin. Her hair was tangled but her eyes
shone radiant blue.

"Hello," Meagan called nervously.

The young woman's blank expression did not change.

"You don't seem like one of ... *them*," Meagan said politely,
forcing a smile. The girl was frail and thin, Meagan reassured
herself, hardly someone to be afraid of. "Maybe you could help
me. I'm looking for my horse. She ran off and is probably
scared. It was her very first ride." She hesitated. "Actually, I
hope you *haven't* seen her."

The blue eyes watched intently.

Meagan pointed to herself. "I am *Mea*-gan." She smiled
expectantly but the girl remained silent. "Excuse me, do you
have a name?"

Behind the girl, the strongest male claimed the feast for himself. He waved his arms and threatened any who came too near
the sputtering bonfire. One of the hungry creatures darted in
and snatched a fallen scrap, and the bully lunged after the thief
as others dashed in from all directions, snatching what they
could before the tyrant returned. The furious strongman chased
them away while others dashed in ... and so the process continued. Everyone was eating except the bully.

"Please talk to me," Meagan called to the strange girl. "I
don't know where I am, and there is this ... *thing* that I did.
Maybe I shouldn't have."

The girl watched Meagan raptly, and mutely. Behind her, the
bully caught and injured one of the feasters. The injured
man's disability seemed to enrage the others and they piled
onto the victim, clubbing. The idiotic beating continued while
the feast burned in the fire and spoiled on the rock. Birds descended for their choice of scraps.

"Never mind," Meagan told the girl, "you don't even know
what I'm saying—" She stopped, turning pale with a horrified
realization. "Oh, *no!*" she gasped. "I've made everyone
primitive. You're all *cave* people again. I really did bring the
world into darkness!" She backed miserably to the cliff wall and
hugged her knees, tearfully listening to the screeches and

howls. "I should have listened, I should have known. I'm *so sorry*." Meagan bent her head. "Come back, Promise. Please, please, come back." The legend was true, it really was. *Please, Promise, I'm scared and I want to go home.* Why, *why* hadn't she listened to Mrs. Bridgestone?

Long hours passed before the grim feast was over. The glutted creatures grew sleepy and searched for comfortable places to sleep. This naturally led to more fighting and more howls until all were unconscious for one reason or another.

Meagan sat up on the ledge, peering periodically over the side at the creatures laid out like slugs on a sidewalk. She shuddered each time and sat back. Of course, having an Angel for a horse makes something like this quite normal, she rationalized. The whole experience was like a ... a *gift*. Yes! A not-very-good one. Maybe now was the time to find Promise, while the slugs were asleep.

"Oh!"

A sudden thump on the rock announced one of the creatures, and Meagan was looking into the intense blue eyes of the staring girl. Meagan backed against the cliff wall. "Hello. Nice to see you again." She looked up. There were no heads, at least none visible. "Why aren't you sleeping like the others?"

The girl stared back silently, but made no noise or motion.

I want to go home, Meagan thought desperately. She glanced cautiously over the edge. Only bones, ash and lingering smoke remained of the bonfire. Pecking birds scoured the rocks. The only sound was a singing breeze.

Meagan turned back to the girl. "This is all my fault and I know you can't understand, but I am very, very sorry. You were probably going to be a schoolteacher if not for me, weren't you? Or an astronaut, or ... oh, *please* don't be mad!"

The girl watched silently, moving her eyebrows to mimic Meagan's.

"It won't be hard to start over," Meagan said reasonably. "The horses are still here ... or, well, they *were* before you ate them. But you could find more and, and, build a corral. It's simple once you know how. Horses are horses. Your family or what-

ever that is could do something with their lives instead of—"
Her hand went to her mouth. "I sound just like my mother."

The girl's hand went to her own mouth. Her eyes were wide
and unaccusing.

"All I'm saying is, you don't need much to start with. Some
leather straps is all. I'm sure you can figure it out. It doesn't
have to take thousands of years again." Meagan looked down at
the sleeping bodies. They twitched in their sleep, bothered by
flies. "Except you probably kill most of the smart ones." The girl
scowled like Meagan was doing, several times in succession.

People would have to go through history all over again,
Meagan thought dismally. No, she could never face the guilt—
she simply *had* to find Promise and put things back. "I'm sorry,
but I need to go." Meagan swallowed, seeing the girl's lips moving in odd contortions as if mocking her. "I will find my horse
before everyone wakes up. Thank you for not attacking me."
She stood and took a step toward the edge.

Without taking her eyes from Meagan, the girl laid a dark
scrap on the rock between them.

It was a careful moment. Meagan picked up the strip with the
ends of her fingers and held it out. "Burned horse meat ... why,
thank you." She wanted to hurl the meat off the ledge, but po-
liteness and precaution made her keep it instead. "I hope this
won't come in handy," she said with forced cheerfulness.

Stepping to the edge, Meagan let herself over. She slid down
and dropped to the top of the next boulder. Above her, the mute
girl crawled up to the edge, preparing to follow. Meagan
climbed down faster. "I don't want to be rude," she called over
her shoulder, "but I'm trying to get away from you. It's nice, but
please don't follow me." She made the last feet in a jump. The
girl landed a few moments later. "Thank you so much for coop-
erating," Meagan said tightly. "Look, I am sure you are very
nice, but you don't have a shirt and, well, you are wearing
blood. I will find Promise and then this can all go away. I really
am sorry. It's all my fault."

A movement attracted Meagan's eye and she looked past the
girl. Several of the glutted clan of horse-killers were watching

with unfocussed eyes. Meagan backed away and turned to the open field. She looked back only once. The girl was still staring.

———

It was some time before Meagan would admit she was lost. She had tried to make a large circle around the canyon cliff, hoping to see a landmark or maybe a Great Horse. But now it was getting dark and the canyon was not where she left it.

Besides being hungry and thirsty, and barefoot in her nightgown, she was growing rather frightened. There was nothing to be seen of civilization—no buildings or roads, no power lines or airplanes. In all directions were endless grassland and ridges of rocky hills, all under a brilliant clear sky. A low breeze floated over her, heavy with the sweet scent of vegetation.

At least it smells nice, Meagan thought, breathing deeply. *Maybe I could live off the land.* Of course, she had not the slightest idea of how such a thing was done: she was the primitive here. Uneasiness hummed beneath her consciousness like a low bass note.

Meagan passed a mammoth stack of manure, a pyramid where generations of stallions had dropped to mark their presence. To her, horses had always been some kind of domesticated, almost manmade beings—beautiful, disciplined and familiar. But this pile was a clear warning, made by and for other *wild* animals.

At dusk, Meagan saw movement in the haze ahead. At first she stopped in fear—she did not want to meet any more horse-killers. But as she studied the haze, the patches resolved into silhouettes of grazing horses. A herd stood against the fading sunlight. She hurried after them.

———

Hours later, Meagan was still walking. "I *hate* horses," she grumbled as she trudged through the dark, echoing millennia of unseated riders in pursuit of their mounts. She had dogged the herd for hours, sometimes coming close enough to see their manes and tails lifting in the breeze. Each time the horses had snorted and moved off, leaving their dust to settle slowly over her.

Meagan was discouraged. She strained to see the tall, sleek form of Promise, but it was obvious the young thoroughbred was not one of the evasive herd. In fact, these were the smallest and shaggiest horses she had ever seen. As the last sunlight faded, the horses joined in a final chorus of whinnies and galloped away. She was alone in the darkness.

I will not panic, Meagan told herself bravely. It is only the legend. This was supposed to happen. She scanned the horizon for a city's glow, but there was only darkness behind the brilliant haze of stars. The only sound was the brushing of the long grass against itself.

Scents of grass and earth washed around her as the hard earth gave way suddenly to mud. Water squished through her toes. A sheen of moonlight glimmered over a strip of river shrinking to its deepest parts. A small *ka-thunk* sounded in the darkness. A splash ended in a swirling sound. There was another splash in the distance, and then a light, distinct *plop*. Meagan froze. Shadows were moving around her. She jumped back and instantly the ground began to rumble as the darkness erupted around her. She hugged herself as the ground boiled beneath her feet. Shapes lunged past her in the dark, so close she felt the breeze of their passing.

Then Meagan recognized the sounds of a herd settling in the distance and almost laughed in relief. It was only the horses. Hearing their comforting snorts and nickers in the dark, she felt civilization upon her.

"Bring on the empty horses!"
- director Michael Curtiz cueing (riderless) horses during
the filming of Charge of the Light Brigade *(1936)*

Meagan KNEW THE horses could see her quite well—equines can be as active at night as during the day. She had frightened them away from their water hole, but if the herd stayed they must be thirsty. Good.

She would wait.

Meagan settled on a dry piece of ground and waited for dawn, hungry and tired, slapping moth-sized mosquitoes that swarmed from the darkness. She didn't know what to believe. The normal horse sounds in the distance were reassuring enough to push her first dire thoughts away.

"I'm coming to my senses," Meagan announced to the silent air. She spoke out loud because horses like noise: only predators are silent. "Promise ran off with me, that's all that happened. I fell off ... and I have a *concussion*." Yes, exactly! Those primitives were just homeless people—who knows what they do? There are lots of empty places like this in California. She swallowed, looking at the glowless horizon. *Lots.*

"What I need to do," she argued soberly, "is to follow these horses. Surely they belong to *someone*." Feeling more brave, Meagan now realized she was thirsty. Her throat was tight and dry, and visions of cool streams burbled into her thoughts. "It's like layers. Solve one thing and something else is right behind it, making you just as miserable as before." She knelt at the muddy edge and studied the tiny bubbles clinging to debris in the water, glistening. "A little dirt never hurt anyone," she told the emptiness. "I'll just have a sip." She leaned forward and paused.

The edges of the water were becoming distinct in the gray light of morning. Animals were materializing around her. A horse with the unmistakable girth of a broodmare was stepping haltingly to the water's edge. When the mare lowered her head, blowing softly across the water, the whole band flowed in, heads high and ears taut. The stallion stayed back from the edge and paced the dark shore.

The horse herd spread along one bank, interspersed with small creatures that drank cautiously at the edge. One small gray horse began moving further into the riverbed in search of clean water, its steps comically high. "I think you have the right idea," Meagan told the animal quietly. She stepped further into the warm water, feeling mud flow around her bare toes. If there were danger, the horses would know.

The gray horse's soft eyes fixed on Meagan's progress. Her grandfather often called horses the "nosiest animal in Creation." He called curiosity a fatal weakness of the species ... well, that and a fondness for oats.

Meagan waded into deeper water and sipped from cupped hands. She meant only a few swallows, but the water was sweet and she gulped greedily. The little horse watched as if taking notes.

In the growing light, Meagan could see the horse was a mare. The animal's round belly was tucked into thin, drawn quarters and her cream-colored coat was mottled with patches of darker gray. The scrubby mane and tail were chewed off in spots, and her coat was covered in scars and puffy lumps. Faded in the pre-dawn, the mare reminded Meagan of the squat, huge-bellied horses portrayed in cave paintings.

"Poor thing, no one's taking care of you." Meagan's voice was loud in this quiet place and many small eyes were quickly upon her. She decided to rinse off her coating of dust and grime, and knelt in the cool water to gently splash her arms. She inhaled deeply, drawing in rich scents of animals and earth.

Warm breath smelling of cut lawn blew on her neck. Meagan blinked in surprise but did not move. She thought of something else her grandfather used to say: "Horses are as unpredictable as people, only they have more sense."

Meagan let the flutter of horse nostrils explore her hair as she reached slowly for the mare's shaggy withers. The small gray horse half-closed her eyes as Meagan scratched gently to imitate the nuzzling greeting of equines. "A horse got me into this," she told the mare softly. "Maybe you could get me out..." An unwelcome thought intruded: *was it risky to mount again?* Meagan pushed it away as silly nonsense. She had a concussion, that was all, and only needed to find a way home.

The first thing would be to halter the horse, but Meagan had nothing to use for restraint. "I am not letting you get away," she whispered to the mare. "I'd never catch you again." She was positioned on the horse's right side, of course—the wrong side to mount. Meagan's next move was bound to be unwelcome.

Mounting in deep water is an old riding trick, or so Meagan had read. The idea sounded logical and, if nothing else, water was a softer landing than dirt. She took a breath, hitched up her nightgown and gently closed her hands around the horse's knotted mane.

The first broodmare waded out of the water with a snort. This was the signal to depart and each horse ducked its head for a last drink. The little gray horse started back to shore, but before the animal could swing away Meagan pulled herself up and threw her leg over. She clasped her feet around the little horse's belly and waited for the explosion.

It came quickly. A horse's greatest fear is a predator on its back, the only place unreachable by a bite or kick. The frantic mare hunched herself and heaved in the water as the other animals darted and fled, but Meagan was a good rider and the water slowed the mare's efforts. "Easy girl," she urged the mare as they thrashed in circles, "I'm not going to hurt you."

The other horses splashed through the shallows and kicked back in irritation once they gained hard ground. Reforming into a line, the band trotted away and began receding into the distance.

Churning in panic, the mare gradually realized her attacker was not attacking. She was a practical soul, and if her passenger was causing no injury there was no reason to be left behind. The water made a surging sound as the mare galloped from the riverbed after the others.

"It's all right," Meagan calmly told the wary circle of horses. She moved slowly as individual horses stepped closer to sniff suspiciously. "I'm not going to hurt you." She stroked the gray mare's neck to show her good intentions.

The herd's stallion trotted fretfully around the edges of his band. A stallion may choose his group but he is *not* the boss. Equine society is based on friendships and roles—the stallion was waiting for the group's leader to make a decision, and he wished she would hurry.

The actual chief was a squat sorrel mare. She paced around Meagan with tight steps, her head held stiff and high. She was not pleased. Yes, this noisy pale monkey was interesting, mildly, taking a predator's position to do nothing but gurgle. But the mare was impatient. She had a specific destination in mind today, a sheltered area with quality grass. The clinging creature was plainly too clumsy to be a concern, so perhaps a good day's grazing could still be had.

To Meagan's relief the sorrel mare snorted and swung around. The stallion moved to the rear as the herd fell into a brisk trot. "Really, I won't be any trouble," Meagan assured the horses as they moved off, patting her mount's coarse neck. The little mare flattened her ears and crow-hopped.

The ride was rapidly turning into a challenge for Meagan. A cease-fire had been reached, but the little horse still made testing bucks. The mare's gaits were unschooled and poorly bred, so the sensation was like riding on square wheels. Also, Meagan's legs hung almost low enough to have used roller-blades.

More disheartening, she was able to see a bit farther now that she was mounted. In all directions, the only sights were rolling grass and hilly ridges of rock. No plastic cups blew through the grass, nothing was mown or dug. The world seemed to lay empty and expectant; a quiet prologue.

A craggy tree bent in the distance. Meagan squinted, trying to decide what the tawny, stretched shapes under it could be ... *No,* that was being silly, she told herself quickly, and looked away.

And even if those *were* lions—*which they were not so there was no need to look again*—they were safe at this distance. She patted the gray mare for reassurance, and the mare answered with a half-respectable buck. Reseating herself, Meagan realized that the mare was unfortunately improving.

The chief mare led the herd into a grassy basin surrounded by hills of sheered rock. The long grass was brittle, but many stalks were green near their base. The horses nickered softly as they trotted in and lowered their heads to graze. "Another lovely view," Meagan complained aloud to the grazing horses. "Nicely private, thank you." She looked around with the idea of dismounting ... but where would she go?

She scanned the hills. The sides of the rocks were smooth, and colored moss grew along the base. Something was vaguely familiar about this place. She looked again, and with a shock realized she was not looking at moss at all: the colors were a mural of some kind, reaching five feet up from the ground and covering the rock. Crude figures of horses were drawn in rich oranges and reds. Etched people danced among drawings of horse herds in poses of grazing, of running, of ... falling. The paintings marked a corridor into the canyon.

Meagan scanned the open landscape in dejection. *There really is a lot of empty space in California,* she told herself. Then a shape caught her attention: a person was squatting in the grass. One of the horse-killers. Meagan tensed and instantly every horse's head was up. The lead mare froze and looked past the squatting figure as she tried to get a scent in the calm air. A horse's eyes are made to detect motion, and if the man made the slightest tremor the mare would recognize the danger. But she required that tremor.

Another man lay behind the mare, prostrate a hundred feet away. He crept so slowly Meagan could track his movement only by marking the grass's separation. Another man was beside the others—and another. The horse-killers surrounded them.

Looking again at the canyon walls covered with paintings, Meagan realized why it looked familiar. She had seen these canyon walls—from the other side of the cliff.

"*Run!*" she shouted. The horses could escape if they would only gallop away. "Go *on!*" She urged her mount forward but the untaught gray mare only balked. Then the stallion nipped the furthest horses to herd them closer and caught the scent of the hunters. His shrill trumpet cut the air and the electrified band swerved to take flight—but the men stood all at once and the startled horses wheeled to the center.

The tribe advanced, slowly tightening their circle as the herd milled in confusion. The only apparent escape was the deadly corridor between the rocks. The lead mare paced, trying to find another way before committing to the canyon's blind entrance.

Meagan swallowed, remembering that horses were a delicacy of primitive man. Prehistoric bands of humans had ranged near such rocky formations, luring herds into blind alleys and driving them from cliffs. She remembered the caves of Lascaux in France which held the remains of thousands of horses killed some fifteen thousand years before. Thirteen millennia before the Year of our Lord. She wished she had not read so many books.

A wisp shot past the men, a figure—a girl—running alone into the circle. Horses shied from her path. The figure slowed to a walk, approaching Meagan and the frightened mare. It was the silent girl who had tried to follow. Her crystal eyes held wonder. Thin fingers stretched to touch the gray's matted coat, stopping short.

"Don't be afraid," Meagan said, encouraging the girl. The mare shifted nervously. "She is not going to hurt you." The girl grasped the mare's coat, clutching; the mare flinched and a ripple went through the herd. "Softer," Meagan said, leaning to stroke the mare's trembling coat. "Like this." The girl began to mimic the motion, her eyes wide with discovery.

Meagan watched the dark men tightening their circle. She wanted to believe they were anything but what they seemed, anything but primitives on a well-scripted hunt. The girl followed Meagan's gaze and in sudden understanding gave a chirp of alarm. She sprinted back to the circle to stop the hunters. Her thin cries sounded as she waved her arms, but her efforts only served as a trigger. The men sprang forward and overwhelmed her shouts with their own.

The spooked horses stampeded into the deadly corridor. The gray mare swung with the herd as Meagan grabbed mane and fought to stay mounted. Packed bodies crushed against her and she was carried with the torrent. Walls of rock blurred as the band plunged down the canyon. The close-running her squeezed against her legs, threatening to pull her into the flashing hooves. There was no way to stop and a fall would mean a trampled death. The corridor curved ahead, and Meagan felt the ground begin to slope. The left wall vanished as the first shrill screams tore the air.

"PROMISE!"

The gray mare collided into the horse in front and scrambled to remain upright. Meagan buried her face into her mount's neck, closing her eyes for the impact from behind. She fell into the rolling mass, holding the gray tightly as they were torn from the earth.

Black Sea
700 B.C.

North America
20,000 B.C.

Escort

EVERYTHING STOPPED, WITH neither a bump nor a sensation of falling. Meagan tried to clench the horse underneath her, but there was nothing to hold. The winged horse had flickered into view, swooping her up—and had vanished.

Meagan rocked back onto her heels. The horses were gone. She stared at the dusty ground, feeling vertigo from the sudden stop. Around her, the landscape was changed from its flat, rock-studded panorama, folding now into gentle hills that rolled into the distance. A gusting wind carried the sharp tang of salt.

"Is anyone here?" she called nervously. Only the empty breeze answered. A line of trees, obscured by fog, marked one of the distant hilltop silhouettes washing against the sky like waves. The closest landmark was a steep, flat-topped hill rising behind her.

I need to calm down, Meagan told herself to avoid panic. I have a concussion and that's *all*. This was strange, yes, but legends don't happen—that is why they are called legends. She looked around the landscape, so alien it could have been a set for a foreign movie ... *of course!*

She thought quickly. A film studio near my house, one I never knew about ... yes, certainly, a movie set! After all, I am in California, where they make movies. Why didn't I think of that before? She would soon find Promise and everything would be back to normal.

Meagan saw motion on the horizon. The distant line of trees seemed to shimmer and sway. A wispy film lay above them, as if the trees were on fire. *No,* she scolded herself, not everything has to be a disaster. The wisps were just rising dust.

She studied the raised hill behind her and walked closer. The surface was of barren, fresh earth, as from an excavation. Dirt on the mound was darker than the ground around it. A series of pegs had been driven into one sloping side of the hill, making a vertical line up the incline.

She reached to feel the flattened top of one peg. It was solidly imbedded in the hillside. On impulse, Meagan reached above it and pulled herself up, standing on one of the lower pegs. It's like a ladder, she realized, reaching to the next in the line of pegs.

This will be a great story, she thought, hearing herself tell it: *'And then I climbed the hill and saw the camera scaffolding. No, I wasn't really scared. Well, maybe a little, until I was sure.'* And then we will laugh...

She climbed up the face of the hill until she could peer over the top. The open hilltop had been scraped flat. Its only feature was a circular pit dug in the hill's center.

Oh, how funny this will be.

Meagan crossed the hilltop. The pit was a shaft bored into the mound, its narrow walls defined in flickering orange light from below. She leaned closer. Another set of pegs led into the murky depths. Warm, ripe scents of decay rose from the pit.

"Hello," she called nervously. "Is anyone down there?" Her words made a dull echo. *"Hello?"*

A tinkling swept over the hilltop, a musical sound that vanished with the breeze. Meagan looked up to see the line of burning trees had expanded. Its edges were blurred and moving. Growing.

Another round of chimes played in the gusts of wind, and Meagan caught a flash in the corner of her eye. A stream of movement emerged from a dip in the landscape. She stared in astonishment as horses and riders rose from the dip as if bubbling from dry ground.

Meagan crouched on the hilltop as the disorganized procession jogged and bobbed closer. Perhaps a hundred strong, the field of riders was a carpet of color and glinting reflections. The horses were unruly and barely contained. Hopping sideways, they battered against each other. Their riders sat atop their mounts' croups—far back—holding twined leather straps as reins.

Those must be the movie extras, Meagan reasoned, noting their authenticity. The horses were small and wiry, and of every color and shade of bay, tan or white. Crowning each horse's head was a patchwork of gold and leather supporting a fantastic headdress of golden antlers or curved horns of mountain sheep. Everywhere gold trinkets moved and flashed.

The riders could have seen Meagan exposed on the hill, but they passed at an angle, eyes glazed and mouths open. A thousand tinkling gold pieces played in time with the horses' gaits. Fractured sunlight from the metal-encrusted mob showered the ground. It was clearly a big-budget film.

A rumble started low and rose to shake the air. Meagan turned and saw that the "burning trees" had grown to a blackness swallowing the horizon. Instead of smoke, what she had actually seen was the wall of dust rising behind an approaching mass of galloping horses. Now visible were men standing on flimsy carts, their whips flashing through air filling with screeching metal and pounding hooves.

Chariots.

The golden mob shouted to each other for courage and flailed their horses into erratic gallops to meet the charge. Meagan blinked as her "extras" were dispersed like scraps of colored paper as the chariots ran pell-mell into them. Flashes of sunlight swirled from ornaments as the riders were annihilated in convulsions of horses, wheels and breaking leather. As the wave of chariots hurled into the fight, it was clear each unit was unstoppable even by its pilot—perhaps especially by its pilot—for chariots do not stop destroying in death but come apart in deadly pieces, releasing with each horse a new force of chaos.

A rider stopped on the ground below. Until that moment Meagan had been too stunned for fear, but she looked into the man's slitted eyes and backed away from the edge. *He saw her.* The rider's thin arm motioned and an object whistled past her. Two yards away a spear jabbed into the bare ground. Its end rocked. Another spear shot up. Meagan scuttled for the center pit as the new missile streaked overhead. She caught the edge of the pit and lowered herself, kicking for a peg. Another spear arced up, but she did not wait to see where it fell.

She stepped down, bare foot waving until she found a peg. Heavy air insulated the sounds of battle as she descended the dim tunnel. One peg gave slightly and shifted. Meagan froze. She flattened against the side of the pit, testing the nub with her weight. With a sudden twist Meagan's support was gone. For a brief second she hung in space, scrambling against the scraped earth. Her toes dug into the crumbling indentation left by the fallen peg, kicking dirt away before she fell.

Wherever man has left his footprint in the long ascent from barbarism,
we will find the hoof print of the horse beside it.

- John Trotwood Moore (1852-1929)

THE DROP WAS not far, not more than ten feet. For a time Meagan
lay with her eyes and hands clenched shut, trying to make sense
of recent events. Slowly she opened her eyes and let her vision
adjust to the dim light around her. A hoof stood inches from her
face. Meagan jerked away, but another solid limb pressed
unyieldingly into her back. She was surrounded by a forest of
horses' legs.

Meagan expected the horses to whirl away, erupting in stam-
pede. She scrambled to avoid being trampled and was stopped
by a wall of packed earth. But no horse wheeled and ran, no
horse gave alarm. All stood in rigid silence, immobile, and she
did the same.

Shadows from smoking torches shifted as she stared through
the gloom. Each horse's tail was tightly wrapped and each mane
was pulled short. Crude, stirrup-less saddles made of stuffed
pillows were held in place by a girth, breast collar and crupper.
The horses' heads were topped with headdresses made of
leather or fur, spouting feathers and links of gold. The effect
was garish and otherworldly.

All the animals obediently faced the same direction. *Very well
behaved,* she thought, impressed with the horsemanship. In the
middle of the dim room, two horses flanked a kind of carriage,
harnessed with roughly cut straps across their narrow chests.
Only a few horses had riders; these sat mounted, staring ahead.
But no one acknowledged her.

Meagan looked carefully around her. The walls enclosed a
space the size of small warehouse. A rank, sickly sweet smell

permeated the air. Wisps of smoke from the torches rose and disappeared into the round shaft above.

Uneven light and moving shadows made it hard to see clearly. Meagan moved towards one of the horses. She reached out and stroked its hindquarters as she tried to study the carriage more closely. Though it was in the darkest part of the room, she could see two wheels and a light cab, like a trotter's buggy. The cart was made of wood and the sides were mounted with gold decorations of griffins, eagles and predator cats.

It could almost be the inside of a kind of a tomb, Meagan thought. She swallowed, thinking it seemed recently finished, if so. The torches had not even gone out.

"Hello ... Promise?" she called softly. No tail swished, no ear pivoted. She spoke louder: "Please, Great Horse, you can take me home now. I have seen the darkness, thank you, I don't need to see any more." She edged toward the center carriage, moving past one of the motionless riders on his equally quiet mount. Even now the rider ignored her and did not look down.

It's like everything is frozen, Meagan thought nervously. Which wasn't fair, if true—the spears were moving perfectly fast outside. "Nice horse," she said, crossing in front of a motionless mount to look for a way out. She patted the horse's neck gently. It was a piebald, speckled black and white. The animal's eyes were dull in the torchlight.

Meagan froze with her hand on the horse, having a gradual realization she was touching cold flesh. She backed to the wall. In the dim, red light she could see foreleg-sized posts set into the ground beneath the horses, impaling them, supporting their corpses. Now she saw the horses' bodies were subtly misshapen, deflated, twisted in grotesque angles by the beams that skewered them into place.

She moved along the wall, her back to it, facing the grisly mannequins. The wall was smooth. She pounded her fist against it. Solid earth. Scraping, letting it tear at her hands, Meagan moved along the wall. *Why did Promise bring me here?* The stink of the room seemed to rise from the ground and overwhelm her.

She remembered the headdresses of the horses from magazine pictures, excavated from ancient tombs filled with horses ritually massacred for the funeral of their leader. Meagan was surrounded by the gold of a long vanished nomadic people—a dead entourage escorting their passing king to the underworld.

If this was such a place then she was no longer home, but in a long-dead past. The words of the legend swirled in her mind ... *eclipsed by shadow...* She was in the darkness. The room seemed to close in as she sank down, fists clenched against her head.

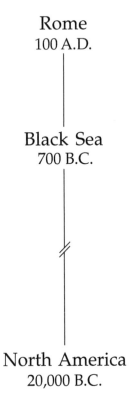

Rome
100 A.D.

Black Sea
700 B.C.

North America
20,000 B.C.

Savage Nation

*H*ABES SPEM NATANDI!"
An icy blast of water filled Meagan's eyes and nose. She tripped among wet bodies as she was drenched by another downpour. A crowd of ragged people crouched around her, soaked and shivering within a circle of steel spears. Men in rags stood close with brimming buckets.

Where am I now?

Another bucket was tossed. Meagan gasped under the spray and stood to escape. Metal-tipped points blocked her way. Bronze-helmeted men came closer, shouting furiously at the people cringing within the circle of spears. The prisoners were men and women both, mostly young, and all were filthy and sodden. A few bled diluted streaks into the rags they wore. Sweat, garlic and leather mingled with the scent of animals and dung.

Meagan knelt in her tattered nightgown, barefoot on wet, cement-like flooring. *This is not happening,* she repeated, keeping her eye on the soldiers. The group was forced to its feet and she was shoved forward with the others. Incredibly, Meagan heard something she understood just as another bucket drenched her. It was a fragment of a language heard only in a classroom, but the words were well-formed and clear: the words were Latin and they meant, *you have hopes of swimming.*

Soldiers forced the group against a wooden wall until splinters pressed into Meagan's forearm. Suddenly the wall gave way, swinging open. She was pushed into open space.

Sound rose and shook the air. Filled bleachers banked a vast four-story amphitheatre. Tall masts soared to spread a high awning over the stadium. A moat circled the inner arena floor, and beyond it smooth marble walls were topped with elephant tusks and netting. Cherub-winged boys suspended by rope swooped over white sand and arced high above the audience. Near the opposite end of the stadium, a team of mules was lashed to something dark and slack. It took a moment for Meagan to recognize the shape of an elephant.

Some of the ragged people threw themselves onto the sand. One woman walked as if sleepwalking, tears running down her face. The wooden doors groaned back together behind them. Points of spears filled the narrowing gap as it closed.

New gates opened, tall iron-banded doors that swept outward. The cheering was too loud for any other sound to be heard, but Meagan felt a familiar rumbling. Her stomach chilled to icy jelly as horses thundered from the gates in teamed pairs.

The dazed woman looked up to the sky, thin arms outstretched. Meagan saw a chariot bearing down on her, and she screamed into the crowd's roar as the woman went under hooves and iron-sheathed wheels.

There was everywhere and nowhere to run. People scattered before the galloping horses and their bristling chariots of bronze. Meagan leapt out of the path of an oncoming team. Hooves pounded across her footprints.

Others tried to climb the smooth mortar walls, but spectators beat them back. A chariot rode along the inside wall, sparks and masonry flying where its spiked wheel made contact. One man climbed high enough to clutch the arm of a spectator—the crowd tossed both over the wall. A woman from the stands threw herself onto the netting, writhing in the passion of bloodlust.

Meagan saw a chariot fishtail, throwing plumes of sand as it straightened towards her. She turned and ran blindly, hearing the thundering gallop grow distinct from the crowd's noise as the chariot gained. Ahead, blurred by the effort of her run, she could see a platform rising from the arena floor. An iron-barred cage appeared from under the sand. Meagan dived in a last effort to reach the platform, shrill whinnies screaming behind her.

A bellowing roar ripped the air. The pursuing horses shied from the sound and their chariot flipped, snapping the yoke and shearing the traces. One horse's reins tangled in the wreckage and the trapped animal reared in a frenzy to escape. The driver was pulled from the chariot's wreckage by the reins around his waist.

The iron-banded gates were opening again. Chariots arced toward the exit. Across the arena, people were kneeling in exhaustion among the crumpled bodies. Meagan stood trembling in her torn nightgown, barefoot and exposed on the sand.

The cavernous amphitheater quieted to random shouts. Stonework draped with burgundy cloth framed a pitiless crowd. Their glazed eyes were glutted but still ravenous.

The fallen charioteer lay close to his overturned chariot, groaning but alive. The coal-black horse to which he was tied squealed piteously and paced around the wreckage.

In the crowd's expectant hush, a high, piercing sound came from the island cage. Iron scraped iron as the cage's bars slid open. The audience roared with new hunger. Tan shapes bounded into the arena and the sand erupted into a riot of running people. Meagan scrambled under the chariot's twisted cab to escape. Her nightgown caught metal and tore as she pressed herself against the cab's front piece and pulled her bare feet inside.

She peered from beneath the twisted chariot. Outside was pure bedlam. Spectators cheered as lions scattered across the ring, at first skulking, hiding, and then pouncing as they grew bold.

The fallen charioteer struggled to his side and seized the reins around his waist. The horse he was tied to backed nervously, provoking laughter in the stands as the straining driver was pulled across the sand. His knife came out and flashed in the sun—too late.

One of the lions streaked towards the charioteer. The horse bolted away and pulled the man behind him: the knife flipped away and stuck in the sand. The lion sprinted and pounced,

clenching the driver and swinging the horse around. The savage
cat released its hold and the man was snapped away once more.
The stadium vibrated with cheers. A second lion joined in,
chasing and worrying the now limp form as it bumped behind
the fleeing horse.

From the corner of her eye, Meagan saw two metal-helmeted
men jump from the platform and run towards her. She struggled
out of the twisted chariot and scrambled to escape—but the men
were not coming for her. She ran a short distance and crouched,
clutching sand, exposed again. The men crowded one side of the
wrecked chariot and pressed it up and over. Meagan realized
why the men had come: she would be more entertaining without a place to hide.

The chariot's motion attracted a pair of lions. The cats
lowered themselves, tails twitching. The men raced for the
safety of the platform, their helmets dropping as the tawny
streaks ran to intercept. Meagan turned away. The roar of the
crowd told her everything.

She stood alone in a whirlpool of despair. *This is not happening,*
she told herself, *this is not...* The stained sand was dotted with
lions feasting. Some of the animals laid a casual paw over the
meal as they gnawed, others fought a gruesome tug-o-war. A
few lions gazed in her direction, but none rose from its meal.

The chariot horse, still tied, galloped across the stadium floor
with his driver's body dragging behind. The animal's black coat
was lathered with sweat. The second, free horse galloped to
join his partner, and together the horses wheeled and dashed,
trying to find safety among the lions.

The horses' act of self-preservation stirred Meagan. Even if
she *was* imagining a nightmare, the prospect of being made into
a meal was something to resist. She forced herself to step towards the driver's knife protruding from the sand. She made
slow, even steps as the feeding lions watched with undulating
tails.

As the horses circled close, she moved for the trailing reins.
Averting her eyes from the mauled driver, Meagan grasped the
leather straps and pulled the reined horse into a spiral. The
horse turned to face her as she desperately sawed the thick

leather until it was cut through. Dropping the knife she reeled the black horse closer, talking to the frightened animal as she worked steadily up the reins. The horse spun in a circle as Meagan gripped the horse's mane. She hopped and pulled herself up, slipping on the horse's sweaty coat as he bolted to rejoin his teammate.

The main gates opened to trumpet blasts. Soldiers poured into the arena, a marching line of breastplates and laced sandals bristling with spears and swords. They circled the lions, javelins high, while the predator cats blinked in confusion at their formerly helpless prey.

The crowd began laughing at the terrified girl clinging to her fugitive mount, the only entertainment remaining. Spectators pointed and mocked her frantic ride. Meagan tried to coax her mount down to a slower pace, but the frightened horse fought every pull. The animal's breath came in short, explosive bursts. Flecks of foam covered Meagan's legs.

The crowd's roar surged as her mount stumbled and pitched. Meagan's shoulder hit the sand as the horse fell, and she rolled to escape being pinned. She pulled herself to her knees.

The fallen horse lay heaving. The sight reminded Meagan of Moose lying stricken in her stall—the horse's black coat was curled from sweat like Moose's had been. Going to the animal's head, Meagan spoke gently, huddled against the sound of the crowd. Around her were only the dead and dying and panting soldiers leaning on spears. The crowd clamored for more blood, but the sound receded into the background of her mind.

A uniformed man strode towards her and the fallen horse. He wore no helmet and his hair was plastered in sweat. Scars slashed his face, and one slash intersected the place his left eye should have been. The man ignored Meagan and stood over the horse's head. His living eye was filled with hard passion. She shouted to him but the man did not hear. He was savoring the moment, the glory. He lifted his sword over the horse's neck.

Even in this dark dream, Meagan did not want to see another death. She forgot danger; she reached over the stricken horse and touched the soldier's arm. The eye in the scarred face fixed on her. The granite look of victory flickered as the crowd fell silent. The stricken horse lifted his neck and rose in a series of well-timed jerks. Shouts began to rise across the stadium as the pardoned horse jogged stiffly away to find his partner.

The soldier lowered his sword. He looked to the sky and moved his lips as if in prayer, and then looked down again at Meagan. He strode forward to snatch her hand and lift it high. A roar went up from the stadium. As far as she could see in the afternoon sun, hands were outstretched with fists raised. A chant began rolling through the crowd.

The disfigured soldier pulled Meagan to her feet. She half-jogged to keep up with the man's purposeful strides as he brought her to the side of the arena. On the platform above her, a robed man stood. He waited a moment, listening to the ovation, and thrust his fist into the air.

Far back, far back in our dark soul the horse prances...
    - *D.H. Lawrence (1885-1930)*

FOR A LONG time Meagan remained in the position the soldiers had left her, stunned and afraid to move. She huddled alone in a cold, gritty underground cell, buried in catacombs beneath the amphitheater. Her shoulder ached from her fall, and her forearm was raw from a soldier's hard grip. Her nightgown was torn and filthy.

Muffled cheering surged at intervals, coming from all sides of her prison. Meagan hugged her knees and rocked when the sounds came, reliving the images in her mind. *I've seen the worst that people can do,* she thought numbly. *People can do anything.* She rocked as another roar rose to surround her. Things could never be normal again.

In time the cheering ended. Long hours passed in silence. Scurrying cellmates skittered around her, tiny shadows in the gloom of flickering torchlight. *This isn't real,* Meagan still told herself, making it a mantra. *Promise will come back for me. She will come back...*

The scraping of a latch startled her. *"Salve!"* a voice greeted her gruffly. Two men entered, their armor gleaming dully in the torchlight. Meagan recognized the one-eyed soldier from the arena, the man whose sword she had stopped. He seemed almost unblemished in the dim light.

"Ut vales?" the soldier asked curtly. *How are you?*

Meagan stared and nodded dumbly, too frightened to answer.

The soldier looked to his mate and shrugged. He knelt and spoke slowly, using gestures. Meagan was made to understand she was not to be afraid. She would not be hurt.

"Gratius," she thanked him, head low.

The soldier pointed to himself. "Horace," he said in a gentle baritone.

"Gratius ... Horace."

The second soldier grunted and moved closer to grasp Meagan's gown. Horace growled and struck the man's hand away. Both men squared off with heated words as Meagan backed further into her cell.

There was lunge and a skirmish. The soldier Horace rushed the other man against the corridor wall and held his forearm across his throat. Gagging, the trapped man dropped his sword with a clatter. A second weapon fell.

Horace shoved the man a final time and released him. Leaving his companion to cough and reclaim his blades, Horace turned back to Meagan. In slow, considerate words, he asked her to follow.

She nodded and walked out, crossing her arms as she walked past the second man. *They act as if nothing happened,* she thought dully, *as if they hadn't just tried to kill each other.* Force and fear surrounded her—she was numb from more than the cold. *Promise will come back, she will come back, she will...*

The men escorted Meagan through dank corridors that wove underneath the amphitheater, emerging finally into overcast daylight. She blinked in the weak sun, breathing in the strange, rich scents that blew over her. People and animals jostled through cramped streets, and beyond, hills of classic architecture rose among grids of cluttered tenements. She swallowed at the sight of ancient Rome come to life.

Her first impression of history was nothing like she had imagined. The scene was drier, grittier, with more color and *certainly* more smell. The biting air was ripe with the scents of spiced food and sewage.

The soldiers marched down stone-paved boulevards with Meagan between them, entering a street whose backdrop was a hillside of bleachers filled to capacity. As they approached, she could see a vast, sandy oval within a massive stadium that literally lined the interior of a valley.

Meagan and the two soldiers marched past lines of people fil-
ing into entryways. Spears uncrossed in synchronicity as they
approached. She followed her escort through a guarded entrance, and a harsh clatter sounded behind her as the spears
rejoined.

Marble stairs led up to a tile platform decked with garlands
and branches of laurel. The floor was a mosaic sunburst over
skies of sapphire-colored chips. Dwarfs crossed the tile, balanc-
ing silver trays of wine and delicacies upon their heads as they
weaved through rows of stone benches set like pews. A chained
crocodile lay expiring in the sun; food tidbits and crumpled
linens were strewn across its back.

The platform was perched like a splendid bubble over the
milling masses, commanding a perfect view of the track below.
The sandy raceway circled a long central spine, or *spina*, cluttered with painted statues, altars and spurting fountains. Tinted
water rose in columns of blue, red, green, and frothy white.
Fires raged in open pits and, high above the spina, a giant
golden ball gleamed in the sun.

Robed people mingled inside a perimeter of guards. The
marble benches were filled with patricians chattering in foreign
tongues. Everyone was small in stature; Meagan was among the
tallest. At fifteen she was a full-fledged adult, already older
than most people of the time. The few women present wore in-
tricately layered hairstyles. Flowers were worn on garments
and in hair. One stern-looking woman waved a fan of short pea-
cock feathers—her face seemed to be coated in chalk dust.

Horace led Meagan to a line of people who were also in torn
clothing, also frightened and shaking. An olive-skinned man
darted forward and placed her in the line, dismissing the soldier curtly. Horace gave her a brisk nod and walked to stand
with the perimeter guards.

The olive-skinned man spoke to Meagan and, when she did
not answer, turned her roughly around. His eyes narrowed and
he spoke more slowly. She recognized a word, then another: the
man was asking if she spoke the language.

"Dico," she answered hesitantly. "Tarde." *I speak slowly.*

The man frowned and unfolded Meagan's arms, clucking at her torn clothes and bare feet. He produced a damp cloth and dabbed Meagan's face before tying her hair back with cord.

The sound of steel striking steel caused heads to turn. Soldiers approached the platform clanging swords against shields. All eyes went to a single man walking imperiously in the center of the entourage. His robes were brilliant white over a leek-green tunic, and around his slim weathered neck shone a collar of gold.

The man strode across the platform and seated himself beside the stern, peacock-fan-waving woman. Attendants flocked around the man as he calmly scanned the area. He raised his voice, speaking words Meagan later recalled: "How are the omens, my Master of Horse?"

A puny man near the front of the platform jumped as if prodded. He stood quickly, his oversized garments in disarray. "Very good, Caesar, very good. The horses are ready and the omens are with us, favored son of gods. Victory should be ours."

The platform's audience clapped dutifully. The man called Caesar shifted in his seat. "So you always say, Master of Horse. So it never is."

Trumpet blasts sounded across the stadium. On the sand track below, men in red tunics marched forward pounding drums and cymbals. Chariots entered, appointed in red and drawn by surging teams of four horses. The drivers turned and saluted the platform as they passed.

Another wave of riders filed into the stadium, these wearing the color of blue. Chariots of the Blue faction pulled beneath the platform to low thunder. Anxious as she was, Meagan was stirred by the pageantry flowing across the track.

Cheering rose for a new entering color. Caesar stood as riders in green tunics rode forth between columns of marching men. The first chariot to appear was pulled by four black horses, their manes woven in matching emerald ribbon.

A gasp went up from the spectators as one of the horses rose in his traces. The animal was satin black with the thick crest of a stallion. The horse struck his partner and the team swerved out of line as kicks hammered the chariot. Dull thuds echoed across the field. Men flooded the track and stretched ropes before the fighting horses.

From the raised center of the platform, stone-faced Caesar watched.

The chariot's driver thrashed his whip to no effect and finally threw it away. He sliced his reins angrily and abandoned his cab. Without looking back at his horses, the driver jogged to the wall, his clean-shaven jaw clenched under his leather helmet. He ran beneath the platform and was lost from view.

As those on the track worked to subdue the fighting horses, the man called the Master of Horse groaned piteously and covered his face. Caesar gave the shriveled man a long, chilly stare, then abruptly stood and made his way across the deck, followed by his guards.

"Emperor Trajan..." the olive-skinned man beside Meagan called respectfully. "We have the slaves you pardoned. Will you assign them?"

Meagan felt a hand at her back as she was pushed forward. She had read the name "Trajan" before, but remembered nothing of his reign. Whatever else he might be, the Emperor was a pale, plain man with a weak chin and large ears.

"Send them all to my gardeners," the Emperor said dismissively. He stopped before Meagan. "Oh, this one, the rider girl. Give *her* to my Master of Horse. Tell him I wish to have someone successful with horses in my stable." He gave one more look to the horse riot on the field below: chains and whips now tangled the confusion. With a final cold glance at the groaning Master of Horse, the Emperor departed.

The abandoned chariot's driver soon reappeared, mounting the steps in agitation. Dirt covered his arms, broken by streaks of sweat. As he pulled off his helmet to reveal black hair plastered against his scalp, he glanced at Meagan with eyes as gray as the unpainted stone around them. She flushed with the sensation of being caught.

The Master of Horse lifted a shaking arm to the driver. Giving the field a final squinting glance, he and the driver departed.

*Grooming: the process by which dirt on
the horse is transferred to the groom.*

MEAGAN LAY CURLED on an uncomfortable cot. She had been numb since her arrival; the cold was not intense but it was seeping and damp. Her extremely *un*private quarters consisted of a row of filthy beds crowded into a low room. The cracked cement walls were coated with dirt and scratched graffiti. Meagan's cot was only a foot above the floor, but it was a crucial distance. She felt about the floor of her living space as she would the underside of a rotten forest log.

For clothing she had been given a wool tunic with holes for her head and arms, and a tie-cord around the middle: only people of distinction wore togas, and she was clearly *not* one of those. She waited for the meager candlelight to be put out before crying softly, missing home.

Meagan hugged her knees, listening to the rattling sleep of the other slaves. She struggled to understand what was happening: *does the legend mean I just go from place to place?* When she had tumbled off the cliff with the gray mare, Meagan had been scooped back into the air—and from the tomb there had been another brief flash of white.

The details were familiar, as if the flights had been a normal ride over the top of a jump ... then Meagan hugged her knees tighter, feeling ridiculous to find herself rehearsing the finer points of *riding a flying horse.* No, she could not be where she seemed to be, shivering on a cot in the ancient city of Rome. This experience was clearly the result of reading too much history and getting a bump on the head. She needed to forget the tomb and the arena—if she could.

It was only an accidental fall, Meagan told herself. Poor Promise had been so frightened ... and anyway, nothing in this strange place mattered because it was only a kind of dream. The flying horse dream, *that's* what it was! A *dream*. She was coming to doubt there had even been two armed men in her backyard when she finally fell asleep to snores and scurrying sounds in the darkness.

The next morning her roommates failed to show the courtesy of ceasing to exist. Instead they resumed talking as if sleep had been a polite interruption, and after a few disoriented moments Meagan sat up groggily. She tried to pick out Latin words she knew from the confused conversation, but the talk was too fast to follow.

Conversations halted upon the arrival of a man wearing a dingy toga. He was apparently a supervisor, and from his tone Meagan inferred a toughening of policies. She stood barefoot on the cold, gritty floor—this fact was not addressed, nor was breakfast. Her conviction that she was only dreaming was again challenged as her group formed a line and followed the supervisor into the damp morning: she could see puffs of breath as they tromped across the chilly courtyard and past iron-grilled gates into the stables.

The sand aisles were well raked and orderly. Mortar walls were punctuated by a series of reinforced doors, and helmeted soldiers stood along one side. Meagan and her group were assembled between them. She heard her name called softly.

"Mea-gan."

The gentle call came again, and she recognized the soldier Horace standing in the guard line. His helmet's shadow obscured his scarred face. Glancing to make sure the supervisor was not looking, she gave him a quick wave.

The first worker was called. The supervisor pulled a pin from one of the doors and swung it around on enormous hinges. A narrow closet of a stall appeared, presenting a black stallion's muscular hind end. The chosen worker looked dumbfounded as he was handed a woven basket and scoop. *Stall cleaning,* Meagan thought resignedly. Some things never change.

The stallion shifted in the narrow confines of his stall as the shaking worker knelt beside the open door and began to delicately scrape the closest clods. Exasperated, the supervisor raised his voice and gave the horse's rump an ill-considered slap.

The enraged stallion bunched his hindquarters and launched a kicking barrage. Chain broke from the masonry and the horse rushed backwards like a dam giving way. Meagan flattened against the wall as men came from both directions. The stallion lunged at a nearby groom—alien behavior for a horse—and wheeled to attack another. Men scrambled to escape the deadly hooves.

Grooms ran and tossed ropes until the raging horse was trussed like a fly in a web. The scene had almost quieted when a piercing whine filled the stable aisle. Workers and guards came to attention as a pale, puny man in an oversized toga entered, flanked by armed men. The Master of Horse had arrived.

The man pointed and shouted and called out instructions until the scene was more confused than before. The stallion renewed his fight and pandemonium filled the aisle. Restraining chains were linked. In the end the black stallion was safely conducted outside, leaving the dazed grooms staggering as if on a battle-field.

The horse was clearly a product of harsh treatment, Meagan thought. An emblem of Rome's brutality. She watched the Master of Horse angrily confront the supervisor, who pointed first to the abject servant who crouched, cowering, and then to Meagan who remained standing. The Master of Horse took measured steps to stand in front of her, coming only to her chin but managing to look down on her. She did recognize the Latin words for "pain" and "punishment," since they were repeated several times.

—————

Meagan had never been homesick before, but it descended upon her like an illness. The new and simple reality of hunger pains ended her belief she was only dreaming. Meagan finally accepted she was exiled in history. Now her tears started at the slightest things—a mother holding a child's hand, a certain color or scent, or even hoofbeats crossing the courtyard.

Something else descended upon Meagan like an illness: an actual one. Without heavy clothing to protect her from the chilly weather, she developed a fever and a lingering cough. There was a small fireplace set into the grimy walls of the slave quarters, their only ornament. She often struggled to feel the thin warmth, but she was a stranger and most of her fellow slaves pushed her away. In the Roman era of "Might Makes Right" the milk of human kindness had curdled.

As the shock of recent events faded, Meagan saw things that in her haze of fear she had not noticed. The courtyard was paved in red stone, and from it could be seen the massive hindquarters of a colossal pair of marble horses that guarded the iron-grill gates. Great men live in Rome, the stone horses silently told the commoners. Great men whose protection they needed.

Entering the front gates, the barracks and workers' quarters were to the left, the stables' gates to the right. A blank cement wall opposite the entry was softened by a garden of slim-barked trees beside a fountain. Mosaics of green-colored tiles filled the walls of each entryway, and the arches over the stable gates were inscribed with a quotation from Homer: *A Multitude of Rulers Is Not A Good Thing. Let There Be One Ruler, One King.*

It had not always been this way. Rome had once grown the world's first middle class, since lost to the depredations of commerce. Wealthy merchants of the Roman Republic had formed corporations to buy up land in central Italy, forcing middle class farmers to compete against the slave labor they employed. The bankrupted citizenry drifted to cities to become "the masses" while merchants tore up food crops to plant more profitable wine vineyards. To prevent riots from starvation, grain was shipped from Africa, and the dispossessed mobs were distracted by chariot racing and the ever-increasing violence of the Games: these were the 'Bread and Circuses' that averted Rome's gaze from its own steady demise.

The Emperor's chariots belonged to the Green corporation, and it was impossible to forget. Green banners flapped against squat mortar buildings and green ribbons adorned iron-grilled gates. Guards and supervisors wore leek-colored tunics and the horses worked in green-dyed wrappings and pads.

Inside the Emperor's compound, stern horsemanship was executed with clockwork precision. Daylight hours were filled with the rumbling of chariots and shouts of men. First feeding was sharply at dawn and repeated at regular intervals throughout the day. Fresh water was supplied continuously and the stalls cleaned in rotation.

Horses helped Meagan through the dark days. The familiar rhythms of their care was an anchor to the world she had always known. Stall cleaning was her duty: slaves of better rank carried out feeding and grooming. The horses' mangers were stuffed with fragrant hay and grains, but every morning a stained cart was wheeled down the rows, from which meat and eggs were distributed to mix with the feed. Romans believed feeding sparrow's eggs, ground feathers and birds' blood logically made a horse run faster.

"No, they do not," Meagan had protested in broken Latin. "Horses are … are…"

"Horses are what?" asked a sneering voice behind her. She turned to see the baleful gaze of the Master of Horse. A waft of pungent perfume seeped from his toga. "Please, tell us. Horses are … what?"

"I-I don't know," Meagan said, flustered. She wanted to say "vegetarian" but could not think of the Latin word.

The man blinked up at her and wrinkled his nose. "Better not to offer opinions in the Emperor's stable, I think. Others might find out we use idiots here."

Meagan observed the other workers' downcast eyes and remained silent. Later, she would learn the Master of Horse was called Posthumous, a name commonly given to a son born after his father's death. Others' descriptions of his character added colorful phrases to her vocabulary.

Horses thrive on steady routine, but Meagan did not. Uneventful weeks passed, each gray as the cold mortar walls. She brooded, and grew angry at Promise for leaving her in this grim place. This was not like Promise, she told herself; apparently the Great Horse was a big Great Jerk. And always her thoughts wandered home. *Where are Mom and Dad right now? Did Mrs. Bridgestone know about this? Do they miss me—are they looking for me?*

As her homesickness receded to a dull ache, Meagan realized the horror of slavery was not the work but the drudgery. She was simply to mark time until she perished. The courtyard gates were open and she could have slipped out, but to where? Hunger was the unseen chain.

It was surprisingly easy to adapt to a new, if horrible, human condition and new—if horrible—ideas about life. The standard of living here was the highest so far achieved by mankind, and it would be more than fifteen centuries before it was achieved again. Meagan thought it appallingly bad as a high point.

In contrast to the well-groomed horses, the human scenery was an unlovely sight. The people were a catalogue of deformities, and lesser imperfections like moles, rashes and scars were alarming in their degree. She was most disturbed by the dental defects, in every state of decay—except for the eye problems. She shuddered to think of those.

She was horrified to discover her sickly, bent fellow slaves were mere teenagers. The lifespan of a Roman slave was less than twenty years. Such facts had been glossed over in the history she had read, but for Meagan the gloss was gone. It was clear why slaves were mostly ignored in books and movies—the practice was excruciating to contemplate. She watched the people working fearfully, heads down, and saw that tyranny was mostly mundane evil. There was nothing she or they could do, no recourse. The Republic was lost and every hope of man screamed, "too late!" but now the scream was silent.

On certain days she was sent out with a group to collect the corn dole, which soldiers poured from sacks into troughs in the marketplace. On the way she passed men standing on podiums or outcroppings of rock, orating on the decline of Rome. These speakers harangued their dispossessed listeners about the need for "Good Romans" to stand firm against the onslaught of impure barbarians. These speeches found listeners in the ragged mobs, who sensed in the words a dark hint of advantage.

Even so, as Meagan began to better understand the simple talk around her, she was struck by how people of different times and places are alike more than different. Her fellow slaves were childlike, but she could recognize the scolds and complainers, the troublemakers and peacemakers. Among the petty intrigues and gossip were acts of kindness and warmth.

A secretive whispering passed among her fellow slaves. Talk of a new creed circulated in the shadows, speaking of redemption and love of one's fellow man. The new faith had been taught by a prophet crucified in Jerusalem a generation before, and the words found audience in the downtrodden, yearning people. Roman law persecuted the new religion and its followers, called Christians, for it threatened the rule by force of the prevailing government. Conversations ceased when guards were about, but the nighttime simmered with excited, suppressed speech among the lowly workers.

When she was not being reprimanded or ordered about, Meagan was generally considered not to exist. The fact of her station was impressed upon her by the Emperor's driver. Handsome and popular, the young man was a celebrity. Well-dressed businessmen accompanied the star athlete at all times, and groups of admirers waited for him outside the courtyard gates. The first time Meagan saw the gray-eyed driver, she gave him a nervous greeting. The driver strode past her without the slightest acknowledgment.

Someone did notice her, however. The scarred soldier, Horace, came to talk whenever he saw Meagan in the courtyard. Sometimes he would be gone for days and reappear with a new limp or nasty cut. "These scratches?" he would say, joking. "I get them training. Careless of me."

At first the man's hulking presence frightened her, and she avoided looking at the dried, shriveled place where his eye should have been. Still, his was the only friendship Meagan could claim, and she learned simply to look at the eye that was looking at her and to avoid the map of scars.

"You take many baths," the soldier told her one day. (Actually, he pantomimed the splashes Meagan took in the courtyard's fountain.) "You are so clean. Not like the others."

She smiled and nodded, her usual response to the language. Classroom Latin had not stressed conversation.

Horace bent down to unlace his sandal and nudged it towards her with a mud-spattered toe. "Like my new sandals? I got them from a Macedonian cobbler. Good, no?" The man flipped the sandal over to show an underside studded with iron nails. "They have hobnails too, for a practical Roman. It saves the soles."

Meagan nodded blankly.

Horace sighed and picked up his sandal to show her. "*Sandalio,*" he said in a good-natured baritone, and knelt to lace it. He stood and plucked his garment. "*Tun-i-ca.*"

"Oh! Your tunic is ..." Meagan searched vainly for an adjective.

"*Elegans,*" Horace prompted her, grinning. Then he held up his thick fingers, counting patiently, "*Unus, duo, tres...*"

With his eye-patch, Horace was remotely handsome in a mashed sort of way, and Meagan tactfully encouraged him to wear it. Regardless, when Horace made her laugh she found it easy to forget his imperfections. Soon Meagan forgot academic Latin terms such as *imperfect* and *present tense*—words that described imperial Rome quite well—and instead rehearsed the names of things explained by Horace. During meal-breaks she huddled as close to the fire as allowed, listening closely to the conversation. In time she came to understand all but the fastest speech.

When Meagan could find no place at the hearth, her favorite spot was the grove planted along the courtyard wall. The place was dedicated to a minor deity, and for that reason she could sit on the grass without worrying about sanitation. There were few such places.

Most children were warned away from Meagan for her crime of being a stranger, but there was a boy, an orphan, with no parents to forbid him. The child approached one gray afternoon while she was brooding in the grove.

"What are you doing?" the boy asked boldly.

"Waiting for gruel-time," she replied in halted Latin. Hunger was a common denominator and she felt it as keenly as the cold.

"There is a fight behind the grain bins after the guards change. Want to watch?"

"No, thank you." Fights were semi-daily occurrences. "I am Meagan. What is your name?"

"Xerxes," the boy said suspiciously. "My father was from Persia. He was in the cavalry before. He was a driver for the Greens."

"Shouldn't you be in school, Xerxes?"

The boy shook his head vigorously. Meagan frowned. Rome had no education system: the common mind was dark and filled with superstition.

"Why do you not see fights like other people?" the boy asked warily.

"It just seems so silly," she answered. "This place is hard enough without fighting."

"Do you have the Evil Eye?"

"No, I do not have the Evil Eye. What *is* that, anyway?"

The boy kicked the dirt and shrugged, careful to keep his distance. "I do not know, but everyone says you have it."

The Lupercalia arrived, the "Festival of the Wolf"—an occasion Meagan was determined to avoid. There were over a hundred holidays in the Roman calendar, and on these days most workers rushed off after first feeding. Meagan never followed. She had some idea what made them return with such wild, excited eyes.

On the Festival's race day, the horses of the Emperor were led through the courtyard gates accompanied by a swarm of grooms and spectators. After the horses and workers had gone the stables were deserted. Meagan sat in her grove alone, glad the cold benches were empty of sprawled guards and their leering catcalls. Cheering drifted on the morning breeze. Closing her eyes, she listened to the familiar sound she remembered from home. She appreciated her own time more and more, and was immensely impressed mankind had ever escaped such an encompassing evil as Imperial Rome.

Meagan had arrived at several conclusions about her situation. Most importantly she had determined she was not going to die. The Great Horse had saved her before—both from the cliff's fall and from the tomb. This cannot be the end, Meagan reasoned. Even if this experience *was* more than a dream, there was an Angel watching, she reassured herself. The thought made her much more brave.

She surveyed the deserted courtyard and eyed the unlocked stable gates. *Could Promise be here?* She hesitated. Most of the horses seemed to be stallions, anyway. Which was nonsensical, she thought, because a horse with an aggressive temperament was dangerous to himself and others. Male horses were usually castrated, or gelded, to live happy and productive lives.

She looked at the stable gates again. The aisles were usually guarded, so this was a rare chance to look inside. She could just slip through and check the horses while the grounds were quiet. Perhaps she needed to take action to bring back the Great Horse, and in any case she had to do *something*. It was an unlikely chance, but no one would ever know...

Nervously she stood and crossed the courtyard, looking from side to side. Stepping fearfully past the stables' gate, she hurried into a vacant aisle. The rows were silent except for the companionable sounds of horses. She unlatched the first unknown door and swung it open to find a thin bay croup. She shut the door and moved quickly to the next.

Meagan peered hopefully in each stall before moving on. She was almost to the disappointing end when a noise made her stop. Voices were entering the courtyard. She hurried to stand beside the gateway, hugging herself nervously and hoping not to be seen. A whine rose from the tangle of voices. She recognized the thin voice of the Master of Horse.

"I wish they would not throw eggs. Fruit does not bother me so much."

"There is always another race," soothed another voice.

"Stop consoling me! We all know there is only so much patience in an Emperor. My poor beauties. Tragedy, woe! To think the world could lose such a horseman as *me*."

"It was only a stallion, good Master of Horse," said the second voice. "You will find another, and perhaps Fortuna will smile on this one."

"No, the other factions are keeping black horses from us! This is a conspiracy ... *how dare they!*" The Master of Horse's tone rose angrily, then broke in despair. "The crowd *booed* me," he sniffed. "The rabble blamed *me* for this disaster. *Me!* This is jealousy, I tell you. *Jealousy.*"

Suddenly a hand seized Meagan from the side. She tried to resist, to explain, but the thick-necked guard pushed her into the courtyard. She stood barefoot and embarrassed within a circle of soldiers. The Emperor's gray-eyed driver was present in his green racing tunic. "*Salutare,*" she said in a small voice.

Unfriendly faces glared at her, except for one: Horace merely gawked. The Master of Horse pushed between the guards. "What is this? Sabotage, no doubt." An opportunistic gleam came into his expression. "Yes ... *sabotage!* I expected no less. What success can I have if all Trajan sends are rabble and slaves?" He came to stand at Meagan's chin and looked up at her without pity in his puffy eyes. "What have you to say," the man hissed, "that you should die in less pain?"

"One of the horses was sick," she said, putting on an easily evoked look of concern. "I was looking for ... for..." She tried to think of the word for medicine.

"Who can listen to this gibberish?" Postumus spat. "Barbarians cannot speak. Why am I wasting my time?" The man pointed a bony finger at her. "Emperor Trajan's little gift is a troublemaker. You can see the treason in her eyes!" He looked her up and down. "Skinny, too. I see why the lions didn't bother."

"May I speak, Master of Horse?" Horace stepped forward respectfully. "The woman has always done her work. We have no proof of sabotage."

Meagan nodded vigorously in agreement.

"You and your broken-winged birds, Horace. What sort of guards do I have?" The Master of Horse crossed his arms petulantly. "Do we need a confession? Very well. My guards that are loyal, torture the girl until she admits the sabotage."

"I was not!" Meagan protested, frightened by the glowering men. "I was just looking inside. That's *all*."

Horace spoke with his head lowered. "Perhaps we might wait to hear her story, honorable Master of Horse."

"If she could speak that might be a plan. You hear the mush that comes from her mouth. *Bah-bah-bah*—why do you think we call them barbarians?"

"Our Emperor spared this slave for her good fortune with horses," Horace said softly. "Use her knowledge. Trajan could not complain."

"Oh *yes* he could complain. You do not know him as I do."

"Hold your tongue, Horace!" the Emperor's driver added, his voice shrill and frustrated. "No one needs advice from paid swords!"

"Jove's *Beard*—or advice from *drivers!* Watch yourself, whipsnapper!" The Master of Horse reached to snap his fingers in the driver's ear for emphasis. "You have not been winning and no one would miss you—maybe if you would listen instead of talk our team would make it past the Emperor's Box!"

The driver gasped. "I followed your instructions to the letter! *To the letter!*"

"Is that so? I do not remember asking your horses to fight in the entrance tunnel and overturn your chariot and stop all the races for half the afternoon." The Master of Horse sniffed. "Go. Get out of my sight."

The driver pushed angrily past the guards and was gone.

The Master of Horse appraised Meagan as she tried to look as wise as possible. He wrinkled his nose. "These Greek slaves are overvalued. All their logic and learning, what has it done for them? We Romans know how to show who is in charge. I will have this slave sent back to the Games for her sabotage against the Emperor. And this time she *will* die."

Meagan haunted the courtyard as a homesick shadow. The Master of Horse had issued her death sentence and with those words, it was as if her substance had evaporated into the cold evening air. The other slaves left her alone. She ate supper in a corner and went to lie in the small grove beside the courtyard. Why shiver in a filthy bed? It would be better to listen to the icy wind in the trees than her roommates' snores.

The grainy clarity of the moon and masses of stars were an overwhelming presence. Looking up, hands tight around her knees for warmth, Meagan imagined falling into the blackness if only the earth would release her. She argued, bargained, cried and pleaded—*did the Great Horse see her, or even care?*

She thought about the sight of the Emperor's bedraggled stallions coming back from the last race. One poor horse had limped to his stall, staggering on three legs from the classic strain of a bowed tendon. Leg injuries are a horseman's nightmare, for a horse is only as good as his legs. Meagan had wanted to run cold water over the tendon, but her request went unheeded.

She adjusted her bare feet within the filthy piece of cloth she used to keep from growing numb. A horse kicked in the stables and an answering chorus of hooves struck iron-strapped doors. She sneezed in the cold night air. Her throat was getting sore again. It would be wonderful to see Promise, she thought for the thousandth time.

A lone shape approached from the shadows of the barracks. "Of an evening!" the dark figure called. "May I join you?"

"Of course!" she called back. Horace usually retired early, but she would be glad of his company.

Instead it was the Emperor's chariot driver who approached. He knelt, two eyes shining in the moonlight. "Are you planning your place among the stars?"

Meagan swallowed, unable to think of anything sensible to say in English, much less Latin.

"I have seen you here before. You like this little grove. Are you a worshipper of wood nymphs?"

"Oh, I am. They are so clean." When the driver did not leave, Meagan sat up straighter. Maybe *some* Romans were friendly, she thought. One shouldn't judge based on a few. "Have you been a driver very long?"

"All my life. I have driven three seasons for the Emperor. I drove Cerberus to his greatest victories."

"Did you say 'Sir-Bearus?' Is that one of the horses?"

The driver laughed. "I do not mean the demon hound that guards Hades! Of course Cerberus is a horse!"

"Oh," Meagan said politely. "You named a horse after a demon?"

"Yes, the three-headed dog-beast who devours all who try to escape the Underworld." The driver spoke with admiration. "Our stallion Cerberus does the same to any who try to pass him."

"I *see*," she answered, trying to sound impressed. Then she asked casually, "have you seen any new black horses lately ... say, a really tall *mare*?"

"We keep no mares in the Emperor's stables," the driver said curtly. "We favor stallions." He lowered his voice. "I wonder, how does it feel to know the time of your death?"

A flash of panic went through her. "Well, I do not know that yet."

"The Festival of Mars begins in six days. Are you not sad, not miserable?"

"I suppose." Meagan felt a chill beyond the cold. "Are you trying to be nice?"

The young man's teeth shone in the moonlight. "It is a jest. The Master of Horse always promises punishments but never does them. He enjoys the thought but not the act."

"Oh." Meagan's first reaction was relief, then confusion. "He was playing a joke on me?"

"No, I was." The driver chuckled. "I waited to tell you. Do not worry, the Master of Horse is very flexible in his feelings. Like a snake."

The night air seemed to grow a degree colder. Meagan saw no reason not to worry.

A scuffle rose above the normal whinnies and sounds of the compound. It faded into steady clopping down an aisle. "The great stallion Cerberus," the driver said respectfully. "He kicks in his stall and has to be taken out."

"Oh, *that* horse," she sighed. "A demon's name might have been a bad choice. There is a lot to a name, you know." The driver ignored the words and she began to feel awkward. "Not to be impolite, but why are you talking to me? I mean, why now?"

"Because you were watching the stars, as I do." The young man edged closer. "I missed seeing your escape in the arena. It is said you rode a horse to its death. It was said to have been glorious."

"The horse *lived*, as a matter of fact, and it was *not* glorious. I could not make the horse stop."

"Perhaps it was said to make the story better." He stood and offered his hand. "Would you like to see Cerberus? I will give you the honor." His handsome smile was warmth in the cold air. "My name is Braedin."

She took his hand casually, but the heat of his grasp went through her. "Braedin! I like that. My name is Meagan. They rhyme, sort of … Meagan, Braedin." She bit her tongue to stop talking.

Together they walked out of the compound, past the curved hindquarters of the marble horses protecting the gates. Beyond them, the outline of buildings topped the surrounding hills, a moonlit cityscape framed by stone. Hard-packed road passed between a circle of pens and an adjoining work-shop. Inside could be seen a shadowy row of neatly stowed chariots.

They passed the workshop area and approached the paddocks. Out of the darkness a stallion's scream pierced the night air. A horse charged the fence. The driver smiled as dirt flew around him and announced, "The warrior Cerberus!"

Meagan watched in disapproval. "Horses do not have to be like this, Braedin. You would be amazed what some carrots and a nice bridle can do."

The driver watched the angry stallion with admiration. Hooves smacked against the wood fence in front of him. "The greatest son of Pegasus, the Thundering Horse of Jove! If I had three more like Cerberus our team would win without challenge!"

"Actually Braedin, I think you would have four dead horses."

"You are wrong. Were the others as strong as mighty Cerberus, he would pull with them. Cerberus is a warrior. He only hates weakness."

Common horse sense told Meagan that the stallion only hated rivals, but she decided against pressing the point. Instead she watched a small shadow dance toward them in the moonlight, approaching with a comical jig. A goat came up to the fence and shoved his wiry neck through the timber poles, hoping for a handout. It is not uncommon for a horse to bond with a smaller animal, and a transformation came over the stallion as he sniffed his tiny companion. Meagan reached to pet the goat and Cerberus laid back his ears. She stepped back. "So, they do not fight because this is a strong warrior goat? I mean, the horse does not hate everything. You can see he has a nice side."

"We are not interested in the stallion's *nice* side," the driver said sharply. "Cerberus is not the Emperor's favorite stallion for his *nice* side."

"*This* is the Emperor's favorite?"

"Yes. From the day Cerberus savaged Titus' Blues and scattered them across the track. A glorious day."

Meagan made herself stay silent.

"It was the same month the horse became a *centenarius!*" The charioteer's voice was a boast. "Emperor Trajan gave orders that Cerberus would always run in his team. Trajan was a general of the legions, and Cerberus is to represent the military strength that now rules Rome!" The boast died. "Of course, that was many months ago. And many horses."

"I am sorry, what is a 'centenarius?'"

"A horse that has won a hundred races. I drove Cerberus to half of those victories before he became too fierce." His voice grew boastful again. "One of my fans is a poet named Martial. He gave me an epitaph for when I am killed." The driver stood straighter and recited: "*Here lies Braedin, the glory of the roaring Circus, the object of Rome's cheers and her short-lived darling. The Fates, counting not years but victories, judged me an old man.*"

Meagan listened appreciatively. "That is very nice, Braedin, for when you are killed." She watched the goat grazing quietly by the stallion. At least the horse was not insane, she realized, ending doubts. "I think Cerberus wants friends. Horses do, you know."

The driver laughed. "He has Rome, he has the Emperor. What friend could matter? Though, it *was* misfortune his partner Celeris was hurt. He lasted longer than any other."

"What will they do with the horse?" she asked with misgiving.

The young man shrugged. "Celeris is valuable breeding stock. He will be retired to father more champions."

"Well, that is something. But it is horrible what they did to him, Braedin. You cannot keep destroying horses."

"Of course we can, if the Emperor wishes it! Though perhaps you say truth. We have forfeited all of last season's races because of fighting. We have no more horses."

"But there is a whole *stable* of good horses."

"No, the Emperor favors blacks. We have used them all."

"You mean crippled them," she said darkly.

The driver's tone was dismissive. "Whatever the word, we have no more."

"Braedin, you do have another black horse, a nice one. I clean his stall every day." She was referring to a coal-black horse on her row, one of the few geldings kept. "In fact, I probably shouldn't tell you. The horse is very sweet."

Braedin's laugh was derisive. "You mean Helios. The horse stays in the Emperor's yard because we need a quiet teacher. Helios is not a stallion."

"He is a *gelding*, you mean. Stallions only fight for mares, so geldings don't fight. People are supposed to be smarter than animals."

"Do you suggest the Imperial chariot could be pulled by anything but stallions? *Never!* My last race will be run with warriors!"

"Your last race?"

The driver laughed coldly. "The Emperor has no more patience. We were ordered not to embarrass him again under threat of death, and Trajan keeps his promises." He lowered his voice. "I would be quite an attraction at the Games ... of course if you *did* join me, the crowd would watch you instead. An escape has never happened twice."

Meagan swallowed. "No, probably not."

He looked at her, a thin smile curling his lip. He took a step closer. "Trajan has promised the people he will execute the Master of Horse on the track after his next loss. They are going to circle him in a chariot first so everyone can have a throw. Amusing, is it not?"

Meagan leaned against the railing. She truly failed to appreciate Roman humor. Cerberus flattened his ears and she moved back. She sneezed; the frosty night air was not helping her lingering cold, though she felt energized talking to the handsome driver and warmed by the subject of horses.

The stallion *is* impressive, she admitted, mentally checking the animal's conformation as he paced in the moonlight. The horse's chest was broad and his barrel was deep; this coupled with short, straight legs gave the animal brutish authority. There was symmetry about the dark beast. Balance. Presence. His viciousness was only a product of his treatment and it was a shame, for with proper training the stallion could have enjoyed his life's work.

"Where are you from?" the driver asked, his voice becoming husky. He moved closer. "The women must be very beautiful."

"Thank you, but it is very far away." She sneezed and hugged herself, shivering. "What about the other two horses in the team? They were hurt, too."

"Not badly. They will be ready to run." He playfully brushed back a strand of Meagan's hair.

She sneezed again and sniffed loudly in a rather unladylike way. "Sorry, I have a cold." Embarrassed, she changed the subject. "Braedin, have you *seen* the horses? They were very scraped up."

The driver stepped back and watched her sneeze yet again. "It does not matter," he said abruptly. "Let us go back. It is late." He turned and began walking to the compound with long strides.

"But the grooms are not taking them out." Meagan followed the driver back to the courtyard: he seemed suddenly impatient. "You should see the horses yourself, Braedin."

"The Master of Horse gave a hundred denarii to Neptune!" he said over his shoulder.

"Well, of course, *Neptune*. But the men are leaving the horses inside. That is not what they need."

"You are speaking foolishness. It cannot be so bad." Braedin crossed the road and marched into the silent courtyard, bellowing to wake the sleeping workers. Within moments a dozen groggy grooms emerged. The two injured team horses were brought out, limping and swollen. Each stallion stared dully ahead as the driver walked around them, inspecting. "This is Saxon," Braedin said unhappily, watching the horse give a feeble toss of his puffy head. "The other is Ajax."

"You should not leave them standing," Meagan said politely. The horses' hind legs were fat, swollen posts. "They need to walk."

"Are they ruined?" The driver's voice was tight. He was shaken by the two horses' condition: that they could soon pull a chariot seemed impossible, even with Neptune's assistance.

"The scrapes do not matter so much." She ran her hand down one thickened foreleg. "Heat would be good for the swelling, though. Of course no one will listen."

"You know of these things?"

"I know they need to be walked and rubbed down. And heat will make a huge difference."

"They say you are Greek, and Greeks make the best doctors. I can have the men assist you."

"Oh, Braedin! I would be happy to!"

"I will tell the grooms. What do you need?"

Meagan studied the horses again. They had both walked sound after the accident: the swelling made them stiff. "The best thing would be to turn the horses out into the paddocks and treat them there. I need hot water and bandages."

"It will be done."

THE DAYS GREW more cheerful. New duties gave Meagan a goal and kept her from thinking about home. The weather was warming, and now she could stand close to blazing fires as they heated water for the horses. Her chills receded with the coming spring.

A small army of helpers nursed the two equine patients toward recovery. The horses were lathered daily in butter—actual butter—head to hoof, and rubbed for hours. Though the treatment was unusual to Meagan, both stallions soon began trotting sound.

Now the stables awoke to become a production line of chariot horses. Meagan was allowed as far as the practice track: from the rail she could see young horses pulling single hitches, and four—six—even *ten* horse teams practicing flying turns at a gallop. Flocks of yearlings were wrestled into halters and given the rudiments of manners.

There is more to chariot racing than its appearance of runaway horses, Meagan soon learned. The game was more about survival than speed. Charioteers rode as upon a galloping skateboard, using their weight to change direction. Communication with the horses was limited to slaps and pulls. Of course, the true horseman's challenge of chariot racing was in keeping the animals sound. The most popular chariots were teams of four horses, the *Quadrigas*, which meant sixteen delicate legs exposed to overreaching and missteps, apart from the disaster of collisions. Because of these risks, chariot horses were not raced until five years of age.

As spring took hold the workout track was swamped with spectators hoping for a glimpse of the Emperor's team. Ajax and Saxon were now sound, with only bare spots to mark their injuries. Trotting out with floating strides, the recovered Saxon was applauded for his beauty. With his large eyes and dished profile, the sleek stallion resembled an Arabian, the oldest pure breed of horse. He had been born in the fiery deserts of Persia, and each year a fleet of mares sailed the fabled stallion's blood back to his homeland. Indeed Saxon had one of the most beautiful heads Meagan had ever seen, if the horse would only stop tossing it.

Ajax was a special favorite of the guards. The men stiffened in salute whenever the stallion jogged past, as if to a wartime hero. The short-backed, burly horse had been raised in a barracks in Gaul. He was trained to a simple, brutal code, and was eager in the extreme.

The stallion Cerberus was a daily spectacle, scattering grooms into his flocks of admirers. The Emperor's infamous favorite had been born free in a Greek village's semi-wild band of horses. In his youth the stallion had been allowed to choose his mares peacefully, but when the new Emperor Trajan's preference for black horses was made known the stallion had been hauled away to Rome. It was clear from the stallion's flashing limbs and teeth that Rome was not forgiven.

Though he was not a member of the Quadriga, Meagan's personal favorite horse was the gelding Helios. The coal-black horse was named for the god of the sun, and possibly, she thought, for his bright disposition. His gentle manners reminded Meagan of her beloved Moose.

As a gentleman with consummate manners, Helios was also a favorite of the grooms. Even fighting Cerberus liked the quiet gelding. If another stallion was placed in an adjoining pen, Cerberus would charge the fence repeatedly; to avoid conflicts the grooms turned Helios out next to Cerberus. The two horses stood across the fence, neck to neck, friends. There was no rivalry between the two horses, only the usual friendship bond. It gave Meagan the beginning of an idea.

Helios impressed in other ways. Only non-threatening geldings were teamed beside Cerberus for practice, and during his turn Helios always cantered a steady pace and gave a good example. For this he was a favorite with drivers, too: horses influence each other, so it is important to have at least one well-behaved horse in every group. Overly-spirited teams were prone to bolt headlong through the gates or into the spina.

In fact each of the positions of a Quadriga team required special abilities. The two center "yoke" horses, or *iugales*, provided the chariot's power and stability, and were of necessity strong, steady and responsive. The two outer horses attached only by their traces were called the *funalis*. Cerberus held the crowd-pleasing place of fame as the inner *funalis*, a dramatic role which required great strength and spirit to anchor the chariot around each turn. Flighty, surefooted Saxon held the outer position requiring lightning-fast reactions and speed.

The driver Braedin came to see the horses every day, striding up to the paddocks in a green cape, his handsome features stern and proud. A crowd of admirers followed behind, but these were smaller crowds than the driver once had. Charioteers were popular celebrities in Rome—winning ones, that is. Braedin's once-rising reputation was a dull memory. People now knew him as the driver who cut his reins, race after race, and jumped out of his chariot.

Meagan overlooked the brash charioteer's aloof manners. She overlooked many things about the abrasive, handsome young man. She liked Braedin's passion for the sport, and she wasn't the only one. Women watched him, some overtly. He did not seem to notice, which Meagan found charming.

She found herself organizing her days around Braedin's visits, and recalling his rugged features and bold speech in his absence. Her extracurricular feelings found no expression, however. Roman opinions on romantic love were influenced by the ancient Greeks, who believed that passionate love was a form of madness. The first bout of passion was considered the worst and, like a respiratory ailment, its effects most dangerous to the very old and very young. The theory was not helpful to Meagan, who ignored it; this too was in keeping with the symptoms.

"Braedin, I have an idea," Meagan told the driver one day as he visited the horses. "Why not put the gelding Helios beside your horrible stallion?" Her plan so obvious that anyone could see the logic.

"It is tradition to use stallions," he replied gruffly. "I will not be laughed at."

"But Braedin," she persisted. "You cannot get anywhere if you are always fighting. Besides, there is nothing in the rules against geldings."

"I said *no*," the driver snapped. "We have a stallion arriving from Africa."

"Very well, but if there is a problem would you *please* tell the Master of Horse about my idea?" She smiled winningly, or so she hoped. "Please?"

The driver's smooth face grew dark and his jaw set. "Look after the injured horses and do not speak of the eunuch again! If Greeks are the best doctors, remember—Romans are the best warriors."

The incident shocked her. How could people have such ideas? The charioteer's attitude was not unique, unfortunately. Roman horsemen shared an outlook based on force: their crude horsemanship was not so much the product of Greek enlightenment as an ancestor of medieval brutality. Meagan knew the Emperor's stallion in a very different way than a Roman horsemen could understand. She realized what they did not, that a horse was not a primal force to be contained, but a being with thoughts and fears of its own. Civilization had made real advancement in ways of thinking, and she knew more about horses than any Roman, fundamentally. Her idea was better for the goal as Meagan understood it—victory—it truly was.

Would Rome accept a better way?

On the first day of March, a loud commotion rose throughout the city. Meagan joined the workers standing on fences to watch priests leaping through the streets banging swords on their shields, followed by laughing crowds of children. The Festival of Mars had begun.

The month of March is named for the Roman god of war, for it was traditionally the first month when the weather was suitable for legions to march out of Rome. Mars' festival was the longest in the Roman calendar. All the month's days were filled with feasts, gladiatorial contests and races. The most popular event was the *Equirria*, a day of chariot racing and equestrian games in honor of war's insatiable god.

The *Equirria* was the beginning of Rome's annual racing Circuit. The races were held outside the city's walls, on the ancient military grounds of the Campus Martius. Top chariot teams traveled the empire, underwritten by wealthy sponsors whose names were trumpeted across the known world. Famous horses and drivers raised spectators' passions beyond the flashpoint. Despairing losers threw their clothes onto the field and wandered the streets in misery. It was grumbled that Romans showed more grief for a favorite chariot team's loss than for a defeat in battle.

Meagan lay in the dark the night before the Quadriga's race. Candles and oil lamps were costly, so the common people retired at sundown. Living by moonlight and candles was not quite as romantic as she would have thought. Without radio or television or engines of any kind, the silence of ancient Rome could be deafening.

At night when all was quiet, old nightmares from the Games haunted her. She was revisited by images of things she had seen but not seen: hacking guards, gore-splattered lions, pitiless faces. In her mind, she could not turn away from the crazed spectator—a woman—who had fought onto the field to drink pooled blood from the sand.

Meagan always did the same thing when those red images crowded her thoughts: she thought of riding. Her memories were strong enough, the sensations sufficiently ingrained. She remembered trotting into a better kind of arena, looking along the fence for a parent who would always be present.

What would my mother say about this? Meagan wondered. Mostly she would be sorry for doubting Mrs. Bridgestone, of course, but her mother would want to stop the horses' fighting too, if she could—it was the horseman's view.

That night Meagan had a vivid dream, the first such in many weeks. Words of the legend chanted around her ... *The Four Winds swirled into a shape of beauty that moved to thunder...* A distant beat drummed the ground until the sound burst into a stallion's scream. The Emperor's chariot appeared with Cerberus raging beside the calm gelding Helios. When Meagan awoke, her last memory was of a winged horse carrying her aloft as words of the legend faded ... *the Great Horse comes to men once more.*

She sat upright in her cot. The Great Horse seemed suddenly close—and if the Angel now lived, where *was* the Great Horse of Rome? Who personified the ruthlessness and aggression so worshipped in this doomed society? *Cerberus!* Son of the Thundering Horse of Jove!

Mrs. Bridgestone had said the Great Horse comes through dreams, so perhaps the Great Horse had spoken. And perhaps, having spoken, it was expected for Meagan to act. The myths of Greece adopted by the Romans gloried in tales of brave feats required of heroes. She might not be much of a hero ... but if she tamed Cerberus, could that be the answer to the legend?

With these thoughts Meagan marched into the courtyard, newly resolute. The morning was already alive with the sounds of men swarming the complex and chariots being drawn from the yard. Meagan hurried to begin her duties. She had a convincing speech prepared for the Master of Horse, but by the time she finished her work the courtyard was quiet. She found Helios standing in his paddock alone, ears pricked, gazing into the distance.

She hurried to the barracks and approached a guard, stopping at a respectful distance. "Excuse me, sir," she asked timidly. "Have you seen the driver Braedin?"

"Drivers are gone to the Circus," was the gruff reply.

"Did they bring an extra horse ... in case the new stallion fights?" The guard looked away but she was persistent. "Please, it is very important."

Horace came to stand in a side doorway, dressed in a rumpled tunic. His marked face was unshaven.

"Horace!" the guard called. "Can you answer this girl? She asks to go to the Circus."

"Meagan?" Horace narrowed his single gaze. "You are not confined to the compound."

"I want to bring Helios," she answered plainly. "He might stop all this fighting. Braedin will not listen to me."

"The driver listens to no one. Fame has deafened his ears." Horace stepped into the early morning sun. His marred face was ugly in the naked light and Meagan fought her urge to step back. He led her a short distance away from the gates and lowered his voice. "If you are planning to escape you will have no interference from me."

"I am *not*, Horace, I promise. I just want to help the horses." She saw his quizzical look and corrected herself. "Help the Emperor, I mean."

"Good. Helping the Emperor cannot be wrong. It can even bring you freedom." Puffed from sleep, the man's pale gaze was unnerving. "You are different than other women, Meagan. I want to ask..." His voice became carefully impassive. "What will you do if you receive freedom? Will you go home?"

"I don't know." Quick tears formed which she wiped away. "Sometimes I don't think so."

Horace rubbed his face and looked at the morning sky. His profile was clean and unblemished. With quiet conviction he recited, "*And yet more bright shines out the Julian star, as moon outglows each lesser light...*"

"That is nice, Horace. What is a Julian star?"

"The moon at its fullest. Or, one who outshines."

"Where did you learn it?"

"My mother. She believed in education."

"My parents did, too." She hurried to change the subject from home. "How old are you, if you don't mind?"

"An old man. I have twenty years."

"That isn't *old*, Horace. You be anything."

"And I would be, now. 'A good scare is worth more than good advice.'"

She nodded. "I understand that. I really do."

"That quote was the real Horace," he said softly. "Quintus Horatius Flaccus, the favorite poet of Emperor Augustus. I was named after him. Rome wants another Horace, my mother used to say."

"Your mother sounds very sweet. I think it's nice to be named after a poet."

"Thank you. I didn't used to be so courteous about it. 'Adversity draws out talent,' my mother said to me, over and over. I found my own favorite lines. *'Seize the day!'* I told her when I left for the legions. Wasn't I a bright boy?" He gave a dry laugh. "Father approved of the legions. Men of honor find their reward, father said. Homer was *his* man." He lifted his face again to the sky. "'A vase is begun—why, as the wheel goes round, does it turn out a pitcher?'"

"I'm sorry, Horace."

"There is no need to be sorry. I give Rome their poetry." He grunted dismissively. "Trajan's ascension was kind to our family." He gave Meagan the grin that made her forget his scars. "I have heard that horses talk to you. Is that to be your secret to help the Emperor?"

"Actually, I do the talking," she said, smiling back. "They mostly wiggle their ears. Do you ride?"

"No, I cannot. It was above my class and was forbidden. The magistrates did not mind boxing or sword play, or for that matter slaughtering for crowds. We were not allowed to learn horsemanship."

"I'm sorry they didn't let you ride horses, Horace. That wasn't right."

He shrugged. "At least the equestrians have standards. But I would like to have ridden. It is said when you gallop the wind rises like a gale in your ears."

"That was very poetic, Horace."

"Was it? I read too much as a child." He reddened as if embarrassed. "I didn't see your escape at the Games, but I have heard. They say you must be nobility of a cavalry nation."

"Why, thank you, Horace! My coaches would be glad to hear that."

"Woman warriors can be fierce," he said appreciatively. "Queen Boudicca fought in Britannia in my father's time. And you saved yourself from lions, Highest Lady."

Meagan straightened. "I was so scared I barely remember it, Horace. We never talked about that day, but I want to thank you for saving my life."

"The bosses like twists of fate," he said modestly. "They please the crowd." He watched her a moment. "You would have survived without me. Lions are cowards. They only become fierce if they see weakness." He grinned. "Like politicians."

"Well, I do appreciate it, Horace. Did you say you were in the legions?"

"I was, until we were ordered to torch a village that lay on a merchant's route. We were to kill the witnesses. Sometimes to lay down your weapons is bravery. Rome's wars are fought for rich men now."

Meagan was alarmed to see veins standing on the man's neck. Horace was clenching his fists methodically; his lip was slightly curled. She had a mental flash of the fallen horse and the blood-smeared sword lifted high. She avoided her sudden urge to look at the short sword by his side—refused to search for evidence upon it. "You don't have to explain, Horace."

"Mine is not a rare story. They wanted my right hand, the deserter's punishment. Trajan was coming to power, and he brought leniency. They lashed me instead and sent me home. Then I learned what fighting was."

"They made you become a gladiator?" she asked, shocked.

"No. I was not forced." He laughed without humor. "But when you leave the legions, what do you find? Money is king in Rome. Paunchy thieves have ten villas and loyal farmers are penniless. Between tax collectors, bill collectors and landlords, our farm was always in danger. Never a spare denarius. You know what poverty is like."

"I do now, Horace. I know very well."

"So you'll understand my feelings when a man came to me with an offer. He was a trainer of gladiators, a *doctores*. He would give my family title to our land. I was the price. I spat on the man's feet, but then he pointed out the legions are the same as the pit—entertainment when we are winning, forgotten when we are not."

"The 'pit' means the Games, doesn't it?" she asked in a small voice.

"It does. The trainer explained it to me, and I saw it was true."

"I'm sorry, Horace," she said sincerely.

"When Trajan took power, gladiators of military background were called up. I was proud to serve in Trajan's Praetorian Guard and as a lictor for the Master of Horse. I could go home to be received with respect at last. But it was a quiet homecoming. My father was dead. He and my uncle had been trapped in a slave-gang on our family's farm. The *doctores* had cheated me. My mothers and sisters were living in..." The gladiator's breath caught.

"I'm so sorry."

"*Do you say nothing else?*" His hand gripped the hilt of his gladius.

Meagan glanced finally at the sharp sword he carried: its double edge was nicked but well-honed. "I am on your side, Horace," Meagan said calmly, trying to placate him. As with a horse, it seemed best not to tense.

"We are in good company, you and I. We are brothers to the slaves in Spartacus' army! They were hounded by the richest man in Rome, an inhuman who hung six thousand prisoners on crucifixes from Capua to Rome. In crucifixion you can only breathe by grinding nail on bone. It takes three days to die as your enemies watch you suffer agony and terror of death. I say any who turn away allow it!"

Meagan stood frozen. She suddenly realized no one could reach her in time.

"I was a good fighter." Horace began pacing. "I held my own. My scars make me distinctive and I had a new cause, hatred of

Rome. I was trained to fight human beasts, and I would destroy the howling creatures screaming for blood. The *gods* see their evilness, sitting and watching. Many die in the stands and I can tell you, the screams sound no different because no one applauds."

"*Please*, Horace!"

The man did not hear, trapped in his own grief. "Have you ever seen someone in the bloodlust? Free of conscience, inhuman. It looks like ecstasy but is only madness. Their souls are dissolving. When you watch violence, it takes your soul until you never want to stop. It drives you to see murder, over and over. A simple death must be followed by a decapitation. You want to see two men die—three, *five*—now all at one stroke! Gushing blood is counted upon fingers. That was only four fingers, but there! Look how the elephant squashed that old man—wait, he's ... no *he's* dead. That was seven fingers, the right scream would have made it eight."

"Horace, *please* stop."

"Stop my visions—how? Tell me that! I have seen wealthy men's lovers tied by cords to the top of the amphitheatre and jerked off their feet to dangle and be dropped over and over while the crowd rolls with laughter. I have seen worse, I have seen—"

"Horace, I don't want to talk about this." She backed a step, mentally tracing a path out of the courtyard.

"Then what can we talk about? I know nothing of horses." Horace's good eye glared. When he spoke again, his tone was more controlled. "Do you know I am blind in my left eye?"

She nodded stiffly. "I ... have seen it."

"It was green. Not unlike the color of yours."

"Horace..."

"Do you want to know how I lost it? You will never ask, but I will tell you. This is what happens when Rome singles you out. You will know what pain is, bound to a post, covered in blood from the eye they lashed out. They go for the eyes, so you must keep the other one against the pole, no matter the pain." He caught his breath, and once more.

Rome was a nation of psychopaths, Meagan thought, pressing out hot tears. *Creating more.* "I'm sor—I mean, Horace, why do people go to the Games? I've never understood."

"To feel immortal." The man's face was a dark mask. "You live, they don't."

"I'm going to have to hear the rest later." She kept her voice steady. "I hope you don't mind."

The man's expression registered shock. "No, I—I didn't mean—" He swallowed. "I shouldn't have talked so ... I have not been trained to hold my temper. Don't leave. Here, you want the horse. I am about to leave for the races myself, we will go together." He barked at two guards standing at the gate. "Catallus, Terence! You will accompany me and this slave to the Circus. Find some workers to help and do as the woman says."

One of the guards leaned and spit. "We are off duty."

"You are back on. It is to help the Emperor."

The guards looked at each other and grumbled.

"Thank you, Horace," Meagan said meekly, "but I do not want to make trouble."

"It is no trouble. I have been a member of Trajan's Praetorian Guard. My words have volume." He kicked off his sandals. "Here, take these. You cannot go barefoot."

Meagan looked longingly at the worn leather. Men and women wore the same style of sandal, and the prospect of being immune to pebbles was tempting. "Thank you, Horace, but—"

"I have many. Your foot is small, so lace them tightly." He gave a short lecture as she complied. "Keep your head high and look at no one. We will follow the crowds and if we are stopped, remember I am Horace Campangus Livio of the Ludus Magnus School. Gather some workers, not fewer than five—ten would be better. And remember..." His gaze was hard. "You have only the authority you take. Take much."

Such is the general decay of manners that on the longed-for day of the races the public rushes headlong to the course ... as if they would outstrip the competing teams.

- Marcellinus (330-395A.D.) last historian to write in Latin

"Please ... anyone? I only need ten people to help." Meagan stood with Helios before a small crowd of ragged workers. The gelding scanned the assembly with interest; the people stared back with bored expressions. "Or maybe five?" She smiled hopefully.

"We are going to watch the races, not work at them!" one of the workers called out. A thin cheer greeted this, and people began drifting from the group.

"How about just three or four?" Meagan pointed to the two guards recruited by Horace. "These nice men will protect us."

"They protect us from bread, that is all!" ranted a worker. "I am safe from meat and cheese!"

"Yes," Meagan said politely, not intending a rally.

The young boy Xerxes scampered forward and puffed out his chest. "I will lead the horse! I will do it!"

"You are nice to offer, Xerxes, but you are a little ... young." She did not want to say small, but he was.

"I am nine!" the boy insisted, holding up six fingers for emphasis.

"That is very nice," she said sweetly. "Are you not afraid I have the Evil Eye?"

"I will stand far away. Let me take him!" The boy grasped for the lead. "I know this horse, I know all the horses! My father was a chariot driver before!"

Meagan looked at the eager face unevenly coated with grime. His tunic was stained and torn in places, like her own. She sighed and handed Helios's lead rope to the boy. "Okay, Xerxes. Thank you for offering." The boy patted the horse's neck with a proud smile.

Horace arrived clean-shaven and grinning, wearing an olive mantle and matching eye-patch. He looked to be in a jovial mood. "Where are the workers?"

"No one would come," Meagan said matter-of-factly. "It is only me and the boy."

Horace looked at the two guards. "And you did nothing?"

One of the men spit. Neither replied.

The air tightened with sudden tension, until Horace turned back to Meagan. "I remember *this* horse! A fortuitous choice, Meagan—the one you saved! You rode this mount in the arena to escape. Why did you not tell me before?"

"I had ... forgotten about that." In truth Meagan had never realized the black gelding was of the chariot team that had almost trampled her. In truth, she had tried to block the entire experience from her mind.

"Will he remember my intentions?" Horace stood well back as he spoke. "My role was not one the horse would appreciate."

"I don't think he understood, Horace." She bit her lip as she looked at the placid gelding, wondering. No, it could not be: fearsome Cerberus was the vaunted celebrity of Rome. Helios, however sweet, was far too innocuous to be Great.

The tiny contingent started out the stable gates to join the crowds streaming outside the walls of Rome. The slick, mud-scored road sloped out of the city. The black gelding clopped along sedately, each leg wrapped for protection. Meagan's group walked through the arches of the city's high walls and crossed the muddy plain towards a gathering crowd.

The *Equirria* was this Circus venue's largest race of the year. Columned grandstands and temporary bleachers circled the freshly sanded track. Coming to the special entrance for horses, they were made to halt before a group of soldiers. Hearing the name "Ludus Magnus School," a soldier waved them on into a carnival of colors and smells.

The area was packed with people and horses. Whinnies mixed with the cries of men. Long banners of cloth in the four Colors—

Red, White, Blue and Green—draped walls of smooth mortar. Pockets in the crowd formed around the chariots and horses. A familiar challenge trumpeted in the air, and Meagan pointed in the direction of the sound.

Horace cleared his throat suggestively. "Comrades?"

The guards opened a path through the crowd with shoves and sharp commands. As the group approached the corner, the black head of Cerberus could be seen rearing high, nostrils flared crimson. A swarm of attendants held his ropes.

"Wait here," Horace told Meagan. "I will check in and return." He disappeared into the crowd.

Meagan scanned the scene and found Saxon within a flock of attendants. Veins stood on the horse's sleek black coat and nervous sweat darkened his neck. Even at standstill, the long-legged stallion snatched the rope so it jerked the groom's arm. Beside Saxon, the stallion Ajax danced at the end of his lead. A third, unfamiliar stallion was being led in circles. The horse hung his head low as he walked. A scattering of scars and white hairs marred his ebony coat.

A chariot was wheeled out. The wicker cab had a cutaway back and thin wheels. Four sets of reins and harness were separated and held aloft. Men swarmed like a pit crew, attaching traces and readying for the horses.

With a rush of excitement Meagan saw Braedin deep in conversation with a circle of men. She waved over the crowd and caught the driver's attention. His eyes widened and the driver quickly excused himself from the others and strode over, concern on his face. "*What are you doing?*" he asked in a hoarse whisper. "*You could be flogged for trespass.*"

"I am sorry to bother you, Braedin. I brought Helios in case you might try my idea."

The driver grimaced. "I told you to forget the eunuch. Take it away."

"But this could stop the horse fights."

"I will not discuss it," he said harshly. "We have a new stallion!"

Meagan followed Braedin's gaze to the unfamiliar coal-black horse being walked in circles. Showing the white of his eyes, the horse made a vicious kick at one of his handlers. "It is only going to be another fight, Braedin. Please try the gelding."

The driver walked away with his jaw clenched as the new stallion was led to the front of the chariot and into position. Men darted around the animal, running straps and harness under and around. Ajax and head-tossing Saxon were hitched to the third and fourth traces. Each stood fidgeting and lurching in false starts, straining the chariot forward in jerks.

Men stood holding the traces, waiting for Cerberus. The stallion stood on his hind legs. Ropes were taut about the raging animal's head; every few yards the horse lunged and struck. Cerberus lived in a world of containment, the most primitive form of training: when the stallion saw the chariot he rose high, landing to whirl and kick. The stallion's hooves slashed empty air. The handlers acted quickly, bringing the belligerent stallion into the far-left position. Trumpeting a shrill challenge, Cerberus struck the air. His new partner lifted his head and flattened his ears.

Meagan could see the tightly focused faces of the men as they worked, professionals. "You have to stop!" she pleaded. "You will hurt them! *Please* listen!"

A harness was flung over plunging Cerberus. Straps were slid deftly into place. Men darted in and caught a front leg, holding it so the stallion could only hop. The grooms kept the situation under control, one man at the head of each horse, twisting ears, pushing and slapping the animals into momentary submission.

"Please listen!"

The men disengaged on a signal. The chariot lurched convulsively as the black team of horses writhed together. Shrill screams filled the air. Hooves clattered on stone. The new horse flung himself backward into the chariot with a metallic thud. Traces twisted—the harness was coming apart. The chariot cab groaned under the strain. One wheel snapped. Ropes and buckets of water were tossed over the horses, which only increased the fury.

"What is the meaning of this?"

Meagan turned to see the scrawny form of the Master of Horse standing in shock, watching his team disintegrate. "I *said*," the man screeched louder, *"what is the meaning of this?"*

One of the grooms answered over the angry screams. "The slave-girl cursed us!"

"I did not!" Meagan shouted back, but accusations swirled and piled over her. The horses were separated as she stood defiantly.

"How did *she* get in?" The Master of Horse walked closer and glared malevolently up at her. He was dressed for the occasion in a leopard-skin tunic and an Egyptian hairpiece. He addressed the guards impatiently. "Take this little Myrtilus back to the compound and confine her there. *Another* chariot gone. Trajan will not like this month's bill."

"I have an idea, Master of Horse, sir," Meagan said respectfully in her best Latin. "Excuse me, but if—"

"It is a shame she is learning to speak. They pick it up, you know, like parrots." The man turned away and motioned Braedin to follow. "They do not understand a word they are saying."

Soldiers in green livery closed around the boy and the gelding. Meagan felt a rough grip under each arm as her own escorting guards lifted her and carried her along. "No, please don't send me with these men!" she cried out. "You do not understand ... *please*..." The crowds of people seemed under orders to ignore her desperation.

"I said the day would be looking up, Terence," grunted one of the guards.

"Why do you not scream louder?" the other asked, speaking into Meagan's ear.

She kicked at the ground but could get no traction. They were through the thickest part of the crowd when Meagan heard a welcome voice behind her.

"Going so quickly, Catullus? I do not think this the escort our friend requested."

"Leave us be, Horace." The guards tightened their hold. "You cannot protect her now. We have orders from the Master of Horse himself."

"This reminds me." Horace followed, his voice calm and pleasant. "I am in charge of recruiting for Galas next month. Catullus, your brother once belonged. I can give you a chance to defend his memory."

The men increased their stride. Meagan twisted in their iron grip.

"And Terence..." Horace followed more closely. "I can promise that if you kill Catullus without too much trouble, I will bring you on as a full recruit. Mass assembly, of course."

"We have orders, Horace. Leave us be."

"The Master of Horse's whims change with the breeze ... do mine?"

Meagan felt the men hesitate, and she struggled with new energy.

Horace lowered his voice. "Bring her to Galas' area, I will join you after the entry parade. The woman is to be *untouched*—in this way you will do as ordered *and* avoid dying for the pleasure of Rome."

Meagan finally wriggled out of the wavering guards' grasp and darted away. "Thank you, Horace. Thank you *so* much."

"Are you hurt?"

"No, just scared. I am okay." She watched the two guards warily. "Those men were ... I am so glad you came."

"You do not seem to be having success," he said mildly.

"I wanted to put Helios in the Emperor's team, next to Cerberus." She rubbed her arm, trying not to let tears start. "No one will listen."

"It seems a poor thing to do to the horse."

"It know it sounds silly, but the horses are friends." She wiped away an embarrassing tear.

"Do not cry," Horace said solemnly. "I will help." He called to the waiting guards. "You will follow us now, and escort the slave-girl to her seat when we are finished."

The two guards grumbled but obeyed, following as Meagan and Horace searched the swirling crowds for Helios. The gelding was found standing within a circle of disinterested soldiers. Young Xerxes still held tightly to the horse's lead.

"Comrades!" Horace addressed the soldiers boisterously. "We are on a happy mission to save the Emperor's horses. We need this fine specimen. You may go about other business." When no one moved, a feral gleam came into Horace's eye. "Just the men I was looking for! Staunch soldiers who hold to their duty. If you will stay a moment, Galas needs only six. Or better, any who care to remain."

One by one the guards evaporated into the crowd, leaving the boy and Helios alone.

"I did not let him go," the boy said proudly. "One of the men tried to take his rope but I did not let him."

"Very good," Horace said approvingly. "Honor does not depend upon size."

The boy beamed and gripped the lead rope harder.

"Thank *both* of you very much." Meagan rubbed the gelding along his crest. "This will be your moment of glory, old boy. Show them how good geldings are."

Horace reached to stroke the horse's sleek neck. Helios turned and lipped the man for a treat, and the soldier snatched his hand away.

"He is not trying to bite, Horace. He is just begging." Meagan pushed the gelding's head straight. "Now, listen, Helios. Do not let mean old Cerberus bother you. Stay sweet and stay friendly."

Horace watched curiously. "You truly do talk to horses?"

"In a way. Now please, Horace, be sure the horses have time to greet each other first, before you put them together."

Horace shook his head. "I think you misunderstand my abilities. I will find others to help. And, do horses talk to you?"

"All the time." Meagan gave Helios a final pat. "Thank you *so* much for helping, Horace. Good luck. May Fortuna smile."

"If he cannot, I will do it!" young Xerxes shouted, still flushed with achievement.

Horace looked at the boy staring up at him and the gelding quietly watching the crowds with a faraway gaze. "The horses must greet first, I will remember. The boy should come with me. I have little experience with horses. And I will accept your good wishes."

The two guards made no effort to be gentle while escorting Meagan into the stands. When she tripped on the stone stairs, they simply grabbed her hair and lifted until she regained her footing. Coming into the weak sunlight of the open stadium they shoved her in the direction of a low bench.

I don't like them, Meagan thought darkly, watching the men join a larger group of soldiers. She surveyed the sun-drenched stadium, thinking the reconstructed photographs of the Circuses of Rome did not do justice. Then a loud burp and a woman's giggling shaded Meagan's reverie. A splash landed on her and she chose not to look for the source. She moved down the bench, thinking photographs were nice too.

Hawkers called among the milling crowds, offering drinks, seat cushions and programs inscribed on clay tablets. Meagan squirmed on the baking rock, wishing she had coins for such luxuries.

There was an uptick in the general murmur. People were finding their seats. The crowd applauded—and booed—as a line of bronze chariots entered the Circus: the "opening credits," as it were. These hired chariots carried waving officials who had paid for the opportunity: the races offered the very best in political advertising.

"Marius Priscus, the great merchant!" A patrician official wearing a politically correct green toga stood to greet a stout, red-bearded man wearing military sandals and an ornamental sword. "I missed you at yesterday's Games," the official called. "That is not like you, Priscus!"

"I do not bother with the Games anymore!" the merchant roared back contemptuously. "All you get these days are rickety gladiators and broken-down slaves—blow and they fall over!"

"But you *will* like Athens this year," the official gushed. "The governor has a hot temper and a heart of gold. He will have something to show us! None of your common gangs of gladiators, no! Most will be freed men!"

"That is the thing!" The merchant clapped his hands, making his jewelry jangle together. "All I want is the best of swords, no backing out and bloody butcher's meat to feast my eyes on!"

Meagan watched the politicians' chariots with a critical eye. Rome had advertising, taxes, courts and contracts, free market capitalism, corporations, seven-day weeks, holidays, welfare, organized religion, spectator sports, running water and sewers, fine roads, literature, cultural arts, and a well-run military—none of this would save them. The world was about to slip from Rome's grasping fingers into an abyss of dark centuries. Meagan could see it in the darting eyes: the people could sense it. Evil had taken hold of power. Commerce and blood had Rome on its knees.

She recalled a story that illustrated the grip chariot racing held on the public mind. A harbormaster in the time of Emperor Nero, it was told, sent a message that the Roman fleet was in Egypt, ready for loading. The harbormaster informed the Senate 'the ships may carry corn for the starving or special white sand for the Circus. It cannot be both ... which shall it be?' The Senate cried to the harbormaster, 'Has your sanity left you? The Emperor is mad, the legions are restless and the people revolt—for the gods' sake, man, bring the *sand!* We must get their minds off our troubles!'"

In a far corner of the stadium, a troop of men in golden armor marched onto the sand, blowing deep notes on long trumpets. Applause mounted as horsemen rode forward to begin the entry. A standing cheer greeted the competitors. Meagan's heart began to pound when she saw the emerald banner for the Emperor's team. All in the stadium rose, necks craning.

A phalanx of mounted horsemen poured through the entrance, trotting onto the sand to deafening cheers. The Greens' marching band entered now, followed by soldiers in matching sashes. Meagan strained to catch a glimpse of the Imperial chariot but spectators stood in the way. She stood and pushed further down the row, enduring the jostling to find a clear view.

A hush fell on the packed stadium. The parade for the Greens was on the field, but a long gap stretched from the last soldier to the chariots' entrance. The Emperor's Quadriga had not entered.

The other chariots reined to a standing halt, their horses tossing heads and making false starts. The eerie afternoon quiet was like a song cut off mid-chorus. No one sat down, no one talked to his neighbor. In the silence, the massive crowd seemed a sea of cloth and flesh.

An eruption of applause broke the spell, swelling as the Imperial team galloped onto the arena floor. The Emperor's black horses cantered into the throng: the Serpent Cerberus, Saxon Head-Thrower, Dancing Ajax—names known across the Empire. The hair on Meagan's arms prickled as she watched the four horses pulling the Imperial chariot as if it were the very Coach of the Sun. As the team rocked in their traces, she could almost understand why men wagered their lives on this surging, sublime force that brought glory even to an Emperor. The driver Braedin held out one hand to the crowd as he glided past. He leaned against the reins, a flash of green rippling under his leather vest as spectators tossed flowers and even clothing onto the track.

"Meagan!" Horace pushed into the space next to her, grinning. He had a spot under his left eye that appeared to be swelling.

"Horace! Were you able to do it?"

"I was. I had the horse switched while they were dealing with the Emperor's Serpent. Have you noticed how fast those chariot men are with those straps? When bribed they are even faster."

"Is it really Helios?" Meagan craned her neck to see the field. "These seats are so far away."

"It is. The hardest part was getting the boy to let go of the lead rope."

"What did Braedin say?"

"I had the new horse taken away before he realized the change." He pointed to his darkening eye. "Although he did express his feelings."

The Imperial chariot was moving close enough to show Helios in the traces next to Cerberus. The black stallion had his ears pinned back—but he was cantering forward.

The most famous chariots in the Empire rolled before the crowd, four-horse teams jogging in tight formation. These well-known stars were competitors in a yearly series of races which circled the Mediterranean through cities such as Rome, Syracuse, Carthage, Alexandria, Athens, and Constantinople. The yearly "Circuit" bound the empire together in the imaginations of the ragged, dispossessed masses, and no lavishment was too grand. Genuine emeralds and pearls were even woven into the horses' manes; some gems always fell into the trailing dirt which ensured the presence of throngs of followers.

As the Imperial horses circled to the starting gates, Cerberus gave a savage kick that glanced Helios, earning an indignant squeal from the gelding heard all the way to Meagan's seat. Mollified, the stallion pawed and did not kick again.

The chariot teams maneuvered into a line of ornate starting boxes. The cheering dipped as the last chariots pulled inside, and exploded as the gates swung open and twelve chariots surged forward in a ragged line.

Two teams tangled in the opening rush and faltered as the Imperial chariot surged forward. From Meagan's distance the field was a pack of scrambling color, but the Imperial black horses were easy to spot. She leaned in sympathy as they galloped to the first turn. Braedin cut back and Cerberus dug against the traces—the crowd roared as the Emperor's chariot tilted and skimmed across the flying sand. Saxon leapt around the turn, gouging up great sprays before heeling to the inside track. The chariots scattered across the curve and disappeared around the turn.

Chariot racing was more like sledding than a race of speed. Horses were never able to reach top speed in the heavy sand, so the teams jostled for position as they galloped from end to end, braking and wheeling around each turn. The center spina obscured the view of the horses galloping on the opposite side of the track, which added to the tension as half the crowd screamed in imagination of the unseen action. The crowd was caught in the fever of a new fanaticism: chariot racing was the world's first major spectator sport.

Meagan waited anxiously until the field came back into view. Progress of the horses on the far stretch of track could be followed, for the chariots raised clamor and dust as they passed. Workers darted out of the way of the chariots, while behind them others worked to clear the fallen. Water boys ran up and down the center spine, wetting the track.

Horses streamed into Meagan's view amid plumes of sand. The Emperor's horses swung out of the turn as two chariots collided behind them. The cab of one twisted and cartwheeled; the other teams streamed past, sand skidding from their wheels. The fallen driver darted to safety as workers ran to pull his chariot clear.

A Red chariot led the field—the Emperor's team was a distant third. Newly recovered Saxon and Ajax were flagging, and Helios was not in racing shape. The team ran wide on the next turn, lengths behind the two leaders and losing ground.

"How many times around?" Meagan asked nervously. She had not even thought about the race itself.

"Seven circuits. Watch the dolphin-counters on the spina."

The two lead chariots ran well ahead of the Emperor's team, but the trailing field was bottled behind the Imperial horses, reluctant to meet Cerberus. One team tried to pass, making an attempt to come inside. The crowd rioted to see the gains the rivals were making, four horse heads stretching in unison, moving up with each stride. Braedin slashed his opponent with his whip and ducked when his turn came.

When the advancing team was close enough Braedin edged Cerberus to the inside. The stallion lunged, and the surprised rival horses swerved to foul *their* inside neighbors. Chariots locked wheels, and the collision cleared a section of chariots in a series of crashes that each earned a shocked scream from the crowd. The survivors swept from sight around the curve. A roar greeted the horses on the other side of the stadium.

Meagan strained to see the heads of the drivers over the spina, but all she could see was rising dust. "S-P-Q-R," she read, squinting at letters scrawled across the arena walls. "Horace, what does that mean?"

"Senatus Populusque Romanus," he answered. *The Senate and People of Rome.* Though the Roman Senate had abandoned even the pretense of representing the people, hopeful citizens still scrawled these hopeless words.

A full minute later the horses drove around the far turn. The leaders were the same two teams, a Red and a Blue, and they were halfway down the stretch before the Imperial Quadriga swung into sight. The remaining field was trapped behind.

On the straightaway, the leading Red team's driver looked back to see one of his color-mates making an attempt to pass the Emperor's team. The driver braced his feet against the front of his chariot to choke his horses down.

"What is he *doing?*" Meagan shouted above the crowd. The leading Red chariot was slowing directly in the path of the Imperial chariot.

"Taking us out of the race!" Horace shouted back.

The Emperor's horses raised their heads as the back of the Red chariot's cab drew close. Spectators who could see the challenge roared and the other side echoed in frustration. Braedin swung outside to block his oncoming rival, a swerve that brought Cerberus directly behind the back of the lead chariot's driver. The stallion flattened his ears and lunged—the lead chariot careened sideways into the passing Reds. Meagan watched through squinting eyes as the two opposing chariots cartwheeled into a pile of horses, leather and metal. The Imperial Greens narrowly missed the wreck, fishtailing out of the sharp turn before vanishing behind the spina.

"Are you holding our seats?" asked a slight woman holding a baby. Behind her was a man with a bored expression.

"No, I am sorry," Meagan answered, trying to concentrate. There were no assigned seats here, and plenty others available. These charming people merely wished to exert authority.

The woman reached down and shook Meagan's shoulder. "Young woman," the woman said again. "I think you are in our seat."

Horace looked up. "Could I have your name?"

"Certainly, and I will have yours. She is obviously a slave and *I* want to sit there. My name is—"

"I do not want your name, I want his." Horace grinned at the man. "I am recruiting for the Galas School. We are a few short for the tomorrow's melee."

The man's bored expression faded and he pulled the woman away.

Meagan laughed. "Do you ever get tired of doing that?"

Horace shook his head. "These worthless citizens would fill bleachers on a battlefield but never fight."

The horses swung back into view. The Blue team were now the sole leaders, and they dashed alone down the straightaway before spinning out of sight. The second-place Emperor's team appeared late, more than a half-lap behind the leader ... and fading.

"The Emperor's chariot may be lapped," Horace grunted. "That should have the Master of Horse groaning."

"At least the horses are not fighting. Maybe the Emperor will see they are trying." She ignored Horace's laugh.

Before the laboring Imperial horses had reached the midpoint of the straightaway, the leading Blue chariot dashed into view behind them. The first-place Blue team was almost a circuit ahead of the Emperor's chariot and coming fast to pass them. The Blue fans were exultant. Support for a color showed allegiance to certain senators or factions, and lapping the Emperor had clear political overtone. Some would consider it an omen.

Foam-flecked Ajax snatched uneven strides between Helios and Saxon. Only Cerberus was fresh and pulling. Braedin let the team drift out, and the crowd screamed as the Blue team surged inside to pull even with the wheels of the Imperial chariot, then alongside the pumping hindquarters of the struggling horses.

The crowd rose to its feet. The challengers came alongside the Emperor's horses as they gave a last effort. Braedin looked over his shoulder and edged his chariot closer to the passing inside team, and laid his whip deliberately down Cerberus's side to slash the black stallion along his inside flank. Cerberus curled around the lash in fury and charged into the pain, breasting the Blue team's outside horse.

The desperate driver beat Cerberus away as the black stallion tunneled savagely into the rival team. The Blue's horses were caught between the barrier and the jaws of Cerberus. The driver pulled frantically to slow his horses, throwing himself sideways and back, over and over, as the Imperial team forced them against the spina's wall. Shrieks of metal pierced the stadium's inferno of sound. The stadium's stone benches vibrated from the cheers.

In the last seconds before the vanishing turn, Meagan saw the driver slashing at the reins that tied him to running death. The Blue chariot's yoke snapped and the chariot sagged—the front of the chariot dipped and caught the dirt, flipping the vehicle high. The impact spiked the roar of the stadium, and the sound bounced and rolled like the collision itself. The Blue driver disappeared into the wreckage as the spectators on the other side of the stadium greeted the Emperor's chariot with a roar.

The Imperial Quadriga rolled on to victory, limping home to the riot of Rome.

***Caveat emptor** [Latin for "buyer beware"]*
- Ancient Roman law to limit fraud cases involving horse trades

In the moments after the cheering slowed to a chant, Meagan simply sat, disappointed. She did not think much about victory—the wrecks had pretty much ruined *that*. But in last night's dream, everything had changed the moment the race was over: a winged horse had taken her away. She looked despondently at the celebration.

Horace knelt between the benches. "You have been blessed!"

"Excuse me?"

"The god of war has blessed you, Meagan. This is his day and he has spoken on your behalf!"

"That is silly, Horace. The horses are just friends. I tried to tell everyone."

He prodded her to stand. "Come, we should make an appearance at the Emperor's Box."

Meagan looked over the crowd. People were standing and shouting, jamming the stone aisles. "You cannot be serious, Horace. Why would the Emperor want to see *me*?"

"Trajan is a good Emperor who honors Mars. He will want to greet the person responsible for ending two seasons of losses on this day. If he spared you once, for this the Emperor may give you freedom."

Good could come from the victory after all, Meagan realized. She assented, and Horace took her hand and pushed through the multitude. In places where the crush was very great he went first, opening a path for her to follow. Almost an hour passed before they reached the marble steps to the Emperor's Box.

Meagan surveyed the ocean of people surrounding the Imperial platform, held at bay by lines of fierce-faced Roman guards.

They were the infamous masses, remnants of Rome's once-proud middle class made destitute by their own merchants: the "decadence" and decline of Imperial Rome came not from leisure, but impoverishment.

Guards acknowledged Horace and began shouting orders. He turned to her; his expression had grown solemn. "You will have to go on alone, Meagan. They will not let a gladiator on the platform."

"Wait, Horace! Will I see you back at the stables?"

"If you wish. After you receive honors from the Emperor, you may be subject to new desires."

Heavily-scented guards pressed around Meagan. *No wonder claustrophobia is a Latin word,* she thought as they jostled her. This was happening too quickly. "Of course I will visit you, Horace. Do I have to go?"

"We could escape." The baritone voice was husky as he leaned close. "I have family in Lazio. We could be married. We could..." Horace stopped himself, seeing her head shake slowly.

Meagan was surprised by the matter-of-fact proposal. She had not until that moment fully realized she was of marriageable age. Of course she would be considered mere property in the arrangement, but the offer touched her. "Horace, I can't. It's not my choice. I ... I don't belong here. Please understand, I *cannot.*"

Horace raised his gaze to the sky and recited softly, "*Her voice rings through me like a song on a lyre, yet it is only an echo on the wind.*" He looked down again, his expression carefully composed. "Does it sound like the great *Horatius,* even a little? It is mine, for you."

A tear streaked down Meagan's face. "Please, Horace ..."

"You make me think of the dog of my boyhood, Highest Lady. I always thought my Hercules was very stupid because he chased birds. Now I know why."

"Horace," Meagan smiled as she wiped her eyes. "As advice, never tell a girl she reminds you of a dog."

The expression on his ruined face was soft. "It is to see them fly."

A tightness grew in Meagan's chest. "You saved *me,* Horace. Don't forget that."

"It was only my destiny. I will remember you." Horace stepped forward and kissed her forehead. He bowed as guards pushed her on.

A cleared space followed Meagan like a spotlight as she was escorted through the tight crowd. A beaming Master of Horse called warmly, hurrying closer. "There she is, Excellency! My *assistant!*" The man's voice was familiar but his manner was not: he was being nice. "Are you well, sweet child?" the man doted. "I hope you had no trouble with the Blue fans!"

Seated on the high bench was a smiling Emperor. His voice was gentle. "Bring the slave closer, Cornelius."

A stout, clean-shaven man approached Meagan. His hair was cut short and brushed forward. "Good woman, I am Cornelius Tacitus, former Consul of Rome and advisor to the Emperor." He opened the arm that held the fold of his toga and gave a short bow. "It is said your assistance was responsible for this glorious victory. Our Supreme Leader would like to acknowledge you."

Meagan wondered how carnage could be interpreted as glorious victory, but when the man held out his hand she took it. Warm fingers folded over hers and led her to the raised platform.

Emperor Trajan appraised her impassively. "Greeks are always interesting, are they not, Cornelius?"

"Yes, Caesar, though not always so entertaining."

Meagan stared into the black eyes of the man seated above. No detail in appearance was notable in any way, yet palpable tension surrounded him. In the sudden silence she realized that his statement was a compliment. "Thank you, Caesar," she said quickly.

"My Master of Horse tells me you played some part in today's triumph. He arrived before the race and said there was a change due to a slave-girl's notion. We have not heard the details but I look on this victory as rain after a drought."

Tacitus gave Meagan's hand a squeeze. "Yes, Caesar," she answered.

Cheering erupted outside the platform and spread across the stadium. Tittering and excited clapping grew around her. An escort of green-sashed men in bronze breastplates marched onto the platform, eyes forward. Behind them strode an angry-faced Braedin.

Tacitus dropped Meagan's hand to join the applause as a path cleared for the Emperor's driver. Eyes hard and focused, Braedin walked past Meagan without acknowledgement. She could see the Master of Horse waving desperately to get Braedin's attention, but the driver ignored him in the heat of his emotion. He came to stand before the Emperor, bowing as his ovation died.

"My driver." The Emperor's speech stifled the last applause. "How pleasant to greet you in victory."

"The honor humbles me, great Caesar. I pray forgiveness for this one episode. It was a mistake and will not be repeated."

The Emperor's face clouded. "Mistake?"

"I knew nothing of this. I could not prevent it."

"Prevent what ... victory?" The Emperor's soft voice hardened. "Are you mocking me?"

"No, my Emperor! Victory is ever your rightful possession."

"Then say what you mean, driver. Do not depend on such recent favor."

Braedin lowered his head. "Racing with the eunuch was advice given in ignorance and taken in ignorance. I was too late to prevent it, Supreme Leader."

"The eunuch?" The Emperor looked to those standing beside him. "What is my driver saying?"

The Master of Horse scampered forward to stand beside Braedin. "Glorious Trajan, your esteemed driver is saying that a *eunuch* horse pulled in the team today! It was a trick of the slave." He pointed to Meagan. "She mentioned the idea to me and of *course* I forbade it. I would permit no such dishonor to you, great Caesar. She fooled a simple guard into replacing one of your fine stallions. This was *treason*."

The Emperor's expression darkened as he listened. "One of my team was a eunuch?"

The platform was silent. Posthumous' arm remained outstretched and accusing. Meagan felt herself shrinking. She had committed the worst crime of the times: she had embarrassed an Emperor.

Trajan turned to her. "This was your idea?"

Meagan trembled under the black eyes. "It was the only way to win, sir," she said in a small voice.

The Emperor's eyebrow eased a trifle. He could appreciate expediency. "And it was worth my disgrace?" The voice was softly menacing. "Take care, the next words could be your last..."

Meagan swallowed. "Sir, is it a disgrace if your team is better than the others?"

The Emperor shifted in his seat, glancing at his attendants. His smirk passed to other lips. A murmur started, a chuckle and finally laughter. Meagan was not sure of the joke, but made herself stand straight among the stares. Perhaps her "crime" was forgiven...

"So, my Cerberus has gained a noble partner in victory. Such an exception requires sacrifice. Mars requires it." The Emperor flipped a finger and guards surrounded Meagan. She felt a stab of fear as her hands were roughly tied by the Emperor's guards. The surrounding people watched in obedience to the first rule of the imperial citizen: stand idly by.

Meagan held her voice steady and did not struggle. It was all a mistake. "Emperor, sir—"

"*Enough!*" Trajan snapped. Hissing from his attendants filled the air.

Meagan froze in silent realization: decadent Rome sought conquest through conflict, not cooperation. Horace had been mistaken about the worthy judgment of his rulers. Boos were being shouted from the stormy acres of spectators. The woman seated beside the Emperor cleared her throat. "Brother, it might please the crowd if they could see the slave..."

"I do not feel like pleasing the mob today, sister," Trajan replied testily.

"Remember your promise? Blood ruins the tiles, and they were just redone."

"*Bah!* Very well!" Trajan barked impatiently, "Take the slave down and put her in view of the people!"

The crowd's tone simmered as Meagan was led out. The Emperor's sister called a hard command after the guards: "She may remain standing!"

Meagan was propelled through a corridor of patrician's eyes. She was taken down the privileged steps and into the dark passageways under the stadium. Torches made flickering shadows as they marched through damp darkness.

Meagan entered the Circus floor bound and flanked by guards. She was taken to the edge of the track. The crowd began twirling garments and reaching for her with wide fingers: a foolish people, in thrall to the power they sustained. A people who had surrendered their commonwealth and their peace, surrendered their liberty ... and ultimately their humanity.

Promise, you have to come now! Meagan thought desperately, feeling herself grow numb with fear. Commercial chariots entered to customary booing. They passed before her, one after the other, close enough to feel the rumble of their passing. Politicians stood beside the charioteers, ducking.

The crowd's roar started at one end of the stadium valley and built into a deafening cheer. Trumpets sounded an entry processional as soldiers uncrossed their swords in synchronicity. Percussion boomed as banners for the victorious Imperial Quadriga unfurled above the entrance. The dark head of a horse flipped above the marching men.

Clammy terror enveloped Meagan as the Imperial horses circled their victory lap. Cerberus plunged beside Helios, nostrils wide and red. The horses were pitching with the rising emotion in the stadium. The crowd's clamor rose to hysteria as the Emperor stood and raised his hand to the turbulent crowd. A shock of cries descended upon the track. Cerberus reared, his whirlwind of mane circling like black flame. Saxon scrambled in his harness as Helios and Ajax held the yoke.

Now, Promise. It has to be right now.

Thousands of voices shook the mortar of the stadium and fevered spectators rushed the track and clashed with soldiers. Guards scattered to meet the onrush. The Imperial chariot lurched as Saxon shied and broke formation, leading his teammates in a charge. Men scattered from their path as the horses accelerated.

Meagan saw the galloping darkness come, but the crowd was growing more distant. The stride of the horses was slowing to still frames in sequence. Time was beginning to shudder. The cries and the crowd's noise stretched into a long roar. Four sculpted heads thrashed against their pull. No one pointed, no one seemed to see the transformation.

The Great Horse comes to men once more...

Wings rose amidst the galloping horses, rising high and unfolding, brightening to shining white as Helios rose from his traces. A gust swirled around Meagan as the winged horse swept overhead. Stallions' screams echoed as the chariot consumed the ground where she stood.

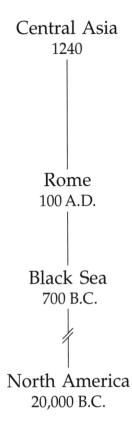

Central Asia
1240

Rome
100 A.D.

Black Sea
700 B.C.

North America
20,000 B.C.

Damsel

NOTHING HARMLESS FEELS so much like dying as having one's breath well and truly knocked out. Heaving for air without result, Meagan fought panic as she waited for a breath. When it finally came, she leaned onto her hands and panted in great gulps.

Sounds of men came through the darkness, their speech fast and urgent. Meagan steadied her breathing and listened as words rose and fell around her, foreign words spoken in crisp, rapid strokes. The voices approached and hands gripped the fabric of her tunic, inspecting, pulling at the folds and letting them go.

A light colored horse was led forward, a faint apparition glowing in the darkness. Meagan reached out a hand and ran it along familiar contours. It was a pony, a short but fully grown equine. She was lifted and pushed onto the pony's back, where she instinctively reached for the reins lying low on the animal's neck. The stadium and chariots had evaporated into the night air. The last Meagan remembered was the rush of white wings, and the world seemed to melt and reassemble into new solid forms. Now Rome was a memory.

A knot of horsemen rode past Meagan. She could see faces in the light of the torches they carried, Asian faces, parched and grim in the flickering redness. Her pony mount swished its tail impatiently, and Meagan automatically reached to pat the animal's shoulder. Her hand felt an irregular patch in the hair, and she leaned over to see. Branded on the shoulder, barely visible in the torchlight, was a crescent symbol over a circle.

Now voices were receding into the night. Meagan allowed the pony to join the sound of hoof beats flowing through the warm darkness. All she cared to know was that she had moved closer to her own time—so far, there was no evidence. One thing was certain: she was not yet back home.

The group cantered miles before dawn broke. A glorious, cloudless sunrise could be seen over Meagan's shoulder, though she was too out-of-sorts to appreciate scenery.

The sky is as empty as the landscape, she thought irritably. If these people were riding through the middle of nowhere, they rode through it with purpose. There was no stopping for items as trivial as food or water. Meagan's saddle possessed a single skin canteen of water, which she had ineptly doused over her face and clothes while attempting a drink.

Meagan had a complaint, or rather a series of them. There seemed to be no rules to this legend, and it was very disorienting to keep changing places and time periods, to say nothing of being snatched away at the last possible moment—was it to be a deathmatch every time? *This is the worst possible legend,* Meagan told herself, sulking. It was more like a curse. *Of course, I could have listened to Mrs. Bridgestone,* added an unwelcome thought. She pushed it away.

The memory of Rome haunted her and even the brisk rushing air could not cleanse it. Meagan was still in disbelief that the Great Horse had been Helios. Nothing made sense. There must be another Great Horse in whatever place she had come to. She ran her hand down the bristly mane of her mount. *Could the Great Horse be a pony?*

When the other riders spoke, of course it was a language she could not understand. Also, Meagan was out of practice and the pony's backbone was growing more distinct with each passing mile. She could not guess how the group of horsemen knew their way. The land was nothing except rolling grass in all directions. A line of dark clouds hugged the hazy horizon ahead, offering the hope of cool rain. Uncharacteristically, she thought dismounting would be the best relief.

Strangely, though, on closer inspection it seemed the bottom of the clouds hung *below* the horizon. Meagan's pony suddenly raised her head and whinnied into the wind, and hundreds of answers echoed across the empty grassland. The trumpeting of horses filled the open plain as if the land ahead were welcoming them.

Riding on, Meagan could see the approaching black cloud was actually an enormous congregation of horses and riders spreading across the horizon, waves of bobbing movement stretching beyond sight. In all directions a herd of free horses nipped the beaten earth. Dust rose in a column that clouded the sun to a dull orange ball.

The air thickened with dust and scent as they rode closer. A tremendous sound of insects' buzzing met them at the edge of the moving population. Meagan drew her tunic over her face until only the barest slit enabled her to see, and brushed away flies that boldly crawled in to find her eyes and mouth. Horse tails flicked in concert around her.

All of the sea of equines were pony-sized, with shaggy coats and brushy manes. Meagan shielded her eyes to look over the endless congregation of weathered people riding in loose jackets and pants. A tall, dark thoroughbred would be easy to pick out, but of course was nowhere to be seen.

Little spurs of grass began to appear on the flat ground, sprigs not yet trampled into dust. As Meagan's group passed into the main body of the herd, campsites appeared with horses staked in rows, grazing and swishing flies. Meagan's group halted and she felt herself being watched. The glances were not threatening; other females were present. Various races were represented among the people, including Europeans. Even so, she wished for anonymity and wrapped her slave's tunic close around her, thankful the dust had transformed it to the universal khaki.

When Meagan opened her eyes, her first thought was she had been beaten. Heavily. A horn sounded at close proximity and pain blossomed throughout her body in an amazing bouquet. *Maybe I was run over by a chariot after all*, she thought, wincing.

Others were sitting up and stretching. All around her, lines of horses were being groomed and tacked. Meagan groaned to think of getting on a horse. The mere effort to sit up made her gasp. A bow-legged man was walking through the camp knocking pallets of late sleepers. "No, thank you," Meagan told him. "No riding today."

She flinched as the man kicked her pallet. He pointed to the line of horses. "Targ ha!"

"Yes, good morning," she said politely. "I am really quite sore."

"Targ *ha!*"

"Thank you for understanding." Clenching her teeth, Meagan kept herself well wrapped as she stood.

"Aieeee!" The man grasped Meagan's thin tunic and dropped it in disgust. He stamped away and returned to thrust a packet of clothes into her arms. She was sent to dress behind a curtain of skins. Worn boots sailed over the top.

The standard set of garments was loose trousers and a coat with a flaring skirt and long sleeves. The coat's front fabric was crossed and tied. Meagan studied the crude tailoring. Her abiding hope was that she was traveling forward and not to someplace older than Rome, but she still could find no reassurance.

She stepped timidly from behind the skins. There was no need to be self-conscious, for no one was looking. The camp was a bustling hive of activity: she was only to conform and not ask questions, and her anonymity was assured.

Surveying the field of small horses, Meagan was unsure which mount was hers. She limped after the bow-legged man. "Excuse me, which—"

"*Targ ha!*" The man shouted, and exploded into a string of words that were not enlightening in the least.

Meagan smiled and retreated. She listened as a bent man, somewhere between aged and ancient, whistled to the vast herd grazing behind the camps. As the note went from low to high, several horses picked up their heads and trotted into camp. Men and women swarmed over them as they arrived, checking the animals for injuries before tacking up.

"Targ ha!" the bow-legged man shouted again, right behind Meagan. The man took her arm and propelled her toward one of the horses tied on the line.

"Yes, I see. Targa. Thank you, you have been very helpful." She rubbed her arm. The offered animal certainly *looked* like the pony she had ridden yesterday. Of course, so did fifty or eighty thousand others. Meagan walked around the horse to see if it was a mare—it was. Good, she had been riding a mare. Also, the animal had the identical crescent brand on her shoulder, though that proved nothing. All the camp's horses had the same brand.

When the little mare was not watching Meagan, her gaze seemed fixed on a distant horizon. Her pony-sized ears were cocked at an ill-tempered angle. There was a small nick in her right ear, and suddenly Meagan knew. After staring at that nick for hours, it was imprinted on her brain exactly.

"You *are* Targa!" She reached to stroke the pony's neck, but the little mare laid back her ears and snapped. *Lovely attitude,* Meagan thought as she looked the mare over. The mare's small ears flipped back and forth as if she were inspecting Meagan, too, and taking a dim view of what she saw. The pony was a sandy brown color and sprouted a bristly mane from both sides of her neck. Her legs were short and thin beneath a shaggy coat: a standard issue pony and not very friendly. "Good girl. Don't bite and we will get along fine."

"Aieeee!"

Meagan flinched to hear another call from her tormentor. The man approached, this time carrying a flimsy saddle that seemed hardly more than a device to hook the crude horn stirrups onto. She beamed to see it: stirrups were not invented until after Roman times—finally here was evidence she *was* moving closer to home!

She copied her neighbors and began tacking up the pony, avoiding the mare's peevish nips and stamping feet. Though seemingly an insignificant detail, the stirrups of Meagan's saddle were one of three equestrian innovations that changed history. The first great advance of horsemanship had been the bit and bridle, which replaced nose rings and transformed skulking nomadic tribes into invincible raiders. The second major innovation was the horseshoe—an iron-shod horse can cross miles of rocky ground that would splinter a bare hoof, making possible far-flung battlefield campaigns and long-distance communications. (Roman horsemen experimented with iron "hipposandals" lashed to hooves using cord, until it was discovered a metal plate could be nailed painlessly and securely to the dead outer horn.)

The straggly stirrups on Meagan's assigned saddle looked to be a puny afterthought. They were indeed an afterthought, but a powerful one, for the third of the great cavalry inventions was the stirrup. This obvious addition to a saddle—indeed the seeming purpose for one—did not appear until well into the Dark Ages. The stirrup revolutionized war, for it allowed a rider to withstand shock without being thrown and to swing a sword without becoming dislodged. With stirrups to brace him, the impact of a knight's own lance did not knock him backwards off his horse. Stirrups were the millennium's most transforming military invention, and they were born on the plains of Asia.

> *I hear an army charging upon the land,*
> *And the thunder of horses plunging, foam about their knees...*
>
> *- James Joyce (1882-1941)*

MEAGAN FELT HERSELF floating. *I must be moving again,* she half-dreamed. *To somewhere else, another time ... maybe I am home. Home!*

A fly landed on her nose. It was a horrible disappointment to open her eyes and see people sitting on their mats beside lines of tied horses. She and the vast company had ridden the entire day and well into the night. Meagan tried to sit up, but pain shot through every muscle. She was sure she felt a twitch in her eyelids.

She sleepily watched two men arguing. Apparently there was a question of ownership of a certain pony, since both men gripped the animal's reins and neither would let go. Each took turns yanking the bridle to illustrate his point until the pony soundly bit one of them. Meagan sat up at the man's cry. The pony looked suddenly familiar.

Painfully she stood and marched up to the men. "Pardon me, but I think there is some mistake. This is *my* pony, Targa."

A booming voice made Meagan jump. The bow-legged wake-up man was coming. For once she was happy to see him, for he knew the truth. She expected to be handed the reins; instead, the man led Meagan away by the sleeve to an ancient, decrepit pack pony. *"Targ ha!"* the man shouted. She had been unceremoniously reassigned to another horse. Disappointingly "Targa" was not even the pony's name, but only a verb, or at best a noun.

Meagan felt reprimanded for imagining that she, a mere woman, could have claim over property desired by a man. She bent to greet her new horse, though "new" was a description hard to apply to the aged beast. "Are *you* the Great Horse?" she asked doubtfully. The animal bore her greeting with the interest he would have shown a bundle of sticks.

Meanwhile, the two men reached a conclusion over possession of the pony she had dubbed Targa. The victorious claimant tossed the reins across the mare's neck and threw his leg over with practiced ease. With equal ease, Targa twisted away and dropped him onto the ground.

People stopped and stared. The man covered his embarrassment by leaping to his feet and grabbing the pony roughly by the reins. Using a time-honored technique for mounting difficult horses, he tightened the outer rein, bending the mare's neck so she could only step toward him. Targa knew the trick too, and she moved under the man so quickly he slid over the other side.

A fall among these people was uncommon, particularly one from a standing mount. A crowd was gathering.

From where Meagan stood beside the pack animal, she could plainly see her former pony was in a sour mood from being abused during the argument and was not interested in being ridden. The best thing to do was find a treat for the mare and walk her out quietly. Instead, the man found a switch and laid it sharply along the mare's side.

Seeing the mare's ears lie back, Meagan almost felt sorry for the man. He did not have the opportunity to yank the reins again. As he held the rough leather straps, Targa struck, seizing the man under his arm. The man wrenched free and collapsed in the dirt, holding his side.

The second man came forward now, ready to claim his prize by default. The pony mare flattened her ears and swished her tail. The man lunged in and grasped her reins tightly. He looked at his audience to make sure they were observing the *proper* way to mount a troublesome horse, and lifted his leg an infinitesimal degree before Targa's hind hoof struck his left calf. The man went down with a cry.

Another man started forward hesitantly. The pony cocked a leg in anticipation and the man stepped back into the crowd. Everyone turned to look at Meagan. The wake-up man gave her a short nod.

"Oh, sure. *Now* she's mine." When Meagan took a step, the mare shifted ominously. A field of spectator's eyes waited expectantly. Meagan stopped with an idea. She bent down and pulled a handful of grass—her old game with Promise—and held it out.

Targa laid her ears back. Meagan watched carefully: a mare in this temper was unpredictable. Horses have a sense of fair treatment, and the pony's had been violated.

"Hello, Targa," Meagan said sweetly. "What did I name you, I wonder? 'Get over here' or 'stupid girl,' probably." She stopped well in front of the mare to avoid crowding her. "You don't seem much in the mood for a ride. Me either. See, we have that much in common."

Like all horses, Targa had a photographic memory. She remembered Meagan quite well. The mare had never before been ridden by someone who did not kick or yank as a matter of routine. Targa stretched her neck and took the crushed grass. Meagan bent down for another handful. The mare sniffed the second offering of grass and blew it out of Meagan's hand. Meagan let Targa smell her.

The pony's tiny ears twitched forward, signaling the mare's change of mood. Disappointed, the crowd began dissolving into their normal routines. Targa stamped her foot in irritation at whatever was taking Meagan so long to mount.

As days and miles passed, Meagan's soreness subsided and new loneliness settled in. Memories of Horace took on a rosy glow while those of Braedin faded into a lesson. At least she could communicate with the Romans, who were, after all, her own culture's fatally flawed ancestors. Alone in a sea of harsh faces, Meagan almost missed the infuriations of Rome. Almost.

To make matters more unpleasant, the days were filled with dust and swarming insects. Her hair was a tortured mess and she was sunburned and sore. *I hope the Great Horse doesn't know what I am thinking,* Meagan grumbled to herself. The unanswered question was, *why was she here?* She had to believe she would see her family again. If there was a reason for the journey, she could not detect it—but instead of looking back sadly at home she would look ahead to it. As with riding, plan and adjust. With thoughts like these she let her mount's gentle rhythm pass the miles beneath her.

The pony mare was quite a reasonable ride once mounted. Targa had a natural desire to go forward, and her workmanlike conduct reminded Meagan of her best former competitive mounts. The pony's trot was a low vibrating ride and her canter flowed over the ground. Meagan had always liked ponies, and the little mare was everything she remembered and missed about her childhood mounts. Of course, the way her feet hung below Targa's girth would have been considered ridiculous back home.

A pony is a fully grown equine that never exceeds fifty-eight inches measured to the top of the backbone. Though equines, ponies are different than horses. While some are cranky and mischievous, ponies are also courageous and sensible about their well-being. Many children instinctively want a pony and in this case children are wise. Equines and children have a special bond, and good ponies are natural teachers who take excellent care of their young cargo.

It fascinated Meagan to watch the horses being summoned each morning. It was usually the same old man who called, and when he cupped his hands and blew his whistle, heads popped up throughout the ranging herd. Some horses came immediately; others took longer, snatching last mouthfuls of grass as they came.

Each band had its own call, and each foal was trained at its mother's side as to which call was its own. Meagan practiced her camp's whistle, imitating the low-to-high pitch. Targa was always one of the first to answer, coming with head high and nostrils flared, snapping impatiently at loafers moving too slowly.

Two things were always in demand: firewood and water. Meagan enjoyed the daily expeditions to hunt for supplies, conducted in slow gallops across vast stretches of plain. She soon found the landscape was not featureless as she had first thought, but rather too subtle for eyes accustomed to manmade structures. She began to notice undulations and colors in the emptiness, and to see the variety and richness of the plains.

Occasional puffs of dust appeared in the landscape, puffs that grew into riders wrapped up like mummies. These were messengers that galloped into and out of the horde, running from horizon to horizon, providing a lifeline of communication to the world. With growing respect, Meagan realized these were not mere wanderers but true nomads. This was a nation on horseback, a laughing, squabbling realm.

Whether hitting a goat skin in a game played like polo or running a spontaneous race, a serious edge underlay the fun. The nomads had given up their lives to the horse and in return had become superhuman. The people could survive for a time without food, but they could not survive without horses. Every rider groomed and fed his mount before taking his own meal, which include dried meat and barbeque, as well as fermented mare's milk, something Meagan tasted only once.

Gradually Meagan learned the different camps, knowing them by their banners. The entire mass was an assembly of such camps, and each had a place within the larger whole. The vast majority of people were of Asian descent, but there was an in-mix of Europeans, Turks and Arabs as well. Women were somewhat respected in this mobile society, and Meagan found a romantic current of shared destiny in these people. The rhythms that bound them marched to hoof beats and were measured in miles.

Meagan knew little of Asian horsemanship, but she did know that in her own time, of a world equine population over seventy million, ten million horses lived in China alone. Nomads from that region once held history's largest land empire—from the Sea of Japan to Western Europe—and they did it on horseback.

Hast thou given the horse strength?
Hast thou clothed his neck with thunder?

Canst thou make him afraid as a grasshopper?
The glory of his nostrils is terrible.

He paweth in the valley, and rejoiceth in his strength.
He goeth on to meet the armed men.

He mocketh at fear, and is not affrighted;
neither turneth he back from the sword.

The quiver rattleth against him, the glittering spear and the shield.
He swalloweth the ground with fierceness and rage...

- Holy Bible, Job 39:19-24

Meagan sensed excitement in the camp. An undercurrent ran through the people and the horses pranced nervously. Throwing her saddle pad over Targa, she saw something had been added: an odd-looking pole now hung from a loop of leather on her saddle. Then she saw the sharp point and realized she had been given a spear.

Leaders rode through the lines of horses, each with a string of knives hanging from one arm. Meagan took one and examined it, confused. The others were sliding theirs into belt pouches. It seemed a dangerous place to carry a knife, but she did the same.

Horn answered horn throughout the camps. A rippling change went through the horse nation. The few not yet mounted swung aboard. Meagan's group moved out. The camp leaders rode ahead, each holding a blazing torch.

The pitch of the horns was changing, signaling back and forth down the black mass of horsemen covering the plain. The tight lines of the nomads were dissolving into chaos, melting and running in streaks. Horses were breaking from easy canters into

full gallops. When the call reached Meagan's group, Targa
sprang forward, her legs stretching in exhilaration of the run.

One in a sea of horsemen, Meagan saw buildings of a
settlement ahead. Tendrils of smoke rose pale against the clear
sky. A shrill scream rose. At first she thought the cry came from
the town. Then she saw the spreading blackness of horsemen
and knew worse.

Meagan checked Targa when she saw the tide of torches reach
the town like a flow of lava exploding everything in its path.
The stream of nomads swirled thickly around points of resistance. Horses crowded Targa and pushed her into the mob.
There was no way to stop as all sides closed in and pulled them
forward. Screams of horses gave voice to the terror around her.

She and Targa swam through the men and horses. The ground
was no longer visible below. They flowed with the current into
the center of the town. Looking at the faces of her fellow riders,
Meagan saw there was no fear—only hatred and greed and the
raw flush of victorious emotion. She had never known triumph
could be ugly.

Warmth splashed across Targa's neck, and Meagan's left side
was suddenly slick with others' blood. Her reins slipped and
Targa plunged forward, wading through the pack of flailing
men. Meagan's legs were scraped backward—she had to pull
them up to avoid being dragged off the pony's back. Fires were
starting all around them. The morning had become hell, the nomads its demons.

The river of horseman poured through the settlement.
Meagan tried to pull Targa to the side to avoid a pileup ahead.
She urged the mare toward a side path but the flow carried
them beyond. Horses were coming in behind, overwhelming
her. Bucking in the thickening brawl, Targa was pressed against
a building. A knot of men on foot clubbed their way forward
and a horse wheeled away, falling against Targa and bringing
her down. Meagan slid hard against the wooden wall, scraped
between the wood and her struggling mare. Her arm fell free
into open space, and she pulled herself off the pony and through
the opening of a doorway.

Inside, she watched the wall shudder with the weight of horses trapped against it. Meagan jumped away as one board splintered, then another. Backing behind a table, she heard a whimper and turned to see two children crouched under a crudely made chair. They were boys, hardly more than toddlers. Meagan made a move to comfort them but they flinched away, huddling tighter. She stopped, realizing that she was the enemy.

The wall was coming apart. A section bowed in. Beyond it Meagan saw her mare lying on her side, the top of her hindquarters trapped underneath another horse. Targa was kicking in her efforts to rise, but the mare could not move her head and lay helplessly whinnying.

Meagan wrapped her arms around her knees and screamed into the inferno around her. Targa thrashed against the dirt in desperation. Meagan felt sick, knowing she should put the horse out of her misery; sicker to remember there was a knife in her belt to do it with. She crawled toward the mare and reached out a hand to smooth the dirt from the pony's face.

The mare was lying on her own reins, making it impossible to raise her head and get up. Meagan was furious with herself for not thinking of it. She pulled the straps from under Targa's head and instantly the horse was scrambling to her feet and kicking her way free.

Meagan pulled the pony away from the chaos and led her over the broken boards into the room. She left Targa and went to the cowering boys, roughly tearing strips from her clothes. It was only knowing they would surely die otherwise that enabled her to tie the children together forcibly, back to front. The boys did not struggle as she lifted them onto Targa's back. Meagan led the pony to the back door and pushed it open.

Men and horses ran in open streets. Meagan guided the boys' hands to Targa's neck, making sure they clenched tightly to the mane. Whooping bands on horseback whirled through the dying settlement slashing all that would not burn. The town was engulfed in riot. Meagan mounted and clutched the two boys in front of her as the pony jogged through the chaos.

They were passed on all sides by galloping madmen silhouetted black against their inferno. Meagan dared not dismount, for anyone on foot was marked for slaughter. The children sat huddled and still, with only their tears giving any sign they were alive. A horseman's fluttering banner was held high in the wind, mimicking the flames around her. Chilling screams of *"Genghis!"* hissed around them. Meagan squeezed the boys softly. She no longer wondered why other races lived among the nomads.

Meagan knew something of the name, Genghis Khan. The good news was that hearing the name gave solid proof she was, in fact, moving closer to her own time. The bad news was everything else.

In the first years of the thirteenth century, the squabbling nomadic tribes of Mongolia found a leader. United under their great Khan, the Asian hordes rode again as in previous centuries, leaving flames and desolation in their horses' dust.

Under Genghis, the Mongolians battered and broke the Great Wall set against them by their northern neighbor, China. Sweeping through India and Turkey, they struck far into the Holy Lands and laid waste to Russia. Sacking Baghdad, descendents of Genghis dealt with a common superstition about shedding a caliph's blood by rolling the hapless man in a carpet and having him trampled by horses.

The Mongolians at their zenith held the greatest land empire in the history of the world, reaching from the eastern shores of China to Western Europe. The Mongols sent an armada against Japan, but that nation was spared when the Mongolian fleet was destroyed by a hurricane—which the Japanese afterward named their "divine wind," or *kamikaze*.

The eyes of Genghis' sons turned west. The Black Horde plundered through Poland, laying siege to and destroying Russia's Golden Kiev in December of 1240. Before the frost of the following year, they would be camped outside the walls of Vienna.

———

Meagan came to learn other truths about the nomad horde. The constant low rumbling of thousands of hooves was an echo of doom: their column of dust darkened more than the sun. Settlements that surrendered were pillaged; settlements that did not were massacred. Riders near the front made the attack, leaving those trailing to ride past scorched remnants. Gruesome pyramids of human skulls marked those who resisted.

And yet, every day, the horses were brought to clean pastures to be fed and rubbed down while children played and men joked.

When Meagan's group galloped to attack, others were so eager they never noticed she rode to the sides to avoid the fight. But she could never escape entirely. In one attack, Meagan veered to escape the main fight. Turning a corner, Targa slid to a stop. A group of fleeing men cowered, looking up with hand-covered faces. They did not see death coming behind them, the nomads with short spears held high. Meagan wheeled and galloped away and did not look back.

She saw too much. At first Meagan tried to save children, swooping them from the street. But this only brought the children into slavery, and soon more prisoners were being taken than the nomads wanted. When the children she had tried to save began falling under knives at sunset, she stopped. She could block out most memories, but not all.

Memory had become Meagan's enemy. Her dreams were now nightmares. She survived in small steps, from moment to moment, veering from fresh-seen atrocities to remembered shreds of old ones. Brief instants of gentle sanity such as Targa's nicker, or even a cleansing breeze, became islands in the madness to be cherished and nurtured into hope.

The horses were instruments. But though the war ponies of Genghis Khan were taught to attack, they never learned malice. During battle Targa might lunge at helpless villagers, but when Meagan pulled away the mare obeyed without question or regret. When it was over, Targa whinnied and nuzzled Meagan for treats. The horses were innocents.

The army sped its pace now, leaving the camps behind. Horses were rotated, turned out into the roving herd behind them and exchanged for others. Meagan rode Targa during the day, setting her loose to graze at night and recalling her in the morning. She rode other horses on night treks, but it was always Targa that came to the morning whistle.

Seldom now did anyone dismount. Only delicacy moved Meagan to find shelter for rest stops; most simply urinated from horseback. Meals were eaten in the saddle, and in time she became used to catching snatches of sleep while her pony jogged across the miles.

Once-enjoyable forays now became grim spy missions. On each ride Meagan prayed they would find deserted fields, but the countryside was becoming populated and seldom did an expedition fail to find another victim to pillage.

There were more hills now, and brush and scraggy trees. Most settlements on the edge of the grasslands were tiny, with only ten or twenty families scraping an existence from the thin soil. These were wiped out in the rush of a single division. Larger towns were given the chance to be sacked without loss of life—a chance regretted if not taken. The Mongol's purpose for holding prisoners of other races was soon made clear: they were fodder for the front lines.

There could be no resistance to a galloping wave of horsemen launching arrows from all directions, except perhaps to wait out the onslaught in an impervious fortress. Meagan realized that walled medieval castles were more practical than she had once thought.

From the top of a rise she could watch the moving nation on horseback spreading across the plains further than could be seen. In what had first appeared to be a teeming mass she now saw purpose and structure. Open spaces were corridors of supply lines, like arteries in a living creature. Before the black throng of horsemen lay clean grassland—after it, lifeless desolation. The Horde moved across the plain like a dark, seeping creature.

On a clear morning that smelled like early summer, Meagan's camp was sent to scout ahead. They had not cantered far when Meagan saw a flash of color fluttering in the bright sun. Nomad riders pulled up around her as Meagan stared.

A band of men rode along a distant dirt road, mounted on heavy horses much larger than the nomads' ponies. Their reins were beribboned and they wore helmets. The men wore linked mail rather than shining armor, but they could not be anything else: Meagan had seen her first knights.

The Mongolian riders circled and galloped on, giving the knights a wide berth. She looked back in fascination as long as the heavy horses were in sight.

Coming over a ridge, Meagan's party met a wide river flowing brown between sandy shores. Birds flew overhead in the trees lining the bank. The leader turned to trot down the banks. A path was beaten alongside the river, and it dipped into a hollow filled with trees and denser vegetation.

She saw motion. People were coming down the path. Five or six were on foot, but Meagan had time to notice only the two on horseback: a lady and a man. The woman was draped in a soft cloth of light blue; the man wore crimson clothing and a cap. A single red-dyed feather arced forward over his head.

The nomads gave a cry as their horses leapt forward. The people on foot fled down the bank toward the river. Some nomads galloped headlong through underbrush to intercept the men on foot, as others rushed the woman and the man on horseback. The woman fell from her mount with a scream that was quickly silenced. The man was killed where he sat, still urging his heavy horse forward. Screams and splashes from the riverbank told the end of the story.

The nomads stripped the slain people. The heavy mounts were judged too slow and released. The leader of the troop trotted from the trees surrounding the hollow and gave a shout. He pointed into the distance.

A town was ahead, the largest yet seen. Buildings of two and three stories crowded behind stone walls alongside the river. A low bridge swarming with ant-like people jutted from the city. Adjacent fields framed the town with squat huts—huts, Meagan knew from experience, that burned easily.

A nomad rode up beside her, a man Meagan knew for his polite manners and quick smile. Around his horse's neck hung a cord used for souvenirs of war. On it was strung a new prize: a small human ear. Gore, stamped with a woman's earring.

Meagan looked away. The city beside the river seemed utterly peaceful ... and vulnerable. She realized her chance. Saying nothing she casually pushed through the nomads onto the open road toward the settlement. Once free of the band she suddenly lay her leg on Targa.

She looked back only once. The surprised Mongolian patrol stood looking after her in confusion. It occurred to Meagan that they looked like mere boys on shaggy ponies, harmless.

No man ought to looke a given horse in the mouth.

- John Heywood (1497-1580)

THE CITY'S BASE was raised earth, with ramps leading to open gates. Men shouted from the top of the wall, and a troop of horsemen cantered out of the main gate to meet Meagan. Each wore a bright red tunic draped in chain mail and carried a shield and sword.

Meagan slowed Targa and waited. She stroked the pony's thick mane nervously. *Finally*, she thought, *civilized people.* The knights rode huge, powerfully muscled horses so different from Targa they could have been different animals. The chests of the knight's horses were broad enough to lay the flat of a shovel between their forelegs, whereas Targa's slender chest could hardly accommodate a hand. The pony mare was a terrier confronting a pack of bulldogs.

Meagan held up a friendly hand as the men drew close, and did not react when two of the riders leveled dull-pointed wooden lances. One point glanced off her shoulder and the other caught her ribs, spinning Meagan over Targa's croup and onto the ground. She lay stunned in the dirt, too dazed to move.

The men circled and grabbed Targa's reins. Meagan tried to stand, but another blow came and she hit the ground with her chin. A forest of horses' hooves moved around her as she listened to the unintelligible voices.

Her arms were yanked backward and bound by cord. After weeks spent on horseback it was disorienting to walk, but she was forced to stagger up the road to the town she had hoped to save.

The sun seemed to fall behind a cloud as they approached the gates of the city. The stench was worse than the nomad camps, worse even than the squalid valleys of Rome. Meagan was pushed along a rutted, muddy street through man- and animal-made puddles, and into a courtyard surrounded by buildings of oversized hewn beams. She was dragged to a set of stocks mounted along one end of the courtyard. Heavy iron clasped over her head.

"I am trying to save you!" she protested, her face mashed into the beam. Metal burrs sliced small wounds into her neck. "*Please* listen or we are all going to die! *Listen to me!*"

"Oh ho, 'tis ferly! Have someone say die?"

Meagan stopped pleading. She was almost sure she had heard English.

A man stepped up and squatted, peering into her face. A blast of noxious breath billowed over her. "So said verily, this Tatar be a she." The words were thick, beyond the thickest brogue or British cockney she had ever heard. O's were ah's and ah's were o's—but it was *English.* "You be of England?" the man exhaled. "Answer."

"Yes, sir, I—" Meagan's feet were abruptly swept out from under her. The iron dug into her neck as she scrambled to stand. Shouts and arguing boiled around her.

"*Belay!*" bellowed the English-speaking man. He crouched near Meagan. "Unwittily said."

"This is *very* ungrateful," she mumbled to the beam. The metal felt imbedded in the back of her skull.

"They not like aliens, these." The man leaned his breath closer. "It be not them what decides." He smiled, showing colors of yellow, black and brown. "I was alien beforetimes, and English as you be. Now I be *they* maister. I be Marshal." The man nodded to the others. "The Tatar wench be mine. We gluppen and speak."

Men came forward and released the iron clasps. For the first time Meagan was able to face her captors. Like the nomads they were unwashed, but where the skin of a nomad was clear and smooth, the faces of these men were bearded and blemished. Their clothing was varied and colorful, but it fit less well than the nomads' clothing and was less well kept. Like their city, these men looked better from a distance.

The English speaker indicated for Meagan to follow him across the courtyard and up a flight of uneven stairs. They arrived on a platform overlooking the city's wall. Men sat at tables taking meals. When the Englishman offered Meagan a place on a bench she hesitated.

"Make shrift," the man said roughly. "What journey brings you?"

"I-I came to warn you an army is coming. There is not much time."

"Be you a Tatar?" the man asked.

"Pardon me? I don't understand."

"You wear Tatar clothes. You ride a Tatar horse. For the nones, say thou be not a Tatar!"

"I was captured and I escaped," she said plainly. "I am telling the truth, an army is coming! They have seen your city!"

"Why would I take the word of a Tatar?"

"I told you I *escaped*. Please listen! If you do not resist they will leave you alive. I have seen it. You *must* surrender to them."

"You would have us lay down arms?" His voice dropped. "Had I these words sooner I would have left you pilloried, English or no. Others arrived beforetimes." The man strode to railing overlooking the city wall and pointed below. Meagan followed with foreboding.

Open fields surrounded the town. The horizon blurred into trees and hills, and behind it a dark column of dust rose like black smoke. A troop of knights stood in a loose formation around a band of perhaps twenty Mongolian ponies. Only one nomad sat upright—every other rider lay sideways and motionless across his mount.

The Englishman snorted. "Tatar messengers, asking for surrender." He gave a signal and a call went out. The knights parted ranks to let the single nomad pass. The man galloped away towards the horizon.

"You *killed* them?" she asked incredulously.

"Oh, ho, yes. For the nones, they die as other men."

"You can still escape," Meagan said urgently. "We have to leave now. There might be time to get away."

"Mayhaps. Or mayhaps I have your rusty bayard carry your body back, what the rats leave." The Englishman swaggered back to the table. Servants began to rush about, bringing out pitchers and bowls. "I have waited my bread long enough. To gluppen."

Meagan thought anxiously about rats and her 'rusty bayard.' A goblet filled with wine was set before her. She picked it up and drained it.

The man was delighted. "A witful act for a wench, such a draught! There be English in you still! Which be you, North or South?"

"Oh—I was—"

"I hail from South, therebefore. Long live King Henry the Third, if he lives. Could be Henry the Fourth now or Fifth, being I not seen the shores of England for fifteen years, nigh."

"Long live King Henry," Meagan said politely. Shaken and afraid, she still watched the approach of a well-cooked duck with interest. The roast was falling off its bones, held in place by carrots and other boiled vegetables surrounding it. She made an effort not to grab.

The Englishman winked. "Aghast are thee, alien, to think we men might pluck a likerous rose as you be?" His eyes wandered over Meagan but kept snapping up like a leashed hound jerked to attention. "Fear not lewid men. The Lord's word is counsel here."

Meagan swallowed, looking at the unsavory collection of people around her bearing limps, pockmarks, warts, and filmed-over eyes. Here she was a goddess of beauty.

"Enough the nonsense of surrender! It was not meant, so we talk of other things." The man took a handful of meat and chewed it, open-mouthed. "How best to skathe a Tatar be a matter. Tell us this."

Skuthe a Tatar? Meagan looked at the man. He wanted to know how to kill a nomad, but how could she make him understand? The coming army was too numerous, too fast and too seasoned. She could say that nomads struck from all sides, setting fires, wheeling away shooting arrows on the attack and the retreat.

She could tell this man his city was doomed, but his eyes said the truth would not be welcome.

Panic began pooling in Meagan's chest. If these people were not going to surrender, she had to escape. A thought came to her … if she could only get close enough to Targa. "I don't know about the Tatar *men*," she answered innocently. "But their horses have a weak spot. I could show you. Take me to any horse with a bridle on it, say … oh, the pony I was riding would be perfect. For a demonstration, I mean."

"So, the devils ride a tainted bayard! Oh, *ho!* 'Tis ferly never to have heard so." The man reached for his goblet. "Tell on."

Meagan breathed easier, pleased with herself. She would only need a head start. "It is a place on their horses' neck. If an arrow hits it, the horse—I mean *bayard*—dies instantly. I can show you. It would be better to do it outside the city, really. We will need some room."

"Nay, the courtyard below will serve. And we shall use your own Tatar bayard." Juices ran into the man's beard as he chewed his food. "My archers will aim where you show us and we shall see how it dies."

Meagan choked on her drink.

"How is this? I think you be glad to see the foul animal die!" The man leaned closer. "*If* you be a Tatar prisoner, as so you say."

"Well, of *course* I am," she sputtered, red-faced. "I … I was just disappointed the animal is still alive. The sooner she is eaten by crows, the sooner I can forget everything." She smiled weakly.

"Better this," the man grunted, and motioned to a guard. "Find the alien's bayard. To-luggid hither to the courtyard."

A horn sounded from below. It was taken up in quadrants all around the city, until the rooftop platform was surrounded by a chorus of trumpeting. The Englishman rushed to the railing and began shouting orders.

Meagan followed the confusion to the platform's edge. Knights were pouring out of the city gates below; already the fields were filled with their color. In the distance, on the edge of the horizon, a black flood could be seen flowing through the trees.

"They take not our answer." The Englishman gazed in satisfaction. "They shall see our manner of surrender."

Meagan watched the knights gather into formation, massing close to the city. The first offensive rode out in ordered rows. The line of knights swept across the field, lances lowered.

The front line fodder for the nomads came shrieking from the horizon, plunging headlong into the line and impaling themselves into annihilation. Meagan could have been in the charge had she remained among the Mongols. The survivors tried to counterattack, desperately shooting arrows, but their arrows glanced from chain mail and armor while the knights' swords met no resistance. The heavy mounts trampled the fallen with spike-studded iron shoes until the battlefield writhed with the remnants of the nomads' attack.

Closer to the city, another cavalry battalion of knights was riding into formation. The remaining nomads retreated, shooting futile arrows in their wake as they ran for the plains. A roar went up as a new division of knights took the field, row upon row gaining speed with each stride. Shouts of victory rose from the battlefield as the knights chased their beaten enemy.

"No!" Meagan cried. "Call them back! Do not *follow*, that is what they want you to do!" She tugged on the sleeve of the Englishman. He turned to her with eyes drunk with conquest, unseeing, and then looked back to the battle.

The man would not listen, Meagan plainly saw, and there was nothing he could do anyway. Victims were only allowed to surrender because the Mongolians did not want to reveal their battle tactics, but once the nomads attacked, they killed to the last defender. There were no witnesses to an attack by the horde, ever. Meagan thought furiously of how to escape.

Determined to chase their beaten enemy into oblivion, the knights below were being drawn into the nomad's trap. As they galloped, the battalion of knights loosened and drifted apart, and their lines became thinner.

Swarms of horsemen emerged from the horizon like black claws as the trap began to close. The main force of nomads encircled and engulfed the knights, discharging volley after volley of arrows, turning away so fresh riders behind could launch still more. Wherever the knights drove, the nomads dashed away and wheeled back with reinforcements. Knights and their heavy horses began to fall. The horde continued to flow onto the battlefield like floodwater rising.

Meagan turned from the rail. Stunned by the disaster below, no one noticed her walk quickly to the other side of the platform. The stairs were in pandemonium. Men pushed in both directions and fights were beginning to break out. She looked over the railing. Except for prisoners held in the stocks, the courtyard was almost empty. Her heart caught when she saw Targa. The pony was dancing short, nervous steps around a man who held her lead.

The platform was perhaps ten feet above the ground. Meagan looked back at the men watching the battle. Slowly, the truth was dawning on them. It would not be long. Slipping over the railing, she dropped, sprawling upon landing. Guards crowded the platform above as she recovered and sprinted toward Targa. Men pointed to her and shouted.

The mare skittered sideways, wheeling around her handler. Meagan caught the pony's mane and leaped across her back, stomach across the saddle pad. Men were coming at a run. She swung her leg over and grabbed the reins, pulling Targa's head around and closing her heels. The handler dropped the leadrope as Targa bolted past and Meagan leaned forward to take it up.

She steered the pony for the street. Men blocked the way but she held straight, guiding Targa so there would be no mistake. The pony drove through, hitting exactly between them. A sword grazed Meagan's arm and caught in her clothes. It clattered to the ground behind her.

Meagan remembered the city's bridge over the river and turned the pony toward it. People shrieked and ran from her, thinking the horde had broken through. *No,* she thought grimly. *Not yet.*

A flood of people poured from the city. Meagan could see the bridge, but she had to slow to a walk and thread through the crowd. Guards were controlling the flow of people, holding spears high. The bridge was clogged with traffic of people, carts and horses. They would never get across in time. Targa pranced and plunged against her tight hold as Meagan studied the bridge entrance. Stone walls curved to the gate, forming low barriers on each side over the river.

Water was Meagan's least favorite obstacle. To her, landing in water and its sudden deceleration was like feeling the floor fall out. But the bridge itself was impassable and growing worse. A crowd was building behind her. Meagan did not know her mount's attitude or ability over fences, but Targa was capable if only she would try. Her grandfather had a saying: *sometimes you can trust a horse and sometimes you can't—and sometimes you have to.*

Meagan gauged a line to the bridge's wall and released the reins. The mare sprang forward like an arrow. Guards yelled warning but the pony and rider were already in motion. Targa's hooves scrambled in confusion at the low barrier, but Meagan held the mare's head and urged her forward. The pony hesitated, looking for another way, then gathered herself and skimmed over the low wall. They plunged into the water below.

The river closed over Meagan's head. She pushed off Targa's back so the mare would not sink. Hooking an arm over the horse's withers, she let the mare pull her to shore. When Targa's hooves caught the river bottom, Meagan remounted.

Water streamed off them as Targa rose onto dry land. Whatever her faults, the little mare was one of those most valuable of animals: an honest pony. Meagan leaned forward and kissed the mare thankfully between her wet ears.

The Knights are dust...
and their good swords are rust,
Their souls are with the saints, we trust.

- Samuel Taylor Coleridge (1772-1834)

MEAGAN WAS STRETCHED in cool grass looking at tree limbs above. Something had awoken her. For safety she had decided to travel the past two nights and sleep during the day. Now the sun was still high in the sky. She listened, then closed her eyes. Whatever had awakened her seemed to be gone.

A muffled cry made her sit up. She scanned the open field, a tiny alarm sounding in the back of her mind. She expected to see Targa, but the field was empty. This was strange because the mare always grazed nearby, and horses are animals of exact routine.

Concerned, Meagan picked up Targa's bridle and stood. The knoll she had chosen was a mile from the road she hoped might lead to a city—and something to eat. Hunger, familiar from her slavery days in Rome, was returning with its lightheaded gloom.

The muffled crying sound came again, from just over the hill. Meagan crept forward. A man was crouched at the base of the knoll, sobbing. He wore chain mail over coarse brown fabric. Next to him lay a shield and a long, tapered, brightly-painted wooden pole: a knight's lance.

She cleared her throat delicately. "Excuse me, is something wrong?"

The man whirled and rose to his feet, and Meagan saw two things immediately. First, the man was not much more than a boy, and second, there was a sword strapped to his side. The young man brandished the metal blade, then on another thought grabbed his shield. He took a fierce stance, wiping his red eyes discreetly.

"I am sorry, I did not see you before," Meagan said cautiously. "Are you lost?"

The young man sniffed. He was blonde-haired and his plain, wide features were raw from rubbing. "Cheval go," he said miserably.

Zhivago? Meagan enunciated clearly: "Do you mean as in 'Doctor,' by any chance? It's one of my mother's favorite movies."

"Nie, nie!" He pointed to the bridle Meagan carried. *"Cheval!"*

"Oh, this?" Meagan held up the simple headgear. "It is not a shovel ... it's a *bri*-dle. For my horse."

"Tak, tak! *Horse!*" The young man launched into an excited string of what sounded like gibberish.

Meagan held up her hand. "I am sorry, I do not understand. Do you speak English?"

"Small!" The young man nodded eagerly. "English mother once."

"English. Mother. Once," she repeated.

The young man pointed off into the distance. "Horse go. Mens."

She straightened. "What do you mean, horse *go?* My horse or your horse?"

He pointed at himself sadly, saying, "Horse go." Then he pointed at Meagan. "Horse *go.*" He made an angry face and pantomimed kicking, as if imitating a certain ill-tempered pony.

This person had no idea what he was saying. Meagan put her hands to her mouth and whistled the call that always brought Targa trotting. The pony did not come. Again she tried ... the call sounded shrill and futile.

After a moment silent except for sounds of birds in the trees, the young man shyly cleared his throat. He pointed to himself apologetically. "Henryk."

"Oh, I'm sorry, Henryk. I am a little upset. My name is Meagan Roberts, and it is nice to meet you."

"Polacy," he said, pointing to himself and then to the horizon. "Polska go."

"Polska? You mean Poland?"

"Tak! *Po-land*." Henryk shrugged and trailed off. He turned away, sniffing.

Meagan began bundling Targa's crude saddle and bridle to carry. She had become attached to the pony and felt vulnerable without her. Part of her—the saner part, it seemed—would not believe Targa could be gone. "Really, there's no sense in crying," she told the young man brusquely. "Unless you are broke and lost like me." She sniffed then herself, realizing it was true.

Henryk stood quietly, his plain honest features clouded. She looked at the striped wooden pole beside his shield and a frayed coil of rope. Apparently he was a knight without a horse.

"Where is Poland?" she asked more sympathetically.

Henryk pointed to his right, rubbing his eyes.

Meagan bit her lip, deciding to trust the hapless knight. Her options seemed limited. "Henryk, we both lost our horses. Should we go together?" She gestured. "You and me, Henryk, go together, find horses?"

The young man's expression lit up. "Tak!"

Dusk was falling when Meagan and Henryk passed a pair of squat dwellings that represented an inn. The young knight stopped and made motions to indicate sleeping.

"I have no money, Henryk," she told him with a shrug.

"Tak!" he said firmly, stamping the end of his lance in the dirt road.

The action reminded Meagan unpleasantly of a certain arrogant chariot driver. "'Tak' yourself. I can't. I am hungry and…" She had no further answers.

"Nie!"

"What do you mean, '*nie?*' I have no money, Henryk! And I wish I could tell you how ridiculous you look walking with that stupid lance or whatever—" She stopped herself. *This is not Rome, I can be nice.* "What I am saying, Henryk, is that I cannot pay to stay anywhere." She opened her hands for effect. "See? No mon-ey."

Henryk smiled and patted his waist pouch: metal clinked inside. The young knight hoisted his lance onto his shoulder and started toward the ramshackle inn.

"Oh." Meagan relented. A meal and a place to sleep would be quite welcome. "You pay, then." She followed the knight past what she thought was the inn but was actually the stables—the shack *behind* the horse livery housed the travelers' lodgings. Both buildings were in equal states of cleanliness and repair, or perhaps the stables were the better of the two.

Henryk knocked at a poorly fit door. It opened to a middle-aged woman with suspicious eyes. The young knight greeted her pleasantly in Polish.

The woman narrowed her eyes and said nothing.

"Ma'am, do you speak English?" Meagan asked. The woman's eyes narrowed further and the door began to shut.

"Français?" Henryk suggested.

The door stopped. *"Oui..."* the woman said suspiciously.

"Merci!" As if given a signal, the two set instantly into what Meagan gathered was intense bargaining. At the end of the transaction, coins exchanged hands and Henryk stepped triumphantly through the doorway, indicating for Meagan to follow.

A bald man sat in a corner of a dark room, arms folded and eyes staring. He gave no greeting. The woman clucked under her breath as she walked across the dirt floor and began struggling with a door shorn of hinges. Grunting, she slid it aside to reveal a tiny, dismal closet of a room.

Henryk removed his cloak and tossed it inside. He gave Meagan a shrug and walked outside for his shield and lance. She stepped gingerly into the dark room and took careful inventory.

The air carried the inviting scent of moldy clothes. Along one side, taking fully half of the room, a lumpy pile of matted straw was covered by unspeakably soiled cloth. Meagan looked vainly for a place to set down her saddle and pad. "Where is my room? I am *not* sleeping in here—" She was interrupted when the bald man entered, pushing past Meagan and grabbing Henryk's pack and her saddle. Meagan followed him outside in time to see the man heave their belongings as far toward the road as he could manage.

She scowled furiously at the man. "Now that's just *rude!*"

Hissing metal brought silence. Meagan looked past the bald man to see Henryk standing with sword out. On the ground in front of him were his pack and Meagan's saddle—and beyond, two robed men mounted on donkeys. It seemed they were being evicted in favor of the two robed men, and Henryk was reacting to the slight. The knight's method was admittedly more satisfying than a scowl.

One of the men dismounted his donkey and handed his reins to the other. His brown hair was cut short, and a clean goatee marked his square jaw. "Lorenzo, we have surely not pleased the Lord in so upsetting one of his servant knights."

Meagan's eyes grew wide. The man spoke clear English. Henryk waved his sword menacingly as the robed man approached.

"Your gesture may be mistaken, Excellency," said the second man still mounted on his donkey. "A rogue knight may be provoked to do anything."

"So why provoke?" Within reach of Henryk's swing, the first man stooped to pick up Henryk's belongings from the dirt. A silver cross fell from his robes and swung in the air.

"Bardzo mi przykro!" Henryk cried, dropping his sword and falling to one knee.

The robed man straightened. "Do you know what our knight is saying, Lorenzo?"

"He is asking forgiveness, Excellency."

"Tell him forgiveness is not required. Explain that we are sorry to have caused this trouble."

"But Excellency, it is almost darkness."

"Please tell the knight what I have asked you to say, Lorenzo."

"Yes, Excellency." The man translated quickly, and a relieved expression spread over Henryk's face. The first robed man made a sign of the cross before returning Henryk's belongings and returning to his donkey.

"Excellency." The mounted man looked anxiously toward the road. "It is dangerous to travel at night. Reports of mercenaries have been numerous."

"We asked if we could stay in the stables, Lorenzo." The robed man approached his donkey and gathered the reins. "The innkeeper refused us. Come, let us trouble them no more."

"We were not refused, Excellency. The hostler merely insisted we stay in his house for protection."

"Yes, and by evicting this good knight and his Lady. We will pray for the Lord's protection and seek lodging elsewhere."

"I will stay in the stables!" Meagan offered. She smiled at the confused expressions. "I will be happy to. Really."

"Am I mistaken, Lorenzo?" the first man said, still standing while holding his donkey's reins. "Were we not told no one here spoke English?"

"We were, Excellency."

The man turned to address Meagan. "Are you offering your room, Daughter?"

"Oh, yes, I insist. Take it. It is the broom closet behind the leaning door." Meagan took a step and felt Henryk's firm tug on her tunic. The young man blurted out a line of Polish gibberish.

"Lorenzo?"

"The knight asks us to excuse the wench for speaking out of turn, Excellency. It seems the knight found this woman in distress."

Meagan shrugged off Henryk's hand. "He found *me* in distress?"

"Does our young knight say why the young lady is eager to spend the night in the stables? I do not wish to believe he has been untoward with the maiden." The first robed man contemplated Meagan with a soft eye. "Perhaps we should make introductions. I am Aurick Bartholomew, a Brother of Saint Francis, and this is my apprentice, Lorenzo. Tell me your name, Daughter."

"I am Meagan Roberts, sir." The man had an intelligent gaze which held compassion, an expression unseen since she had left home. Meagan had not realized how much she had missed kindness: she would never call it "simple" again.

The clergyman glanced at the knight and back to Meagan. "And you are well, Daughter? Unharmed?"

"I am fine, thank you. I am *so* glad you speak English."

The man smiled. "Meagan, did you say? That is a pretty name, and one not taken by a Saint if I am correct. Are you far from home?"

"Yes, sir. Quite far."

"And you truly wish to spend the night with your animals?"

"Actually our horses were stolen. But, yes."

"Stolen! The story becomes less clear as it is told." Brother Bartholomew stroked his chin, contemplating. "Lorenzo, tell the hostler the stables will do as accommodations for all of us. It is clearly the Lord's will. Have him bring our meals there after he has seen to our animals."

Brother Bartholomew walked purposefully to the stables, his brown robes billowing behind. Meagan moved to follow, but Lorenzo stopped her with a glare. "Wait, unless you are heathen! The Brother must give his blessing."

Meagan was cautious of the men, but also respectful of their chosen path. Rome's violent corruption had degraded the human conscience and ended in centuries of Dark Ages when the population lived like animals, trapped in a warlord culture based on fear. This brought a time of religious conversion, when young men took vows of poverty and ventured forth to live as apostles of a new Christian creed. They roamed the countryside as monks or lived as hermits, and spread the Gospel of their new faith by example.

She waited for the blessing of the stables, and then waited through the ritual prayers at sunset. She waited through Henryk's special request for delivery of the stolen horses, and finally, hunger pains in her stomach, listened to the entire twelve-minute blessing of the dinner brought by the innkeeper. Twice Meagan thought the prayer was done and reached for the thick slab of cheese in front of her, and each mistake earned a special two-minute plea of forgiveness by Brother Bartholomew on her behalf.

Finally able to take the piece of cheese that had been tormenting her, Meagan began devouring the simple meal. Brother

Bartholomew bowed his head. Meagan stopped, putting down her food in expectation of another prayer.

"No, Daughter," he said gently. "Continue eating. I am asking forgiveness for keeping food from one so clearly in hunger."

Meagan tried to eat more slowly. "Where are you from, sir?"

"I was part of the Yorkshire abbey of Meaux in England, until the blessed St. Francis was revealed to me. Now I am Franciscan, of the Brothers Minor. I took my traveling vows two summers past. Where the Lord sends me, I go."

"Where is the Lord sending you?"

"Perhaps here, Daughter. Tell me, how did your horses come to be stolen?"

"I am really not sure. When I woke up, I found Henryk cry— shouting. He knew enough English to tell me the horses were gone, but not much else."

Lorenzo had one eyebrow raised. "Are you not wedded to the knight?"

"Married? Of course not! We just met."

The other of Lorenzo's eyebrows lifted and his voice hardened. "Perhaps the search for your horses had best begin within your heart. Have you begged the Lord's forgiveness for your bed-bourd?"

"My what?"

"Your carnal sins. Or has the part of temptress become too natural to cause shame?"

Meagan was stung from the accusation. "We just *met!* We did not have carnal sins."

Lorenzo eyed her skeptically.

"*None.*" Despite her innocence, she reddened under the cold gaze.

"You wear strange garb for a chaste woman."

"Oh, this?" Meagan looked down at her nomadic vest and trousers, no doubt aberrations in female clothing for the times. "They are just for riding."

"Enough, Lorenzo," Brother Bartholomew interrupted. "As the Lord has made the world wondrous in variety, we should let it be so. We will not put our new friends on trial. Perhaps you could ask our knight how the horses came to be stolen?"

"Yes, Excellency. I understand the knight is coming back from a pilgrimage to Jerusalem."

"I prefer not to be called Excellency, apprentice—we are all nameless in the service of God. The knight is much to be admired, undertaking a journey to the Holy City."

"Of course, Teacher. But it was a troubled journey, from the knight's tale. Most of his companions were stricken with sickness or accident, save two who were captured and held for ransom. He lost his squire and two best horses on the road." Lorenzo paused while Henryk corrected him. "Sorry, Excellency. This was the third horse lost."

"He must be a strong servant of the Lord to be given such trials," Brother Bartholomew calmly observed.

"It seems the knight stopped off the road for a bite of bread, where he saw a free-running jennet." Lorenzo gave a nod in Meagan's direction. "Her horse, Excellency. Men were chasing it around the meadow. The knight believed the horse to belong to one of the men. He never thought them to be thieves."

"Such thoughts never entered his mind?" Brother Bartholomew's expression was dubious for a moment, but returned to serenity. "I suppose it is to his credit. The chaste mind does not contemplate deceit."

"The knight tried to help, and the men thanked him very much, but said what they needed most would be a length of rope."

Meagan gasped.

"So our good knight gave the men his only rope," Lorenzo finished solemnly. "They used the rope to catch this woman's jennet, and then tied him up and took his horse as well."

"You gave them a *rope?*" Meagan asked loudly of Henryk's bowed head.

Brother Bartholomew held up his hand. "Let us hear no more. To pollute the world with a rehearsal of the crime would serve no purpose but the Enemy's. The facts are plain. The nature of our good knight has been preyed upon and our Daughter suffers with him. We shall leave it to the Lord to right these sins. It is time for evening devotions, and then to sleep."

That's just *great*, Meagan thought, stuffing a last piece of fruit into her mouth. She could happily kick Henryk, and might. *Men.*

The others stood, leaving her surrounded by the remains of the meal. *If they expect me to clean up,* she thought irritably, *they are very much mistaken.* Angered by the very idea, she picked her up her saddle and looked for an empty spot to unroll her sleeping mat.

Poor Targa. It was quite understandable why they hang horse thieves, Meagan decided. She folded her outer tunic to use as a pillow. Poor me, poor everything. Suddenly a prayer sounded like a very good idea.

———

The noise could have been a mouse, it scraped so softly. Meagan sat up. The stables were bright, with cobwebs outlining the rafters. The stable door had been partly opened and moonlight filled the barn.

The noise came again, closer. A footstep crunched softly and whispered words sounded somewhere close by. Shadows moved past her. Amid the whispers, Meagan could hear the stall doors of the clergymen's two donkeys being unfastened.

Meagan listened to the tiny, clopping footfalls. These men of the Church were leaving without paying! Pulling on her tunic, she angrily walked outside to confront them—and stopped in surprise. Standing between the livery stables and the road were not Brother Bartholomew and Lorenzo, but a band of men on horseback. They held a number of unsaddled horses, including the two donkeys. She stared at one of the unmounted horses being held by a rope around its neck. The shaggy coat shone faintly in the moonlight. It was Targa.

Men were quickly dismounting. Metal gleamed.

Meagan ran back inside the barn and held the door tightly. There was no latch. "Henryk, get your sword! They have our horses!" The young knight's sleep-laden voice came as the door shuddered. A knife blade slid through the crack of the door.

"Henryk, *hurry!*" She struggled as the door was pried open and wrenched from her grasp. Meagan was struck and thrown roughly aside. She curled and rolled across the dirt floor as men rushed inside, pushing past each other. She looked up to see a swinging pole and heard a dull crack. A weight fell over her and slumped to one side: the warm, heavy body of a man. She heard grunts and the ring of metal on metal as she wrestled from under the body and looked fearfully at the face of the fallen man. Thankfully, it was neither Henryk nor a clergyman.

The fighting moved outside into a confusion of shadows. The men on horseback were escaping to a field across the road. Meagan could see her pony in tow beside a lanky, dark horse— Targa was going willingly, for she knew no better. Meagan watched helplessly as the thieves faded into the night. She brought her hands to her mouth and imitated the nomad call. Its whistle pierced the night.

Targa's ears pricked. She whinnied and tried to turn back, but the mounted horse beside her would not slow. The pony knew the call was to be obeyed and that only the lazy dawdled when called: in the pony's eyes this horse was showing very poor breeding indeed. She pinned her ears and bit hard, catching the sensitive skin of the loafer's belly.

Now a second horse's squeal was heard in the dark. Meagan ran to follow and saw a horseman alone in the moonlight, fighting with her pony mare. The man's fellow thieves were escaping into the field across the road, shadows into shadows. The pony whirled and let her hindquarters fly. The bigger horse ducked away, and his rider let go of Targa's rope rather than be pulled off.

Free now, Targa stopped and shook her head. Meagan whistled again. The pony nickered and trotted forward, holding her head sideways to avoid the trailing rope. In the moonlight, Meagan saw the highwayman turn and spur his horse. Cold gripped her spine. On foot before the oncoming charge, Meagan understood the great truth of cavalry and why history was decided on horseback: a galloping horseman was almost impossible to evade or stop before he struck.

Targa laid back her ears when she saw the oncoming horse. She was not going to let this latecomer pretend he was better than she was, coming now at a gallop. She squealed indignantly and showed her heels. The horse recognized the insane pony and swerved away in alarm. Meagan reached for Targa's trailing lead rope. In a leap, she was up and running away into the night.

———•———

Heavenly Father, I come to You in shame and sorrow. Thieves came in the night, and I sent one into everlasting fire. I read Your Word without hearing. I hear and do not follow.

Two travelers have come onto me and my apprentice, a knight and a young woman. The knight is as all knights, a servant of man and God, whose virtue is humility under the burden of the sword. The woman is a question. Lorenzo mistrusts her, though I see no darkness in her.

It is true the woman's horse returned in the night strangely, as if by witchery, and that the animal is in appearance like a lady's sweet jennet yet has the temper of a demon.

Yet I must not judge. I accept that I do not know the intentions of this woman, and I will do what is required. I can only add penitence to my rituals and remember with what lies the Enemy surrounds us. There is no hope for any man but what hope You give.

I am, by Your Grace,
Aurick Bartholomew

Men are not hanged for stealing horses,
but that horses may not be stolen.

- George Savile, Marquess of Halifax (1633-95)

Bʀᴏᴛʜᴇʀ Bᴀʀᴛʜᴏʟᴏᴍᴇᴡ sᴛᴏᴏᴅ looking up at his three messengers and spoke in a tone of command. Meagan had never before seen men cower on horseback; she almost felt sorry for the thieves. "Remember, one of the donkeys has a white spot on its muzzle, and the knight's palfrey is liver chestnut. Deliver these descriptions to the monastery of each town you come to as an edict of the Brothers Minor. The thieves are to be held in stocks until my arrival. God bless and protect you."

Thus recruited, the messengers spurred their horses and galloped away, fanning out across the fields. Brother Bartholomew did not watch, but joined Lorenzo to walk through the arched stone doorway of the church. Iron-strapped doors closed behind them.

Henryk and Meagan waited outside. They had arrived at this settlement as the afternoon heat was subsiding. The sweet smells of grass and trees were overcome at the town's limits by the sour scents that now bathed them. The day had been long, beginning with eulogies for the slain highwayman. Meagan had noted that commending a thief's soul to his Maker took less time than blessing a meal of bread and cheese. She had not interrupted once.

On the road, Meagan learned more of Henryk's story through Lorenzo's translation. The young knight's father was a Polish nobleman, Baron Bialaskorski. As third son Henryk would inherit no property, so he was given the choice between the church and chivalry. Henryk was a mischievous, light-hearted boy who—with encouragement from the local clergy—chose knighthood.

Henryk soon made a name for himself in a game of dummy jousting called the *Quantain*. His father had encouraged him with a string of six knightly mounts specially trained for "The Lanes." As proof of valor, when the Holy City of Jerusalem called for salvation, fifteen-year-old Henryk joined a contingent of knights bound for Constantinople.

Unfortunately a fever hit the group as they waited for a vessel bound for the Holy Land, carrying off several to an early reward. Some lost armor and horses by gambling; others left secretly in the night to return home. Henryk himself suffered heatstroke in his helmet during jousting practice and missed his appointed ship sailing for the Holy Land. A kind clergyman pronounced Henryk's duty complete.

His Crusade ended, Henryk was now a "free lance." He was homeward bound, he said, and would be there already if his last horse had not been stolen. The truth was that Henryk, like many free lances, considered destination less important than diversions met on the way.

In summary, Henryk's career as a knight was going poorly. He was unhappy about losing his horse to thieves a third time, and when Meagan introduced Targa, he broke his well-traveled lance into two pieces with his foot and stormed away. Lorenzo had mumbled something about witches and their familiars. Seeing the mood of the trudging men, Meagan decided to lead Targa on foot.

The doors to the church opened and men spilled out, Brother Bartholomew and Lorenzo among them. They talked over each other vigorously while milling about the steps.

"We missed a sermon given by Brother Ignacious," Brother Bartholomew told Meagan and Henryk. "It has given the flock inspiration."

A monk clasped his hands and beseeched the heavens. "Words as from blessed Francis himself! He speaks of the purity of animals, who do only God's will because they know nothing of evil."

"Excuse me, Brother," contradicted another member of the flock, "it is not that animals do the will of God, but that they may not be condemned for failing it. Only Man may be condemned to Hell Eternal because he has eaten of the Tree of Knowledge and knows the evil he does."

"That is what I meant, Brother," the first monk sniffed defensively.

"If Eve had not tempted Adam," a third monk added, "the apple from the Tree of Knowledge would never have been tasted, and Man would not have fallen. The woes of the world come from women."

"Which is to say," another agreed sagely, "animals live in the blessed state of obedience to God which was denied to Man by the temptress, Eve."

The eyes of the flock turned to Meagan who, as a female, was apparently a stand-in for Eve. "If I might say something," she said respectfully. "Why was it worse for *Eve* to give in to temptation than it was for Adam?" The monks stared at her, not answering. She smiled sweetly. "I am just asking."

One of the monks cleared his throat. "The temptress Eve fell to temptation and lured Adam into falling from grace."

"Does Adam have any responsibility?" Other monks hearing the exchange came closer. Meagan suspected she should keep quiet, but she was too irked to stop. "Maybe the serpent went to Eve because *she* was the hardest one to convince. Men would just go along."

A definite mood change came over the Brothers. Lorenzo held up his cross and chanted in Latin, as if to ward off evil: "*In principio erat Verbum et Verbum erat apud Deum!*"

"That is a nice passage, but it is not an answer," Meagan replied. "It means, 'In the beginning was the Word, and the Word was with God.'"

A gasp went up from the Brothers.

"She knows the Mass!" shouted one in alarm.

"She speaks the Holy language!"

One of the Brothers called out, "Lorenzo, you said she was heathen!"

Meagan found Lorenzo's eye. He looked at her calmly. "Even the fallen can mimic the righteous."

Brother Bartholomew's voice rose above the rising conversation. "Brothers, the woman and knight are our guests! Do we tell lies of those God has placed in our care?"

The Brethren fell silent. It was the first time Meagan had heard Brother Bartholomew speak sharply. "I am disappointed in you, apprentice! Lies are the Enemy's words."

Lorenzo watched Meagan as he spoke. "I apologize, Excellency. I must have been mistaken."

"Kyrie eleison, Christe eleison, Kyrie eleison."

Of the Church's eight daily services, Meagan preferred the dawn ritual of Prime to the crowded morning mass of Terce, or the midday worship, Sexts. Even these were quieter and more contemplative than the later services of Nones and Vespers, during which men conversed and held business.

"Sanctus, sanctus, sanctus. Dominus Deus Sabaoth."

Meagan knelt with the congregation. She enjoyed the services in Latin. The ancient language gave the Mass an otherworldly beauty and lent the shuffling clergy a much-needed impressiveness. The first prayer was short, and afterward she settled back into the pew carefully to avoid splinters. She looked at the uneven timber and small windows of the church, and the dirt floor with stones beat into it. It did not compare to the ostentation of Rome, but there was a solemn spirituality in the soaring roofs and silent spaces. In this place and time, man's most inspiring structures were places of worship. Everything else had decayed, and there were many centuries yet to pass before society reached the standard of living once achieved by Rome. "Might makes Right" proved horribly wrong. The fall to brutality had been complete.

In the short time they had been at the monastery as guests of the Church, Meagan had been transformed into a proper young woman of the day. She was wearing a long gown and covering given to her by the Order to replace her nomad clothing. Again, it was hard not to compare the coarse material to the silken fabrics of Rome. She now kept her hair in the current fashion, braided and coiled on each side of her head and held with knitted nets.

She had not told anyone about her experience riding with the Mongolian horde. People seemed suspicious enough of her motives. When pressed, Meagan replied that her city had been attacked and that she had acquired Targa from a trader.

A middle-aged man stood by the altar. Such an age was rare in an era depopulated by disease. The man was tithing money before his death, for special placement in the afterlife. Monks raised their hands in prayer.

Meagan's thoughts wandered, traveling back home as always. How long had she been gone? Perhaps four months in Rome, and two-and-a-half months since? Though she was at a disadvantage without a calendar, her calculations suggested her sixteenth birthday was about three months away. Meagan knew what her wish would be.

A robed figure came to sit beside her. "Daughter..." he said quietly.

"Good morning, Brother Bartholomew!" She smiled at the man.

"I am sorry to disturb your meditations, but a messenger has arrived, perhaps with news of our animals. I have had the knight Henryk summoned. Conclude your prayers and meet me in the cloister."

Meagan finished quickly, adding special thanks for Brother Bartholomew. After the Romans and the nomads, she was grateful to meet a gentle man. Too, an idea had formed in her mind. Mrs. Bridgestone's library held copies of medieval writings about the Great Horse. She planned to ask Brother Bartholomew discreetly whether he knew of the legend, in hopes of finding a new clue.

She made final absolutions and hurried outside. Two wings, the Brothers' dormitory and the stables, wrapped behind the main building. When Meagan came out into the sunlight, she saw Henryk and Brother Bartholomew standing with a group of men on the inner courtyard's stone pavement. The group was addressing a boy on horseback in what sounded like French. As she came closer, one man reached up and dropped coins into the boy's outstretched hand.

Abruptly the monks turned and walked toward the dormitory. Meagan started to follow, but Henryk rushed to hold her back—laymen were not allowed in the Abbey's quarters, much less lay*women*. The messenger boy counted his money and slumped on his horse to wait. Moments passed quietly as the sun beat onto the monastery as if seeking its dark interior. Whispers and sounds of slippered feet could be heard in the hidden halls of the dormitory.

A horsefly landed on the messenger horse's shoulder. The boy slapped it away. Typical of the heavy European breeds, the boy's mount was a burly animal with a stocky neck and barrel. The horse's eyes were half-closed and the congregating flies seemed not to bother him, but when the horsefly landed on the horse's rump he swished his fly-swatter tail expertly. The insect fell to the ground and buzzed in jerky circles.

Slippered feet moved through the halls. Brother Bartholomew and two men strode from the quarters, their whispers becoming talk as they crossed the threshold into the cloister. Deep in conversation, they passed Meagan and Henryk without acknowledgment, walking determinedly into the Abbey's main hall.

Meagan watched them go. "Isn't that strange, Henryk? Brother Bartholomew asked us to meet him here and now he's going away." The knight shrugged, half-comprehending her words. She approached the messenger. "Did you bring news of our horses?"

The boy only blinked in answer.

"Henryk, I think they were speaking French to him. Ask about the message ... *Français.*"

Henryk stepped forward and spoke to the boy. Meagan could not understand the whole exchange, but she recognized one deadly word: *Tatars.* She looked up and froze. Over the Abbey's pitched roof was a column of dust rising like thin, black smoke.

"Don't stand here!" Meagan gripped the messenger boy's tunic. "*Tell* people! Warn them to escape! *Hurry!*" She released the boy and slapped his horse's hindquarters. The confused youngster grabbed the reins and circled. "Henryk, *tell* him! There is no time to waste!"

Shouts came from the dormitory. At the sight of angry clergy, the boy at last dug his heels into his horse. With a clatter they were across the stones and out of sight.

The monks rushed forward. "What have you done, imbecile child? You had no authority to release the messenger!"

Others were coming from the buildings surrounding the cloister. Hands clutched for her, groping. Meagan twisted away from the shouting men and was glad to see Henryk's tunic forcing through the pressing monks. The knight stood close to her, his hand on his sword. They were trapped within a fence of brown robes.

"Desist!" The stern face of Brother Bartholomew pushed through the crowd. "Enough, Daughter!"

"But the Tatars are coming! We have to warn people! We have to escape—*Look!*" She pointed at the rising column in the clear sky. *"They are coming!"*

Brother Bartholomew took Meagan by the shoulder and propelled her forward. She started to pull away but he whispered, "Silence, Daughter. There is little time."

Flanked by clergymen, Meagan allowed herself to be taken into the Abbey and down a black corridor. Candles lit the passage; the sudden change from sunlight to darkness blinded her. The winding corridor opened into a cramped room filled with robed men. Dimly lighted walls held books of heavy binding, maps and scrolls. In the center of the room were two chairs. In each a man was tied.

"Abbot!" cried one of the monks. "This woman sent away our messenger!"

"Send for another. Quickly."

The monk kissed the wooden cross around his neck and hurried off.

The man addressed as Abbot stood and walked slowly to Meagan. His flesh was well tended and pasty-white. "You have been a guest here these past days," he said slowly, "enjoying the benevolence of the Church."

Meagan swallowed and nodded.

"You see, I know these things. They are mine to know, for I am the Abbot." The man's voice hardened into a demand. "*So, guest of God, what have you told our messenger?*"

"I tried to warn people about what is coming."

The Abbot leaned close to her face, bringing the scent of cloying decay. "To what purpose?"

"I was only… I was trying to save people."

"The Tatar locusts could never be this close to Christendom. What foulness dares you to this lie?"

"It is not a lie." Meagan held her ground. "I have … *heard* they burn cities to the ground and kill people even if they beg for life. We *have* to warn people to escape!"

The Abbot looked prayerfully to Heaven. "She speaks with the tongue of the Enemy. It matters not, Your wrath will prevail." He addressed the Brethren. "The danger to the Church is not that detestable race of Satan. It lies closer." He pointed to the two bound men in the middle of the room.

The men twisted in their chairs and looked wide-eyed around the room. "We are no danger, Brother! We are only here because the Church needs protection!"

"The Church needs *nothing!*" The scream vibrated in Meagan's chest. The Abbot's voice lowered, becoming soft and gentle. "Except obedience. You come with demands to surrender our Lord's temple to your forces. Prithee, by what authority do you issue such a command?"

"Brethren," a voice interrupted fearfully. Eyes went to a monk standing in the doorway. "The city guards are outside. They are demanding we leave the Abbey."

The Abbot clenched a fist and reopened it. His gentle tone tightened to a rasp. "They *claim* it is for our protection. Do you see how they wait for a chance to usurp the authority of the One True Church? The Enemy never rests. Do you see the danger?" The Brethren were silent as the Abbot's challenging glare made a slow sweep of the room. "Tell the commander he may enter to discuss this matter of our eviction. *Alone.*"

The monk in the doorway disappeared. The Abbot waved a hand toward the two tied men. "Remove them and send in the Abbey Guard." As men moved to follow the orders, he pointed to Meagan. "Take her also."

"A suggestion, Brother." Brother Bartholomew's hand tightened on Meagan's shoulder. "The woman was only trying to do good as she saw it. Under the circumstances, perhaps the Church may be better served through clemency. Let us use mercy to show our strength."

"Use mercy..." the Abbot said it slowly, clasping his hands behind him and looking up at the black rafters. "Perhaps. Hold the woman here. We will await the commander."

Soon footsteps announced another a group of monks. Dressed in the same brown robes as the others, their faces carried harsh lines the others lacked. These monks spread themselves along the walls of the room as the Abbot seated himself. Two new monks came to stand behind Meagan.

It was not long before voices were heard in the passage. Soldiers burst into the room. One strode forward, a short man with sharp features. His hand was on his sword, where it remained. "You are ordered to leave instantly! We must prepare for attack!"

"Lower your voice." The Abbot spoke levelly from his seat. "This is a place of worship."

"You are under *our* orders now," the soldier retorted. "We need this building for defense of the town."

"This is God's dwelling and He takes no orders. Are you the commander of the forces outside?"

"I am. My men surround you. The dark clouds in the sky are the dust of the invaders."

The Abbot looked past the speaker to the soldiers beside him. "The invitation was for the commander only. The others may now leave."

The commander walked forward and slammed his hand down on the table. "They will *stay!*"

The Abbot looked at the hand splayed on the surface before him, then slowly raised his eyes to meet the commander's gaze. "I have one question. Do you know *God?*"

The room erupted into action. The men along the wall moved quickly, pulling the soldiers from the room and surrounding the commander. A short scuffle ended with the man's sword falling to the ground. A chair was brought forward and the commander bound roughly to it. A gag was wrapped tightly over his mouth.

The Abbot stood slowly. He walked to the soldier and stood in front of his chair, looking down at the man without emotion. "Who of us can say he truly knows God? Not while we live, certainly. Yet God is close. This the scriptures teach." The Abbot leaned down to the commander's face. "You may blaspheme God. You may presume to defy His will. But God is close to you, Commander. Closer than you may realize." He reached a hand to the bound man's face and pinched his nostrils shut.

The commander struggled, eyes wide. Hands held his head still.

"God gave His glorious breath to lift you from dust. Without it, worm, to dust you will return." The suffocating man began to kick and wring his tied hands. "When you see God, will you tell Him of your authority? Will you *order* Him to preserve you from eternal damnation?" The Abbot held the commander's nostrils and calmly watched the man's terror. "Do you see God, Commander?"

He released his grip. The commander's chest heaved as the Abbot walked around the chair slowly, waiting for the man to catch his breath. "We will let you go, but your excommunication rites will begin the moment a soldier steps foot into my Abbey. They may be said very quickly in time of need." He took a step back as the commander was untied. "A pity—you soiled yourself. Perhaps it was not our Heavenly Father you saw after all." The Abbot gave Brother Bartholomew a nod. "Take the woman out with the commander. Explain to the soldiers they are being released through the benevolent grace of the Church."

Brother Bartholomew took Meagan's hand, following the monks through dark passages. Coming into the bright sunlight, the man stopped. "Find your knight companion, Daughter. Your horse will be brought out."

"I know this is a bad time, Brother Bartholomew, but I have a question. It is about a legend..."

"There is no time, Daughter. There is a castle north of here, perhaps a day's ride, not more than three on foot. Follow this road and ask directions. The Castle Sobrezy should stand against the locust army." He pulled a few coins from his robe and handed them to her, and kissed her forehead. "Remember God has a plan for you, Daughter."

"You must escape too," Meagan protested. "Before they come."

"If God wills it. Now, go."

"*Please* come with us, Brother Bartholomew!"

"Go with God, Daughter."

Meagan and Henryk left the Abbey on foot, with the knight's shield lashed across Targa's back. The last words they heard were those of the reprieved commander, ordering his soldiers to retreat.

I write this in haste, Father. The enemy approaches. So many voices around me. Some shout, others whisper. The Abbot ever seems tainted by concerns of this world. I am sorry, Father, to have such doubts. I pray to know Thy will.

The knight and the woman Meagan have left us. The woman pleaded for our escape. So full of life, she can see only its preservation. Have I fulfilled my duty to them, or am I so blind I cannot see the woman was sent to me, not I to her? I pray for guidance, Father.

- A. Bartholomew

"The great art of riding," the Knight began in a loud voice, waving his right hand as he spoke "is to keep..." Here the sentence ended as suddenly as it began, as the Knight fell heavily on top of his head exactly in the path where Alice was walking.

- *Lewis Carrol (1832-98)* Through the Looking Glass

THE VILLAGE BARELY deserved the name. Goats and geese poked among impoverished buildings huddled about an algae-covered pond. Yet all was peaceful under the morning sun, and the smell of hay and horses overpowered the usual stench.

"*Pferd zu verkaufen!*" a roadside vendor called out. Horses for sale!

Henryk looked longingly at the line of horses picketed in the grass, and then at Meagan. She could only shrug. The knight's money and the few coins from Brother Bartholomew had been spent on bread and cheese.

A man in a battered hat waved to them. "*Zu verkaufen! Pferd zu verkaufen!*" Meagan kept walking, leading Targa on foot and going a good distance before she realized Henryk was no longer with her. He was examining the line of sale horses.

Henryk *did* need a horse, of course: the nomads were certainly not coming on foot. Meagan looked to see which horse might be lively enough to keep up with Targa. She saw the young knight abruptly stop before an enormously fat brown horse whose drooping head hung inches from the ground. Walking slowly around the big animal, Henryk started to nod.

"Oh, *no*. Come on, girl." Meagan pulled the pony back toward Henryk. The trader was already untying the big horse to lead forward. "Henryk?" she asked sweetly. "Shouldn't we be looking for a faster horse?"

"Ah, the woman!" the trader called loudly. "You speak the English—*wunderbar!* I speak the English too!" The man seemed to
be having difficulty waking his enormous horse, and finally re-
sorted to kneeing him in the side. The horse grunted and raised
his head. "*Ach,* see! Much the calm horse!" Gathering that
Meagan was still unimpressed, the trader bore his attention
down on the young knight. Great gestures accompanied an
inventory of the horse's virtues, given while Henryk ran a hand
down each of the horse's stovepipe legs and nodded appreciatively.

"Henryk," Meagan complained, "this horse would be much
too slow."

The trader wagged a finger. "*Fraulein, bitte!* Of course, knight
he needs such horse. How so he conquest Tournament St. John
and no horse?"

Henryk looked up with a new light in his eyes. Meagan softened. Perhaps, she thought charitably, the horse's lop ears did
not hang out of laziness. Perhaps the white blaze across his forehead made him look simpler than he really was.

"*Ach! Der holzkopf!*" the trader screamed as the huge animal
settled on his foot. After being slapped repeatedly, the horse removed his hoof reluctantly, as if being deprived of a soft place
to stand. The trader recovered and patted the horse's shoulder
as if nothing had happened. Tears stood in his eyes.

Henryk crossed his arms, still nodding in approval.

"Henryk," she pleaded, "remember we have no money."

"*Fraulein, bitte.* Pleasing." The trader spread his arms.
"Knights need horse."

Meagan walked around the huge beast. The horse's eyes were
small in his coarse, heavy head. His throatlatch was undefined
and the upright "mutton" shoulders meant he would offer an
uncomfortable, jarring trot. "No Henryk, I think you can do better."

"The horse from this finest bloodlines!" the trader insisted
with a flourish. "His fathers have sweep this infidel from Holies
Lands! *Ach!* See the chest, it is large—so! This animal can carry
too much weight. He stop at nothing."

"He is about to fall over asleep. Henryk, please warn the man about the Tatars, and we should go."

But Henryk was stroking the horse's nose with growing confidence. The animal's eyes were half-closed and he was beginning to doze.

Seeing the knight's interest, the trader dismissed Meagan. "Now we set price," the man said firmly. The trader's eyes alighted greedily upon Henryk's garment of chain mail, and the two began negotiating in earnest.

No day can be good that begins in a tree, Meagan thought irritably, *I need to remember that.* The sun gave no indication of breaking through the overcast skies, and the night's drizzle seemed a prelude to more rain. Hungry, sore and sunburned, Meagan was annoyed by Henryk's new habit of continual singing. She reached up to the wide bough on which she had balanced through the night and retrieved Targa's bridle. She struggled to tie her gown up so that she could ride. Her ankle-length garment seemed designed to inhibit motion, and she wished again she had not let the Abbey take away her comfortable Mongolian trousers.

She tried to ignore Henryk's garbled stream of broken English, French, and Polish tunes. "Oh, *will* you shut *up*, Lancelot?" She had called him far worse. She tripped over Henryk's helmet and kicked it towards him, then eased the bridle onto Targa's head. Honestly, the knight had been better company when he was sulking.

Henryk slipped down from the tree and stretched luxuriously. His new horse lifted his enormous head, nudging the young knight and pushing him off his feet. Henryk gritted his teeth as the horse used him for a scratching post. "Chouchou, no," he said mildly, pushing the horse's head away and accepting its immediate return.

"Chouchou? Is that what you named him?"

"*Tak*, Chouchou! You enjoy?" Henryk murmured something in his horse's huge, floppy ear. Chouchou—the name meant "teacher's pet" in French, Meagan was to learn—delicately sniffed in Targa's direction. The pony flattened her ears and snapped. *"Visqueux!"* Henryk sniffed, and gently soothed his mammoth horse's supposedly-hurt feelings.

Meagan rode out into the muddy field, leaving Henryk to follow. The German horsetrader had promised the nearby road led to a castle, and she was determined to find it in the rain if necessary. She turned back and saw Henryk hopping up and down beside Chouchou.

Oh, yes, she remembered crossly. Henryk could not mount his elephant without a leg up. Meagan turned back, deciding there was nothing more useless than a knight. Fairytales could talk about shining knights riding up on white steeds, but she was beginning to think their fabled rescues could do without the knight if one had the horse. If knights were not the only people with swords, she was sure no one would pay them the least attention.

"Merci bien!" Henryk said merrily as she helped him aboard.

"You are welcome. Now please, Henryk, no singing, at least until we get back to the road."

"Certainement, Meagan!" Henryk looked odd in his helmet without chain mail, but he had gotten a fair price for the armor, and Chouchou had come equipped with a saddle. Worn straps of crisscrossing leather held its creaking pommel and cantle together. The saddle reminded Meagan of an exaggerated cowboy's saddle with the horn and outer layer stripped away.

Targa jigged impatiently as Chouchou sloshed through the field's rocky muck. Henryk had a proud smile pasted on his face: he was quite happy with the snail's rate of speed.

"Henryk," Meagan complained. "Horses sleep standing up, but I think yours sleeps while he walks. We could move faster on foot."

Horses can be divided into those that need urging to speed up and those that need urging to slow down. Forward-moving Targa, bred on open plains, was an example of a hot-blooded horse. Henryk's new mount was decidedly in the cold-blooded category.

The large animal stopped to snatch a mouthful of grass. "You shouldn't let your horse eat under bridle," she warned. "It is a very bad habit."

"*Merci*, Meagan!" Henryk agreed as Chouchou clipped the top of a passing bush.

She was happy to get back to the road, even if it meant another ballad from Henryk. The path splayed over rolling hills of knee-high grass, then dipped as they entered a thicker part of the woods. It was dark beneath the trees and the air was heavy.

Henryk stopped singing when Targa raised her head and whinnied. A horse's neigh answered from within the woods. The young knight snapped his head around, looking for the source. Targa pranced in a circle, and as she turned, Meagan looked down the part of the road they had just traveled. Someone was following them. Someone who had not been there before.

Black shapes moved quickly in the far trees.

"Meagan!" Henryk urged Chouchou forward. "We *go!*"

Crashing vegetation and cries sounded from the right, and Meagan saw distant forms leaping through underbrush. Chouchou continued his leisurely walk, undisturbed by Henryk's efforts to accelerate.

Meagan hesitated, afraid to leave them behind. Henryk and Chouchou were a waddling target. "Hurry up, Henryk!" she screamed. "They are coming!"

"I try!" Henryk was flailing his legs without result.

On the road behind them, their pursuer dropped to one knee and reached for the bow behind his back. Meagan turned and closed her legs—Targa leapt forward, and before the man could string his arrow the pony was coming fast upon him. The man leaped out of their path, dropping his bow on the road. Meagan pulled up and turned back, deliberately taking Targa over the bow until she heard a sharp snap.

Further up the road, Henryk was still trying to kick his mount into something faster than a slow jog. Meagan galloped back again, passing men just breaking free of the trees. She pulled up beside the hapless knight and together they looked back. Eight men were gaining quickly, brandishing staffs and long knives.

Henryk's face was blotched with exhaustion. Giving up on Chouchou, he stopped kicking and drew his sword, holding it out and waiting for the attack. On impulse, Meagan reached out

and grabbed the sword from him. It was heavier than she realized and the blade drooped.

"*Arrêt*, Meagan! No!"

Circling Targa, she wrestled with the sword before swinging
the flat of the blade across Chouchou's hindquarters. The
startled horse shuffled forward a few steps and slowed again to
a creeping walk ... and then Targa pinned her ears and bit down
on the base of the waddler's tail. The pony had had quite
enough of his dullness.

Chouchou gave a squeal and tripped into higher gear, with
Henryk holding on as if riding a runaway. The horse rumbled
down the dirt road, his eyes ringed white with fear, as Meagan
kept Targa close behind him for motivation.

Their pursuers fell behind. The path rose and trees thinned
into open land. Safe now, Henryk pulled on the reins and nearly
bounced off as Chouchou broke into a rough trot. He took his
sword from Meagan sheepishly, deliberately giving Targa a
wide berth.

"That was a good girl," Meagan said, patting Targa's neck.
"Never mind them."

Henryk smoothed the ruffled tufts of hair on Chouchou's
plump hindquarters. "*Lunatique*," he murmured privately to his
scandalized mount. Both sent offended looks in the pony's direction.

———

In places the road dwindled to a bare line in the grass, in others it became a muddy bog. By late afternoon the path began to
travel past cultivated fields and thatched houses. Coming over a
hill, Meagan and Henryk saw a village ahead. The road ran
through the settlement and up another hill, disappearing under
a stone archway—the walls of the Castle Sobrezy.

There was no drawbridge, though the stone walls were
square and crenellated, and towers rose from the corners.
Guards walked the parapets and flags waved from high turrets.
Below, men on horses practiced archery before the rampart,
cantering across the green in a display of rolling color.

"*Allez!*" Henryk called, slapping Chouchou heartily. Meagan hesitated. The stone fortress seemed to forbid visitors, not welcome them. She looked up; the overcast sky hid any sign of the nomad army. She gave Targa a reassuring pat—for herself—and started towards the castle.

No one challenged them as they rode past fields of men swinging rakes. A gray ox pulled a cart across the shorn field as hands heaved bundles of hay aboard. Swarms of children gathered scraps.

The road through the village was rutted and foul. Buzzing hornets and flies, squealing cartwheels and babies' cries filled the air. Geese flapped from round poultry houses, bells hanging from their outstretched necks. A pond lay at the bottom of the hill, with a trough dug into one end. The horses nickered at the sight.

Meagan steered toward the pond. "We should water the horses here, Henryk, before we go on."

Women gathered in groups at the edge of the brown water, washing laundry with hiked skirts. Henryk lifted his sword to them and kissed its hilt before dismounting. The women tittered and whispered to each other as Meagan rolled her eyes.

Arriving at the trough, Targa made dainty sips while watching the women carefully. Chouchou dunked his head into the green water and took long draughts, his ears moving in time with his swallows. Targa suddenly lifted her head. The mare's tiny ears strained forward, nostrils wide and testing the air. Henryk's smile faded and he pulled Chouchou from the water.

Seven horsemen riding massive horses moved ponderously toward them across the field. Meagan could see it would be minutes before the slow horses arrived. "Let the horses drink a little, Henryk. It has been all day."

The knight watched the oncoming riders. "No, Meagan," he decided, gesturing for help to mount.

Meagan sighed as she led Targa away from the water. She interlocked her fingers to give him a lift, grimacing as the knight used it as a stepping stool. "Henryk, I've shown you how to take a leg up—*ow!* It is not a climb—*jump!*"

A long note sounded as the knight squirmed aboard. One of the distant riders held up a horn and blew a call that rolled across the fields. Pulling on his helmet, Henryk pointed to his shield lying on the grass. Meagan handed it up. Henryk dropped his visor and began adjusting his equipment. "Not friend," he said ominously.

She looked again to the oncoming band. Their visors were down, a sign of hostility. The riders stopped in a line thirty yards away. One of the men shouted words unintelligible to Meagan, words that seemed to challenge. Henryk shouted unintelligible words of his own.

"Tell them the Abbey sent us," Meagan suggested. The exchange grew heated, and she swallowed hard as one of the men pointed to her. It seemed their conflict was not with Henryk at all. Targa was clearly a horse of the enemy. The riders started forward.

"Henryk," Meagan said nervously. "I think we should just go. We will find another castle."

"No! I safe!" Succumbing to the taunts, the young knight lifted his legs wide and clapped them to Chouchou's broad sides. The horse grunted and sauntered off to meet the line of horsemen.

"Of all the ... *Henryk!* Come back here!" A chorus of shouts came from the horsemen, and one shrill battle cry from Henryk. When the young knight raised his sword, it dawned on Meagan that Henryk was truly attacking—though his charge was scarcely a walk. "Oh be serious, Henryk! There's seven of them! And they can't catch me anyway."

The knights charged on.

"Please, Henryk. Let's just go. You don't have chain mail, remember? *Henryk!*"

The horsemen clashed in brief anticlimax. Henryk batted a lance away with his sword, but then Chouchou stopped completely. Henryk was left kicking to restart his mount while the seven continued on, coming for Meagan.

Wonderful, she thought, turning Targa in the other direction. *I hate knights.* She cantered over the top of a hill and glided down the other side. At the bottom she slowed, hoping the men had stopped. Moments passed before Meagan heard the rumble of hoof beats. Rising over the hill came the horsemen, swords out, lumbering in slow motion.

"It is too ridiculous!" Meagan said out loud in frustration. Clucking to Targa, she skirted in front of them and cantered back up the hill, leaving the horsemen to interfere with each other as they tried to turn. She cantered over the hill and almost collided with another band of riders.

Targa ducked away from this second wave of horsemen. Looking back, Meagan expected to see her pursuers toiling away in the distance—instead, three galloping riders were coming up fast behind her. These were not armored knights on slow heavy horses, but caped men on sleek runners.

Meagan clamped her legs around Targa and gave the pony her head. Across an open field they ran, the pony mare stretched out in a dead run. Meagan saw a line of woods and turned toward them. The pony was fast and the long-legged horses did not gain—but neither did they fall behind.

After the day's travel Targa was beginning to tire. The racing mare's breath came in bursts. A shadow darted to the side of them and stopped—they were past it before Meagan realized it was an arrow striking the ground. Another sailed past, closer. Crouching, she drove the pony toward the trees. Targa responded, pounding the ground in lightning strides. Ducking low, Meagan checked as she passed the first branches. Targa sailed over fallen trunks and crashed through brush as they fled through the woods. Meagan heard the fading shouts of her pursuers. Their large horses could not follow.

For a long time, Meagan walked to listen for followers and to let Targa cool down. Her attackers plainly thought she was one of the nomads. It did not matter that she was a woman in commonplace clothing—they saw only a barbarian's horse.

Meagan finally relaxed and slid off the pony's back. She untied her skin canteen and shook it as the mare bent down to nip the thin forest grass. There was enough for a few swallows. The water was too precious to let drip through a cupped hand, so Meagan found a depression in a flat rock and poured a stream into it. Targa leaned down and sniffed gently before sipping the spot dry. Meagan refilled the depression until the skin was empty, upending the last drops into her mouth.

———

Dusk was nearing when Meagan and Targa came to the edge of the woods. She mounted and rode out of the forest.

The pony raised her head, ears taut. "Easy, girl." Meagan looked around her, wondering why the mare was skittish. They were lost, true, but there was no sign of people, only alternating patches of meadow and wood. Targa shied from the darkening forest, so Meagan let her jog to the crest of a long hill to settle. The pony refused to go further. It was then she saw men in the trees.

"Barbarian! Stand firm or be killed!"

Targa half-reared as the sound of a gallop rushed up behind her. Meagan froze, holding the mare still, and felt a sharp punch to her back. The world spun and she was on the ground, stunned, felled by a dull-tipped lance—these men wished for a live captive.

A shadow fell over her. "My apologies," said a man in cultured English. "We thought you were a Tatar warrior since you ride astride. We did not realize it was only one of their wenches."

There was laughter from men around her. Meagan tried to sit but could not yet straighten. She probed where she had been struck and felt faint.

A man caught Targa's reins and twisted the bridle. The mare opened her mouth in pain.

"Let her go!" Meagan shouted. "We are not the enemy!"

"Oh ho! The barbarian speaks. So the better—she can beg for mercy."

The man who held Targa's bridle feinted to make the pony flinch. Targa laid her ears back and snapped.

"Leave her alone!" Meagan shouted again, trying to stand. The flat of a blade knocked her back.

"Cease at *once!*" came a clear voice. "By the Church's authority, strike again and it shall be your soul!"

Meagan looked up. A brown-robed man knelt beside her. "Hail thee, Daughter."

"Brother Bartholomew!"

Making a short sign of the cross over Meagan's forehead, the clergyman smiled. "Thus come the sheep to pasture." Lifting his voice to the men, he announced, "The horse is under the protection of the Church, in God's love as St. Francis has shown us. If the animal runs away, none shall rest until she is found."

"In God's love," murmured the subdued men.

"Was it you who escaped pursuit near the village, Daughter? We were told one of the infidels escaped into the forest. We have been searching."

"It is my horse. We look like Tatars."

"In these times, men see enemies. They have reason, Daughter." He glanced at Meagan's gown, tied for riding in a manner that made it apparent she had two legs. He said nothing about the immodesty.

Meagan rubbed her back. "I am so glad to see you, Brother Bartholomew. I was afraid you ... I thought you stayed behind at the Abbey."

"Providence intervened. The infidels arrived soon after you were away, and Daughter, every word you spoke was true. There were those who believed the Abbey could protect the town, but I heard another call. I left with these men, and we saw flames before we reached the first hill." He spoke softly. "There were many who escaped, Daughter, because of your warning."

While they were speaking, Targa terrorized the circle of men corralling her, kicking the air and lunging when any came too close. The men looked helplessly at Brother Bartholomew. "Excellency," a soldier said respectfully. "Forgive me, but we await instruction."

"If the animal has been provoked," he told them calmly, "you reap what you have sown. Now come, Daughter, we are guests at Sobrezy and we should proceed. Can you stand?"

Meagan nodded and took his hand to stand up. "Thank you, Brother Bartholomew." She stretched stiffly and eyed the mounted knights.

Brother Bartholomew warned softly, "Vengeance is the Lord's, Daughter. Practice forgiveness and take nothing on yourself. All the world loves a maiden sweet."

"Maybe they do, but that is the *second* time I've been lanced off a horse, and in case no one has noticed I am *not wearing armor!*" She limped purposefully to the circle of men being harassed by Targa and whistled the signal. The mare flapped her mane and snorted, waiting to let Meagan take her bridle. "It helps to be nice," she explained to the perplexed men around her. She joined Brother Bartholomew, leading her incensed mare a safe distance away from the others.

"How long will you stay with us?" a man asked the clergyman.

"We will not be summering, so fear not," Brother Bartholomew answered. "We are in pilgrimage to the Feast of St. John."

"Henryk has been talking about that ... what *is* it?" Meagan asked.

"A jousting tournament in Lublin, three days from Crakow. It is heresy to put the name of a Saint upon the devil's games, but even so there will be a Midsummer's Eve gathering of monks from Poland and Germany. Dominicans, Cistercians, Franciscans, perhaps even Benedictines."

"Really, even Benedictines?" she replied with forced cheer. The thought of a gathered multitude of monks and knights made her latest lance-injury twinge. "Have you seen Henryk? We were watering the horses when we were attacked."

"Perhaps, yes. Lorenzo spoke of a knight traveling with the barbarian. He is being held under suspicion of having a demon."

"That's probably him."

"We should be able to right the situation. It is a blessing to see you again, Daughter." Brother Bartholomew put his hand on her head. "We shall take the pilgrimage together. You and the knight Henryk will come with us. As God has brought us together a second time, it would be unwise to ignore His will."

The warhorse is a vain hope for safety,
by its great might it cannot save.

- Holy Bible, Psalms 33:16-17

Eᴠᴇʀʏ ɴɪᴄᴇ ᴛʜɪɴɢ Meagan had ever thought about castles was wrong. Standing inside her quarters (which she shared with four others), she could hear things crawling in the sweet-smelling rushes laid over the floor. Her newly-corrected wardrobe, a light gown, left her shivering in drafts or roasting beside fires. The best thing about a castle was probably its view, Meagan decided, if only you could see it. The heavy glass over the room's single window had the transparency of milk.

"*Madame?*" came a maid's voice from the doorway. "The meal begins."

Meagan smiled politely and followed the servant into the smoky hallways. Rush torches made shadows dance along the stone walls, bringing the rich tapestry to life. Woven scenes of Demons and the Heavenly Host seemed to watch them pass in the flickering light. Suddenly all was brightness and sound. A large bonfire burned on a ledge above a great hall. Racks of candles hung over the room. One long banquet table was set upon a wide stage, with gaily clad occupants lining the wall to face the crowd below. Perhaps two hundred people milled about the floor, eating, drinking, shouting, singing, and throwing bones to dogs. Odors of spices tangled with those of spoil and sweat.

"Meagan!" The voice was nearby, but it took two more calls before she saw Henryk standing on a bench waving, obviously inebriated. A mild-looking man sat beside him. She made her way across the room.

"Sitting, Meagan," Henryk slurred, pointing to the table's community bench.

Almost faint with hunger, Meagan wiped off a used spoon. *This is how people manage to eat with this smell,* she told herself— *they are starving.* There were no place settings, but there were piles of trenchers made of brown bread lying on wood platters. She scooped thick stew into one from a central basin and tried not to slurp, not that it mattered to the gobbling crowd. Roving servants traveled the tables with large pitchers, sloshing wine into outstretched goblets. Others carried trays of cut fruit. People began grabbing pieces before the tray was set down and Meagan, too slow, went without. The cold nose of a dog pressed against her leg, and Meagan handed down a scrap of bread.

Henryk walked around the table with his new friend behind him. "Meagan!" he shouted into her face. She waited for more, but the tipsy knight was apparently through.

Henryk's new friend leaned close and said in a soft, cultured voice, "My name is Janek. May I sit next to you?"

"Of course." Meagan moved to make way.

"Do you not speak Polish?" the man asked courteously. "And not even a little French? It is a shame. Your friend has much to say."

Next to Henryk another man talked blearily to the air. He winked at Meagan and lifted his glass.

"You make friends easily," Janek told her mildly. "Your friend says you were attacked on the road. I know the place. It draws thieves, and flushing them is great sport. You will feel safe to know a group went out immediately." Janek looked at Henryk. "Your friend must be a stout fighter to have rescued you from highwaymen. Is he a knight of renown?"

Meagan shrugged. "I suppose."

"I have seen his horse. A goodly sized mount."

"He is a mountain. Why does everyone want such huge horses? It seems the bigger, the better."

"It used to be said the bigger the horse, the better to trample peasants."

"I see," Meagan smiled, thinking the man was joking.

"Now it is because armor is so heavy." Janek squatted to pet the dogs pressing around the table. They jumped on him, licking his face and wriggling in excitement. "Your knight friend said you escaped the locust horde."

Meagan caught her breath. She had not told anyone about her ride with the marauding horsemen—that is, no one still alive.

"He said they attacked your town. You were staying at their Abbey."

"Oh, the *Abbey*. Yes, we escaped."

"What did you think was meant?"

"Nothing, I was just confused. Janek, the Tatars may not be far. They move very fast."

"Come, Meagan! Have you forgotten? Tomorrow is the Sabbath! Enough worry of this!" He leaned over and kissed Meagan full on her surprised mouth. "What is the matter, maid Meagan? Ha! Shall we call you Maid Meagan?"

"No, please don't." Something about the man reminded her of Braedin, unpleasantly. "I think a person should not kiss someone unless they expect it, and without dog drool all over them."

"Maid Meagan! Take no offense where none was meant!" Janek lowered his voice. "One would not wish to offend an Tatar's wench."

She pulled away sharply. *"You?"*

Janek stood and began an impromptu dance around the table. "Maid Meagan! Hah! Maid Meagan! Come, it is the time for song! It is time for dance!" Henryk stood with the others, joining in.

They are all insane, Meagan thought, as she felt the coldness of a dog's nose press against her leg. She started to pick a scrap of bread to throw when the coldness squeezed her knee. She jumped and slapped the man's hand away. Grabbing a last piece of food, she stood and walked quickly out of the banquet hall, ignoring the pleas for her return. It was time for bed.

Meagan heard the bells in her dreams long before she opened her eyes. The white glow of the room's opaque window showed dawn was approaching. Meagan heard shouts from the Great Hall below.

Her first thought was that breakfast was even louder than dinner. Then she heard something else, or rather felt it. A tremor was coming through the stone floor, the rumbling of a hundred thousand hooves.

Shouting was in the hallways now. Meagan pulled her gown from a clothes pole and dressed in the half-light. She followed a stream of people into the hallway and through winding corridors. Bells rang from the towers as she crowded with others onto the battlements. Meagan strained to see, but all that was visible was a placid dawn sky. She pushed her way to the edge and looked across the fields.

The ground was black with horsemen. Galloping shadows swirled through the flaming village below. Black lines streaked across the green rampart. Mist rose in places to give glimpses of the nomads pausing to devour the village.

Men ran through the courtyards and lined the battlements, but they were pitifully few against the onslaught. A shrill scream drifted on the wind, a sound Meagan remembered with a knot of terror. The massed horde surged up, spreading as it came and circling the castle like a rising tide.

Thin flames streaked through the air as galloping riders shot burning darts over the stone walls. Castle archers returned waves of arrows. On the balcony, tonsured men began sacraments against the attackers as others backed away, ashen.

Yet the flaming arrows landed harmlessly among the stone buildings. Massed horsemen stormed the closed gates to no avail. Meagan watched the smoke rising from the village as the nomads' strength was wasted against stone. The tide retreated. The locusts could not enter the silo.

The castle was quiet by sundown. The day had been filled with such smoke and screaming that the balconies could have overlooked Hell—but the tide had dashed harmlessly against stone, and now the marauders were gone.

Meagan remembered reading stories about medieval times, which were called the Dark Ages not because the period lacked lighting, but because it was marked by impoverished illiteracy and left little record of itself. Before the Dark Ages, books and dramatic works were produced—but the Western record fades with the fall of Rome and remains dark until the intellectual flowering of the Renaissance.

It was true that Europe could never resist the Mongolian tide, but neither could the Mongolian armies hold their gains. Their equestrian strength was also their weakness. The massive cavalry needed a constant supply of fresh grass: it was impossible for the nomadic army to stay in any region for long. The Black Horde indeed passed through history as locusts—unstoppable in destruction but quickly fading away.

Dinner in the castle that night was somber, and afterwards men retired to their beds in exhaustion. Meagan had seen Henryk only once. He had been in a company of guards, engrossed in the battle. She was not worried, for few in the castle were injured. Thousands of arrows had rained over the fortress without finding a mark. In contrast, horse and nomad corpses littered the rampart, and the village was a silent, smoking ruin.

Meagan's thoughts returned to the Great Horse. Sleepless, she wandered the castle corridors. There *must* be a way to summon Promise, she told herself. Some way to go home. The Great Hall was silent and few torches were lit. Dogs slunk along walls beneath dark gargoyles. Only the rats were emboldened, scurrying on tables, climbing tapestries and running across wooden rafter beams.

"I see one infidel survives." The dark form of Janek stepped out of a shadow and stood before her.

Meagan jumped at the voice. "You frightened me, Janek! I didn't see you there."

"Really, Maid Meagan, you must be more observant." He stepped closer. "For your own sake."

"Thank you, Janek. I will remember that."

Pattering footsteps approached. A group of clergy entered the corridor, carrying candles close to their hooded faces. It was the Brotherhood on their way to the candlelit midnight Mass. This unsettling rite was feared: the service was also called the Dark Choir.

"Hi Lorenzo, how are you?" Meagan called, for once glad to see him. "Is Brother Bartholomew with you?"

"This is not so high a place. My Teacher is at counsel." The face of the apprentice was barely visible in the flickering light. "You are found in strange places, Daughter of Eve. You are ever a seeker in darkness."

"I suppose you might think so. Well, I think I will call it a night." Meagan said it nervously, backing away from Janek. "Sleep well. God bless."

She walked quickly to her room, stepping carefully over the sleeping forms of her roommates. The single window glowed with moonlight. Meagan lay on her straw mat and stared into the darkness, trying to calm herself and not listen to the castle's noises.

A random incident drifted into her mind as she waited for sleep. She remembered when, among the nomads, two men had tried to mount Targa and failed—lifetime riders, unable to mount a pony. The memory brought back the words of the legend, that no one could ride a Great Horse without the owner's permission ... *save conssente by hir maister wille.*

That night Meagan dreamed of her own golden foal running and kicking in the backyard. The image transformed into the sleek frame of an older Promise running with her pasture mates. Stretching her limbs and pouring across the ground, the filly turned toward the sun and was transfigured into whiteness, unfolding bright wings and lifting into the air. Soaring aloft, Promise galloped across the sky with thunder in her wake. Circling, she glided down and splashed into water. She stood to her knees in a murky waterhole. Small now and aged, her shining white coat was mottled gray. She watched Meagan curiously with friendly interest, and then Promise again changed color, first to piebald and then to black. Pawing the water, she bounded forward in a splashing surge as Helios—then Helios too brightened into shining white and rose up to the sky.

Meagan opened her eyes. It was morning.

She was still in her clothes, but she felt lighter, energized, because at last something about the legend made sense. Though she had first looked for Promise in the lanky form of a young thoroughbred, the Great Horse had other lives in other times. Promise had been Helios, and perhaps even the curious gray mare from the watering hole. Meagan shuddered to remember the poor piebald horse entombed in the Scythian crypt.

Targa. I have to go see her. Meagan hurried down the halls and stairways and through dark passages to the castle stables and its dim row of stalls. Horses began a nickering chorus as she walked slowly, peering into each dank enclosure. Meagan finally found a tiny head with perked ears looking back.

"Well, good morning, girl. Are you or are you *not* the Great Horse?" The pony only remained watching Meagan expectantly. Sighing, she took the bridle from its hook and went inside. Targa butted her head against Meagan's stomach. "Maybe we should call you the Great Pony. Okay, okay. We are going outside."

Nothing seemed special about Targa, nothing more or less than usual. The little mare was eager to leave the stall, and pulled down the aisle into the breaking sunlight. Meagan led her through the courtyard. A sleepy sentry stood by the half-opened gate and let them pass.

The grass was gone, trampled into earth. Nomad bodies had been gathered into high piles of corpses that were scattered across the hill. Even so, the morning air was fresh and the sun shone with the same warmth as upon yesterday's violence. Targa nosed the bare ground and snorted.

"We will find grass," Meagan promised, putting the reins over Targa's head and jumping on bareback. After last night's dream she had a *slight* hope the pony would turn white and sprout wings, but disappointingly the mare merely opened into a jigging trot.

Meagan pointed Targa down the hill, keeping away from the piled corpses The village was charred wood and ashes. She rode past the desolation, remembering the laundering women Henryk had flirted with at the ash-blackened pond. She thought sadly about the people in the fields, the oxen, the other animals. She had seen so many of these burnt remains. There would be no one alive, nothing left.

Targa grew restless. Meagan skirted the hill but found only more ruin, so she rode the mare over the still-warm ashes toward green countryside. The pony stepped gingerly across the blasted ground, blowing in dismay.

Gradually the churned earth gave way to grass. Meagan steered Targa toward a open place between trees, looking for a place to graze. Riding under the foliage, she saw dark forms of men underneath a large limb. Meagan turned quickly and trotted away. She looked back, but the shapes remained motionless until a gust of breeze moved the leaves. One of the shapes twisted slowly, then twisted back. Nine men were hanging by the neck. Highwaymen.

She leaned down to Targa. "If you are the Great Horse, can we *please* go home now?" But the pony only continued trotting, unchanged, ignoring every plea.

———

Father,

I come to You with doubt confusing my thoughts. My Brethren suspect the woman Meagan to be of the Enemy. Indeed, she is shrouded in mysteries.

Her horse comes whither she summons, a thing to be seen in familiars of witches. The woman is fair of look and strange of speech but comes without a past, or none she will speak of. She rides a pagan's horse, and this too well, as if the animal and she were truly of a kind. She warns of doom yet she escapes its fire, and she knows the language of the Mass.

She has a protector, a chaste knight. He has pledged her safety in confession, and I pray he can assure it. Father, I see no darkness in this woman's eye, and her warnings have been true. She has saved lives, and good fruit comes not of a bad tree. She may be a heretic as the whisperers say, but I will not judge this. I pray forgiveness if I am misled.

I am, by Your Grace,
Aurick Bartholomew

Lord Ronald said nothing; he flung himself from the room,
flung himself upon his horse and rode madly off in all directions.
                                   - Stephen Leacock (1869-1944) humorist

TRAVEL TO THE Tournament of St. John would take many days, and the castle grounds were alive with cooking, washing and haggling for provisions. On the morning of departure, Meagan was up early to brush Targa. She enjoyed getting up before dawn and the bustle of preparation—it reminded her of horse competition mornings.

The pony enjoyed being groomed, and her stamping and peevish nips stopped when she saw the brushes coming. Most horses enjoy the simple ritual. Grooming is a healthful ancient practice little changed by the ages, and one of the first skills learned as a horseman.

There is an order to be followed. To begin, the horse must be tied with a special knot that will secure the powerful animal and yet undo with a simple tug. The horse is gone over head to tail with a curry comb to break out the dirt and then a stiff dandy brush to flick it away. Special attention is given to places where tack might rub. To finish, a short-bristled body brush is stroked across the clean hair to raise a soft luster. The mane and tail are separated and combed, and the hooves are cleaned, counter clockwise, in order.

Meagan stood back to admire her work. The pony's coat was coming along nicely. Targa lowered her head and shook, as satisfied as a cat after a morning's cleaning. Vanity has been considered a horse's trait.

"Of a morning, barbarian's fair wench."

Meagan turned to see Janek. The knight was mounted in armor and accompanied by attendants. "You say the rudest things," she told him coolly. "Unless you are coming to apologize, I have nothing to say to you."

"As a man and a knight, it is what I have to say that matters most ... is it not, sweet maiden?"

"I am not dignifying that with an answer. Just because you are a man does not mean you can be rude."

"To speak to a man this way defies the order of nature and rejects the law of the eternal Church! Who are you to ignore what has always been and will always be?"

She sighed. "I am looking for Henryk. Have you seen him?"

Janek lifted an eyebrow to his companions and there was rude laughter. "Is he missing? Perhaps we should look together."

Meagan swung up on Targa—or rather she *hopped* up, for another irritation was having to ride sidesaddle to please the clergy. The fierce taskmasters enforced dress codes and focused their frowns on female comportment. Clothing indicated social standing, and Meagan was displeased to discover that her ankle-length dress, or *kirtle*, was of a drab color and style suitable for a semi-respectable peasant. She did not mind the comment on her station, or even having to therefore wear her hair in tight braids under a short veil, but she did mind the cumbersome gown. The kirtle was as utilitarian for riding as eating salad with a spoon.

Even in the precarious and unfamiliar position of riding *aside* rather than *astride*, Meagan had nothing to fear from these men while mounted. Targa was much quicker and more responsive than any of the huge, manly mounts. If knights did not take themselves so seriously, she would have been tempted to tease them by running circles around their horses. She chose valor through discretion and rode away.

Thin horns announced the first departures, but Henryk was nowhere to be seen. Meagan searched the grounds milling with court attendants, merchants, clergy, and of course knights with their assorted entourages. The benighted medieval period created no formal breeds, instead there were "types" of horses such as the weight-carrying *destriers* whose descendents resemble the Clydesdales and other heavy draft breeds. A wealthy knight also kept a tall, noble *palfrey* as their "High Horse" for parades and ceremonies. Real work of battle was done on light *coursers*, and low-bred *rounceys* and *hackneys* were used for common transportation. Ladies rode fashionable *jennets* not much larger than Targa.

Meagan looked impatiently for Henryk and Chouchou as she watched the first travelers move out. It occurred to her that most knights—including Janek—had a boy to hold the lances, another for blankets, a falconer, a page, a professional armourer, entertainers, and a plentiful collection of huntsmen and hounds. This was not counting squires, grooms, valets, maids and cooks—while poor Henryk had no attendants at all.

"Henryk has us, doesn't he, girl?" Targa flicked an ear back as Meagan patted her. "His sister knights." *I'm sure he would love to hear that,* she thought, reconsidering. The only women in the knightly procession were giggling maids dressed in garlands or those carrying cooking supplies.

Meagan had to admit that if Henryk was unhappy with his situation, he never showed it. The proud knight never tired of brushing his enormous mount, taking great care to rub the giant horse between his lop ears. While others were at campfires telling stories, Henryk grazed Chouchou in the dark, singing Polish ballads.

She and Targa searched the thinning crowds and finally found Henryk in ditch, grumbling and flailing his legs as Chouchou calmly grazed. "There you are! The dynamic duo."

"*Grand limace!*" the knight grunted, terming his beloved a "giant snail." He hauled on the reins to raise Chouchou's head. The horse took only a few steps out of the ditch before plunging for another mouthful.

"Henryk, I warned you about letting him eat under bridle." The equine vice was highly annoying, if less dangerous than bucking or wiping a rider off under a low tree.

"Horses must eat—*oof!*" Henryk lay slung across his horse's neck from the sudden pull. He groped for the reins while Chouchou nibbled a succulent patch.

"You are going to have to be firm, Henryk." Meagan would have suggested spurs, but spurs are properly meant to refine communication, not to cause pain—Henryk was not a skillful enough rider to use spurs correctly. The young knight was not merely bad, he was practiced and diligent in his errors. It was left to Chouchou to decipher which kicks and pulls Henryk intended and which he did not.

"Why don't we change places?" Meagan suggested. "I could teach Chouchou to walk without eating and you could ride Targa."

Alarmed, eyes wide, Henryk began kicking harder.

"No, really, Henryk. Targa is easy once you are up, and riding more than one horse is the best way to learn." Meagan stopped when she saw the knight's white knuckles. She realized then something she could never tell: why Chouchou was perfect for him and why he chose the slowest possible mount.

Knight Henryk was afraid of horses.

———

Meagan enjoyed the road. Her pilgrimage group was sixty members strong, not counting the crowd of horses, donkeys and mules of all descriptions. The clergy stayed together. Whenever she rode past Brother Bartholomew, he waved before returning to his chants.

Food and water were plentiful, and campsites were made every twilight. Stories and laughter passed the time and singing was always in the air. One of Meagan's favorite performers was a minstrel on a donkey who rode back and forth along the procession strumming a lyre. People joined in as he passed, so waves of song passed over the party as they traveled.

When a town was seen in the distance, scouts rode ahead to announce their group's arrival. Always eager for an occasion to celebrate, townspeople filled the streets as the expedition passed. It was the original parade, with everyone waving and shouting. People rushed up with bouquets and gifts of food. Children and barking dogs flanked the procession, and the horses pranced as if conscious of the occasion.

One dark cloud hung over the group—literally: that of the Mongols. Vulnerable on the road, members of the party rode ahead on coursers and returned with news. Once the scouts did not return. That day the pilgrimage rode through a town where the people did not run out to greet them. There, the procession instead walked grimly through the town's ashes, heads low.

On the last night of the journey, the Brothers varied their normal routine. At Vespers, twilight, a table was set at each side of the altar. Instead of devotions, passages in Latin were read aloud as everyone present walked solemnly to the altar. Each was handed a candle and bowed in prayer as it was lit by a clergyman. Afterwards, each placed his or her candle, still lit, upon an altar table. The result was a sparkling display of light around the objects of devotion that accompanied Mass.

The Tournament of St. John had begun.

———

Well before dawn the morning was alive with noise and preparations. Henryk showed up in a freshly washed tunic; his sword and shield gleamed. Meagan left Targa tied to a tree while she helped make Chouchou as presentable as possible.

She began by thinning the horse's thick mane, and then french-braided his tail to show off his wide hindquarters. While she oiled the horse's oversized hoofs, Lorenzo came to stand over her.

"The Tournament evokes each of the Seven Deadly Sins, night-seeker Meagan," Lorenzo lectured. "This dressing and beautifying the corporal body is Pride. Instead of this fleeting vanity, better you should think of yourself as you will be, decaying and putrefying."

"Oh, Lorenzo, *really.*"

"All your work is done to evoke Envy in others, a second deadly sin. And then, there is pursuit of the spoils of victory."

"Which deadly sin is that?" Meagan had to ask.

"Greed."

She bent to oil another of Chouchou's hooves.

"Wrath is brought on by combat, Gluttony in feast. Lust is inflamed by the ladies and their attendants."

Meagan stood up and wiped her forehead with her arm. "Isn't one of the sins Sloth?" She pointed to the teeming camp. "How does a Tournament cause Sloth?"

"The melancholy of the losing participants."

Meagan sighed and moved to the last hoof. "Honestly, Lorenzo. It seems the Church frowns on anything people like to do."

"The Church exists to bring order and must be obeyed. Frivolous pleasure distracts people from giving their thoughts to the Church."

"Lorenzo, if the Church thinks the Tournament is so bad, then why do all the monks and friars come?"

"The Tournament is a bed of vice, but it is at least a time of unification." Lorenzo scanned the camp in dissatisfaction. The road in the distance was filling with gaily costumed people and horses. "It is God's will that His people be united under the One True Church. His wrath is upon us for our failure."

"Don't you mean we are the "Good Romans" against the barbarians?"

"You speak strangely of strange things, night-seek—"

"My apprentice!" Brother Bartholomew called as he hurried to join them. He seemed displeased. "By custom we meet after dawn service."

"Forgive me, Excellency," Lorenzo answered respectfully. "I cannot rest while such sin surrounds me."

"I have asked you, apprentice, to call me "Excellency" no more. Desist. I fear your love is inclined more toward the Lord's power than to His charity as He instructed."

"Again forgive me, Excellen—forgive me, Father."

"We are to call no man Father but the Father which is in Heaven, apprentice," Brother Bartholomew said patiently. "Have you given our Daughter the morning blessing?"

"I was about to, my ... my..."

"I am your Brother in God, Lorenzo."

"Yes, my Brother in God. I was about to give my blessing. I was giving a brief sermon on the Seven Sins."

"Be temperate, Lorenzo. This is a day of celebration."

"You are too lenient, my Brother in God," Lorenzo protested. "Our Lord is one of might and fire—why suffer this foolishness? Proverbs says, 'He who spareth the rod hateth his son.'"

"That is *enough*, apprentice," Brother Bartholomew said firmly. "The rod you speak of is the shepherd's staff, meant for guiding his flock. Do you mean to suggest the Lord's Holy

Word means to strike a child with a *staff*? I think your teaching may be blasphemy, Lorenzo. You are in dangerous territory. Open your heart lest it be snatched from you."

Fear flashed in Lorenzo's eyes. The nether world was very real to him, literally under his feet. He started to stutter. "Forgive me, Brother. I will do more penitence—I will tear the skin from my back!"

Brother Bartholomew closed his eyes wearily. "It is not a matter of exchange, apprentice. You are not grasping the teachings of peace. I am recommending you for mild censure. May it profit your soul."

"I will do better!" Lorenzo wrung his hands together. Meagan was shocked when he glanced her way, for the man's eyes burned in fury.

The traveling party arrived at the Tournament grounds midmorning. Meagan had never seen so much color; even memories of Rome seemed austere in comparison. Multicolored tents set upon boldly-colored carpets spread across meadows to the edge of the encroaching forest, draped in tapestries and hanging baskets of wildflowers. Food spices and perfumes filtered through an underlying scent of unwashed bodies. More people arrived each day, drifting in with sweet ballads or bawdy choruses depending on their taste and sobriety.

A Melee was underway in the Center Court. By the time Meagan and Henryk arrived to watch, horses had been dispensed with, led off the field by each combatant's squire. Now the knights fought with mace or sword, swinging in high strokes. The purpose of a blow was obviously to stagger one's opponent, but beyond this Meagan could gain no insight as to the rules.

Three knights in red tunics descended upon a common enemy, beating until the man fell lengthwise. Then two of the Red knights surprised their third teammate with a double hit to the back of his head, leaving him sprawled on the pile of fallen contestants. Only a knight in green checkers was left standing to face the two treacherous knights. Boos echoed as the man tried to escape. Meagan thought it the most foolish thing she had ever seen. "I am going, Henryk."

"No, Meagan. Begins."

"I just want to check on the horses. There will be more fighting later, I am sure." She walked through the gathering crowds to her tent beside a patch of trees. Behind it, picketed in a grassy clearing, Targa was dwarfed by the grazing Chouchou. Horse companions often stand head to tail, flicking each other's front half to keep away flies. It had taken time, but now the mismatched pair were inseparable.

It was strange to see the two together, these representatives of different worlds. The encounter of the light, fast horses of the Mongolians against heavier, more powerful European types—the fleet against the strong—symbolized a clash of cultures that stirred the tides of history.

Meagan whistled softly. Targa lifted her head and nickered, coming forward.

Two men watched nearby. "Sorcery," one whispered loudly enough for Meagan to hear.

"Not exactly," she said, producing a piece of carrot from her pouch. Targa took it delicately.

"You should not jest about such things," one of the men growled. "There be strange spirits in the air. Just last week a rooster was tried in our village for laying an egg."

"I don't doubt it," Meagan replied pleasantly. The common lack of education seemed to increase superstition—there were no skeptics here.

Targa lipped the piece of carrot before crunching, her ears flicking as she listened. Returning to join Chouchou, Targa gave the towering mammoth a gratuitous nip that the gelding ignored. Eating was the one serious activity in Chouchou's life and he gave it his full attention. The big horse was fortunate to live in a virtual salad bowl.

Meagan encouraged youngsters to pet Targa and bring her treats—under supervision. The mare still snapped at adults but was ladylike with well-behaved children and took their offerings with good grace. In time, Meagan was sure the little war pony would learn manners. "You need to follow Chouchou's example," she chided the mare. "Eat and get fat, so you won't look like a Tatar's horse. Then everyone will leave us alone."

The Tournament's jovial atmosphere was lifting Meagan's spirits. By her calculations her own sixteenth birthday was coming, even if she could not say exactly when it would be. She would celebrate anyway. The sunshine seemed to carry a vibrant, clean smell. She leaned across Targa's back and stroked her thick coat. As the pony bent down to graze, it seemed the good day could go on forever.

Qualifying rounds took place in the outer fields, where the tilting courts took all comers. It was Henryk's chance, and Meagan did everything she could to help. Chouchou had never been sleeker and his old saddle had been soaped and oiled into new life. Looking at Henryk sitting on Chouchou, his blond head sticking out from borrowed chain mail that hung in loops, Meagan felt the glow of a horse show mother.

"Here, Henryk," she said, handing up his shield. "And remember to keep your heels down. That's why you keep losing your stirrups." She took a dilapidated lance with peeling paint from where it leaned against a tree.

"*Merci*, Meagan." Henryk adjusted the lance so it stood straight in the air, balanced on its stirrup rest.

There was only one thing left to do, and Meagan tried once more to persuade Henryk against it. "Do we *have* to, Henryk? It just seems so ... well, stupid."

"*Tak!* Meagan, please the foldblind."

Meagan looked out over the fields filled with contestants on blindfolded horses. There was no barrier between the contestants as there would be in later years of the joust. At this point in history, two knights simply rode their blindfolded mounts together with all possible speed.

"It is just so dangerous, Henryk." Chouchou scratched his massive head against Meagan as she tied the blindfold over his eyes. "It looks silly, too."

Fortunately, all possible speed for a Tournament mount was a slow amble: under nearly seven hundred pounds of rider, armor, barding, gear, saddle, sword, shield and lance, the horses could hardly move. Watching the massive beasts stagger under the weight, Meagan finally understood the preoccupation these men had with their horses' size.

She was not too worried for Henryk. Much of the time the horses passed too far from each other to make contact at all, though occasionally horses sideswiped each other or collided, making a mess of their riders, tack and embroidered robes. Meagan had been watching the contests all morning and, aside from occasional broken lances and a collision, every pass had been a clear miss. As far as she could see the game was a colossal bout of Chicken.

"Of a noontime, Daughter." Brother Bartholomew appeared with Lorenzo standing just behind. "I have come to give the knight his blessing."

"Tak!" Henryk let go of his reins and set down his lance. He wrenched off his helmet and struggled to dismount for the ritual.

Meagan frowned and wiped her forehead. "Is there any way to give his blessing where he is, Brother Bartholomew? You have no idea how hard it is to get him up there."

The dilemma was answered with a cry from Henryk which preceded his long, noisy slide to the ground. He clinked and lay prostrate. Chouchou dropped his head and began to eat.

"The woman wishes to thwart the blessing," Lorenzo said ominously. "Did you not hear, Brother?"

"Our friend is unaware of custom, apprentice. That is all."

Henryk revived and struggled to stand with Meagan's help. "It was nice of you to come, Brother Bartholomew," she said, grunting; the knight was awkward underneath his heavy secondhand chain mail. "I have not seen much of you, sir."

"But you are seen, seeker in the night," Lorenzo commented darkly.

"Silence, apprentice. Our friends need assistance, not trials from us."

"As you say, my Brother in God."

The knight leaned to kiss the clergymens' hands humbly. A few Latin words were said over Henryk's bowed head.

Getting a chainmail-clad Henryk back aboard Chouchou was a daunting project. Earlier, Meagan had recruited porters for the job, who had hoisted the knight up with a shaky pyramid. She looked around for helpers.

"The blessing is finished." Brother Bartholomew spread his hands. "Should you not proceed?"

"We will, it is just ... we are rather short of grooms and squires."

"Very well, we shall assist. Lorenzo?"

The apprentice protested. "This is not our duty!"

"We can hardly leave the knight on foot. As we have caused him to come down, we shall cause him to ascend once again."

Lorenzo began to say more, but he was stopped by the gaze of the senior priest. "Very well, we shall assist."

Neither of the clergymen knew how to begin, so Meagan directed. "Lift Chouchou's head, Henryk." She faced Brother Bartholomew. "Hold my hands tight. Henryk steps here, and we lift him up." The two stood close by Chouchou and held their interleaved hands low. Henryk tried to lift his leg high but could not reach. When Meagan and Brother Bartholomew bent lower, they sagged under his weight.

"More suggestions, Daughter?"

Meagan bit her lip. She did have one. "Maybe if Lorenzo could just, well, lean down."

Lorenzo bent forward. "I do not see how this accomplishes anything. Perhaps this is conjuring, my Brother in God."

"No, I mean get down on all fours," Meagan corrected. "You make a step for Henryk, so he can climb up. It's the only other way he knows."

Slow incredulity spread over the apprentice priest's face as he realized what Meagan was suggesting.

Brother Bartholomew nodded. "Sage advice, Daughter. Come, Lorenzo, offer your back. We must thank our friends for this chance. It is exalted in the sight of the Lord to serve so humbly."

"Yes, my Brother in God. For the Lord." Lorenzo bent down and positioned himself on the ground.

Meagan could not resist wiping a quick hand over the clergyman's back to smooth his robe. "There you go, Henryk. Step right there."

The knight was horrified by the prospect of standing on a holy man's back. He stood open-mouthed, looking from one to the other.

"Go ahead young knight," encouraged Brother Bartholomew. "Tell him, Lorenzo, how welcome he is to use your back in his need."

"Go ahead," growled Lorenzo.

Henryk gently tested Lorenzo's back before applying his weight. Lorenzo grunted as the knight stepped up and into the offered hands of Meagan and Brother Bartholomew. He clambered into the saddle and sat fearfully as if waiting for the sky to open up.

"Nicely done, apprentice." Brother Bartholomew nodded approvingly. "Now, we must go. Others have need of our services."

Lorenzo dusted himself off in ill temper. He gave Meagan a last dark look before turning to follow his senior. Meagan noticed the imprint of a boot clearly outlined on the back of his brown robe. She decided not to mention it.

Henryk's turn was called. "Contestant Bialaskorski, attend!"

Meagan helped to start Chouchou. Henryk clutched the reins as she led him to the narrow rectangle marked in bare dirt. The competitors came to face each other and the start was given. Chouchou shook himself and tried for a bite of grass, but for once Henryk was firm. With the equine equivalent of a shrug, Chouchou started to walk forward.

Henryk's competition was having trouble of another kind. The rider was a portly fellow who had perhaps been too long in his cups for such a contest. He clapped his legs on his blindfolded horse and fell backwards when the animal surged forward. Hauling on the reins to bring himself upright, he caused the horse to turn left. The knight pulled again to compensate and his horse veered right. In this way they zigzagged across the lane, completely missing Henryk and Chouchou and clearing the sidelines of spectators.

The blindfolded horse soon had enough and decided his own path. The portly knight left the tilt lane at a high amble, picking up speed. Onlookers craned their necks to follow the knight's run, flinching as it ended in the boughs of a tree.

Henryk turned in the saddle and raised his visor, beaming. "See, Meagan. I ride the not worst." She could think of no reason to argue.

The two foremost ranks of either party rushed upon each other
in full gallop, and met in the middle of the Lists with a shock
the sound of which was heard at a mile's distance.

- Sir Walter Scott (1771-1832) Ivanhoe

THE RULES FOR jousting were simple: the object was to shiver, or break, one's lance against an opponent. Three runs were made. If both knights shivered their lances an equal number of times, the round was declared a tie. Oddly, unseating a competitor gained no additional points, and *how* a lance was shivered made no difference: a lance held sideways was a legal strategy. Of course, the surest way to shiver a lance was head-on contact with an opponent's armor or shield, but this was difficult because the point of the lance was twelve feet away and its motion was amplified by the distance. Competitors came together at something approaching twenty miles an hour—though in Chouchou's case it was considerably less—so there were many misses and frequent disasters.

As the competition proceeded, Henryk did prove himself gifted with the lance. If Chouchou was started in a straight line and Henryk passed within reach of his opponent, the young knight seldom missed.

The Tournament was arranged so the qualifying rounds took place around the main tilting lane, or Center Court. As a knight rose in the standings, he was able to ride in lanes progressively nearer to Center Court where he might attract the attention of patrons.

"Henryk Bialaskorski, by the Saints!"

Meagan and Henryk turned to see a man draped in yellow-and-black checkered robes. He upended an oversized silver tankard before handing it to a servant and spreading his arms. *"Ami!"*

Henryk returned the greeting and they embraced.

"Your papa would be so proud," the man sniffed, wiping his eyes. The meeting was a fortunate one, for the man was a wealthy old friend of the family. Looking over Henryk's borrowed chain mail in dismay, he barked instructions to a servant. Henryk started to protest, but the man in the checkered robes took the knight by the arm and led him away. Henryk gave Meagan a cheerful wave before vanishing into the crowd.

———

One tent had been set aside as restroom facilities, and Meagan liked to use it early before a line formed. She emerged wondering, as she had in Rome, whether these people even had a sense of smell. Coming back to her shared tent, Meagan found a roommate looking through her things. Privacy was an unrespected concept.

The woman dropped the saddle pad and returned to her mat. Meagan hurried to refold her pad as the snooper sighed loudly and took up her own statuette figure of a saint, a gift from a courting beau. A trumpet blast preceded a call from outside. "Will the Lady Meagan present herself?"

The Lady Meagan? All froze in position. The call came again, and the women made a collective rush for the shared hair brushes. Meagan avoided the scramble and tried to compose herself as she walked outside.

Henryk was mounted on Chouchou in full regalia. The young knight was resplendent in a yellow-and-black checkered cape emblazoned with a white lion over a gold cross. A cream feather capped his helmet. A full complement of attendants circled him: squires, armourers and grooms. Henryk's new sponsor had been generous.

Chouchou's transformation was even more startling. The horse was the very image of a *destrier*. He was draped in *barding*, a giant fabric that covered his wide body and trailed to the ground. It was yellow to match Henryk's tunic and cape, with a broad stripe of checkerboard along its hem. Chouchou's head was encased in a black velvet brocade, with a single silver spike set on his forehead in imitation of a unicorn. The saddle was an enormous leather loveseat over embroidered tapestry.

Meagan had the sudden realization that *she* was the final attendant, the Object of Court. All around the tents, people stopped to watch. "Oh ... my brave knight, how long the time has seemed since seeing you last..." she said dramatically, and hoped it would suffice.

One of Henryk's attendants translated his words: "My lord's request, if it pleases you, gentle maiden, is your graceful courtesy in bestowing upon your servant knight wishes of victory."

"Oh! Of course ... yon wonderful knight..." Meagan winced as she struggled to find the right words. "Go to triumph, bold knight, and go to ... win! Yes, go win! Please!" Conscious of eyes upon her, she pulled down her night ribbon, letting her hair spill over her shoulders. "One moment, oh brave knight. I could not bear you to leave without this ribbon ... to tie on you somewhere ... for luck." She walked over and flamboyantly tossed the twisted ribbon; it fluttered and fell before Henryk could grab it. Snatching it midair without losing her pasted smile, Meagan tied it to the horse's bridle. She turned, pretending not to see the stares, and without a backward glance went back into the tent.

The women inside were speechless, excited to be in the presence of a prosperous knight's formal object of desire. With a flurry of movement they rushed into action, grabbing combs and ribbons and scooping out dabs of coarse makeup. They descended upon Meagan with gusto.

———

Henryk's ability with the lance offset his weak horsemanship, and his successes brought him steadily closer to Center Court. In the tournament's final days, knights on "The List" paraded the grounds in full regalia, each choosing a color and a contrasting black, gold, white or gray. The horses' colorful barding swept the ground; reins were covered in matching cloth. Plumes and feathers so decorated each knight and his attendants that each entourage was a moving pageant.

Four strong attendants were needed to lift Henryk onto Chouchou. Before each match his new shield decorated with standing lions was handed up, followed by a new striped lance.

Meagan wanted Henryk to succeed, but she had doubts. Earlier rounds had weeded out the lesser competitors, and there would be no more wild forfeit rides into the trees. She worried most about Chouchou, for the easygoing animal did not seem to be rising to the occasion. In fact, at that moment Chouchou was losing his battle with sleep. The horses eyelids sagged as Henryk's helmet was lowered.

The signal was given and the knights were off ... sort of. With much help from the attendants Chouchou was stirred into motion. Henryk grasped the reins for balance and began a steady barrage of kicking as his opponent accelerated and crossed the lane. Henryk tried to feint his opponent's lance away, but it hit Chouchou mid-chest and cracked. Chouchou faded to an ignoble stop. His head drooped.

Henryk's sponsor came onto the field throwing his arms and shouting, yellow robes billowing behind. Chouchou watched with perked ears hoping for a treat as the man stopped in front of him and, holding his nose, waved the big horse away. Knight Henryk was pulled from his disgraced mount. Chouchou stood calmly through his humiliation as his barding was removed, and lastly his silver unicorn's horn.

The sponsor shouted orders to his manservants. A bay horse was soon led up to the sidelines: Henryk's sponsor had brought his protégé a proper mount. This new horse made a better impression in every way—he was livelier, cleaner of line and more muscular than Chouchou, his eye was fiery and he gave the impression of knowing he was a knight's mount. The sponsor watched in satisfaction as white-faced Henryk was lifted up and given his lance.

The next round was begun, and at the signal the bay slid majestically into a fast and steady amble. Henryk was relieved of having to kick constantly, and he couched the lance high to expertly hit the opposing knight's inside shoulder. The rival knight twisted and toppled with the dignity of a great oak—and remained as inert. After a short discussion the judges awarded the contest to Henryk.

At the news, Henryk's sponsor began slapping bystanders on the back. His yellow robes disappeared into the crowd. Meagan watched attendants swarm the field. A knight was on one knee before a maiden, his hand on the hilt of his sword. The young woman slipped a small handkerchief from her bosom and draped it over the knight's hand.

Meagan decided to play the part. She retreated to a thick part of the crowd and ducked down, ripping a strip from her linen undergarment. "Henryk!" she shouted, running out onto the tilt lane. She waved the cloth and ran up to him. Henryk grasped it silently, and Meagan was suddenly embarrassed. Had she done something stupid?

Henryk shifted in the high saddle and lowered his shield for his valet to hold. Struggling a moment, he wrenched off his helmet. A broad smile was on his plain face. "*Mademoiselle* Meagan!" he said dramatically, and kissed the fabric. "*Merci!*"

Meagan did not associate with many people. Medieval times were lived in the aftermath of Rome's philosophy of "Might makes Right" and the average person's character had degraded to that of a dull, ill-natured child. Brother Bartholomew was an exception—an early manifestation of a gentle man. The prestige of the early Church was in large measure due to the sincere compassion of such members.

For diversion, Meagan began wrapping and tying her oldest kirtle so she could ride Targa bareback around the Tournament grounds. On the pony she felt safe, indeed *was safe* from everything except an arrow. Her able horsemanship aroused suspicion, however, together with the fact she kept Targa spotlessly clean: a knight's horse was kept polished, like a gem, but never a common animal. Meagan knew it was not "acceptable" for a woman to ride astride, but she practiced her sin away from the tents so as not to disturb the dark imaginings of clergy and tattling commoners. It cheered her to find a clear area and quietly practice Targa's flatwork. It reminded her of home.

There was a problem she hoped to fix. Targa favored her left "lead" in the canter, a gait which, unlike the walk and trot, has two separate patterns of footfalls. A horse is more balanced circling with the inside foreleg leading, but many horses pick a favorite side and seldom change. The pony was, in a sense, left-handed.

Meagan started trotting in both directions to develop flexibility and balance. They made large circles, serpentines and figure-eights, spiraling in and out. She and Targa were practicing the ancient art of dressage, now lost and forgotten in the Medieval era. It would be almost three hundred years before the Renaissance and the rediscovery of this humane, empathetic system of training—so when others laughed or made jokes, Meagan simply ignored them.

She ignored, too, the black-robed men standing in a line who came one afternoon to watch her ride suspicious figures in the grass.

———

The Franciscans had the largest tent, and a multitude of monks busied themselves within. "In the name of the Father, the Son and the Holy Ghost," Meagan murmured as she kissed the steeple of her hands. She enjoyed the religious rituals and the sense of community they offered.

"It is a blessing to see you, Daughter."

She looked up into the kind face of Brother Bartholomew. "Oh, hello, sir! It is nice to see you, too."

"Have you read the letters I showed you?"

Meagan nodded. The clergyman had given her a selection of handwritten letters in his own heavy script: his questioning correspondence to the Lord. She *herself* had been the subject—the man said he wished to keep his conscience clear. "Thank you for trusting me, Brother Bartholomew."

He put his hand out and stroked her hair. "One so young and innocent. Where is your family, child? Are you far from home?"

"Yes, Brother Bartholomew, I would say so."

"We are given many trials, Daughter. We can but ask for guidance."

"I am sorry about getting Lorenzo in trouble, sir."

"He will endure. His censure is mild. As lambs, we must be shorn of falseness. My apprentice will accept his discipline and gain the profit thereof."

"Yes, sir." Meagan smiled. "Henryk did well today, did you know? He is high on the List. Tomorrow he jousts in Center Court."

"I am aware. You have the pledge of a victorious knight. Even a noblewoman could not hope for more." He glanced at the celebration in a nearby tent where Henryk's sponsor had commissioned food and entertainment. Drunken men hugged and wept at a staged play. "Remember, Daughter, the truth of our souls is shown more in good fortune than in bad. Now look up, child."

Her smile widened. "Yes, I have seen! The sky is clear."

"It is, and it will stay so. The Church was given a pagan prisoner to tell us the Tatars' plan. Their goal is to capture Great Kiev. The locust army has gone north."

Meagan nodded in quiet relief. The cracking, thudding sound of clashing knights rebounded in the distance. "Do you like the Tournament, Brother Bartholomew?"

"Why do you ask, Daughter?"

"Because I saw you watching this afternoon. And the biggest tent *is* the Franciscans'."

"It is a gift from the archbishop of Kent, a worldly man. It is said the archbishop's first visit to a cathedral will be his own funeral. You know the Church frowns upon the Devil's Games."

"But do *you* like the Tournament?"

"You ask an unimportant question." He turned away, but Meagan caught amusement in his expression. "Very well, I am forced to say it. I do enjoy the Tilting."

"I am shocked."

"I am not certain what draws me. Not the violence, of that I am sure. It may be the horses. Have you heard of our founder, Francis of Assisi? Animals gathered about him when he preached in the forest. Some believe horses are the gift of the

Creator, showing men beauty without vanity and strength without ambition. The horse has carried civilization upon his back, even to the end times we live in." It was a common teaching of the medieval Church that mankind was living in the fallen aftermath of a sinful world—proven by the fantastic aqueducts and other ruins of Rome. He nodded thoughtfully. "Thinking this way, Daughter, I am sure it is the horses. I find example in their humility. The animal participates not for coin or renown, but because he finds in it our Father's joy."

"Brother Bartholomew," Meagan asked quietly, "have you ever heard of a story about an Angel in the form of a horse?"

"It may be in the old manuscripts. Franciscan libraries have every kind of writing about animals."

"White—and with wings?" she asked excitedly.

"All Angels are white, Daughter, and all Angels have wings. Why do you ask?"

"I wonder if you have read of a horse Angel who left Heaven to help people on earth? It might be written down..."

"It does not sound unfamiliar." The man smiled benevolently. "I do not believe this comes from sacred text."

Meagan bit her lip. "No, I suppose not."

He watched her for a moment. "As I recall, you knew of the Tatars' army as if by prophecy. And yet you are sometimes unknowing of even the simplest customs. Tell me, Daughter, how is it you know so much and yet so little?"

Meagan shrugged unhappily.

"You keep your own counsel, Daughter. It is noticed. There is about you a freedom of thought. I approve of this, in God's love. Others do not."

"Approve of thinking for myself, you mean."

"Yes. Perhaps it is time to consider a new mount, Daughter. I wish to put this delicately ... it seems your jennet reminds others of evil things."

"Targa is just a pony. The trouble is only in their imagination."

"Yes, but those placing their care in the material do not always think of their actions, Daughter, or what they inflict."

Meagan looked away. "I know you are being nice, Brother Bartholomew, but I can't. We've been through a lot together."

Brother Bartholomew took Meagan's chin and turned her to face him. "Beware melancholy, Daughter. Be happy and be light, for all the world loves a maiden sweet."

Meagan nodded. "I will remember, Brother Bartholomew." She watched him move off to mingle with the gathering of soft-spoken clergy. She looked at the fields of tents and boisterous crowds, and felt a wave of homesickness. *A maiden sweet.* She would be sixteen soon—or already was—and there were none of her family or friends from home to celebrate with. She decided to make her birthday celebration coincide with the end of the Tournament: there would doubtless be an excess of partying so some could be spared. Excusing herself as she went, she left the Franciscan tent and cut across a field toward her own.

"Maid Meagan!"

Janek blocked her path. Next to him stood Lorenzo.

"Excuse me," she said coolly. "I have nothing to say to you."

"Oh, but I have things to say to you, Maid Meagan. Many things. My friend Lorenzo has told me of your witchery. We are beginning to understand you, Tatar's whor—"

Meagan impulsively slapped Janek hard enough to leave a white mark on his face. When she saw a glint come into the man's eye, she wished she had not done it.

Janek placed his hand delicately over the spot. "It is true, Lorenzo, this woman needs to learn her place." He smiled before he lunged and caught Meagan's arm. He clamped one hand over her mouth and wrapped his other around her chest. Meagan kicked as Janek propelled her toward the far line of trees. Lorenzo followed silently.

Janek's grip was iron. As hard as she fought, Meagan could not cry out or slow his step. She felt his callused hand between her teeth and bit down. Janek jerked her off the ground and started to shake her—and dropped her suddenly. She scrambled away and was about to run when she saw the resplendent yellow robe of a knight.

Henryk stood before Janek and Lorenzo, sword drawn.

Nothing was said. Henryk's sword remained steady, its steel blade a pure and beautiful plane. Lorenzo excused himself. Janek gave a slight bow and left.

Meagan brushed herself off. Her estimation of knights had suddenly increased. "*Thank* you, Henryk."

"*Prosze bardzo*, Meagan. Careful be."

"I will try." Henryk's look of concern touched her. "Thank you, Henryk. I will be fine." Meagan leaned up and kissed the knight lightly on his cheek. "You rescued me." She tried not to smile when he blushed a dark crimson. Together they walked a long route back to Meagan's tent, taking time to recover from the confrontation. She hoped there would be no consequences from Henryk's intervention, and that Janek and Lorenzo would end their harassment. She hoped so, but the problem with force was repercussion.

They arrived to find Meagan's tent quiet and undisturbed. "Thank you again, Henryk."

The young knight pulled his sword and stuck it lightly into the ground, dropping to one knee. Instinctively she offered her hand. He kissed it and stood, and with a deep bow he departed.

The campgrounds seemed dangerous now. She was disappointed none of her roommates was home; they were agreeable company now she was the Lady of a victorious knight. Meagan lit a rush and carried it to the candle by her mat, trying to relax from the day's events.

Henryk had entered and won two bouts, shivering three lances in six runs—an excellent score. His sponsor had produced yet another horse, a dappled gray possessed of a wonderfully smooth gait. Poor Chouchou was not to be given another chance.

Henryk's skills with the lance had gained the kerchiefs of three other women, including a duchess, yet it was Meagan's gift he wore in the place of honor under his horse's bridle. Meagan smiled to herself and lay back. She had to admit she enjoyed being an object of Courtly Love.

Something bit into the back of her head and she sprang forward with a cry. She clawed at her hair, but whatever it was had fallen away. Voices outside her tent called with concern.

She went to the entrance. "I am all right," she said, thanking the attendants crowding outside. Cautiously she returned to her mat. Something dark was on the rough pillow. She brought the candle to where it lay like a dead thing.

It was only a thistle. A dry sticker-burr had been laid carefully on her pillow.

"Are you certain you are well, our Lady?" a voice called from outside.

"Yes, thank you." She swallowed. "Good night."

Clang! said the armor,
like a motor omnibus in collision with a smithy,
and the jousters were sitting side by side on the green sward,
while their horses cantered off in opposite directions.
"A splendid fall," said Merlyn.

- *T. H. White (1906-64)* **The Sword in the Stone**

THE COURTIERS DID nothing to hide their dismay at being forced to abandon their box seats to a Lady of the Moment simply because her knight was having a good tournament. Meagan had seen such expressions before and knew the way to deal with such looks was to not acknowledge them. She settled down with a half-smile and polite words, giving the impression that she was doing her best to be courteous to people she could hardly be expected to know existed. It was a method that generally worked well with the socially ambitious, and it worked here. She found herself greeted warmly with smiles all around, which she politely ignored.

Meagan was enjoying herself. It was her sixteenth birthday today, she had decided—why not? It was fun to make the neck-craning nobles curious. Was she a merchant's daughter, the niece of a foreign lord ... a princess? The population was young with all the impetuousness and imagination of children, vainglorious in printed linens, gold cloth and embroidered damasks. She herself had been gifted by Henryk's sponsor with a scarlet satin dress patterned with golden griffins and filigree. Fitted sleeves gave final proof of her improved social station to a gossiping world. *Happy Birthday to me...*

The Tournament was not mere competition: it was high theater and everyone had a role. From noblewoman to livery footman, each made the most of their part; jousting was merely the colorful backdrop. Center Court was a turf rectangle surrounded by a moat filled with fresh wildflowers. A strip of tended grass edged the moat for each knight's entourage to parade along and for the victor's gallop. Around that, wooden grandstands were jammed with spectators, though "revelers" would be a better description.

Meagan scanned the pit areas for Henryk. She saw him, a yellow knight mounted on his bay, preparing to enter Center Court for the introduction parade. Henryk's reserve horse was the dapple gray, standing ready and saddled. Tied to a distant tree an unsaddled Chouchou dozed, peacefully reconciled to the arrangement.

Henryk led his entourage around the flower-filled moat, parading a fluttering sea of color. The cavalcade pranced under Meagan's box, and the young knight stood in his stirrups as she dutifully waved a handkerchief.

The opposing knight rode out in colors of red and gold. The middle third of his mount's barding was lined with broad checkers. Dyed plumes cascaded over the knight's back.

The contestants entered the tilting field and the horses were positioned and blindfolded. Henryk's new mount was out of sorts after a morning of being kicked and pulled by his inept rider, and surged into an erratic amble. Henryk swept his lance up and let the opposing knight pass. The blindfolded horses crossed without incident.

The knights were turned. This time Henryk's horse settled, and the young knight leveled his lance to hit his opponent mid-chest. The red-colored rival missed his mark as Henryk's lance cracked loudly and split. The stands cheered at the sound.

In the final run, Henryk started well until he accidentally pulled his reins the wrong way. Chouchou would likely have ignored the error, but Henryk's new blindfolded mount obediently blundered into the Red knight's path. Colliding chest to chest, the horses crumpled together.

Meagan jumped to her feet. Attendants swarmed over the fallen horses and nothing could be seen. The Red knight's horse was up first, standing unsteadily, and then Henryk's horse heaved to his feet. Grooms led the shaken horses out. Henryk's mount walked stiffly with a swelling hock. Though she wanted to follow, Meagan did not think her role as the object of knightly passion included running backstage.

Henryk had scored the only shivered lance in the set, so his name remained on the List while his opponent's was removed. The stands celebrated as Henryk left the Court.

Minstrels meandered through the boxes where gossip, schemes and flirtation raged. Whenever a knight did well, his designated Lady would glow, her eyes flickering among female rivals. The other women's part, Meagan understood, was to clap lightly with a bored expression, intimating dismay at the successes of another. This was done to increase the pleasure of the successful Lady. If her knight was *not* doing well, a Lady would stare straight ahead, stricken, and at such times rivals were free to clap or not—instead flowers and napkins or occasionally pebbles were surreptitiously thrown.

It was late afternoon when Henryk reentered for the concluding joust. He rode his sponsored second mount, the dappled gray. Shadows reached across the beaten grass. His final opponent rode a black horse in barding of dark blue, with encircling horizontal gray stripes. Meagan took in a breath when the rider lifted his helmet and doffed it to the high stands.

The Blue knight was Janek.

The host Queen was roused from conversation to drop the handkerchief, and the joust was begun. Janek started strongly, charging into a fast amble—but at the final moment he swung his lance around and swerved his horse off the line, rapping the side of his lance across the blindfolded face of Henryk's dappled gray.

The horse balked, throwing his head as Henryk held on tightly. Grooms ran onto the lane as the gray shied and kicked into space. Henryk leaned forward and clutched the reins as attendants tried to restore his mount's composure.

Janek rode easily to his place and waited. Now even the Queen's attention was on the field. The kerchief was dropped.

Both horses sprang forward, both knights lowered their lances, but in the closing moment Janek again swept his lance sideways to crack Henryk's horse across the forehead. Meagan gasped with the crowd as the blindfolded horse reeled, staggering to regain balance under his heavy weight. The animal spun in panic, kicking at the unseen men pressing around him. Henryk dropped his lance and shield and crouched to stay aboard.

"His blindfold is slipping!" she shouted, but no one heard, or would listen. Forgetting her prior misgivings, Meagan made quick excuses and flew down the steps. She threaded her way around the grandstands and through the crowd, emerging to see Henryk's mount twist away from a man holding onto his bridle.

She pushed through the attendants and reached to pull the fluttering cloth away. It slid down and off; the horse shook his head and stood trembling. A groom touched his side and the horse flashed out a hoof.

"Easy, boy." Meagan moved slowly as she took the horse's reins. "Someone please help Henryk down." Every man jumped forward at once and the frightened horse wrenched backwards out of her hand. Henryk let out a low moan. "*Stop!*" she hissed. "Everyone get back." Quietly, she moved forward again. The gray flattened his ears and snapped, so she waited. Biting was actually a good sign: an angry horse was more rational—and therefore less dangerous—than a frightened one.

"Hold the reins tight, Henryk. *Tight.*" Meagan came closer to the horse and spoke sharply: the gray raised his head at the tone and she quickly grasped the reins under the horse's chin. Cautiously this time, attendants moved around the gray and removed Henryk's feet from the stirrups. Henryk leaned over and they fell together in a torrent of metal and curses. The stands rippled with laughter.

Meagan handed the reins to a groom and went to Henryk. Dazed and pale, the knight sat on the ground with his helmet in his hands.

Henryk's sponsor marched across the field, stopping once to shake his fist in the direction of the Blue knight. Taking

Henryk's hand and yanking until the reluctant knight stood, the sponsor pointed with a bejeweled hand. A group of men were coming with a replacement mount in tow.

The new horse was a magnificent chestnut. He frothed at the bit; flecks of foam spattered his chest and forelegs. A trumpet chorus began as the powerful animal pranced toward Henryk. The horse arched his neck and rocked back on his haunches, fighting his restraint.

"*Magnifique!*" the sponsor shouted rapturously, kissing the back of his hand without noticing his knight was shaking in terror.

"Or, Henryk," Meagan suggested softly, "you could ride Chouchou..."

I can only imagine what breach of etiquette that was, Meagan told herself as she walked behind the grandstand, ignoring the glances and comments. She reclimbed the wobbly wooden stairs to the Royal Box and settled into her seat as Henryk reentered, riding his old favorite friend.

The now-rapt Queen tossed out a silk. Janek's horse charged out as before while attendants prodded Chouchou into motion. The knights came together to a crescendo of cheers.

Unfortunately the prodding attendants could not follow Henryk onto the Tilting field. Chouchou started down the Lane with promising speed, but when he scented the carefully laid turf—obviously a thoughtful buffet—he stopped and dropped his head. This action collapsed his precarious rider straight down on his neck, causing the point of Henryk's yellow-striped lance to droop to the ground. The hapless knight started to right himself but then, seeing he was helpless before an oncoming lance thrust, he returned to lying flat forward.

Janek held his lance as if for a frontal assault, and at the final moment swept it sideways to knock Chouchou soundly across the forehead. The gentle giant merely shook his mane and continued to graze unperturbed. He could not be bothered about a bump while blindfolded: in his experience such knocks only meant opportunities to eat heartily while the riders recovered.

An uproar of cursing rose between each knight's followers, and the gestures Henryk made could not be nice no matter the language. Meagan jumped to her feet and booed loudly, furious. "Aren't there any *rules* to this thing?" She realized she was the only one standing in the box and sat back down.

Chouchou stood quietly in the eye of the storm, his blind-folded head dipping in attempts to graze the turf bounty. For the start of the final run, the equine giant was turned slowly and with much shouting, recalling a barge being turned in a narrow canal. The stands fell into a hush waiting for the silk to fall.

His opponent was well down the lane before Henryk and his helpers convinced Chouchou to move yet *again*. Barding rippled with the horse's gait as he shuffled Henryk down the lane. The crowd cheered as the mounts brought the knights together.

Janek dispensed with pretense and swept his lance early, aiming it squarely at Chouchou's head—Henryk stopped kicking, unwilling to allow his beloved horse another blow. Without encouragement from his rider, Chouchou slowed; as he did the tip of Henryk's lance caught the chainmail on Janek's chest. The Blue Knight quickly pulled to a stop to avoid being unseated by Henryk's lance, and was implacably pushed backwards as Chouchou plodded the death throes of his walk. When Chouchou finally halted, Henryk's lance held Janek backwards at a severe angle, perched precariously against the back of his saddle.

Neither horse nor knight moved for a moment. Spectators fell silent. Janek started to wiggle impatiently out from his predicament, and contemptuously knocked Henryk's lance away. The pole slipped so that its point stuck into the ground—the lance's sudden movement startled Janek's horse and the animal shied sideways before the Blue Knight could right himself. Janek fell in a heavy crash, snapping Henryk's lance as he landed. He lay in the splinters.

All eyes went to the Tournament host.

The man shrugged. These were unusual circumstances, but the facts could not be argued. The Blue Knight's lance lay unbroken on the ground, while Henryk held only the fractured end of his own. The decision was made.

Henryk and Chouchou were champions of the Tournament.

Mᴇᴀɢᴀɴ sᴛᴏᴏᴅ ᴄʜᴇᴇʀɪɴɢ with the crowd as Henryk circled the List. The crowd laughed as Chouchou made a comfortable victory walk.

The Blue Knight remounted and rode to stand in front of Meagan's box. Uncomfortable under Janek's silent gaze, she sat down upon the wooden bench—and immediately jumped up again from a sharp pain. She thought the cause was a splinter at first, but looking back she saw a crushed and brown sprig. She leaned and picked it up. It was a dried thistle.

"It is her! It is her that did it!"

Meagan turned to see an unknown man pointing at her.

"It is horrible things she did to my little girl. Gave her the fever, she did, on a full moon too!"

"What little girl?" Meagan asked in confusion. "Why are you saying that?"

The man backed up as if in fear. "She is carrying the witch's wort! See it in her hand!"

Meagan looked down at the thistle and back at the staring crowd. She felt herself pushed, and then hands were grabbing her, holding her arms as rough cord was wrapped around them. She was carried and shoved down the steps past leering faces shouting or shrieking with laughter. *"Henryk!"* The crowd's celebration was too loud; her knight could not hear.

A moving corridor formed around Meagan, bearing her past the bleachers and across the field. Everything was unreal. The tents she passed had no substance. Nothing focused until the crowd parted.

She was allowed to stand. The mob fell silent as they waited for Meagan to see. Targa was tied to a tree, but grotesquely, inhumanely. Her head was bent low and she trembled on three legs. One of the mare's hind limbs was flexed and bent forward, caught by a rope that ran from her halter, looped behind her hind leg and back to the tree. The rope was taut, so when the pony moved to hop or lift her head, the rope rubbed the back of her pastern. The ground around the tree had been trampled into marsh.

"Why?" Meagan whispered. "I don't understand."

One of the men stepped forward: Lorenzo. He held out a cross, speaking the Rosary rapidly in Latin. Meagan was afraid to look at the accusing crowd around her. She was afraid of who else she might see.

"Is this horse your consort?" Lorenzo shouted, his eyes fixed on hers.

"The woman is a pagan and a witch!"

"Let her answer!"

"Let the witch answer!"

Meagan's eyes glistened as she watched her suffering mare. Lorenzo held up his hand for silence and came to stand in front of her. "What say you? Are you a witch or a heretic only?"

"Neither."

"Lies!" The man held up a crushed thistle to the crowd. "She bewitched a child with *this!*" A shocked gasp went through the crowd.

"Lorenzo, that isn't anything except a sticker-burr."

He seemed not to hear. "Tell us, be your horse possessed?"

"Lorenzo, you *know* me. Look at my horse! You are torturing her. *Please* untie her."

"It is the horse of the Devil! We have seen the fields of flaming locusts ... *devils* ride these demons!"

"She is just a horse, Lorenzo. It is not her fault."

"What is the mark she wears upon her shoulder?" The crowd fell into whispers, straining to see the brand on Targa's shoulder.

Meagan hesitated. Was it worse to be a Tatar's horse—or a witch's? "I don't know. The mark was there when I got her."

The mob was growing. Many of the shouts were from deep in the crowd, from people she could not see. She shuddered to suddenly recall primitives from the cliff howling amid burning chunks of flesh...

"Your familiar comes to you in the moonlight! *Say* it!" Flecks of foam dotted Lorenzo's lips. "Admit the beast consorts with you, brings you to dance with the Devil! *Say it!*"

"Burn her!" started a chant. "To the trial!"

A new group of men with black robes over vestments approached. Each clasped a cross before him. One pushed Lorenzo aside. "Under God, it is *our* duty to determine the guilt of a witch! When deemed guilty she will be given to the people for justice. Now take the familiar away and have it slaughtered."

"*No!*" Meagan screamed as men surrounded Targa. She worked her arms unconsciously, fighting her bindings. The rope had been poorly tied in the rush to take her and was loosening under her efforts. Men in black robes lined themselves before her, but she did not see them. She was watching her little mare stagger, holding her leg high off the ground as men crowded around her.

"Confess thy foul deeds, sinner, that thy death be swift..." intoned the black-robed men. The men were speaking ritually, heads bowed. "Gone be the demons that hold thee in thrall..."

New violence erupted. The pony was not going gently to her fate: in fact the decision to untie Targa was unraveling the enterprise. The provoked mare returned her mistreatment, snapping and kicking with fury that did, admittedly, imply the demonic. The chaos was not eased by shrieks from Lorenzo: "The *Devil* is come—*the Devil himself!*"

The black-robed clergy increased their invocations. The sun was setting in high clouds and a shaft of light drenched the pasture. As the pony fought the men away, Targa's pale coat began to glow in the dying sun. Meagan had a feeling of familiarity ... of time changing, shifting, slowing. Her bindings uncoiled and finally fell away. She pulled her hands free of the rope to give Targa's summoning whistle.

The mob behind her gasped to hear the pony's whinny of rec-
ognition. When Targa aimed a last kick at her tormentors and
began trotting to Meagan, the crowd—primed by Lorenzo's
shrieks—fled as from hosts of the netherworld. *At least they are
sincere about being afraid,* Meagan thought, noting the clergy were
foremost sprinters in the rout. When the pony arrived, she and
Meagan were quite alone.

The mob milled in the near distance, regrouping as their fears
were unmet and bloodlust returned. Time was short. Meagan
hurried to take her mare's lead rope. She looped it around the
mare's neck and quickly checked Targa's pastern for rope burn:
it was mercifully mild. The crowd's babble rose louder, feeding
itself.

"Daughter!"

Meagan mounted and turned toward the people. One latecomer pushed hurriedly to the front of the crowd. He watched
her a moment and mouthed the word, "Forgive." She nodded
and silently said goodbye to Brother Bartholomew. He had not
betrayed her; it mattered a great deal he had not.

The crowd's emotion was making an ugly change from fear to
fury. A few men were beginning to run, trying to surround her
and cut off escape. She leaned forward and whispered to Targa,
"Please, girl, let's go now." The pony stepped into a brisk trot
and broke into a canter, and in a few strides they were past the
clutching mob. Meagan buried her face in Targa's neck and felt
the mare's stride become free and strong. The sounds of the
angry scene slipped into the wind of the gallop as the ground
faded to a blur.

The journey has just begun...

Please join Meagan and her ride through history in the second book of The Legend of the Great Horse *trilogy. The adventure continues as our homesick traveler encounters Spanish Conquistadors, rides with the Court of Versailles, and helps a family with a struggling farm in Merry Olde England.*

The second book will be available in 2009. Please visit www.TheGreatHorse.com *for more information about the books and to sign up for notification of the upcoming release.*

⚔ Glossary of Terms ⚔

Amazon race of female warriors of Greek mythology.

amble one of several four-beat gaits, usually faster than a walk but slower than a canter.

bareback riding riding without a saddle.

bedding wood shavings, straw, sand, peat or other materials used to line the floor of a stall.

bit mouthpiece of bridle.

bridle horse's headgear which carries a *bit* and *reins* for guidance by rider.

buck movement in which a horse lowers his head and raises his hind-quarters into the air. A natural equine defense that may become a vice.

cannon bone bone of the lower leg between the knee or hock and the *fetlock*.

cantle the raised rear part of a saddle.

canter natural, controlled three-beat gait of horses, slower than a *gallop* but faster than a *trot*. The speed of the canter varies between 10-17 mph.

Cerberus (sir-BEAR-us) Black three-headed hound of mythology who guarded the entrance to Hades. All were allowed to enter, but Cerberus devoured any who tried to escape.

cold-blooded horses known less for speed than stamina.

Colosseum Roman amphitheatre built for public entertainment, which for four hundred years hosted gladiator fights, mock naval battles and exotic animal combats. The oval four-story stadium had a capacity of 50,000 spectators. Underneath the flooring were tunnels and cells where gladiators and animals were held. The well-designed passageways could fill or empty the stadium of spectators in ten minutes.

conformation the structure and general make-up of a horse.

coronet bands growth line at the top of the hoof.

crenelated pattern of multiple, regular, rectangular spaces cut out of the top of a wall.

crest top of a horse's neck between the *poll* and *withers*.

cross-ties method of securing a horse with two ropes or ties, on each side of the halter. Used to avoid provoking a horse's fear of being trapped.

crop short riding whip with a loop rather than a lash. Properly used as an extension of "driving aids" to signal a horse to move forward.

croup the top of the horse's hindquarters.

crow-hop action by horse of jumping slightly off the ground with all four feet.

crupper equipment used to keep a saddle from sliding forward on a horse's back, tethered to the root of the horse's tail.

dam mother of a horse.

denarius silver coin the size of a dime which was the main denomination of the Roman Republic.

destrier medieval war horse, selected for strength and a calm nature.

dressage (French term meaning "schooling") a humane system of developing a horses communication with the rider, balance, gymnastic ability and natural expression.

equestrian of or relating to horses or horseback riding.

equine horse.

farrier person trained professionally to tend to a horses hooves, make horseshoes and shoe horses. The modern equivalent of blacksmiths.

fetlock lowest joint in a horses leg; the ankle.

filly female horse less than four years old.

foal young horse up to the age of 12 months.

forging action of a horse's hind hoof hitting the bottom of a fore hoof.

Fortuna Roman goddess of luck.

freeze-mark unalterable identification applied with symbols on the neck that identifies an individual horse.

frog rubbery, wedge-shaped projection at bottom of horse's *hoof*.

gait pattern of footfalls of a horse in motion. The natural gaits are: *walk, trot, canter* and *gallop*. Additional gaits such as the *amble* are seen in various "gaited" breeds.

gallop fastest gait of a horse, averaging between 25 to 45 miles per hour. An extended version of the *canter* with four-beat footfalls.

gelding castrated male horse.

gladius Latin word for sword; name of common Roman short "thrusting" sword used by legionaries.

gray color that ranges from white to dark gray, including dapples.

groom person who looks after horses; a stable-hand. Also the term for brushing and/or cleaning a horse.

grooming the care and maintenance of a horse's coat. Includes washing, brushing, trimming, and the treatment of hooves, mane and tail.

halter headpiece harness that fits over a horse's head, used in leading or securing a horse.

hand unit of measurement equal to four inches, originally derived from the average width of a man's hand. A horse's height is measured in hands from the *withers* to the ground.

hipposandals Roman horse sandals.

hock the center joint or "knee" of the hind legs.

hoof horses 'feet'.

Homer (ca. 8th century B.C) by tradition considered the ancient Greek author of the epic poems the *Iliad* and the *Odyssey*.

horn hard, insensitive outer part of hoof.

horseshoes Iron or alloy horse-shoes fixed directly to the dead horn of a horse's hoof by *farriers*. The horse-shoe equips the horse to handle different types of terrain, as the human shoe does for humans.

hot-blooded typically horses with ancestors from hot climates in the Middle East. High spirited but not necessarily flighty.

lame disabled in the feet or legs; term used to describe a horse which is limping or has difficulty walking properly.

lead term to designate which foreleg "leads" or advances further in a gallop or canter. On the "right lead" the horse leads with right leg.

legion Roman military unit which varied in strength from 4,000 to 6,000 heavily armored foot soldiers. Their weapons were javelins and the short thrusting sword called a *gladius*: source of the word gladiator.

lictor bodyguard in ancient Rome.

longe / lunge exercise in a horse's various paces on a circle using a longe or 'lunge' rein, with the horse circling the trainer.

mane long hair growing down a horse's neck and on top of the head.

manger trough to hold feed or hay.

mare adult female horse; commonly defined as over three years of age.

Master of Horse (*magister equitum*) high Roman official associated with cavalry. The office was appointed; it came to hold ceremonial importance and possessed imperium.

meridian the hour of noon.

monk (*derived from Greek: monos, alone*) general term for a person living a religiously ascetic solitary life.

mount the action of getting onto a horse. A rider may mount from the ground, a mounting block, or by receiving a "leg-up" or assistance from another person on the ground.

mucking out removal of soiled bedding and replacement with clean bedding.

Muses Greek goddesses who govern the arts and sciences and provide creative inspiration.

Myrtilus turncoat chariot-boy of Greek legend who put wax axle pins in his master's chariot for a bribe.

nicker common 'friendly' sound a horse makes, usually low and welcoming.

paddock enclosed area used for pasturing or exercising animals.

palomino a gold colored horse with blond or white *mane* and tail.

pastern the area on a horse's leg between the *hoof* and *fetlock* joint

pedigree list of a horse's ancestors.

Pegasus the immortal winged horse of Greek mythology. Cared for by the Muses; a symbol for the arts, especially poetry. Commonly portrayed as white, but has also been described as black, 'red as the sunrise,' or as having wings of another shade or color.

piebald horse whose coat consists of patches of black and white.

poll area between the horses ears.

pommel the upper front part of a saddle.

pony horse under 14 hands.

Praetorian Guard special bodyguards used by Roman emperors.

proud flesh 'exuberant granulation tissue,' which is prone to occur in a equine wound, especially near a joint. Overproduction of scar tissue.

rampart defensive wall of earth topped with a protective barrier.

registry breed organization which holds a horse's registration papers.

reins part of a *bridle* consisting of a pair of long straps attached to the *bit*, used to direct and control the horse.

shy sudden evasive action a horse takes, usually sideways, due to being scared by something real or imaginary.

Silk Road longest trade route in ancient world, from China to Rome, earning its name from Rome's demand for silk.

silphion now-extinct herb indigenous to North Africa. In Roman times the plant was valued as spice and for its medical properties. Called by famous naturalist Pliny the Elder "one of the most precious gifts of nature to man." Silphion was exploited and finally exterminated because of its high value (worth its weight in silver).

solstice when tilt of the Earth's axis is at its most extreme orientation towards or away from the Sun. This occurs about June 22nd and December 22nd to begin summer and winter in the northern hemisphere.

spina separating wall in the center of the oval track. It was a major showpiece in the larger venues, with fountains and other effects.

stable a building in which horses are kept. Usually divided into separate *stalls* for individual animals.

stall individual enclosure to house horses. Typical size for an adult horse is 12' square.

stallion male horse aged 4 years or over.

stifle joint in horse's hind leg analogous to knee, close to body under the croup.

tack saddlery or horse equipment, such as the saddle and pad, *bridle, reins,* and *halter.*

Tatars one of the founding tribes that united under Genghis Khan, which was conflated by Westerners to mean the entire Mongolian horde. Most current-day Tatars live in Eastern Europe, numbering more than 10 million in the late 20th century.

Thoroughbred athletic, hot-blooded breed of horse descended from three Arabian stallions given to Britain in the 17th century.

trot a stable, two-beat gait in which the horse moves its legs in unison in diagonal pairs. Faster than a walk but slower than a canter, the trot averages 8 mph but has a wide variation of potential speed.

toga article of clothing distinctive to Romans, worn draped around the body. Only citizens with voting rights were permitted to wear it. Color and decoration was strictly regulated according to social status.

Trajan (Emperor of Rome A.D. 98-117) the second of the so-called "five good emperors" of the Roman Empire, and the first Roman Emperor not born in Italy. Under Trajan's rule the empire reached its greatest territorial extent. Closely linked with his wife and female relations, Trajan's administration enjoyed his good relations with the Senate. Every new Emperor was honored by the Senate with the prayer, *'felicitor Augusto, melior Traiano,'* meaning 'may he be luckier than Augustus and better than Trajan.'

Virgil *[Publius Vergilius Maro]* (70 B.C. -19 B.C.) Roman poet called by Tennyson 'the wielder of the stateliest measure ever molded by the lips of man.' The poet was a favorite of Rome's first Emperor, Augustus.

vetting a veterinary examination of a horse's health and soundness.

vice a bad habit learned by a horse, including bucking, head tossing, rearing, etc.

walk the slowest natural gait of a horse, a four-beat gait averaging about four mph.

withers the highest part of the horse's back, usually seen as a slightly raised area above the shoulders.

yearling a horse between one and two years old.

The author currently lives in Boston, Massachusetts, where he first discovered a love of history. His experiences with (great) horses gave him a love and respect for the animal.

It is Mr. Royce's dream that American culture will rediscover its equestrian heritage. He also wishes Latin would again be taught in grade school. These hopes qualify him to write fiction.

You may contact Mr. Royce through the website, www.TheGreatHorse.com. Inquiries are welcome. They may not be answered correctly—or at all—but inquiries are most welcome.